MW00816599

AUCTION OF SOULS

Pixel Dust Book Three

D. PETRIE

MOUNTAINDALE
PRESS

ACKNOWLEDGMENTS

I started this series because I wanted to tell a story. A story of friends saving a game that they loved. I wrote it for myself because, well, it was fun.

To my surprise people liked its quirky characters and ridiculous action. Now, with all of your support, I get to do more, and the world of Noctem gets to grow. For that I am grateful. So thank you to everyone who picked up a copy, left a review, told a friend, or commented on a post. It's because of all of you that I get to do this.

In addition, thank you to my betas Andy, Tara, Kevin, Sean, and Caitlin, as well as my amazing wife Sam and everyone at Mountaindale Press who keep me motivated.

CHAPTER ONE

Coping is never easy.
Some people accept the things they can't change, while others…
Well, others fight.

Farn's hair clung to her face as she sprinted across the rain swept rocks of Altum Cove. A trail of crimson light spilled from her clawed hand.

"Eat death!"

The Deep turned its writhing mass of leathery tentacles to face her as she slammed her fist into the Nightmare's oversized beak. A wave of heat and power exploded from her hand, a life consumed by the Death Grip bound to her body.

It felt horrible.

Impact staggered the four-story Nightmare and blew away the rain, creating a pocket of dry space within the storm. An acrid scent filled the air before the downpour crashed down again. Farn landed in a roll, her wet hair flinging water in a circle around her head like a halo as she righted herself. She brought up the Death Grip's barrier a heartbeat later. A plate of crimson light appeared on the back of her clawed gauntlet, no bigger than a hubcap. She braced and shielded her head as the Deep slammed a black tentacle into her stomach.

The barrier was just too small.

She couldn't protect anyone.

Not even herself.

Waves crashed against the rocks as Farn soared into the jagged stone at the water's edge. Her health, displayed on the tattooed stat-sleeve on her exposed wrist, slammed down to half. The surf crested over her head, filling her mouth with the sea. It burned her nose as she coughed the salty water back out.

Suddenly, the light of a fairy's wings streaked the sky, causing a momentary swell in her chest for an instant before her mind stomped it back down. It wasn't really her friend.

No.

Kira had been stolen from her.

The small figure spiraled down toward Farn, the spitting image of the fairy she'd loved, and lost. The avatar's cheerful smile shined, but the dull, lifeless blue of her eyes told the truth.

There was nothing inside.

Her avatar should have destabilized months ago. Instead, the system kept it running, drawing input from the minds of those who knew Kira best. The result was a memory, a representation of a player who had passed away while logged in. Whether that was true remained to be seen.

There was still so much that they didn't understand about what Nix and Carver had done to her friend. About what Kira had become in the end; a digital entity capable of breaking into every database in the world. Her real body had been abducted, and without it, there was no way to be sure if she was really gone.

At least, that was what Farn had been telling herself. Kira had to be alive somewhere out there, and Farn didn't want to keep her waiting. It was the only thing keeping her and the others going.

Farn couldn't bring herself to call the system's imitation by her friend's name, so she just called it what it was: Echo.

It was a name that stuck.

Farn shook her head. None of that mattered now, not while she was face to tentacle with yet another Nightmare, the second of a new expansion of three.

The fairy above spun, releasing a shower of pixie dust on Farn to bring her health back up. It was what Kira would have done, so it only made sense that Echo would do the same.

It didn't last.

A glistening, black tentacle whipped through the air, catching the small avatar in the side. The light around her winked out before Farn's health could climb to full. Echo shot across the cove like a poorly-aimed firecracker before plunging into the waves.

Farn suppressed the urge to pull herself off the rocks and chase after the fairy. It wouldn't have mattered; Echo wasn't really a player. No, she was a glitch and, apparently, glitches didn't take damage.

Noctem's system didn't seem to know what to do with the mindless avatar, so it kept her impact on the game to a minimum. Echo couldn't cast spells or join a party. All she could do was fly and take up space.

Farn blew a lock of wet curls out of her face and pulled herself up. There was no point in dwelling on the past, the fight now was still winnable. Gunshots barked over the sound of crashing waves and thunder as Max raced to her rescue.

"Good hit. That punch dropped the Deep twenty percent. We'll have to make sure you kill a few more players to feed the Death Grip for the next run, if we don't survive this one." The *Fury's* voice was harsh and callous.

Farn tried not to think about the Death Grip's ability. Necessary or not, of late, she had been using the evil contract more than she felt comfortable with.

She pulled a wooden cylinder from her item pouch and pulled on one end with her teeth. It snapped open, revealing a glass vial full of shimmering light. Tossing it at the rocks by her feet, it exploded on impact. A burst of shining dust rushed out to surround her and top her health off.

Echo might not have been able to help much in battle, but at least she was able to give them a steady supply of healing dust. With a little creativity and the help of a good crafter, pixie-bombs had helped them scrape by without a proper *Breath* mage.

As Farn recovered, a grappling line flew through the air and Ginger, the lady of House Lockheart, swung by with her dagger at the ready. The *Coin* landed a slash to one of the Nightmare's thicker limbs, scraping the length of the beast with a streak of green light. The Deep froze as her passive Venom Bite took hold, its skin lighting up with a variety of debuffs. Ginger leapt out of the way.

"Everyone, let loose!"

The party pounced. Max slammed in a fresh pair of magazines and opened fire. Kegan joined in, the *Leaf* launching a handful of arrows into the Deep's hide. From above, Corvin leaped off a ledge, the *Blade's* sword carving down through the Nightmare with a crimson streak of damage.

Farn glanced at the boss's health, still sixty percent left. It was going to take more than that to bring it down. She slammed her gauntlet against her breastplate to activate her Taunt skill.

"Come at me, tentacle-ass."

It wasn't a clever taunt, but Kira wasn't there to disapprove anymore. The Deep turned to her regardless.

"I'd be careful with that taunt." Kegan dashed to the side. "I've seen what these tentacle monsters get up to on the internet."

"Um, that's not something you should admit to." Corvin swatted at an overly grabby tentacle.

"Cut the chatter and stick to the plan!" Max shut the joke down hard and fired another round at the Deep. "We have to lure it over to those rocks." He hooked a thumb back at a pair of jagged stone formations near a cliff.

Farn took a step back as the beast heaved its body out of the water and crept across the cove. Max held his ground, waiting. It rose up on a few thick tentacles to reveal the massive beak at the center of its mass. Then it dropped back down in an attempt to catch the *Fury* in its ravenous maw.

Max rolled out of the way, a hair's breadth from being consumed. The monstrous form dragged itself closer as Farn and Max acted as bait until, finally, it got into position. Corvin rolled in close to Farn's side just as the Nightmare reared back up, its beak open wide for a meal.

"Ready?" Max shouted as the beast's dripping form towered over them. Corvin answered with an audible gulp as Farn backed up to the edge of the cliff, the waves crashing on the jagged rocks below.

"No way out now." She brought up her gauntlet, ready to deploy her barrier.

"Here it comes!" Corvin ducked under her arm.

The Nightmare let out a gluttonous roar as it came down on top of them.

Moist heat and darkness engulfed Farn's world, slimy walls closing in on her. She threw out her legs and braced her back against a ribbed surface. The sounds of her friends struggling filled the space.

Gah, what just touched my neck? Farn thrust her gauntlet behind her head and shoved, activating her barrier. The Death Grip's glow lit the space within the beast's mouth.

"Oh shit! This is really the plan?"

She struggled to lock her legs in place to hold the Nightmare's beak open, her back pinned against the roof of its mouth. Rows of teeth circled the cavernous throat that hung just above her head as a fleshy tendril licked at her cheek and neck. Corvin's foot held firm beside her, his back braced against the opposite side of the Nightmare's mouth.

"I am really uncomfortable with this plan." He leaned away from another small tendril that attempted to slither into his furry ear while more coiled around his arms. Saliva dripped from his matted hair. The razor-sharp edge of the creature's beak surrounded them, held at bay by their bodies alone.

"Keep it together. We have it where we want it." Max stood between them, his guns thrust up into the gaping darkness of the Deep's throat. He fired.

Bellows of protest drowned out the sound of the storm that raged outside as the beak struggled to close. Farn gasped and thrust her legs out to keep the walls from closing in. Corvin did the same.

"Hold steady!" Max lurched to the side, putting a round into the Deep's jaw as the beast tried to rise up to cough them back out. "Oh no you don't!" He raised his house ring to his mouth to speak to the others outside. "Get it tied down!"

"We did!" Kegan shouted back over the house line, sounding like he was struggling just as much as they were. "This thing is really freaking strong."

Ginger's voice came next. "I have four grappling lines tying it down to the rock, but I'm not sure how long we can hold it. It's snapping them as fast as I can secure them. I'll run out of wire if it keeps up."

"Damn, not enough time." Max switched his pistols to full-auto and unloaded both before holding them out to his sides. "Reload!"

Farn used her free hand to pull a magazine from Max's belt while Corvin did the same. They slipped them into Max's guns in unison and he unleashed another burst of damage into the beast's throat.

"Again." He held out his pistols as soon as their slides locked back. Farn caught the Nightmare's health on Max's stat-sleeve as she shoved in another mag. It was working. The Deep was nearly dead after taking so many critical hits.

Suddenly, the sound of cables snapping all at once struck the air. The ground below fell away as the beast rose up with the three of them in its mouth. Max holstered a gun and grabbed Corvin's legs to keep from being left alone on the cliff-side. The entire space flipped upside down and Farn began sliding head first toward the rows of teeth that circled the Deep's throat. A thousand jagged points waited, ready to tear her apart. She braced with all her strength to keep from sliding further.

"Almost there!" Max slipped down to dangle from Corvin's tail, hanging further into the Deep's throat. He fired another shot down into the belly of the beast as his hand slipped through the *Blade's* slime covered fur.

"Grab hold." Farn reached out for him, hoping to catch his hand before he lost his grip. He ignored her.

"I have to finish it!" Max fired again just as his fingers slipped and he vanished into the void of teeth and darkness.

He was gone.

Farn stared down the beast's throat, her hand still outstretched.

The world lurched again as the creature dove back into the sea. Salt water rushed in, flooding the jaws of the beast past Farn's head. She took a breath just before she went under. Corvin's panicked eyes locked with hers through the murky water. They were out of options. They could move and be crushed by the creature's beak or they could stay and drown. Escape was impossible.

Well, almost impossible.

Farn clenched her clawed fist and fed the Death Grip another player's life. One of the many she'd taken in the last few months. As her health dropped by twenty percent from the lack of air, she slammed her gauntlet into the wall behind her. A blast of power blew the beast's beak open wide enough to fling her free. She kicked off a rock toward the surface with everything she had, Corvin following right behind.

Struggling to swim in her armor, she expected a tentacle to wrap around her foot at any second. Her health dropped another twenty percent, then another. Rain met her as she burst through the surface and gasped for air.

"Where's Max?" Ginger reached a hand down to help Farn up onto the rocks.

"Did he kill it?" Kegan asked as he hoisted Corvin from the waves nearby as well.

Farn's heart sank as she glanced at the boss's status bar on her wrist. It blinked with a sliver of health remaining.

We were so close.

Then she took a sharp breath. Max's health was blinking too. A few hit points hung in the space next to his name. Tension raked across her nerves as she stared at the two health readouts, unsure of which would vanish first.

A flash of lightning blinded her for an instant as the waves swept her and Ginger back to the water's edge. Farn landed on her rear, waist-deep in the surf as a black tentacle rose from the water before her.

No!

It loomed over her, ready to strike.

Then, it stopped and grunted.

Max emerged from underneath a second later, throwing the limp form off his back before collapsing to his hands and knees in the water. He let out a wheezing cough before speaking.

"I had to finish it. We don't have time to keep trying."

"I know." Farn looked off into the storm. "We can't keep Kira waiting forever."

As if on cue, Echo stumbled out of the water and shook off her silver locks like a dog. She wobbled afterward as if the act had made her dizzy. Her dress clung to her skin as she tapped a bare foot on the stone, splashing in a puddle.

"Yeah, hurry up, I'm not gonna wait forever."

"We're trying." Max brushed off Echo's complaint.

Of course, the mindless avatar hadn't actually said anything out loud. Rather, it had mouthed the words. The system couldn't seem to replicate her voice, making lip-reading a new required skill. Farn had trouble, but Max seemed to have a knack for it, always getting Echo's point.

"Okay, everybody get ready to make a contract." Max stood and holstered his weapons before looking back at the rest of the team. "Keep your minds clear, this one needs to count. We don't want a repeat of that last one." He shot Farn an accusatory glance.

She looked away, feeling guilty but suppressing a smile at the same time. They had already taken down the first Nightmare of the recent expansion, gaining a useless contract in the process thanks to her when she had been chosen. Though, uselessness aside, the contract was a great item and Kira was going to love it when they got her back.

"I mean it." Max jabbed. "No one has found the last Nightmare of this expansion yet and Checkpoint can't figure out why, so this might be our last chance. We can't afford any more ridiculous items."

"I know, I'm sorry." Farn took a step away clutching her item bag where the offending contract was held.

"It's okay, just think about Nix." Max took a deep breath. "Let your anger do the rest. We need a contract that can trap her or give us a way to find her in the real world. Focus on that, and the system should use that to create something to help."

The last few tentacles of the Deep sunk back into the waves as a familiar voice boomed across the cove. The voice of mankind's first fear, the Darkness. Echo jumped and dashed to hide behind Farn as the age-old terror dragged out a name.

"MaxDamage24!"

"Here we go." Max clenched his fist.

"Make your offer!"

Max reached into his pocket for the item he'd crafted just for this moment. A bullet with a name carved into it. Nix, the one who had stolen their friend. He had shown the carving to Farn on more than one occasion, as if trying to remind her who they were up against.

"I offer one bullet bearing my enemy's name." Max tossed it into the water. It vanished into the depths as the Darkness answered back.

"Accepted!"

An object materialized on Max's belt, silver glinting in the moonlight as the clouds above cleared. He reached for it without hesitation and snatched his player journal from his pouch, flipping to his item descriptions. That was when he froze, staring at the text in his journal and gripping the contract item in his other hand. It was just a small crafting knife with a blade a few inches long, too small to deliver much damage.

"Will that help us against Nix?" Farn leaned closer to see the description.

"Yeah. This could help us find her." Max snapped the book shut and tucked the knife into his belt next to his ammunition pouch. He let out a heavy sigh. Farn couldn't help but notice a quiver in his voice as he spoke again.

"We're a step closer. Now we need to trap her."

CHAPTER TWO

Damn, damn, damn.

Karen Write rushed up the stairs of the Grand Archway that stretched over the city of Lucem.

Great way to make an impression, Karen, late on your first day.

Well, actually, Karen wasn't her name anymore, now was it? No, that name was a world away. In Noctem, she was known simply as Royal Assistant Seven. A part of her was thrilled to have a new name. Especially after the internet had made a joke of her old one with hundreds of memes declaring Karens the enemy of retail employees everywhere.

Her new name, however, wasn't much of an improvement. It wasn't even a name, just a title that came along with her new job. What would she even call herself for short?

Royal? No, that sounded egotistical.

Seven? Well that's just a number.

Whatever…

It was too late now. She was running late, and being late on her first day was unacceptable.

She cursed herself for taking so long to create her character. Never having been a gamer, she didn't really understand what went into the process. There had been far more options than she'd been prepared for. In the end, she had rushed through the process, leaving her in the body of a human woman with dark blue hair.

The hair color had been an accident.

She'd meant to keep it a familiar black but, in her haste, she had messed up a slider.

Blue hair aside, the only real difference was that she had made herself a little younger. She hadn't intended on it, but when faced with the choice, she'd tapped that option down a few years' worth. It was nice to be under forty again. Her birthday had just passed, and after being laid off last month from the accounting firm where she'd worked, it hadn't been a happy one.

For her class, she had just picked whichever had the most professional-looking attire. A simple green robe seemed best in the end. As far as what a *Venom* mage was, she didn't know. She didn't expect to be fighting anyway. Even if Carpe Noctem was a game, playing it wasn't her reason for being there.

She just needed a job.

With bills to pay and her husband, Todd, incapacitated with a broken hip after a frisbee golf mishap, time and money were running out.

Stupid Todd.

Of course, she loved him fiercely but his timing was terrible, and with a career in roofing, it would be some time before he could return to work. After struggling to find employment herself, she'd turned to Noctem's message boards in desperation.

The job description of the Royal Assistant position post hadn't sounded too complex. Just take care of tasks for the Lady of the House of Silver Tongues, a player named Leftwitch. How hard could that be? Apparently not very, because she had received a job offer a few minutes after sending in her resume to apply. Things must've worked differently in Noctem, faster and less formal.

Unfortunately, with her extensive experience in the accounting field, becoming someone's gofer was a little beneath her. eDsperation was a strong motivator, though, and there wasn't much opportunity in the real world these days.

She panted as she finally reached the top of the Archway's stairs, coming to an elaborate set of double doors manned by a huge player in silver armor holding a spear. The pointy bit at the top of his weapon was strange, like two spearheads bisecting each other to create four bladed edges. She gulped at the sight, unsure if he was a person like her or one of those Non-Player Characters.

"Um, excuse me. I'm running late and I'm supposed to meet Lady Leftwitch for my first assignment." She felt stupid using the title of 'Lady' in a sentence, as if she was a child playing make-believe.

"You must be Seven." The man leaned on his spear.

Ah, I guess I'll be known as Seven then. It's good to have an answer to that question, Seven acknowledged to herself before answering.

"Yes. Would you be able to tell me where to go from here? I'm new and I'm not sure how this all works yet."

"No shame in being a noob." He held out his hand for her to shake. "I'm Cassius, First Knight of the Silver Tongues."

Seven's jaw tensed at the word 'noob.' She had been called it twice on the way to the palace already and it was starting to irritate her. Why these people thought the word was funny or endearing, she had no idea. It was rude, plain and simple. She suppressed any complaint, though.

"Glad to meet you, sir?" She shook his hand, unsure what a First Knight was, or if the title was important.

Cassius eyed her for a moment before letting her hand go. "You're not much of a gamer, are you?"

"Sorry, not really." Seven let her chin fall. "Was it the 'sir' that gave me away?"

"Yeah, not sure if I've ever been called that before." He laughed, seeming friendly enough as he opened the door for her. "Now, let's get you to work."

Seven froze as the room beyond came into view. A gilded throne stood tall at the far end, with beautiful tapestries flowing from behind it to the ceiling. It was impressive, but what really pinned her to the floor was the floor itself. Where stone or tile should have been, nothing but glass lay between the room and the view of the city below.

Lights danced through the streets and buildings beneath her feet. Above, another pane of glass, though smaller, gave her a view of the night sky, its blanket of stars sparkling overhead. Seven gripped the side of the door frame for support as a sense of vertigo swept over her.

"You get used to it." Cassius walked out over the fantastical sight below as if it wasn't there.

"He's right," said a woman standing at the center.

Seven recognized her from the recordings that she'd watched in preparation for her first day.

Leftwitch, the Lady of the Silver Tongues.

As Seven understood it, the woman had carved out a place for her house back when Noctem had first launched and had ruled over the city of Lucem ever since. Her income and need for assistants came from Late Knight, a talk show that she'd been running using the game's recording system.

Over the years, Leftwitch had become so well connected with the current events of the game that her name had become synonymous with the pulse of Noctem. In the last few years, she had carried out interviews with the biggest names, including lords and ladies from all the major houses. Even Alastair Cold-blood himself, the head Checkpoint Systems, had appeared on the show. Through a mixture of comedy and news, Leftwitch had covered events from wars to insane heists, all while staying neutral. Even Seven, who had little interest in Noctem, had known her name before applying for the job.

"You must be my new assistant." Leftwitch gave her a half smile and walked toward the door to greet her. A long coat of gray velvet lined with silver buttons billowed as she moved. Her blonde hair was tied off to one shoulder, giving her a casual appearance that seemed welcoming.

"Yes." Seven tore her hand off the doorframe and marched out onto the glass to meet her new employer. She did her best not to look down and held her hand out to shake. "I'm excited to get to work and see what I can do to help your operation run smoothly."

"Great to hear." Leftwitch gave her hand a solid two pump handshake and let go.

Seven couldn't help but notice a class emblem of a hooked claw surrounded by decorative embellishments on the back of her hand. That was when a large bird dove at her head from where it perched on the back of the throne. A wingspan of black feathers, at least three feet wide, filled her view as talons came at her throat. She flailed and fell backward on her rear.

"Halt!" Leftwitch held up a closed fist and the bird ceased its attack, dropping to the floor at Seven's feet. "Sorry. Ruby here is set to attack anyone that approaches me that isn't part of my house. A security measure, considering I do rule over a city. I'm a *Whip* class, by the way."

"I'm so sorry to have upset your pet." Seven stared at the bird as it paced around by her feet. Its feathers were jet black, save for a ring of red that ran down its chest into a silver breast-plate. The piece of armor looked strange on an animal.

Cassius held out a hand to help her up as Leftwitch pulled a small box from her pocket. She opened it and removed a ring from inside.

"Welcome to the Silver Tongues." Leftwitch slipped it onto Seven's finger without giving her a chance to refuse.

"Thank you." The ring tightened around her finger. "I'll do my best."

"Great, because I have a job to start you off with." Leftwitch spun and walked back to her throne, retrieving an envelope and placing it in Seven's hands. "Have a look inside."

"Good, I can't wait to get started." Seven tried to sound enthusiastic as she opened the envelope and pulled out a sheet of blank paper. She stared at it in confusion for a moment. "What am I supposed to be looking at?"

Leftwitch clapped her hands at the bird pecking at the floor then pointed to Seven. "Ruby, guard." The raven-like avian flew up to land on Seven's shoulder, its talons digging in just enough to be uncomfortable but not enough to hurt.

"Okay, this is… a little…" Seven trailed off as she adjusted her shoulders to offset the sudden weight.

"Sorry, that letter is addressed to me so it can only be read if I've touched it in the last minute or so. However, Ruby counts as part of my character, so he can activate it as well. Just hold it up to his beak."

Seven did as she was told and the bird pecked at the page, causing a design of red ink to spread out across the paper.

You are cordially invited to attend the first annual Auction of Souls

"What is the Auction of Souls?" Seven looked up from the paper.

"How much do you know about contract items?" Leftwitch answered her question with a question.

"Not much. I watched your interview with Lord Dartmouth of the House of Serpents, where you talked about the Death Grip. Contracts are supposed to be powerful items, right?"

"Yes, but that's putting it a little too simply. Contracts are items that can sway the outcome of entire battles, even bend the rules of the game. The Death Grip is a good example, since it gives its owner the ability to rip the life from a player with a thought." Leftwich walked back to her throne.

"But contract items are hard to get, right? So most players don't have them."

"Yes, and most of them are locked to the player who forms the contract. Though, in rare cases, one is listed as unbound and can be sold. And, until now, it has been impossible to straight up buy in-game items with real money. But it seems that the organizers of this auction event have found a loop-hole and gotten their hands on a number of unbound contract items. Contract items that they intend to sell off to the highest bidder."

"And this is a problem?"

"Yes, it's a problem!" Leftwitch stopped in her tracks and gave an exasperated sigh. "We saw what just a few contract items could do six months ago when Lord Berwyn nearly conquered all of Noctem. If it hadn't been for House Lockheart robbing him blind, he would have succeeded. And that would have been a problem for Lucem."

"That's understandable." Seven nodded, a little unsure what the topic might have to do with her duties as a royal assistant.

"Plus, it's wrong." Cassius stepped in.

"How so?" Seven cocked her head to the side, crowding Ruby who perched on her shoulder. The bird flapped its wings, making Seven flinch.

"Contracts belong with the players who got them. They shouldn't be sold off." Cassius slammed the base of his spear down on the glass floor, sending a jolt of tension through Seven's body as she braced for it to shatter.

It didn't.

"What Cassius is trying to say is that contract items are a part of the person who fought to get them. Or at least, that's what many believe." Leftwitch stepped forward to pat Ruby on the head. "Think about it, players fight through Nightmares, some of the most difficult bosses in gaming history. Bosses that represent concepts that we all fear. In the end, we offer something from ourselves in exchange for power."

"And the items created from that exchange often reflect the user in some way." Cassius shifted his spear sideways to hold it reverently in both hands. "I fought for this one and it has served me well ever since."

"It was the same for me and Ruby." Leftwitch scratched at the bird's chin. "He was my first contract and he's a part of me. I would never sell him."

"I can understand that." Seven tried to hold her shoulder still to keep the bird steady. "What do you need me to do to help? Should I accompany you to the auction to manage your accounts?"

Leftwitch let out a sharp laugh. "No, I want you to go in my place."

"I'm sorry, what now?" Seven tried to keep the skepticism out of her voice.

"An auction like this will attract every major house in Noctem. Having that many strong players in one place will be a powder keg waiting to go boom." Leftwitch gestured an explosion with her hands. "I'm not crazy. There's no way I would walk into a situation like that. I haven't kept my throne for almost four years by taking that kind of risk. Which is why I need you to go there and bid on contracts that are too dangerous to let fall into the wrong hands, as well as items that seem particularly useful for our house. My account information has already been sent to the auction, and I authorize you to spend up to three hundred thousand."

Seven nearly choked at the amount of money as her forehead began to sweat. "But am I the best choice, being so new to the game? I believe I made it clear in my cover letter that I lack experience."

"That's actually why you're perfect for this sort of assignment." Leftwitch waved away the concern and turned back toward her throne. "I don't need a gamer, I need someone I can trust. My other assistants are highly capable players, but unfortunately, I'm not sure any of them could resist the temptation that a contract offers. There would be nothing stopping any of them from running off with whatever items we bid on, rather than returning them to me. With one or two contracts, any player could become a legend. So, I need someone that has no interest in power. I need a professional."

"I see." Seven began to understand the woman's thinking, then she shook her head. It was still crazy. "But what about the powder keg situation? I would be unable to defend myself if something were to happen. Full disclosure, I came straight here after logging in. I have no idea what sort of place Noctem is or what my class designation does."

"You'll be fine. There won't be a point in harming you. You're not a top member of our house or anything. Maybe one day you will be but, as harsh as it sounds, being a nobody is your best protection. And just in case, I'll be sending Ruby with you under a guard command. He has no range limitations like most pets do, and he'll make the other attendees think twice about making a move on you." Leftwitch snatched an object off the seat of her throne and sauntered back to the center of the room.

"And just to prove to you that I trust you as an employee, I want you to take this with you as well." She placed a small silver box in Seven's hands. "This is a contract item, one that I obtained recently. It's nothing too powerful. Just a box capable of holding more than its size.

"It basically sucks in anything in front of it when you open it and spits it all back out when opened again. I've filled it with ten thousand worth of hard from Lucem's treasury, so if you run out of money in my account, you may use that as well. Just don't open it until you need it, lest you end up spraying plates of hard everywhere. It can't be stowed in your inventory because of the cap on how much hard you can store, so keep it hidden in your item bag and don't tell anyone you have it."

Seven stared at the box in her hands, hardly able to believe what it held. Ten thousand would be enough to keep her head above water for a few months. A bead of sweat rolled down the back of her neck as she realized how easy it would be to lose the item. She closed her eyes and took a breath before dropping the box into her pouch. What choice did she have?

"Okay, I will do my best."

"Fantastic!" Leftwitch clapped her hands, startling Ruby so that he dug his claws in a bit harder.

"I should try to learn everything I can about Noctem before attending." Seven looked down at the invitation to check the date of the event, but found that the page had returned to being blank. "I'm sorry, when is the auction?"

Cassius smirked as the Lady of the Silver Tongues shoved her hands behind her back.

"Tonight." Leftwitch checked the time on her stat-sleeve. "In about an hour, actually."

"What?" Seven felt her eyes nearly pop out of her head.

Leftwitch gestured to a door. "Cassius, would you mind showing Seven to the transport ship we have waiting?"

"It would be my pleasure." He turned to Seven. "Just follow me and we'll get you on board one of our royal shuttles."

"But what about getting prepared? What about—"

"You'll be fine." Leftwitch slapped her on the back. "Just keep to yourself and bid aggressively." She pushed Seven toward the door.

Seven's feet obeyed her new boss, only letting her turn back for a second to see the woman wave and turn away as if she had something else to do. It was clear there wouldn't be any further arguments. Seven heard herself utter one last, "but…" just as Cassius beckoned her through the door to where a stairway waited.

She found herself climbing each step, unable to speak despite the worry rattling through her skull. Auto-pilot took over, carrying her the rest of the way up to where Cassius threw open another doorway.

Wind blew Seven's blue hair across her vision as the open sky filled her view. A strange craft waited for her, its stubby wings angled upward with a vertical engine attached to each. Ruby, still perched on her shoulder, flapped his wings in the breeze, giving Seven a face-full of feathers. She shielded her head and waited for the large bird to settle down. Finally, the damn thing took flight and soared into the shuttle's open door to wait for Seven.

"This transport will take you straight to the Auction of Souls. It's a royal ship, so it's nice and comfortable. Just relax and enjoy the ride." Cassius stood aside to let Seven board the craft.

"Okay," was all she could get out as her shoulders fell.

Seven crept across the surface of the Grand Archway, surrounded by the city of Lucem on all sides, with no railing for safety. She practically ran the last few feet to the craft, just wanting to feel like she had something solid around her again.

Entering the transport, Seven turned around just in time for Cassius to slide the door shut. She pressed her hands against a small porthole window to watch the airship dock fall away from her. Cassius was gone. He hadn't even waited to see her off or wave.

Seven let herself fall back into the plush leather seats, almost sitting on Ruby who had nested into the space before her. The bird flapped and cawed at her as she leapt back up and toppled to the floor.

"Settle down back there." A man turned around from the cockpit, eying her through a narrow door.

"Sorry." She pulled herself back up to sit opposite the large bird.

The pilot turned back to the horizon. The word 'noob' was said again, just loud enough for her to hear.

Seven took a moment to glare at the back of the pilot's head. Then she remembered her player journal, pulling it out without another thought. At least she could read up on Noctem in the time she had left before reaching her destination. She put everything else out of her mind and focused on the task at hand. The message boards would be able to tell her something about the other houses that might be at the auction.

She wasn't about to let herself be blindsided again.

Suddenly, in what seemed like only minutes, the man in the cockpit rapped on the divider wall. "We're approaching the auction, get your things ready. I won't be able to land for long; they'll need the dock for the next ship."

Seven's heart nearly exploded from her chest as she checked the time, realizing that forty minutes had already flown by while she'd studied the message boards. She didn't feel anywhere near prepared enough for what she had to do. There was still so much to learn.

She wasn't ready.

That was when she noticed that the craft wasn't descending toward land. She leaned closer to the window to get a look at the auction house. Then she pressed her face against the glass in shock.

There was no auction house, nor was there any ground to land on. Instead, a massive airship floated through the empty night sky with nothing below but ocean.

Seven couldn't believe her eyes. The vessel had to be at least three thousand feet long; practically a flying city. It looked like a fantasy version of a cruise ship, with four enormous wings reaching out from its sides. They angled up like a bird in flight, their edges shaped to suggest feathers. Some sort of wheel cut through the vessel's sides, rotating horizontally like part of some kind of enormous engine.

"That's the Night Queen." The pilot banked toward the vessel. "You're lucky. It's the largest luxury airship in all of Noctem. I took the wife once. She'd always wanted to take a cruise, but they're too expensive in the real world."

"Yeaahhh." Seven shoved her journal back into her item bag as her craft dipped below the ship and flew close to one side as if the pilot wanted to give her a better look. She watched as they passed an observation deck near the bottom, in awe of the fantastical sight. Eventually the transport slowed, just before her pilot decided to bring the craft back up to land on the ship's platform.

Ruby flapped to the seat beside her, pecking at her wrist until she held her arm out to give the heavy bird somewhere to perch. The now familiar feeling of talons on her skin reminded her of how lucky she was.

She blew out a sigh.

"Lucky me."

CHAPTER THREE

"I'm starting to feel like we get stuck with all the crappy jobs!" Kegan shouted, having trouble breathing with the wind whipping by his face as the Cloudbreaker approached the Night Queen.

"It can't be helped, we're better at stealth than Max and Farn." Corvin shielded his face, holding tight with his other hand to the leather strap they'd tied to the small ship's roof.

"I don't know, Mom is pretty sneaky and I don't see her up here beside us, strapped to the top of a moving aircraft." Piper slapped her free hand on the metal surface the three of them clung to side by side.

"Ginger is Lady of the House; she has to stay front and center." Corvin huddled next to Kegan. "Can't have our leader sneaking aboard an airship under the cover of darkness with us."

"Whatever." Piper elbowed Kegan in the side as if trying to jab the *Blade* on his other side. "Kegan, can you tell Corvin to move his ass over so I can have more room?"

Corvin let out a sigh and scooted over without argument. "There, happy?"

"I don't know, am I? You know what's best for me, right?" Sarcasm dripped from her tongue.

Kegan closed his eyes and rolled his forehead back and forth on the back of his hand. Piper had been going at Corvin since they'd taken off. Kegan was beginning to question his decision to stay between the pair of younger players.

"Anyway, we have to time this right." Kegan ignored the conflict. "Drake won't be able to slow the Cloudbreaker much without raising suspicion. We're going to have to jump all at once."

The craft dipped down to pass under the Night Queen before heading up to drop off the rest of House Lockheart riding in the cabin below.

"Get ready up there," Drakenstein announced over the house line. "I'm going to bank to the side as we pass the observation deck. Be ready to jump and, maybe, don't fall off, okay?"

"Make sure to get us close. And keep it steady!" Piper jabbed back at her brother.

"Yeah, yeah, I have flown the Cloudbreaker before," he added before angling the ship for an approach run.

Kegan shifted his weight and pulled his knees under him in a crouch, ready to leap with everything he had. The observation deck ran along the bottom of the Night Queen's bow. There would only be one chance to make it. If anyone fell, that was the end of the line. There was no going back to try again when they respawned.

"Here it comes." Kegan took charge as the deck sped into view alongside them, the railing whizzing by at breakneck speed. Suddenly, the Cloudbreaker slowed and tiled to the side. Kegan released the leather strap that he'd been clinging to for dear life and kicked off.

For an instant, he was airborne. The nothingness below threatened to claim him just before he flew over the railing of the observation deck. His foot caught the rail, sending him into a spiral as he slammed into the deck.

"Ow, shit, damn, crap!" He tumbled end over end. The

world blurred but the sound of a second body hitting the deck told him that at least one of them had made the leap. A second sound followed, more hollow than the last, as if hitting the side of the railing.

It was accompanied with a loud, "Omphf!"

Finally, Kegan rolled to a stop, taking a second to let the spinning in his head subside. He checked his health. A third empty from the fall damage. To his left, Piper staggered to her feet, looking like she'd been spinning in an office chair. No one was behind her.

"Damn!" Kegan checked Corvin's health, finding it down seventy percent. "Corv, buddy, you make it?"

"Little help." A grunting voice answered as a hand reached up over the rail.

Kegan glared at Piper, who was closer.

"I might be too young to help." She just stared at Corvin's hand and shrugged, feigning a vapid expression.

Kegan launched himself to the rail, catching his friend's wrist as he struggled to get his leg up and over the side. As soon as the *Blade* was safe on deck, Kegan turned back to Piper. She was gone, strolling down the deck toward a hatch at the end.

Kegan turned his attention back to Corvin, who was twitching one ear that had been flipped inside out by the wind. Then he gave the reynard's fluffy ear a solid flick with his finger to fix it.

"Ow." Corvin rubbed at his head.

Kegan just shook his and checked over his shoulder to make sure Piper was out of earshot. "Okay, spill it man, what happened with you and the angry one over there?"

"Pretty much what you thought was going to happen." Corvin let out a sigh, his body deflating along with it. "About ten minutes before we boarded the Cloudbreaker tonight, she told me she liked me."

"Ah." Kegan nodded and offered him a health vial. "And?"

"And what do you think?" Corvin pulled the vial's stopper with his teeth. "She's underage. I told her no, flat out."

"She didn't take that well, huh?"

"No, no she did not."

"For what it's worth, you did the right thing." Kegan gave the *Blade* a supportive pat on the back.

"I know." Corvin downed the health vial. "I don't blame her for being mad. It's not easy being rejected, but hopefully she can move on and start looking at guys her own age."

"Heh, you'll just have to be the punching bag for the time being then."

"I can live with that." Corvin shrugged. "I'm not anything that special; it shouldn't take her that long to get over it."

"Hey!" Piper called from the far side of the empty observation deck. "If you guys are done whispering about me, we have a job to do."

"Damn," Kegan cringed as she hit the nail on the head. "Did she hear us?"

"No," Corvin shook his head. "She's smart. Probably guessed."

Piper threw herself against the wall to lean with her arms crossed, like a model in a clothing ad, not caring what anyone thought.

"Great," Kegan sighed. "Now I'm in the doghouse too. Thanks a lot."

"Sorry, but she's right." Corvin started walking. "We need to get topside so we can watch everyone else's backs."

Kegan adjusted his bow, slinging it across his chest before making his way to the door where Piper waited as impatiently as possible.

"It's locked. I already tried it."

"Not for me, it's not." Kegan pulled out his journal and scrawled a quick message onto a page, sending it off with a messy checkmark. A minute later the door opened, revealing a tall reynard woman dressed in a skirt and blouse that suggested a naval uniform. A crest sat upon her sleeve with the words 'Night Queen' embroidered beneath it.

"Oh, Kegan, it's you." She almost seemed surprised.

"Damn, Kenzie, who else would it be?"

"Sorry, never mind." She held out one hand. "You got my money?"

"That was quick." Kegan reached into his pocket for a plate of hard worth a couple hundred real world dollars. The crest of Reliqua was embossed onto its surface, a leftover from the heist six months ago that they hadn't exchanged for cash yet. It had seemed wise to keep some of the rare currency in game just in case they needed some off the books services.

He slapped the shining plate in her hand and she bounced with excitement before dropping it into her inventory. Her tail wagged happily.

"Pleasure doing business with you."

"I take it you two know each other?" Piper eyed the tall reynard woman from where she pouted against the wall.

"Yeah, Kenzie is a friend from my PVP days back in Tartarus. She used to announce the cage fights." Kegan gave her a warm smile. "She's mostly trustworthy, if you don't count that time she tried to get me to throw a fight so she could bet on the outcome."

"We could have made a killing, you know." Kenzie shifted her weight and put her hands on her hips. "I had to work something out with that MurderStorm guy instead, and let's just say his elevator doesn't go all the way to the top. I got caught and ended up having to take a real job. I host the stand-up acts that run on the Night Queen's forward deck every other day. It's nothing fancy, but it helps with my student loans and my skirt covers my butt more than the one I wore for the cage fights." She gestured to her rear as if to demonstrate.

"That's good." Kegan ignored the display. "Just don't get caught this time. I assume taking bribes and sneaking us aboard the ship is frowned upon by the management."

"I'll be fine. There's always another job in Noctem." She waved a hand at his warning. "Anyway, let's get you three smuggled topside, shall we?" She spun and headed off down the corridor. Kegan gestured for Piper to take the lead.

Corvin followed behind her. "How come there aren't any other passengers down on the observation deck?"

"Normally there would be, but that auction thing that's going on upstairs has some sections closed off for security." Kenzie turned to walk backward. "I guess the event is a big deal. There's a pair of weird guys running the show. They've taken over the main theater and blocked it off from the rest of the guests."

"What do you mean by weird guys?" Kegan raised an eyebrow.

"I mean they're weird. They're using identical avatars so none of us can tell them apart. I've only seen them from a distance, though. I've just been calling them the twins."

"That's creepy," Piper chimed in.

Kenzie led them down another few hallways, each lined with rich mahogany panels and brass detailing. The corridors were lit by glowing crystal inlays that flowed through the ceiling in intricate patterns of filigree. They reminded Kegan of the delicate design that wove around Kira's wrist to form her stat-sleeve. He hadn't seen it in a while, since Echo didn't have one.

Eventually, they reached a storage area where a platform of solid stone hovered within an empty lift shaft. It must have led to the upper floors, like some kind of elevator. The room was full of wooden crates and barrels stacked in an organized manner. Kenzie hefted the lid off one of the larger creates that sat on a cart. It was empty.

"This is your ride upstairs." She gave Kegan a sly smile. "Hop in."

"And where will our chariot here take us?" Piper kicked at one of the cart's wheels.

"The Night Queen is a fully-functional cruise ship that provides the very best for its guests. Each of these crates are full of food items to be plated up on the service floors before being served topside. There's no need to refrigerate anything since it's all virtual, so we just store it all down here. One of my guys will be down in a few minutes to bring this crate up. They'll take you to a secluded space where you can quietly sneak out. Finding your way up to the main deck won't be hard from there."

"Not a lot of room in there." Kegan flicked his eyes back and forth between the crate and Kenzie.

"Eh, you're all friends." She shrugged. "Won't kill you to get cozy for a few minutes."

Actually, it might. Kegan glanced back at Piper. To his surprise, she hopped into the crate without hesitation.

"No sense standing around talking about it." The reynard girl scooted to one side and tugged on her gun belt so that her pistol shifted to her front, making more room beside her.

"True enough." Kegan stowed his bow in his inventory and swung his leg over the side. "I guess I'm in the middle again."

Corvin stepped in as soon as Kegan got settled, swatting him in the face with his tail in the process. Eventually all three of them were snug in the crate and Kenzie dragged the lid over.

"Everybody comfy?" She didn't wait for an answer before setting the top over their heads and pushing it into place.

Kegan couldn't help but smirk as both Piper and Corvin clasped their hands over their foxlike ears to keep them from being pinched. He hugged his knees to his chest and tried to take up as little space as possible. Though that didn't stop Piper from elbowing him anyway.

"Ouch, you're on my tail."

"Sorry." He leaned to the other side.

"Ah, now you're on my tail." Corvin winced.

"Damn it, why did you both have to make reynard characters?"

"Because they're cool," they both answered in unison before falling silent.

Suddenly a knock came at the lid.

"Hey, shut up in there. Have you guys ever heard of stealth?"

"Sorry," they all answered together.

Then Kegan sat, with nothing but the sound of breathing surrounding him.

Good thing none of us are claustrophobic, like Kira. The fairy had seemed pretty shaken after squeezing through a small space to clear a dungeon over a year ago. It was hard to believe how much time had passed since then. Especially after so much had happened.

Suddenly a masculine voice spoke from outside the create.

"Shit, Kenzie, another one?"

"What? I don't hear you complaining about the payoff."

"True, but it's going to get crowded up there."

"I don't like the sound of that." Corvin whispered.

"Neither do I," added Piper.

"At least you two agree on something." Kegan rubbed his forehead against his knees.

The crate began to move. Whistling could be heard from outside as the familiar motion of an elevator jostled Kegan's stomach. Eventually, the lift came to a stop and the crate began to move again. A new voice came from outside, this time sounding confused.

"Another one? Don't we have enough food for the night already?"

"Ahh, just this one crate left, I think," the voice of Kenzie's accomplice answered nervously. "Should be enough after this."

Kegan held his breath along with the others.

"Whatever," said the new voice as everyone in the crate released a collective sigh.

Finally, the ride came to an end and Kenzie's accomplice knocked on the lid. "Wait thirty seconds and then get out of there. You're on your own after that."

Kegan knocked back in understanding. He didn't bother counting off the seconds, figuring that Corvin already had that covered. As expected, the *Blade* tapped on his knee in time.

"Okay, that's thirty."

"Thank god." Kegan shoved off the lid and stood up, forgetting that the crate was still sitting on a cart with wheels.

Apparently Piper had forgotten as well because she sprang up beside him. The cart veered to one side with the sudden movement, sending the two of them tumbling in different directions.

"Woah—" Kegan hit the floor face first.

Corvin yelped from behind him.

Rubbing at his nose, Kegan stood back up finding the *Blade* frozen in place with Piper in his arms. She stared daggers at him as she pushed herself off.

That's getting old fast. Kegan shook his head at the two of them yet again.

Corvin exited the crate last, stopping halfway as he took in the room. "Uh oh."

"That's not good, is it?" Piper pointed out across the room at four other empty crates, each with their lids haphazardly laying to the side.

"No." Kegan folded his arms, noticing a dagger sitting at the bottom of one of the containers. "I don't think that it is."

Suddenly, a door swung open and a man in black leather slipped into the room, looking back over his shoulder to talk to someone standing behind him.

"Sorry, I think I dropped my dagger…" His voice trailed off as soon as his eyes met Kegan's. Surprise fell across his dumb face.

Looking past him, Kegan saw a large man in a helmet holding a spear and four more smaller men all dressed in black, waiting in the hall beyond.

Corvin's hand crept toward the space where his sword would have been if he hadn't stowed it before getting in the crate. Everyone froze as each of the stowaways began to realize they weren't alone.

"Well, Kenzie has been busy." Kegan shrugged. "Some people never change."

CHAPTER FOUR

Seven ducked her head as she exited the transport and set foot on the Night Queen's landing platform. Polished wood stretched across the deck beneath her feet. The bow, where she stood, sat a few levels higher than the main deck, with ornate staircases leading down from one walkway to another before reaching an open space below.

Beyond the main deck, structures spread across the rear of the ship like a miniature city, each merging together to create a seamless expanse of intricate architecture. It looked like it could offer just about any entertainment that Seven could imagine, all nestled between the craft's four massive wings.

A glass-encased section sat on top like a crown, high above the rest. Seven assumed it was the bridge, as its panoramic windows would give the crew a view of the ship's entire surroundings. Hundreds of lanterns hung across the deck from a canopy of ropes that stretched from the top of the bow to the structures below. They swayed gently with the ship's movement and illuminated the scene with a romantic ambiance that matched the stars above.

It was breathtaking.

Ruby hopped up to Seven's shoulder from where he had perched on her forearm, forcing her to stand at an unnatural angle. She wished the dumb bird would find somewhere else to sit.

"Oh well, let's get going."

Seven walked down the stairs as the transport she'd arrived in abandoned her. Its engines released a blast of air that ruffled Ruby's feathers as it took off. Seven watched the small ship vanish into the night sky. She would have stayed there staring off into space, but another ship seemed to need the landing platform. Several more circled overhead.

Must be the auction's other attendees.

She turned away from the sky and checked the time on her stat-sleeve.

One minute late! Seven let out a sudden squeak and hastened her pace. No wonder Leftwitch had rushed her out.

An escort met her at the bottom of the stairs and led her across the main deck to an opulent set of doors that sat at the Night Queen's heart. A pair of tough-looking men stood guard outside, though one kept checking a page in his journal as if he was bored. Neither seemed like they were paying much attention.

I guess good help is hard to find when you hire players to act as security.

That was when a clean-cut elf in a formal waistcoat slipped through the door to approach her. Unlike the others, he carried no weapon, just a book.

"Welcome to the Auction of Souls." His demeanor was quite professional as he inclined his head.

"Sorry I'm late. It's been a hectic night so far." Seven gave an apologetic bow on reflex.

"Oh, that's quite alright, you're the first to arrive anyway."

"Really?"

"Yes, expecting player types to be on time for an event always seems to be asking a lot." His nose turned up as he continued. "Now if I were a dungeon boss, that might be different, but unfortunately proper business ventures don't rank highly on their priorities."

Seven suppressed a smile at his words. He hadn't been kind. Actually, he was a little rude, but even that reassured her. He was her people. All business. A bit of the tension she'd been carrying in her neck faded.

"I'm glad I could be somewhat punctual then."

"Indeed." He opened his book and glanced down at it. "Now, what house would you be representing?"

"The Silver Tongues."

"Lady Leftwitch will not be attending?" His eyes flicked up to her.

"Sorry, no. I'm one of her assistants. I was sent in her place."

He glanced at Ruby hanging on her shoulder. "And I assume that pet is supposed to be proof of the arrangement."

"Yes." Seven took out the invitation she had been given and shoved it in the bird's face, getting a squawk in her ear in return. Ink spread across the paper as it had before and she held it out for the man to see. He lowered his book to examine it.

"That certainly is a creative use of Noctem's pet system. We didn't realize that they could trigger a private letter for their master like that." He sighed and looked back to his book. "But rules are rules, and you do have a valid invitation. My name is Grindstone." He reached into his item pouch and produced several wooden tiles, each about the size of a credit card. He sorted through them, selecting one.

"This will be your auction tile, simply hold it up if you wish to bid on anything. It will also serve as proof that you are an authorized guest. If you need to leave the auction house at any time, just show it to the guards and they will let you back in. It will also notify you of any changes in the schedule through written text that will appear on the reverse side." He placed it in her hand as a countdown appeared on the back. Each number appeared to burn itself into the wood in real time. "There will be an opening round of items up for bid at the top of the hour.

We added a buffer into the starting times to account for any latecomers."

Forty-five minutes from now. Seven noted the wait time before turning the piece of wood over, where a large number seven was burned into the surface. She glanced back up at him questioningly.

He gave her a smile. "Normally we would assign you number one since you're the first to arrive, but this seemed more appropriate with your designation." He took a step back and opened the door for her. "I hope you enjoy your experience with us at the Auction of Souls."

Seven pocketed the bidding tile and headed inside. Grindstone closed the door the instant she was through. She jumped as the door closing startled her.

Then she jumped again.

"Welcome, welcome!" Grindstone suddenly rushed up to her from inside the room. "That's one magnificent bird you have there!"

Seven's mind crashed to a halt as she spun back to the door, wondering how the elf had gotten inside and in front of her so fast.

"I'm so glad you could make it, miss...?" He leaned toward her expectantly.

"Umm, didn't we just meet?" She backed up as Ruby fluttered his wings and tightened his grip on her shoulder.

"Oh no." He let out a chuckle. "That was my associate Grindstone. I'm Dalliance." He slapped a hand to his forehead. "Sorry, we use the same avatar design. I told him it would be confusing, but he thought it would paint us as uniformed professionals."

"I see." Seven leaned away from the excitable elf. He moved closer.

"And you are...?" He circled his hands around each other as if trying to draw a name out of her.

"Oh, I'm Seven. From the House of Silver Tongues. I'm here at Lady Leftwitch's request."

"Ah, perfect. I thought I recognized Ruby here. Pity Lady Leftwitch couldn't make it. But no matter. As Grindstone might say, money is money, it doesn't matter who gives it to you."

"Thank you for understand—"

"Follow me." He spun before she finished talking and raced through the theater lobby.

Seven followed him across the extravagant room, passing a wide bar that sat at the center of the space like some kind of concession stand. Velvet ropes were set up in front to form a standard queue line. It was actually comforting. Seven liked the organized structure of it all. A part of her could almost forget that she was standing aboard a fantasy airship.

Almost.

"This will be where you'll be spending the majority of the night." A door opened and a curtain parted magically as Dalliance approached. "We've rented out the Night Queen's largest theater, and we've done our best to make sure you have a pleasant time."

Seven gasped at the elegance of the temporary auction house. Velvet curtains hung across a brilliant stage while a wide balcony hung over head. Gold leaf covered the box seats that lined the walls above. Chandeliers hung from the ceiling, bearing glowing crystals to illuminate the space. An impressive buffet table sat down by the stage, out of place in a theater, but just as extravagant.

"I know, right?" Dalliance grinned, prompting Seven to close her mouth when she realized it was hanging open.

"Yes, it's beautiful."

"It made sense to hold the auction somewhere mobile so that we could secure the location easily. I'm just glad we were able to find a venue so fitting." He leaned over to her. "Grindstone thought the Night Queen was too expensive and flashy, but I thought the aesthetics were worth it."

"I see." Seven nodded without actually agreeing.

"Anyway, enjoy the buffet and relax. I have more guests to greet."

She gave him a polite bow and he spun off toward the door. Letting out a sigh, she made her way toward the stage where she went about minding her own business. Ruby did the same, taking flight to perch on the back of a nearby chair.

Good riddance. Seven rubbed her shoulder as she turned her attention to the buffet table.

Normally she would have ignored the food altogether, but she had always been a nervous eater. There would be no pleasure gained from it, but at least it would pass the time and keep her calm. She politely claimed a piece of bread as the blandest option she could find. A tingle ran through her mind as she took a bite and, despite her nature, she found herself smiling.

How?

She pulled the bread away and examined it as memory of her childhood flooded back to her. Somehow it tasted exactly like the fresh-baked bread her mother used to make for Sunday dinners.

It even smelled the same.

Seven had read that the system that ran Noctem sometimes called upon the memories of its users to create a more immersive experience. Supposedly, it could fill in the gaps where its information fell short. She wondered for a moment how much of her mind the system could access? How much it could recreate from her memories?

She took another bite, the taste giving her a bittersweet ache in her chest. She hadn't thought of her mother's cooking for years. Not since cleaning out her parents' house after they'd both passed.

Shaking off the thought, she stole another two pieces of bread and stored them in her inventory for later and moved away from the buffet table to hide near one wall. Taking food from the table for later wasn't the most professional thing to do, but no one was looking and she was bound to feel nervous again before the night was done.

Ah, speaking of being nervous, she thought just as the rest of the attendees began to arrive. From the curtained doors at the entrance, Dalliance led a well-dressed elf into the theater. It took Seven a few seconds to place a name to the face.

Dartmouth.

The elf strode down the aisle with an air of superiority, bracketed by a pair of players. In preparation for her new job, she had watched a number of interviews conducted by Left-witch. Dartmouth had appeared on the Late Knight show back when he'd taken over as Lord of the House of Serpents six months ago.

There was a lot of ill will toward his house thanks to his predecessor's attempted conquest of Noctem. Though, since then, Dartmouth seemed focused on rebuilding the Serpents' reputation more than anything else. He'd even gone public with his real-world identity, a political science major at Dartmouth University. Seven suppressed a judgmental smirk at the egotis-tical nature of naming his character after his university.

Before Seven had a chance to make any more assumptions about the elf, the curtain split open again. This time, a man stomped into the room. He tipped back a drinking horn as he walked, while another pair of players followed him in. He was a huge, lumbering man. Again, she suppressed a smirk, recog-nizing him from one of the most viewed videos ever recorded in Noctem.

His name was Tusker, the Lord of House Boar and ruler of the city of Torn. Three months ago, he had been executed in his own throne room by a member of House Lockheart. Seven had read on the boards earlier that night that House Boar had been recruiting new members aggressively. It made sense, considering a player named Farnsworth had killed him so fast that the difference in power had been absurd. It was like squishing an insect. He must have been looking to prevent something like that from happening again.

The strange thing about him being killed before was that Lockheart didn't even claim his throne afterward. Seven shud-dered as the video flashed through her head. House Lockheart's gunslinger, a terrifying player calling himself MaxDamage24, had stared straight into the eyes of the player recording the video. It was downright chilling, like he was looking through the player at the viewers at home while issuing a threat to someone named Nix. His eyes had been so… angry.

If there was one thing Seven was sure of, it was that she wanted nothing to do with the man, or anyone from House Lockheart for that matter.

Tusker and his Boars, on the other hand, seemed friendly enough, taking seats near the middle of the room and throwing their feet up on the chairs in front of them. They seemed to be putting in effort to act like they belonged there. Seven relaxed a little, feeling she could relate. A moment later she tensed right back up.

Amelia, Lady of the Winter Moon appeared at the back of the room. Her violent reputation had preceded her. Especially since she had been involved in that ridiculous heist half a year ago. It would have been hard not to recognize her. She held an unreasonably long saber sheathed at her side like she was ready to draw it at a moment's notice.

A tall man, Klaxon, if Seven remembered the name right, followed Amelia. Apparently all houses needed an Archmage, and he was hers. The other required position, First Knight, was held by the player beside him, Kashka. Seven's eyes widened to take in the enormous woman, the horns of a ram protruding from the sides of her head.

That must be a faunus, Seven assumed, looking at the woman's features, not having seen a member of the race before. It wasn't too popular from what she'd read, due to a highly specialized racial trait of some kind. Seven let her mind wander back to the character race options she'd ignored when creating hers. Lost in thought, she almost forgot she was staring at the woman. She immediately averted her gaze, accidentally locking eyes with Amelia herself. The predatory woman grinned before breaking the connection.

Seven gulped audibly.

Fortunately, a new arrival distracted the Lady of the Winter

Moon's attention away from Seven's fearful response. Unfortunately, this also elicited an even more embarrassing response from her as she choked on a piece of bread and coughed crumbs into her hand. Seven struggled to compose herself before the newcomer noticed her.

Too late.

Alastair Coldblood stood at the center of the room, looking straight at her. The head of Checkpoint Systems, one of the most influential people in the world, was looking her dead in the face. His avatar, dressed like some kind of glam-rock vampire in a long coat, had a dark presence that seemed to dim the lights in the room. He arched an eyebrow at her, only to turn away to speak to a severe-looking elf standing behind him like an assistant.

"What is someone like him even doing here?" Seven whispered to herself.

"Probably just wants some contracts," a voice suddenly came from beside her.

"Gah!" She jumped to the side, finding a cloaked woman standing next to her. A pair of tall fox ears poked through the top of her hood. They twitched in an excitable manner. The upper half of her face was covered with a simple mask, a black diamond pattern around one eye like a court jester.

"Sorry." The fox-woman threw her hands behind her and bounced on one foot. "Didn't mean to startle you. Just didn't realize you were talking to yourself there."

"Ah, yes." Seven scratched at the back of her head. "I was surprised to be in a room with the head of Checkpoint Systems. It wasn't something I expected to happen tonight," She admitted politely while internally screaming, *Who are you? Go away. Go away!*

The reynard woman did not go away.

"It's not that surprising. Contracts make Noctem go 'round, so of course Checkpoint would want in on that action. If only to keep their world running smoothly."

"Couldn't they just create as many contracts as they want?"

Seven asked, accepting that she was having company whether she wanted it or not.

"Not how contract items work." The strange woman shook her head. "Power can't just be created at will. This is Noctem; there is a price for everything. Be it money, effort, or souls."

"That's awfully dramatic."

"Clearly you haven't been in Noctem for long."

"Is it that obvious?" Seven gestured at the starter robe she wore, expecting to be called a noob any second.

"It's okay, we all were new once." The reynard leaned closer and nudged Seven with an elbow. "I'd say you're doing pretty well for a level one, considering you're standing at the center of one of the most important events to happen in a while." Her comment only reinforced the feeling that Seven didn't belong there.

"To be honest, I'm in way over my head." Seven attempted to joke, inadvertently telling the truth.

"Aren't we all?" The reynard's ears twitched.

"True…" Seven trailed off as a new arrival entered the room, this time unrecognizable to her. He was tall, with glasses and blue hair tied back with a red ribbon. He wore a long cloak made of black fabric, that glistened with a sheen like oil in water. A few of the auction's guards followed him, dragging in several large chests, one after another. Seven tilted her head to the side.

"That's Larkin." The reynard in the mask leaned closer to whisper. "He's a crafter, from what I understand. Didn't think he had an excess of money for an event like this though."

"Maybe he's intending on trading whatever's in those trunks," Seven guessed. Before she had a chance to think any more on the subject, another two groups entered the theater.

One group was led by a deru man with bluish skin and emerald crystals poking out from his hair. He wore robes similar to Seven's, though he stood taller, commanding respect. On his face he wore a subtle frown, as if the rest of the event was beneath him. An elf and a human followed him close. Their eyes scanned the room, their hands on their weapons, as if a threat could be anywhere.

The next group complemented the other, a trio of reynards skulking into the theater, possibly the threats that the previous group was worried about. The one in the lead wore a gun at his hip and walked as if he owned the place, his tail wagging excitedly.

"The deru there is Lord Promethium of House Forge. I forget his companions." Seven's masked friend pointed a finger in his direction. "He's the new ruler of Sierra." She turned to face Seven and hooked a thumb back at the three reynards. "Those sketchy guys are from House Saint, Lord Murph and his brothers. He runs the city of Thrift. Don't let their looks fool you, they're a bunch of kittens. Kittens... well, kittens that sometimes murder people for hard."

Seven committed the names to memory.

"Speaking of who's who..." The masked woman's tail swished back and forth. "I take it you're from the Silver Tongues, right?"

Seven flinched at having her house guessed so easily. "How did you—"

"The bird." She pointed to the chair where the overgrown avian perched. "That's Ruby, right?"

"Yes."

"And I take it you're one of Leftwich's assistants?"

"Number Seven. It's weird to go by a number, but apparently that's my name now."

"Eh, there's worse names out there."

Seven nodded just as the curtain at the back of the theater opened again to reveal a beautiful woman. A wave of dread swept through Seven's body at the sight of her. Even to someone out of touch with the virtual world, her name had become legend.

GingerSnaps, Lady of House Lockheart.

No!

Seven felt her hopes of an easy job crumble as the woman

strutted into the theater. Her gray frock coat billowed behind her with green silk lining the inside. A flag bearing the crest of Noctem's most infamous house hung from one shoulder to cover her sleeveless arm.

The woman radiated confidence and desire. Details about her had flooded the news, even in the real world. And why wouldn't they? Her house had pulled off the theft of millions in virtual currency, all within a loophole that kept them out of jail. Checkpoint Systems had been forced to pay out the money in order to obey the rules of the game.

The real-world identities of Lockheart's members were a mystery, but it had become well known that Ginger had worked at a brothel in Lucem up until last year. The media seemed to dwell on that fact of her background, reporting that she'd entertained thousands of clients over her time there. She had also been banned from nearly every shop in Lucem for stealing everything from consumable items to explosives. How a woman with that kind of past had become the leader of one of the most powerful houses in the virtual world was incredible.

Fear gripped Seven's chest as two more of House Lockheart's members entered the room. They were even scarier in person.

Close to Ginger's side, was MaxDamage24.

Also known as the Pale Rider.

His murderous aura was immense. A scarf of black fabric wrapped his shoulders with a pattern of bones decorating its surface. His chest was covered by dark leather armor and a weathered gray shirt, while a pair of lethal-looking guns hung from a double shoulder holster. A small knife glinted, sheathed on his belt next to his ammunition pouches. His eyes were just as cold as the video Seven had seen him in. He was fear incarnate. Even Noctem had titled him so, labeling him as the virtual world's *Reaper*.

A tall woman followed, Lockheart's First Knight.

Farnsworth, the Death Grip.

The clawed gauntlet for which she was known covered her

left hand. It was a contract capable of draining the life from another player in a slow and brutal death. Though, in the video where she'd killed Tusker, she'd taken him down in a heartbeat rather than dragging it out. The gauntlet had been bound to her when she'd killed the previous Death Grip, making it one of the most unique contract items in the game, as it was passed on from victim to killer.

Farnsworth stopped for a moment to glance back at the entrance, her black, curly hair swept to one side as she stood in profile. A cluster of freckles spread across the dark skin of her cheek. Her armor would have made her seem dashing, what with the cape and fur collar, but the coloring gave her a dark presence. A matte black breastplate covered her chest and a sad smile adorned her face as she looked back.

A diminutive woman in a hooded cloak pranced into the theater to take a place at the woman's side. Her face wasn't visible other than brief glimpses of pale skin, but Seven knew exactly who she was.

Kirabell, Lockheart's Archmage.

Seven didn't know what she looked like under the cloak, but her size made her instantly recognizable. The media loved talking about her as much as they did Ginger.

In sharp contrast to the people she played with, Kirabell was harmless, only being capable of healing. Many had done the math, and from what most could tell, she was the highest level fairy in Noctem. Possibly even the most powerful healer. She'd never made news for any such accomplishments prior to Lockheart's heist. According to reports from those that had met her, she was just a cheerful girl that supported others, usually with a sarcastic remark.

The little mage peeked around the room before drifting toward the buffet. Farnsworth blocked her path as if keeping her from wandering off. The *Shield* stepped in front, hiding the fairy from Seven's view and blotting out the only source of light that Lockheart seemed to contain.

Seven took a few heavy breaths, not sure what she should

do. The auction had just become the last place she wanted to be.

"Damn." The strange reynard beside her gave a word to how Seven was feeling, while tugging on her own hood to hide her face a bit more. She let out a chuckle, sounding like she was amused. "Looks like the auction just got a lot more interesting."

"I hope I don't have to interact with them." Seven turned back to her new friend. "I just want to get this night over with."

"Don't worry, they're not as bad as their reputation makes them out to be. And hey, I'll be right here with you. Well, more like hiding behind you." The reynard gave Seven a warm smile.

"And who are you?" Seven asked, realizing how suspicious it was that the woman hadn't introduced herself. "What house are you from?"

"Sorry, no house for me." The woman let out an awkward laugh. "I'm a ronin."

"Then how did you get an invitation?"

"I'm, ah, not what you would call invited. Just, sort of snuck in." Her ears fell like a scolded dog.

"What?" Seven's throat went dry as she motioned to back away.

The woman waved both her hands in front of her while her furry ears twitched back and forth. "Don't worry, I'm not here to hurt anyone. And I have money to bid. I'm just not important enough to get an invite, that's all. Haven't made a name for myself. But the way I see it, every contract I get is one that can't be used against me, so here I am." She slapped her hands together in a begging gesture. "Please don't tell on me. If I don't make a scene, the twins running this thing might let me stay."

Seven let out the breath she was holding. "It's none of my business."

"Thank you, thank you, thank you." The reynard held out one hand in an offer of friendship. "I'm Nix."

Panic alarms rang through Seven's mind as the name left the strange woman's lips. "Oh no, you're—"

"Nix!" a voice roared through the theater, as if on cue.

The reynard cringed at the sound of her own name. "That didn't last long."

Seven spun to see who was shouting, then immediately wished she hadn't as MaxDamage24 raised his pistols and fired in her direction. She screamed as bullets slammed into the stage behind her, sending splinters of wood showering down around her.

Seven waited for the dull pain she'd read about that came along with the game's damage. There was nothing she could do.

It was over already.

She had one job, and she had failed.

CHAPTER FIVE

"Nix!"

Max's mind went blank as he reached for a gun.

She was right there.

After months of searching and preparing, she was right fucking there.

Nix ducked behind some random woman, a low-level *Venom* from the look of it. What someone like that was doing at the auction, he had no idea.

No matter, it was her fault for being there.

Blind rage squeezed the trigger as every reasonable braincell in Max's head screamed at him to stop. Killing Nix wouldn't solve anything. Not in a virtual world.

His pistol locked back empty as the sound of a lone scream echoed through the room. All eyes fell on the low-level woman standing in the wrong place at the wrong time. She shut her eyes tight while her panicked cry trailed off into an awkward silence. Finally, she cracked one eye open, her body frozen in a wince as if expecting death.

"What the…?" She glanced down at herself, clearly shocked to be alive.

With rage coursing through Max's body, it had taken everything he had to hold back. The wall around the woman hadn't fared as well, taking the brunt of his anger and leaving a bullet riddled outline around the woman's body.

"Get out from behind her!" Max growled, his chest heaving with one uncontrolled breath after another.

"Alright, alright, jeez." Nix's voice came from behind the low-level woman who was still frozen in fear. A pair of furry ears poked out followed by the rest of the evil woman. She wore a mask, just like the one worn by the men that had abducted Kira's body. She pulled it off. "I guess there's no point in hiding my—"

Max drew his other pistol and shot her in the shoulder. "Give her back!"

"Ow…" Nix lurched back, twisting with the impact of the bullet, her shoulder glowing crimson as she placed a hand over the hit. "Little help?"

Suddenly, from one of the box seats above, a familiar horned *Coin* dropped into the conflict. Aawil, the strong, silent faunus, coiled a hand through Ginger's hair and pulled her head back before placing a dagger to her throat.

"Go ahead," Ginger spouted in defiance, "like it matters."

"Now, now, don't be like that." Nix threw her hands up as if she meant no harm. "No one needs to be sent back to spawn."

Farnsworth stepped closer to Echo, the avatar claiming food from the buffet while everyone's attention was on Max.

"Don't you move!" He stepped closer to Nix, holstering his empty gun and clutching the silver dagger he'd received from the fight with the Deep.

"Really?" Nix rolled her eyes. "What can you really do to me here?"

Max tightened his grip on the contract. She was right. *God damn it, she was right.* Her being right there before him meant nothing. He still had no idea how to find her in the real world and with her ability to overpower the system, there wasn't much he could do to her anyway. Her being there now didn't change the plan. They still had to trap her. They still needed to prepare.

"Hey! Hey!" Dalliance ran down the aisle.

"What is the meaning of this?" Grindstone raced into the theater behind him.

Alastair stepped into the middle of the conflict. "You seem to have an uninvited guest. MaxDamage here was just assisting with security." He gave Max a pointed glance and motioned for him to lower his gun.

Max ignored him, keeping it trained on Nix.

Alastair approached him and placed a hand on his shoulder, whispering so the rest of the room couldn't hear. "I know how you feel. But we have to be smart about this. She's too dangerous to take chances with."

"Who are you?" Grindstone stomped over to Nix. "And how did you get in here?"

"I, ah." Nix swiped a hand in front of her face and cleared her throat at Aawil, who was still holding a dagger to Ginger's throat. The faunus released her hair and sheathed the weapon. Nix took a breath as if she was nervous before speaking again.

"I'm sorry, but when I heard about the Auction of Souls, I had to check it out." She gave a low bow to Grindstone. "I apologize for sneaking in, but I have money and I can give you my account information to confirm it. I ask that you allow me to stay and take part in the bidding."

"Absolutely not." Dalliance stomped one foot. "This is a high-class event for Noctem's top houses, we can't let just anyone in—"

"What's your account information?" Grindstone stepped in front of his twin, making it clear he valued money over status.

"Let her stay." Max's eye twitched as he forced himself to lower his gun.

Alastair gave him a nod. "Yes, I'm sure Nix has the funds to make for a lively auction. No sense throwing her out."

"But…" Dalliance glanced back and forth between Grindstone and the bullet holes in the wall.

Grindstone handed Nix his book and a pen so she could give him her financial information. She handed it back afterward and the room went silent for a moment as Grindstone stared at the page. Finally, his eye's widened and he looked up at her.

"Ah, well, this will do. This will do nicely."

"Thank you." Nix's ears perked up like an excited cat with a mouse to play with.

Max clenched his jaw so tight it hurt. His knuckles turned white as he clutched the knife on his belt.

"Fine." Dalliance clapped his hands. "But we will have no more of…" He waved his hand around between Max and Nix "…this."

"Yes." Grindstone snapped his book shut. "I think it will be best if we separate our guests until the auction is ready to begin. You can all use the box seats above to wait, at least that will remove the temptation to fight amongst one another. With so many of Noctem's top houses present, I know how tempting it may be to take advantage of any opening that presents itself." He gestured to a pair of doorways set on either side of the theater. "Those will lead up to the boxes, please refrain from any hostile activities on the way up. We can reconvene down here on the main floor at the top of the hour."

"Don't have to tell me twice." Nix was moving before she had finished talking, disappearing through a door along with Aawil. They both reappeared a moment later in one of the box seats above. She leaned out and waved to everyone still on the floor. It took every ounce of restraint that Max had not to shoot at her.

"Let's go." He turned and headed toward the opposite door, gesturing to Alastair with his head as he walked by. He hoped the head of Checkpoint Systems would take the hint and meet them upstairs.

Ginger joined him, taking Max's hand and giving it a brief squeeze. Farn followed, herding Echo along with her. The rest of the auction's guests split up and drifted toward the doors.

Max headed up a flight of stairs with a red-carpet runner that led to the box seats. Curtained archways lined a hallway every twenty feet with a door in the middle. He picked one at random and entered, finding a space inside with a balcony overlooking the stage. A second curtain hung to block the box from view. Max took one look across the theater at Nix, then pulled the curtain closed.

As soon as she was out of sight, he dropped to the floor with his back against the wall and sunk his face into his hands. Ginger sat down beside him and rested her head against his shoulder.

"Can we really just ignore her?" Farn tapped her clawed fingers against a chair rail that ran along the wall.

Max looked up at the *Shield*. "What else can we do?"

"We can throw things at Nix from here," Echo added, mouthing the words silently and miming the act of throwing something.

Max groaned and gestured to Farn. "Could you?"

Farn reached into her pouch and pulled out a plain velvet pouch, the useless contract item she'd gotten a few weeks prior. Pulling it open, she retrieved a small honey loaf baked into the shape of a lagopin, complete with tiny wings and rabbit ears. She handed it to Echo.

"Perfect! I can hit her with this." Echo tossed the loaf in her hand as if testing its weight. Farn caught it out of the air and pushed it close to the artificial fairy's mouth so that the treat bumped her nose. Echo gave in to the distraction almost instantly, scarfing into the bread without restraint. Farn pulled the drawstring on the velvet pouch, before opening it again to produce a second bunny loaf that she tossed to Max.

"You look like you could use one too."

Max caught it and gave her a sad smile. "That really is a stupid contract item."

"Hey, don't knock the Sack of Snacks, the system just gave me what I wanted, and I wanted a present for Kira. She's going to love it when we get her back." Farn tousled Echo's hair as she ate. "See how happy it makes this one."

"Yes, but she's just an imitation. The system only mimics her using our own expectations. She only likes it because you think she does." Max tore off a piece of the loaf in his hand.

"Farn's right," a familiar voice came from the curtain as Alastair crept into the room from the hall. "Kira would love it."

"Agreed, it's a bag that makes infinite bunny buns. What's not to like?" Ginger held out a hand so Farn could toss one to her.

"Right before we lost her, Kira told me," Farn stared down at the bread in her hands, "that this was the perfect adventure snack. Not too sweet or over-flavored like the junk food in the real world. Just light and fluffy, with a subtle taste of honey. The kind of thing you might actually find in a fantasy world. They were her favorite. I think... I wanted to give her that, and the contract system responded to that need."

"Yes," Alastair sighed, avoiding eye contact with the *Shield* as he brought the subject back to their dilemma. "But about Nix, what do we do?"

"We keep her here, where we know where she is." Max ripped off a piece of bread with his teeth.

"I agree." Alastair leaned against the door. "It's better to keep her where we can see her. And I'm doing everything I can to track her account. I'm not very optimistic about it, since her signal bounces all over the world every time we think we've traced her. But there's no sense giving up." He held a hand out to Farn for a loaf of bread. "How are things going on your end?"

"It's going." Max nodded. "We made some headway taking down the Deep and got a contract that might be helpful against Nix, but it's not a sure thing. And since no one can find the last of the recently added Nightmares, we're out of ways to get any more contracts. Have you had any luck figuring out what happened?"

"No, the Void is no longer available to fight." Alastair

groaned. "We've apparently lost the Nightmare entirely. We know where it should be but it's just not there."

"How do you lose a Nightmare?" Ginger gave him a sideways look.

"A contract item, I assume." He rubbed at his forehead. "The more of them that find their way into this world, the harder it is to run. Most don't present much of a problem, but every now and then a contract catches us off guard. That's the only possibility for the Void's dungeon being empty. We've looked into resetting the Nightmare, but there are still some issues in editing Carver's work. He's got the code all tangled up so we have trouble changing things without breaking other parts of the game. It's all very frustrating."

"That just leaves the Auction of Souls." Max sank against the wall.

"Don't remind me." Alastair folded his arms.

"Not a fan of the auction?" Ginger raised an eyebrow.

"No." Alastair sneered off in the direction of the theater below. "This event is a mockery of everything I've built. Noctem is not a pay to win game. So it stands to reason that contracts shouldn't be bought or sold."

"Then why allow it?" Max asked.

"I wouldn't if I had a choice." Alastair sunk back against the wall. "Dalliance and Grindstone represent one of Checkpoint's original investors. They negotiated for privileges back when we started and, at the time, getting the startup money was more important. Now my hands are tied." Alastair narrowed his eyes. "They're both lawyers."

"Ouch, my condolences." Farn gave him sympathetic pat on the shoulder.

"Yes, well, what's done is done." Alastair shrugged before changing the subject. "Why contracts, by the way?" Alastair stared down at him. "If Nix really does have the same power that Kira had, there shouldn't be anything in Noctem that can stop her. A contract wouldn't be any different, she can just override them too, like Kira was able to."

"Don't say 'was'!" Farn snapped, her mouth curling down to bare her bottom teeth. "Don't talk like she's gone. We're getting her back."

"Wha– oh," Alastair flinched at the sudden outburst before lowering his eyes to the floor. "Sorry. But again, why focus on contracts? Nix is pretty much a god to this world, just like Kira."

"Not quite." Max finished off his loaf, brushing crumbs off his leg.

"How so?"

"Max thinks contracts are different." Ginger stood up.

"Nix isn't the same as Kira. She told me that herself," Max got up beside her. "Whatever Carver did to Kira was successful. Nix said that she was what happens when the experiment fails."

"So you don't think she's as powerful as Kira." Alastair placed a finger against his chin. "What if you're wrong?"

"I'm not. You didn't see her use that power." Max thought back to the moment when Nix had revealed to him the monster she really was. "That power… hurt her. She could barely stay upright. And that was just after altering the game in small ways."

"And contracts are far more powerful than anything else in Noctem." Farn held up her hand, staring at her claws with a frown. "If anything can stand up to her power, it's going to be one of these."

"You said it yourself." Max leveled his eyes on Alastair. "Contracts aren't even stored on the game server."

"You're right." His mouth fell open. "They're stored in the user's brain along with the game's background data."

Max tapped his head. "That's why, when we went up against Berwyn six months ago, we couldn't let him log out. If he had, the book that detailed his operation wouldn't have functioned."

"And you think that having the data stored in your head rather than the system, that Nix won't be strong enough to resist."

"Exactly. And the invitation we received for the auction had an additional line written at the bottom."

Ginger pulled the sheet of paper from her item bag and passed it to Alastair.

You are cordially invited to attend the first annual Auction of Souls
(P.S. We may have a contract perfect for vendettas.)

"I see." Alastair handed it back. "I guess declaring your war on Nix publicly got Dalliance's attention. That sounds like something he would write."

"Let's just hope his note is accurate." Max spun back toward the curtain and shoved it aside to stare out across the theater. "We need to get her this time."

"And make sure she can't slip away." Ginger leaned on the gold railing of the balcony beside him.

"Let's hope the rest of the auction goes smoothly then." Alastair ducked back into the shadows. "I can't help you publicly, but I'll do anything I can from behind the scenes." He slipped out the door behind to the hall, leaving it open to add one last, "Good luck."

"We're going to need it." Farn joined Max and Ginger at the railing. They stayed like that for a few moments before the *Shield* spun around in a panic. "Oh no, where's Echo?"

Max turned around slowly, his eyes falling on the door that Alastair had left open before traveling to the avatar's discarded cloak on the floor.

"That can't be good."

CHAPTER SIX

Nope nope nope nope.

Seven burst through a door, her head on a swivel to make sure no one had followed her from the theater. Ruby squawked and flapped his wings behind her in attempt to keep up.

No way did I sign on for this.

Continuing to run, she blew past a pair of guards then veered off down a hallway until she hit what looked like a lift. It was just an open shaft with no doors. Safe or not, it was better than staying there with Max and Nix at each other's throats back at the auction. She tapped the call button repeatedly, jogging in place like it would somehow speed up the elevator.

Come on, come on, come on.

Finally, a slab of stone covered in magical-looking runes rose up to meet her in the open shaft. She stepped aboard, only remembering to breathe when she was safely down a few levels. Ruby flew down the shaft to catch up. The oversized bird landed at her feet, glaring up at her as if silently judging.

"What?" Seven stomped one foot at the bird and clutched a hand to her chest. "He freaking shot at me! That sociopath actually shot at me. He didn't even hesitate."

Ruby tilted his head to one side like he didn't understand the problem. Seven ignored him.

"What is wrong with these people?"

The elevator came to a stop at a rather ordinary hallway with a few random players milling about.

"Nope." She tapped the button on the inside of the shaft to go down another couple floors. "Too many people." The elevator stopped again, this time to an empty room with a hatch-like door riveted into the wood paneling. Seven dashed into the space and placed one hand on the wall to rest while she caught her breath. Ruby flew up to land on her outstretched arm.

"Gah! What the hell?" She yanked her hand back and staggered away. "Can you just not, right now?"

Ruby landed on the floor and hopped around her feet making annoyed cawing sounds.

"Yeah, you and me both," she spat back at him. *Stupid bird.*

After taking a moment to recover from everything that had happened upstairs, Seven finally settled down, letting out a long sigh.

"What the hell did I get myself into?"

She wanted to log out and fire off a quick email to Leftwitch.

Thanks but no thanks. Not the job for me, good luck finding someone more desperate.

Seven buried her face in her hands. She couldn't do that. It was a job, and she really was desperate. Seeing her task through was her only option.

Maybe she could log out and then come back in a half hour when the auction was about to start. That way she could avoid any and all interaction with House Lockheart and the rest of those whack jobs upstairs. She rubbed at her temples. No, that wouldn't work. What if she wasn't able to get to sleep again so soon? Could the game pull her back in that fast? The workings of Carpe Noctem's system were still a mystery to her. Just how much power did it have?

"Damn it." She kicked at the brass frame of the hatch. "Ow! Damn it!" she said again as the toe of her shoe lit up with a crimson glow. Her stat-sleeve spread across the skin of her forearm to tell her she'd lost six hit points. A strange numbness replaced the sensation of pain before fading to nothing. It was… uncomfortable.

"Stupid freaking game–" she complained before catching the view through the hatch's small porthole window.

"Whoa…"

Seven forgot all about her complaints and pressed her face to the window. Her hands moved on their own, rotating the wheel on the door to unlock the hatch. Opening it, she stepped through and stared at the space beyond.

A cavernous space of wood and metal surrounded her as she stood on a long-railed section of deck overlooking an opening in the ship's belly. The enormous wheel that she had seen bisecting the Night Queen from the outside rotated just below her. The space that housed the wheel was so large that she could hardly believe she was still inside the ship. It was at least a few hundred feet wide, as if part of the vessel was hollowed out to make room for the contraption. Whatever it was, she had no idea.

Maybe… some kind of engine to keep us afloat?

Sparks erupted from the wheel at random intervals as if generating energy, while an electric quality filled the air. The hairs on her forearm stood on end. That was when she noticed its surface was covered with the same runes as the stone slab that floated in the elevator shaft a moment before. It was as if they both operated off the same magic, just on different scales.

Maybe the rotation is needed for stability.

Seven stepped forward and placed her hands on the railing, looking down at the ground below, past the enormous wheel.

She had no words.

As irritating as she found the game, she had to admit that it held some truly incredible sights. Just like the throne room of the Grand Archway in Lucem, the inner workings of the Night

Queen were an impressive feat of imagination. Noctem's developer team didn't do things halfway.

No, they went all out.

Alone, Seven let herself sink down against the railing and watched the wheel turn.

At least there's no one around.

She navigated to the inventory list tattooed onto her forearm and found one of the pieces of bread that she'd stored earlier. It materialized in her hand and she took a small bite.

Ruby fluttered up to land on the railing by her side, pecking at her shoulder and eying the food item in her hand.

"No. This isn't for you." Seven pulled her hand away and bit off a piece. There was no reason she should share with a fictional pet. Especially one as annoying as Ruby. That was when a swirl of sparkling dust drifted past her from the other side. She immediately spun around to find a petite woman sitting on the rail, a gentle glow fading from her skin.

Seven froze, unsure where the player had come from. She hadn't heard any of the hatches open and there was no other way onto the deck where she stood. Unless the girl could fly. No, that was crazy. Or was it?

"Umm, can I help you?" Seven regarded the player with caution, but considering she was unarmed, she didn't seem like a threat. Plus, Ruby hadn't acknowledged her at all. The girl gave Seven a warm smile, then immediately hopped off the railing.

Seven reached forward on instinct to try to catch her but the girl just floated there in space, a pair of translucent wings keeping her aloft. Shining particles drifted around her form, making her white dress look as if was made up of tiny stars. Even her silver hair shimmered.

Okay, that's a yes to being able to fly, Seven thought as the fairy shot up over the railing and back down to land on the deck. The fabric of her dress blew up as she set down, giving Seven an eye full. A sparkling heart with a keyhole at its center adorned the girl's rear.

Seven suppressed a laugh.

"Can I help…" Seven tried to engage the strange character again, trailing off as she followed the fairy's eyes to the half piece of bread she still held. The girl's dull blue eyes were huge, darting between the food item and Seven's face, as if silently asking for some. Seven would have gotten annoyed, but there was something off about the avatar. Something she couldn't put her finger on. She shrugged and held out the bread, offering it to the fairy.

She immediately snatched it and scarfed it down, revealing herself to be a bit of a slob. Seven raised an eyebrow as the player brushed crumbs from her chest.

"Okay, what do you want with me?" Seven placed a hand on her hip, growing impatient with the player's refusal to say anything.

The fairy answered, mouthing a few words but not making any sounds to accompany them.

"Yeah, I have no idea what that means." Seven glowered at the girl.

She rolled her eyes, looking frustrated before mouthing the word 'sorry' slow enough for Seven to read her lips.

"Can you speak?"

The fairy shook her head before dropping eyes to the floor.

"That's weird." Seven wondered what could cause that. *A curse maybe? Did Noctem have curses?*

"Sorry," the girl repeated.

"It's okay." There was no sense getting annoyed if she couldn't help it. "Do you have a name?"

"People call me Gecko."

"Gecko is an odd name." Seven gave her a smile, appreciating the simple exchange where no one shot at her.

The fairy shook her head, then brushed a silver locks from her eyes before giving her name again.

"Neko?" Seven tried to read her lips, an annoyed stomp told her that was wrong.

The fairy placed one hand by her mouth and mimed yelling

something into the distance. Then she turned her head as if listening.

"Oh, Echo!" Seven felt a little dumb.

The fairy nodded happily then let out a long sigh as if she'd just finished a chore.

"Nice to meet you, Echo. I'm Royal Assistant Seven, but most people seem to just call me Seven." She held out a hand, surprised at how sociable she was being. Most of the players she'd met made her want to avoid them, but there was something about the character that made her feel at ease.

Echo shook her hand, then cringed as one of the hatches flew open behind her. Seven did the same as an elf carrying a bow slung across his body burst onto the deck at the far end.

"Oh hi, Echo." He stopped short as a pair of reynard players appeared close behind him.

"They're right behind us!" shouted one of the reynards as he slammed the hatch shut and threw his back against it.

"No crap, Corvin," spouted the other reynard as she spun the wheel on the door to secure it.

Ruby squawked at the intruders just as a loud bang came from the other side of the door, followed by angry voices. The wheel securing the hatch started to turn backward, clearly being spun from the other side.

Seven took a step back, unsure of what to do.

The elf with the bow leapt back to the hatch, kneeling between the two reynards and gripping the wheel to stop it from turning. It slowed but didn't stop.

"Could use a hand." He glanced back at Seven and Echo, then gestured to a wooden toolbox sitting on the deck by the wall with a large wrench sticking out of it.

Seven's first thought was, *Why is there a tool box here?* Did the ship even need maintenance? No, it was probably just there for decoration.

"Sometime today, Echo." The elf added.

The fairy immediately ran in a small circle before grabbing the handle of the wrench while Seven stood by and watched.

With a loud clunk, Echo dragged the tool from the box, dropping it to the deck and struggling to move it further.

Seven tilted her head to the side at the sight. Sure, the wrench was large and looked heavy, but just how weak was the fairy? She shook off the thought and reached out to help, hefting the wrench up for the struggling girl. Seven wasn't sure if she should be helping, but the three new players seemed to know Echo, and the little fairy didn't appear to mean any harm.

"Here!" She held out the wrench to the group.

"Piper, take it." The male reynard, Corvin, grabbed the locking wheel and held it steady.

"Alright, alright." Piper snatched the wrench from Seven's hands and turned to the elf. "Out of the way, Kegan." She shoved the wrench through the spokes of the locking wheel and clamped it in place so that the tool's long handle hit the wall. The elf, apparently named Kegan, released his grip and fell back against the door to rest.

"How is this ship's security this bad?" He slapped his thigh. "I mean, how many stowaways are on this thing?"

"Stowaways?" Seven gripped the railing, wondering what kind of chaos had just found her. The group ignored her, still talking amongst themselves.

"Aren't we stowaways too?" Corvin panted against the hatch.

"Yeah, just how many people did your friend smuggle on board?" Piper made air quotes around the word friend.

Kegan leaned his head from side to side. "Probably a ton. Knowing Kenzie, she just snuck in every player with a bit of hard and a sketchy motive."

"Don't we have a sketchy motive?" Corvin interjected.

"That's a given." Kegan laughed.

"Umm. Excuse me." Seven raised one hand, getting ignored.

"Speak for yourself." Piper shot Corvin a dirty look. "You two are the only sketchy ones here. I'm just here to back up my mom."

Kegan scoffed. "Yeah, but your mother is sketchier than all of us—"

"Hey!" Seven stomped one foot and clenched her fists, getting sick of the inane banter. Finally, the three of them gave her their attention as she pointed at the hatch behind them. "Whoever was on the other side of that stopped banging."

The three of them looked at each other silently then back at the door.

Of course, that was when the hatch on the opposite end of the deck swung open, spilling a group of six players armed with various weapons into the space. They wore all black, as if they were advertising the fact that they were up to no good. The man in the back even wore a helmet as if he was worried he might be recognized. He carried a weapon, but it was hard to tell what it was with the others standing in front of him.

A spear maybe?

Seven tried to remember what class that would mean, then shook her head. It didn't matter, she was level one and a slight breeze could kill her.

She looked to Kegan and the two reynards, the scrappy bunch still pressed up against the other door. Then she glanced back at the black-ops squad that clearly meant to do them harm. She couldn't believe her luck. All she had wanted was to wait by herself until the auction started, but somehow, here she was, standing between three idiots and their enemies.

Silence fell across the deck with only the sound of the ship's enormous wheel rotating through the space just below. Seven's body froze, half of her clinging to the hope that she could just step aside and remove herself from the situation, letting the chips fall where they may. It wasn't like any of this was her problem. Her other half had other plans.

What am I doing? Seven screamed at herself as she pushed Echo toward her friends and kicked the tool box toward the six players in black. A chorus of battle cries erupted behind her only to fall apart when a player in front tripped and fell over the tool box.

Piper and Corvin struggled to get the wrench off the door but it quickly became clear that there wasn't enough time. Seven froze.

"Do something!"

Piper weaved past her, pulling a pistol from a holster and unloading it at the group. Seven covered her ears as the scent of gunpowder filled her nose.

"No good! They have a *Shield*." Corvin reached for a sword as a glowing barrier appeared at the head of the attacking group to deflect Piper's shots. It seemed to be projected from a metal glove worn by a faunus player in front.

"Well I don't see you trying anything." Piper reloaded.

Seven glanced to Echo, as if the silent fairy might have an idea. She responded by hopping onto the railing and leaping off.

"Don't just leave us." Seven's mouth fell open with indignation.

"Good plan, Echo." Corvin sheathed his sword and immediately vaulted the railing.

With horror, Seven watched him fall to the massive wheel below. He hit it and rolled, coming to a stop just before falling off the edge.

"That's my partner." Kegan smiled down at the reynard. "Always ready to improvise."

Piper rolled her eyes, then vaulted over the side as well.

"No sense staying here, right?" Kegan placed a hand on the rail and glanced back at Seven as if waiting for her to introduce herself.

She scoffed at him. "I'm Seven."

"Well, Seven…" He looked back over her shoulder at the players behind her, then back to her face. "Try not to die when you land."

Then he leapt over the side.

She clutched her chest and threw herself against the railing, watching him fall the two story drop to the wheel below. He slammed into its surface like a bug hitting a windshield before staggering back to his feet. She cringed, then looked back at the incoming attack team.

"I didn't sign on for this." She threw one leg over the rail, holding on as she placed her feet on the outer ledge. The wind rushed up to remind her that one wrong move would send her falling straight to the ground. She looked down, her eyes bulging at the insanity of it all.

"I can't do this!" Her legs immediately turned to jelly and her hands clamped to the railing like a vice. She had to take her chances with the attacking players. None of this was her problem. She wasn't involved. Seven closed her eyes. "I can't do this."

"Yes, you can!"

Her eyes snapped back open to find that stupid elf, Kegan, aiming an arrow up at her. He fired.

"Gah, what the hell!" She covered her face with both arms. "Shit!" she screamed as she realized that she'd let go of the railing.

The sound of Ruby squawking filled her ears as she fell forward.

"I didn't sign on for this!"

CHAPTER SEVEN

Pain shot up Seven's legs, replaced by the same numbness as before when she'd kicked the hatch up above. Except this time the unnatural feeling ran up half her body. Unable to stop her momentum, she stumbled toward the empty space beyond the engine wheel. By the time she finally stopped, only her heels remained on the edge.

Seven let out a shrill scream as she fell forward, the ground barely visible through the clouds that passed by below. Suddenly a small glowing form rushed from underneath, pressing its body against her own to hoist her back up. Echo hadn't abandoned her after all. A wave of relief swept across Seven's mind as she began to rise back up to place one foot on the edge on the wheel.

The relief didn't last.

Echo mouthed a wordless plea, struggling to hold Seven's weight. It was too much for her.

Oh no. Seven flailed her arms on reflex as she began to tip back toward the ground, unable to find her balance. The fairy pushed, but could do no more than slow her fall down to an agonizing pace.

"I got you!"

A hand clasped around her wrist. The elf, Kegan, leaned back to counterbalance her weight before she slipped off the edge. She curled her fingers around his wrist as he did hers. The elf yanked her back from the edge, sending her toppling to the metal plating that covered the engine wheel. She came to rest on her rear, her head still spinning.

"What's your health at?" Kegan readied his bow to fire up at their pursuers.

"My health?" Her mind locked up, not understanding what he meant before realizing that she was still playing a game. She checked her stat-sleeve and gasped. "Fourteen out of fifty."

"What the hell? I assumed you were low-level from your gear but damn, didn't you at least use your level one upgrade points?"

"My what?"

The elf's face fell to a blank stare.

"You get one level free when you first log in, which gives you five upgrade points to start your character build with." Corvin helped her up. "If you haven't dropped them into your stats yet, then you're essentially at level zero."

"I don't even know what my class does. Why would I use any of my points?" She got to her feet.

"Why the hell did you pick a class you don't know anything about?" Kegan fired a few arrows up at the deck where they had jumped from to keep their pursuers at bay.

"My name is Royal Assistant Seven. I'm not a player, I'm here to place bids at the auction for the lady of my house. I just got the job and haven't even been logged in for more than a couple hours. So excuse me if I don't know what I'm doing. I didn't know you idiots would show up and drag me into whatever this is!"

"Guys!" Piper stood behind them hooking a thumb back over her shoulder. "We should really keep moving."

Seven followed the path of her thumb, then stumbled backward, almost falling down again.

"Oh hell!"

She knew that the engine wheel they stood on was turning, but she hadn't really thought of what that meant for herself as she stood on top of it. In actuality, it meant keep moving… or else.

Further down, a system of enormous gears turned, pushing the engine wheel through a space in the wall where it bisected the ship. The metal shapes groaned, ready to crush anything that got too close. Only a small, dark gap sat between them.

Seven started running in the opposite direction, just as a man brandishing a sword dropped down to the wheel in front of her. She stopped in her tracks and stumbled back just as a pair of arrows struck him in the chest with a sickening thunk. The wounds lit up crimson for an instant before he staggered over the edge and vanished into the clouds.

Kegan stepped in front of her, firing arrow after arrow. His fingers moved faster than she could track, performing some sort of sleight-of-hand trick to ready each shot. Another player dressed in black vaulted the railing above, only to take three arrows before landing in a heap. He writhed, still alive.

"Damn, missed a critical." Kegan ran forward and hopped over the man, firing an arrow down as he did to finish him off.

Piper and Corvin moved up as well to stay away from the gears behind them. Seven looked back at the corpse of the player Kegan had just dispatched. It began to shimmer just before hitting the gears to one side of the gap in the wall. She winced as the corpse burst into a cloud of glowing particles on contact. Seven blew out a sigh of relief that there hadn't been any gore. That would have been too much for her to witness.

A third player, the faunus with the metal glove, jumped over the side. Two more members of his team followed, using his glowing energy barrier as cover to land safely. They took up a position behind him, ready to force Kegan and the others back into the gears. Piper raised her pistol and opened fire at the trio, failing to land any hits, but keeping them from moving forward.

That was when Seven remembered that there had been one

more player after Kegan's group, the big guy in the helmet. She glanced up just in time to see him take a running leap off the deck above, flying clear over her as if launched by some kind of unseen force. A roar of power erupted from him as he twirled his spear above his head in a blur. A trail of fire swirled above him from the head of the weapon just before he slammed it into the wheel near Piper. A blast of heat and smoke exploded from him in all directions.

Piper let out a howl as the wave of power hit her and threw her into the wall. She fell back down to the wheel's surface, only to be devoured but the gears.

"No!" Seven reached out, knowing full well that there was nothing she could do as the reynard girl vanished into the dark space at the center of the grinding maw.

The large man in the helmet stood and yanked his spear's tip from the engine wheel before stalking toward Seven. With no defense, she just shook her head and stepped back. She was powerless to stop him.

Or was she?

In that moment, she remembered she hadn't been sent in alone. Excitement lifted her up as she thrust a finger in his direction and yelled.

"Ruby, attack!"

The man stopped in place, staring at Seven. A smirk grew on her face as a strange feeling of satisfaction settled over her.

Then it faded. Nothing happened.

The smirk fell off her face as the overgrown bird remained perched on the railing above. He offered nothing more than a disinterested caw.

"God damn stupid bird! What good are you?" Seven shook her up fist at the useless pet.

The man in the helmet shook his head as if unable to believe that she was this weak. He didn't even attack when he passed by, opting shove her down with one hand, like she wasn't worth the effort.

"Sit down before you fall down." His voice sounded annoyed under the helmet.

Seven should've been happy. He had passed over her, only caring to kill Kegan and his team.

She was in the clear.

So why was she so… irritated?

A fire lit in her veins that boiled her blood and clouded her vision. She started to stand as the large man stalked toward Kegan, the rest of his squad holding position behind the elf, cutting off any chance for escape. Seven didn't know what she could do but that didn't change anything. She couldn't just watch.

Suddenly, Corvin placed a hand on her shoulder. She hadn't even noticed him approach. He gestured with his head to his wrist where his health was displayed. At first, she wasn't sure what he was getting at, but then she noticed the name next to his.

Piper's health was still at seventy percent!

Seven spun back to look at the small gap in the wall surrounded by the meatgrinder of gears. Piper had somehow passed right through to the outside. Corvin held his wrist to face Kegan as the unknown man in the helmet approached.

Kegan glanced at his own wrist and gave a slight nod, clearly understanding Corvin's meaning. The elf immediately lowered his bow and held up a hand before him in surrender.

"Can't we live and let live here? You know, honor amongst stowaways and all that."

"Sorry, you're a loose end. Gotta be tied up," answered the man in a gruff tone.

"Ah, okay then, I can understand that." Kegan stole a glance at the players behind him as they crept closer using the glowing barrier as cover. "But I have to ask…"

"What?" The man in the helmet hesitated.

Kegan raised one finger and opened his mouth as if to speak, then immediately drew an arrow and fired it at the man. He dodged to the side, leaving room for the elf to dash past him. Kegan ran straight by Seven and Corvin, only turning back to shout.

"Get a move on, Piper's gonna get lonely out there."

Seven watched with eyes wide as he dove head first into the center gap between the gears. She looked to Corvin bedside her.

"Seriously?"

All she got in return was a shrug before he too, made a break for the wall and disappeared into the darkened space between the gears.

Seven glanced back at the four players pursuing them. They might still leave her be if she just stepped aside.

"Umm, hi. I'm not with them."

She waved, then cringed at her own words as a strange emotion that she didn't recognize tugged at her heart. The four men just looked at her in silence. Finally, she sighed and resigned herself to the only thing she could do.

Give up.

Her feet however, had other plans.

Wait, no, what the hell am I doing?

Seven's body moved as if on autopilot, somehow overriding every logical thought in her head. Her level one starter shoes hit the wheel's surface one after another as she ran toward the gears. Her eyes locked on the gap between them, here heart racing like never before.

I have officially lost my mind.

Dropping to her knees, Seven lay down on the wheel and pulled her arms in as tight as possible. The roaring gears chomped closer with every second. She took a few last panicked gasps before her world was engulfed in darkness.

Metal ground against metal all around her in a cacophony louder than any she had ever heard. Fear set in as the gears bit at her robes, tugging on her sleeves and threatening to devour her right then and there. It seemed to last forever.

Then she saw the sky filled with stars… and a gun.

"Hey there." Piper stood on a ridge of brass that

surrounded the opening where the engine wheel passed through the hull of the ship, aiming down to shoot the next person to appear from the gap. A full moon hung in the sky, silhouetting her foxlike ears as Seven looked up.

"Hi." Seven remained laying on her back as the wheel carried her out of the ship.

"Congrats on not getting crushed." Kegan held out a hand to help her up.

"Thanks." She hoisted her body off the engine wheel, only to realize that her situation wasn't actually better. The surface she stood on passed back into the ship further down, and there was no telling what was on the other side. *More gears?* She really wished she had looked while she was inside.

There was also the fact that there was no railing or safety feature of any kind, not that there had been any inside either. The fact that she was essentially standing on the outside of an aircraft suddenly felt very real. The scene was like something out of a ridiculous action movie. Seven suppressed a shiver. She hated action movies.

That was when Piper spoke again.

"Hey there." She waved at the first of their pursuers to emerge from the gap. Then she opened fire.

The helpless man howled for an instant, then stopped abruptly, his cry cut off by a well-placed bullet. The second of the men met the same fate before the slide of her pistol locked back, empty.

The faunus with the metal glove appeared next, taking an arrow to his shoulder before deploying his barrier to protect himself. The man in the helmet emerged behind him. He stayed low to stay in the cover of his ally as arrows pelted their shield.

Seven wasn't sure if she should take up a position behind Kegan and his friends or stay at the front.

"Fall back, Seven." Kegan shouted.

That answered that. Seven made a break for their back line, hoping the elf and his friends could take care of the last of their pursuers.

The faunus with the shield pushed forward as the man in the helmet used some kind of ability to leap into the air. Again, streaks of fire spilled from his weapon. Seven knew what that meant and crouched down to avoid being thrown off the engine wheel by the blast that was sure to follow. Kegan and his friends did the same.

The man landed with an explosion of fire. Seven felt the heat on her skin even while hiding behind Kegan's party. The scent of burning oil filled her nostrils.

Using the attack as a distraction, the faunus with the shield raced forward, slamming into Corvin and Piper like a plow. He kept running until he threw himself off the edge to ensure his targets went with him. Corvin fell back as Piper's hand shot out to save him. It wasn't enough.

Seven shoved down the fear in her chest and ran as they both disappeared over the edge. She dove, landing on her stomach, her arm outstretched. There was no way she could catch them. She knew that much. If she tried, she would just go flying off the side along with them.

Fortunately, she didn't have to.

"Let go of my tail, damn it!" Piper shouted as she clung to the edge of the engine wheel.

"Sorry, I'm going to have to ignore that request." Corvin responded, dangling in the wind by the fluffy appendage connected to her rear. "'Cause, you know, I'll die."

"I'm fine with that," she called back, her knuckles white under the strain of holding them both.

"Didn't you just try to save him a second ago?" Seven grabbed her wrist, trying to help.

"It was on reflex. I couldn't help it."

"Hey, could you two quit arguing and climb back up?" Kegan deflected a spear that had been thrust at his chest. "I'm not exactly a melee class here."

The man in the helmet didn't stop, making sure the elf wouldn't have time to reach for an arrow. At the same time, he pushed Kegan toward the edge.

Corvin let out a grunt as he reached up for a better hold on Piper's tail only to slip down, catching himself with one hand. Piper let out a yelp as her grip faltered.

"Hold on. Please!" Seven gripped the girl's wrists tighter.

"Thanks." She looked up at Seven. "You're doing good."

Piper's words cut into Seven's heart. She was actually encouraging her while dangling from the side of an airship.

Who are these people?

It didn't matter, there wasn't time to think about it. Kegan still needed help.

"Climb faster!" Seven cried just as the elf ran out of room, with nothing but the empty sky at his back.

"Seven." Corvin made eye contact with her from below. "Listen, I'm not going to make it in time to help. It has to be you."

"What can I do?"

"You're a *Venom* mage. You have magic."

"I don't even know what that means."

"That's okay." His face was calm as he spoke. "I was a *Venom* once. I'll talk you through it, alright?"

Kegan let out a grunt as he fell on his back, his head hanging off the edge with only his bow to deflect the attacks that rained down on him. The tip of the man's spear slammed into the brass edging of the engine wheel over and over, narrowly missing the elf with each strike.

Corvin's eyes flicked to his friend then back to Seven. "Alright?" he repeated to get her attention.

Seven nodded as the wind whipped through her hair.

"Okay, you have to open your caster. It's the bracelet on your wrist."

Seven looked at the leather band that hugged the forearm, a small metal chamber sitting underneath like a watch. "How do I–"

"Just open one hand as far as it will go, that will activate it."

She let go of Piper's wrist with her right hand and followed his instruction, opening her hand and stretching her fingers out as far as she could. The metal chamber on her caster snapped open, revealing a glowing green crystal.

"Okay, good." Corvin smiled up at her. "Now stand and swipe your hand up to open your spellcraft menu."

Seven gave Piper one last look and released her other wrist, leaving the girl to hold the brunt of her friend's weight. Then she swiped upward. Four glyphs appeared before her in a grid, bathing Seven in a gentle light.

"Woah." The word fell out of her mouth as the realization that she had magic hit her.

"That's it, you only have two spells at level one. Pulse and Poison. Go with pulse, it won't hurt him but it will push him back. Move the glyph on the upper right to the selection column in the center. Leave the bottom ones where they are. Then swipe down to cast it. Point with an outstretched hand and it will hit the first available target in a straight line."

"That's it?" she asked as Kegan's bow flittered off the side and into the clouds below. He threw his hands up in a useless attempt to protect himself.

"Shit!" Seven swiped left, then down, letting her fingertips pass through glyphs. Her skin tingled on contact and the spell glowed brighter for an instant before fading away. She thrust out her hand at the man as he raised his spear for a killing blow. "Leave him alone!"

A surge of excitement poured through her chest as a puff of energy burst into existence in the man's face.

"The hell?" He stumbled backward but didn't fall.

Seven didn't stop. Instead, she threw her hand out and raised it to the sky, the glyphs appearing again like before. She swiped left and down, cutting the symbols in half with her hand and stepping forward as if pushing the incantation in his direction. It was like nothing she'd ever experienced.

It was magic.

Again she cast the spell, a ridiculous smile having its way with her as her hand swept through the air.

She felt powerful.

The man tried to protect his face with his spear but another pulse slapped him in the hand, sending the weapon clattering to his feet. Another pulse knocked him back, his balance shifting as he stepped away into empty space.

Seven stalked toward her prey, swiping up again only to find the she was out of mana. A red zero showed on the readout of her stat-sleeve. She didn't stop. The man was teetering on the edge, his arms flailing for balance.

"Sorry." The word left her mouth in a quiet whisper as she placed a hand on his chest and gave him a gentle push.

"Damn it, Seven," the man grunted in a low tone as he tipped back over the edge and fell into the blanket of fluffy clouds.

What?

She stood, frozen, staring at her own hand. The one that had pushed a man to his death.

What did he just say?

She took a frantic step back and clutched a hand over her mouth.

How could he know my name?

That was when she looked down at his spear laying by her feet. The one she had knocked out of his hand. The one... that she recognized.

Oh no. She shook her head. *No no no.*

Seven hadn't been paying attention to details during the fight. How could she? Everything had happened so fast, but now, she couldn't help but stare at the familiar weapon. It's unique bladed tip practically screamed its owner's name at her.

Cassius.

She had just killed the First Knight of her own house.

"Holy crap, Seven." Kegan pushed himself up. "You wrecked that guy."

"Could use some help," Piper called from where she hung off the edge of the still turning engine wheel. "We're gonna get scraped off real soon here."

"Oh damn, yeah." Kegan leaped over to help.

Seven continued to stare in horror at the spear at her feet until a happy little chime sounded in her ear. As it did, the spear began to shimmer and dissipate into glowing particles. Cassius must have hit the ground and been disconnected. She raised her stat-sleeve, barely looking at it. The words 'Level Up' appeared next to her name six times.

"You gonna help? Or just stand there in awe of your badassery?" Kegan gestured to his friends hanging over the side with his head.

Seven snapped out of her trance and rushed to aid the two reynards. Corvin seemed to be making it harder for himself, struggling to climb up Piper's body without touching her anywhere that he shouldn't.

"Will you just grab my ass already?" Piper spat down at him. "I don't want to get killed because you're too afraid of touching a girl."

He rolled his eyes and reached up to grab her belt, inadvertently pulling her pants down a couple inches. Piper let out an embarrassed yelp.

"Sorry." He winced as he pulled himself up further.

"That's fine." Piper growled through her teeth. "It's not like you're enjoying it, remember? I'm too young."

Seven started to understand a bit of why the pair seemed to be at odds just as Echo appeared from the clouds below. The fairy flew up to hover above them, fluttering her wings faster and releasing a shower of shining dust on the both of them. Then, Piper simply let go.

Seven reached out on reflex, though neither of them fell. Instead, they just floated up as if gravity had no effect on them.

"What the…?"

"Flight magic." Corvin pointed to a feather icon on his stat-sleeve as he landed next to Kegan, safe again with his feet on the ship's engine wheel. Well, as safe as he could be with Piper glaring daggers at him.

"Flight is one of the convenient effects of pixie dust."

Kegan elbowed Seven in the arm. "You just have to believe in fairies."

"What?" Seven glanced at Echo, hovering just over the edge with her hands tucked behind her back.

"He's kidding," the fairy mouthed. "You don't really need to believe."

"Oh." Seven folded her arms. "Wait, wouldn't it have been easier for you to just dust these two earlier?"

Echo's face went blank, showing no emotion whatsoever. Even her dull eyes seemed to unfocus in an unnatural way, as if no one was controlling her.

"Yeah, well…" Kegan scratched at the back of his neck and gestured to girl. "This one is surprisingly inconsistent."

Seven glanced to the fairy who snapped back to the present and gave an enthusiastic nod at the fact that she was unhelpful.

"Anyway," Kegan gestured to Echo. "Mind dusting us up too, so we can all fly up to the deck?"

The little mage responded with enthusiasm, darting up and circling above Seven's head. A trail of glittering sparkles drifted down, settling on her hair and shoulders. It felt warm and gentle as it touched her skin. After a few seconds, a feather icon appeared on her stat-sleeve as well, though she couldn't help but let her eyes drift back to where Cassius had fallen.

She would be lucky to not get fired.

"Hey, you with us?" Kegan snapped his fingers next to her ear.

"What?" Seven suddenly realized she was almost out of space before the engine wheel passed back into the ship's hull. "Oh." Her eyes darted to Kegan, who was floating in place a few inches in the air. She looked at his feet dangling. "How do I…?"

"Just look in the direction you want to go and close your right hand."

"Okay, like thi– oh no!" Seven shot up into the air, apparently closing her hand too fast and crashing into Corvin who in turn slammed into Piper.

"Oh, come on!" he squealed as the other reynard swatted at him.

Seven let her hand go limp, coming to a stop in the air, drifting weightlessly. The clouds passed by below her, a sudden jolt of fear pulsing through her before a wave of excitement shut it down.

"Oh. My. God." She threw her arms out like wings. "I'm flying!"

"Yeah, yeah, you're flying." Kegan pointed up. "Now how about we head back to the ship's deck? That spell only lasts two minutes and Echo isn't exactly reliable enough to catch us if it runs out."

"Oh, sure." Seven frowned at having such an incredible experience cut short. Looking at Echo, she wondered why the fairy was so bad at supporting her friends. It was like she just didn't care to put in the effort, though something about that didn't feel right. The girl hadn't seemed that heartless.

Seven shook off the thought and followed the others up to the ship's deck, making a point of landing clear of the auction's guards. Of course, that was when she remembered that she was supposed to be inside the theater for the bidding. That was, as long as she didn't get fired first for killing Cassius. Not to mention she'd left Ruby back down in the engine room. Well, that part wasn't so bad. She was glad to be free of the dumb bird.

"Damn!" Seven caught the time on her stat-sleeve. "Only fifteen minutes. I have to get back inside."

"I can help with that. We have to shift this one back in anyway." Piper hooked a thumb back at Echo. "The rest of our house will be worried about her, and we have to sneak in to help back them up."

"Shift?" Seven tilted her head to the side.

"Yeah, it's a teleport of sorts, it will send us all directly into the theater." Piper held out her hands. "Just grab onto me."

"Umm, okay." Seven took her hand as Corvin reached for the reynard girl's other hand. Piper pulled it away.

"You can hold Kegan's hand."

"Gettin' really sick of this," Kegan groaned and took her hand in Corvin's place, then offered his other hand to the boy. "Mind grabbing that one?"

Seven turned to find Echo, who was staring blankly into the middle distance. She poked the fairy to get her attention, then held out her hand, feeling relived when the mage grabbed hold without argument.

"Okay, let's get in there." Piper moved her hands together without letting go of the others, forcing them to move along with her. "Don't want to keep my mom waiting."

Seven's ears pricked up. "Your mom's inside?"

"Yeah, you'll like her. She's pretty cool." Piper stopped momentarily. "Don't tell her I said that."

"Sure." Seven chuckled, changing her opinion of Piper a little. "Actually, I didn't ask, which house are you guys with?"

Kegan opened his mouth to speak just as Piper's fingers touched a bracelet on her wrist. His words were cut off as the world vanished around them, an endless gloom filling her vision.

In that second, a number of facts began to line up.

The three stowaways.

The shift ability that was used in a heist six months ago.

The heart emblem on Echo's rear.

It had all been so obvious, but she hadn't made the connection.

Oh no!

Seven's blood ran cold as the world blinked back; a small, dark room lined with crimson curtains closed in around her.

Oh, no no no! Seven tried to step away, only to find her back against a wall as the Lady of House Lockheart leveled a pair of green eyes on her.

"Who the hell are you?"

CHAPTER EIGHT

"Yeah, who the hell are you?" Max drew a pistol and raised it to the low-level *Venom* mage that had just appeared in the theater box along with the rest of his house.

"I'm Seven."

"That's a number, not a name." He let his anger drip into his voice, filling it with a menacing quality. "How did you force my house to shift you in here?"

"Hey hey hey!" Kegan jumped in front of the woman, holding his hands up. "Seven is her name. She works for the Silver Tongues. We just ran into her below deck."

"Hello, guys, what happened?" Farn's voice came across the house line. "Why did I shift out?"

Kegan raised his house ring to his mouth. "Sorry, Farn, something came up, we're sorting it out now. Hang tight." He returned his attention to Max. "Sorry about shifting without warning. We found Echo so we thought it was okay to bring her back up here and we took Seven with us to be nice."

"That's what you think." Max kept his gun aimed at the woman despite Kegan blocking his shot. "She's playing you."

"He's right." Ginger added from beside him. "She was with Nix down in the theater when we arrived."

"Nix is here?" Kegan spun back to look at the player he'd shifted in with him, clearly just as surprised as Max that she might be involved with their enemy.

The woman, Seven, finally stomped forward, her eyes burning with indignation. "I have no idea who Nix is and want nothing to do with her. She just walked up to me and started talking when I arrived. I am only here for a job, and the sooner I can leave the better."

"Then why were you protecting her?" Max tightened his grip on his gun.

Seven let out a mirthless laugh. "I didn't have a choice. You just opened fire without so much as a warning. Nix used me as a human shield." She lowered her head. "After that, I ran away to hide below deck until the auction started. I found Echo in the engine room and crossed paths with the rest of your house shortly after."

"That true?" Max glanced to Echo on instinct, forgetting what the avatar was for an instant. The fairy shrugged, the system pulling her responses from either him or Farn, reminding him that she only fed back what they already knew. He redirected his question to the others. "Is it?"

"It's true." Corvin stepped forward.

"Yeah, so put the gun down." Piper pushed the *Blade* aside. "Seven saved our lives down there."

"Really?" Max let his gun fall a little.

"Yes, she did." Kegan lowered his hands as if the confrontation was over. "We ran into a party of stowaways down below. Not sure what they were here for, and they weren't interested in talking. They tried to kill us without asking questions. Seven got caught in the crossfire and ended up saving us when things went south."

"How?" Max raised an eyebrow at the *Venom*. "You're, what? Level one from the looks of your gear?"

Seven scoffed. "I'm level seven, actually."

"She hit a high-level player with pulse spells until he fell off the ship." Kegan added. "She made six levels off him."

Max shook his head, picturing a level one mage taking on a high-level alone. It was technically possible. Finally, he lowered his gun and let out sigh. "Alright, that makes sense. And it is kind of badass."

Everyone in the room relaxed as he holstered his gun. Especially Seven, who let herself fall back against the wall to rest.

"Aren't you going to apologize for shooting at me in the theater?"

"I don't know why I would." Max let his hands rest on his belt. "I missed on purpose. You were never in any danger."

"Why would you miss on purpose? Aren't you after Nix?" Seven stared him straight in the face.

"I am, but I don't want her dead. That would only send her back to spawn." Max growled his last few words. "I want her where I can find her."

"Christ, what is wrong with everyone? This is just a game." Seven shook her head and rolled her eyes. "You people take things way too seriously."

Her words sent a surge of anger through Max's vision. "You don't know what you're talking about."

"What could one player have done to incur such wrath?" Seven raised her head, her nostrils flaring. "Nix didn't even seem dangerous. Honestly, she was kind of dumb."

Max couldn't help but be reminded of himself, back when he had thought the same thing. Back before he knew better. "She—"

"She stole something from us." Ginger stepped forward, cutting him off before he said something he might regret. "Something important to everyone in our house."

Max looked to Ginger, getting a kind smile in return. He was glad she was there to step in. "Yeah, and we want it back."

Seven pushed off the wall and motioned toward the door. "Well, good luck with that. Just leave me out of it. I need this job and I don't want whatever blood feud you have going on putting my livelihood in jeopardy."

"That's understandable." Ginger offered the low-level *Venom* her hand. "You helped our people down below, so consider yourself a friend of our house."

Seven hesitated before taking her hand and shaking it. "What the…" She pulled her hand away and glanced at her stat-sleeve as a message appeared along her forearm.

"That's a friend request." Ginger nodded to her. "You can accept it or not. It's up to you."

"Sure, sure." Seven stepped away clearly intending to decline the invitation as soon as she exited the room.

"Hey." Max looked away from her. "Sorry I shot at you. I was trying to scare Nix, not someone trying to make a living."

"It's… it's okay." She let out a sigh as her posture relaxed. "I get it, Nix is an enemy."

"She is." Max gave her a sad smile. "If you see her coming, walk the other way."

"I will." Seven nodded before disappearing into the hall.

Kegan, Piper and Corvin immediately leaped forward.

"Why the hell is Nix here?" they asked in unison.

"To get contracts I guess?" Max shrugged before changing the subject. "Where did you shift Farn to by the way?"

Kegan's eyes widened. "Oh yeah. She's somewhere on the deck." He turned to Piper. "Do you mind swapping back out? Now that we're inside."

"Fine, kick me out, not like I pull my weight on these missions or anything." She groaned and leveled a deadly stare at Corvin. "I didn't want to hang out here anyway." She touched her bracelet without saying goodbye and Farn appeared in her place holding a mug. Apparently she had stopped at a bar while on the deck.

"Woah." The *Shield* stumbled backward from the sudden shift. "A little warning would have been nice."

"Sorry." Kegan bowed his head. "At least you got yourself a

drink, and we found Echo for you." Farn deflated a little as soon as Echo bounced over to her and tried to drink from her mug.

"Oh, thanks." She pulled the cup away from the little avatar. "No, this is my cider. And you're a lightweight." Echo pouted but settled in at her side regardless.

Max ignored the pair, his mind drifting back to Seven. The idea of sending a level-one into the Auction of Souls was insane.

"You're wondering about that *Venom* mage too?" Ginger let her shoulder rest against his.

"Yeah, she doesn't seem to have any idea what's going on." He stared back at the door that Seven had left through. "Just what are the Silver Tongues thinking?"

CHAPTER NINE

"What else could go wrong?"

Seven broke into a sprint as soon as she left Lockheart's theater box. She'd been trying her best to keep to herself since she'd arrived on the Night Queen. Now though, she'd somehow befriended the most dangerous house in Noctem and killed the First Knight of her own in under an hour.

Also, she'd lost Ruby.

It was probably wise that I didn't mention to anyone in Lockheart that I knew the other stowaways. That could have been hard to explain. I expect they'd have killed me on the spot.

She slowed to a stop as soon as she thought she'd put in enough distance. It wasn't like she had anywhere to run to anyway. Seven cursed her bad luck, then ground her palms into her eyes in frustration.

"How did I get into this?"

Of course that was when Leftwitch's voice filled her ears.

"You've been busy."

Seven jumped a foot in the air at the sudden intrusion, then spun in search of the source. The hall was empty.

"Hello?" she asked quietly.

Leftwitch's voice answered back. "I am going to assume from your silence that you don't know how to use your house ring."

"My silence?" Seven glanced down at the silver band that hugged her finger. She thought back to when Kegan had spoked to someone using his a few minutes ago. He had held it close to his mouth.

"Just hold it close—" Leftwitch began to explain.

Seven jerked her hand up to her mouth. "I understand, sorry."

"Ah, good." Leftwitch paused. "I set up a private chat just between us within the house line so you can talk freely. Our house is a little too big to have you on an open channel."

"Thank you." Seven wasn't sure how to bring up the fact that she had killed Cassius. All she knew was she couldn't hide it. The man would respawn any second and tell on her, if he hadn't already. She reluctantly opened her mouth, "I may have killed—"

"I should mention Cassius just respawned?" Leftwitch interrupted.

Seven's breath froze in her chest. "I am so sorry about that. I didn't know it was him under the helmet. I only realized it when I saw his spear after he dropped it."

"Yes, I'm afraid you're going to have to answer for that."

"I know, I'm sorry." Seven clutched her chest. "I'll make up for it any way—" Leftwitch cut her off with a snort followed by a fit of laughter.

"Wow." Leftwitch took a few audible breaths. "Sorry, I was just playing. You're not in trouble."

"What?"

"It's fine. I didn't want to send you in alone, so I sent in Cassius and his team as back up, just in case. I figured it would be easier for you to act natural if you didn't know about it, and I didn't want them traced back to me if they got caught. Hence the helmet. Cass is too easily recognized as my Knight. Ultimately, you did what anyone would do when facing an unknown group of players. I can't fault you for that."

"Oh, thank god." Seven released the heaviest sigh of her life. "I thought I was fired."

"No way." Leftwitch chuckled. "If anything, you've impressed everyone back here in Lucem. All the other assistants are amazed that you took out Cassius at level one. You should have seen his face when he respawned. He just kept repeating that 'the noob pushed him.'"

Seven cringed at the word noob. "I didn't know what else to do. I just got caught between Cassius and Lockheart's stowaways—"

"Lockheart?" Leftwitch sounded surprised. "The people Cass was chasing were from Lockheart?"

"Yeah. Kegan, Corvin, and Piper."

"Hmm. I haven't heard of Piper, but Kegan and Corvin have reputations." Leftwitch went silent for a few seconds before speaking again. "And you saved their lives?"

"Ah, yes, I suppose," Seven admitted sheepishly.

"Would you say that put you on friendly terms with them?"

"I guess so. Lady Ginger sent me a friend request, but I wasn't sure if I should accept it."

"Yes, absolutely accept it!" An excited tone entered Leftwitch's voice. "Actually, let me add a new objective to your mission tonight."

Seven winced as if waiting for an oncoming truck to slam into her as she responded with a reluctant, "Yes?"

"I want you to get close to the members of Lockheart. All of them. I want you to gain their trust. I've been trying to get information on them for the last six months, everybody has. Unfortunately, they have proven to be one of Noctem's most elusive houses. Any information you can get about them would be a godsend for my show."

Seven sunk her body against the wall. She no longer had a choice in the matter. "But I don't really know what's going on, or how to do that."

"That's perfect. It'll just make you seem extra harmless. They may let their guard down."

"How do you suggest I get close to them?"

"Just go back to them and tell them that you're looking for protection since you're there alone and can't defend yourself. Offer a truce and ask if there's anything you can do in return for protection."

The thought of deceiving anyone made Seven's skin crawl. Especially anyone as dangerous as Lockheart's team of miscreants. Seven was an accountant, not a spy.

Then again, a job was a job, and she needed to make rent.

"Okay," Seven opened her player journal and opened it to her friend requests, staring at the accept option. "I'll do my best."

"Excellent, that's all I ask."

"Oh, I should also mention that I lost Ruby with everything going on."

"That's fine, it was bound to happen. Pets get stuck sometimes and need to be resummoned. It happens. I just needed him with you to get you into the auction, so you don't really need him at this point. Although, I'm sending Cassius back out there on another transport ship to watch your back. I can resummon Ruby and send him out on the same shuttle."

"That's not necessary." Seven hoped to keep the oversized bird away from her for the rest of the night.

"Nonsense, it's no trouble." Leftwitch assured her. "It will take a while for the transport to get out there though, so you'll be on your own until then. Just stick close to Lockheart and everything will work out."

"If that's what you think is best." Seven pulled the small pen from the spine of her journal and drew a check mark over the accept option of Ginger's friend request.

"Perfect, report anything you find out." Leftwitch sounded hopeful.

"I will." Seven turned back in the direction she'd run from just a few minutes ago.

"Good luck. You're doing great." Leftwitch paused. "I mean it, I believe in you."

The line fell silent, letting her faith in Seven hang over her head.

At least that makes one of us.

Seven started walking back toward her new friends.

CHAPTER TEN

"Time to head back down." Ginger held out the wooden tile that showed the auction's countdown clock burned into its surface.

"Okay, let's get this over with." Max shoved his hands into his pockets and headed for the door.

"Wish me luck, okay?" Ginger reached out for his arm.

"Ah, okay, good luck." Max's vision shifted around, avoiding eye contact.

"Not what I meant, Max." Ginger rolled her eyes and pushed up on her toes to bring her lips to his, placing her hand on his chest. He froze for a moment, almost stepping away. Then his body relaxed and his hands found her hips.

Her heart ached as she pulled away.

She wanted to hold him there and forget about everything, but that would be selfish. Instead, she glanced up, catching a glimpse of the warmth behind his cold eyes that had been focused on Nix for months.

The man she wanted was still in there, even if nothing had happened between them since that night back in Reliqua. Back before everything had gone wrong. With everything happening, the timing hadn't been right since. Losing Kira had been too hard on Max. Ginger could understand that, and she wasn't about to try to force something to happen between them if he wasn't ready.

After all, she'd never been needy, so she could give him the time he needed to be ready for something more. Even if she did want to move forward.

Oh well, at least the kids tend to sleep in. I can get a little time to myself in the morning.

"So like, do we all just pretend that they didn't just kiss?" Kegan held his hand over Corvin's good eye. "'Cause now it's awkward."

"Yeah, that was surprisingly passionate." Farn agreed, covering Echo's eyes.

Ginger groaned at Kegan and Corvin. "You two stay here in case we need you. Farn, keep close to Echo so she doesn't run off."

The *Leaf* saluted in an exaggerated manner while Farn tossed Echo's cloak over her head and adjusted it to deter others from interacting with the mindless avatar. Ginger gave Max's hand one last squeeze before letting go. Afterward, she passed through the door only to stop short, finding someone waiting in the hall.

"Hey, ah, hi." Seven, the low-level mage from the Silver Tongues stood there fidgeting with her player journal.

"Oh, Seven." Ginger eyed the woman. "I didn't expect to see you again so soon."

"Yes, sorry. I was thinking about my situation and I was wondering if I could remain with your party throughout the auction." She dropped her eyes to the floor before raising them back up to Ginger's. "I'm alone here, and I don't have any way to defend myself, so…" She trailed off.

"So you want to stay near us so that no one messes with you?" Ginger finished her request as she continued to walk, gesturing for the low-level *Venom* to follow.

"Yes." Seven fell in line beside her.

"Well, you did save three of our people, one of which was my daughter, so I think that we can do that much." Ginger gave her a smile, trying to be friendly. It couldn't hurt to be on good terms with a member of a powerful house.

"Thank you so much." The *Venom* mage let out a relieved sigh. "Let me know if there's anything I can do to help."

Max stepped in, causing the woman to tense back up. "Actually, there is something you could do."

"What?"

"Don't bid on anything against us. The less competition we have, the better." He gave her a friendly smile, clearly trying to put her at ease after pointing a gun at her twice in one night.

Ginger appreciated the attempt, seeing a bit of the player she cared for shining through his hardened exterior.

"I can do that." Seven fell back to walk beside Farn and Echo. "I'm Seven, by the way." She held out a hand to the *Shield* since they hadn't met earlier. Farn shook it, making a good impression that seemed to set their possible ally at ease.

Ginger smiled at her house, appreciating their efforts. They seemed to be getting used to diplomacy. It was a good thing too, because the moment they set foot back in the theater, a familiar face turned in their direction.

"Lady Ginger." Dartmouth, the new Lord of the House of Serpents, inclined his head respectfully. "I was hoping to get a chance to talk before things got underway."

"Of course." She gestured to Farn and Max to find a seat but also to stay on guard. "Though, I can't imagine you would have much reason to be friendly with us, considering we did dethrone your predecessor."

"On the contrary." He waved away the concern with a hand. "Berwyn never had what was best for our house in mind. Now that we're under new management, I would be honored if House Lockheart would consider us allies."

"I see." Ginger gave him a friendly wink. "And I guess it doesn't hurt that we paved the way for you to take control of his house."

"Yes, I'm certainly not complaining about anything." He let out a polite chuckle. "I'm glad we have an understanding. If you need anything, just let me know and I'll see if my Serpents can assist in any way."

"I appreciate that, and will keep it in mind."

Ginger gave him a professional smile, despite the fact that she had no intention of taking him up on his offer. Dartmouth wasn't the threat that his predecessor was, but he was an opportunist that seemed to value appearances more than action. Plus, now that he had gone public with his real-world identity, she trusted him less. Not for any real reason, but he was wealthy and had been since birth. It was probably her own prejudice showing, but she simply didn't trust anyone that hadn't struggled to make rent at some point in their lives.

Dartmouth said his goodbyes and made his way to a chair down by the stage where his housemates were already seated.

Ginger took a moment to scan the theater for Nix, finding her and Aawil seated as far away as they could get. She avoided staring at them too long.

"So that's the infamous Nix, huh?" a friendly voice asked from behind.

Ginger turned to find Larkin. "Glad to see you were able to wrangle an invitation to this thing. I thought we were going to have to pay your way in." She finished with a conspiratorial wink.

"Yes, but it wasn't easy." The crafting-obsessed *Rage* pushed a lock of blue hair behind one ear and adjusted his glasses. "I had to put up my shop as collateral to get the twins over there to take me seriously. It's worth enough to buy a contract."

"But you love that place. Fashion Souls is your workshop, if you lose it, where will you craft?" Ginger placed a hand on his shoulder, feeling guilty considering he was technically there on her request. It was always a good idea to have some additional backup.

"Oh, please." He placed a hand over his heart. "I live for fashion, so I have no intention of risking my workshop. Besides, just look at how much I brought to trade with." His words dripped with sarcasm.

"I see that." Ginger glanced to the back of the theater where several trunks lined the wall. "You must have some pretty valuable things in there to trade." She reached out and touched the edge of his cape which was a new addition to his attire since last they had met. "Nice fabric, what's it do?"

"Yes, it is nice, and it prevents piercing damage." He pulled the garment from her hand and clasped it tight around himself as if not wanting to display something he'd hidden underneath. "I wanted to look my best if I was going to be rubbing elbows with Noctem's elites."

"Ah, well," Ginger stumbled over her words, a little worried that she had offended the *Rage*. "I'd be happy to rub elbows with you anytime." She tried to smooth things over.

He gave her a smile as if there was nothing wrong. "Speaking of, how are the pixie bombs helping?"

"They are amazing." Ginger pulled one of the wooden cylinders from her coat. "Without a healer in our house, these have been the only thing getting us through the last few months."

"Glad they have been able to help." He glanced over to where Farn sat beside Echo. "Actually, I'll need you to bring Kira's avatar by the shop sometime this week. I'm almost out of her dust."

"Already? We just resupplied you."

"Yes, but I recently started a new experiment and I'm afraid it cost me the majority of what I had in stock." He brought his attention back to Ginger. "And if you still want me to keep your item bags full of health bombs, I'll need more pixie dust."

"That's reasonable." Ginger nodded, looking over at Echo, who was staring at nothing in particular. "She may not be good for much these days, but at least she produces a valuable crafting resource."

"Indeed," Larkin nodded. "I'm not quite ready to unveil my

latest masterpiece, but her dust has really allowed me to create something special."

"That's good to hear."

Suddenly the twins appeared on stage, signaling that things were about to get started.

"Well, I should get back to my seat." Larkin motioned to leave. "Good luck, I hope everything works out tonight."

Ginger gave a slight bow as he walked away, before turning her attention to the stage.

"Welcome Lords and Ladies, Knights and Mages," one of the twins announced. Judging from the smile on his face, it was Dalliance.

"Yes, welcome to the Auction of Souls." The other stepped forward wearing a severe frown. Clearly that one was Grindstone.

Together, they began to explain the night's proceedings and how to bid. Ginger walked to her seat next to Max. She would have paid attention to the presentation, but her mind was drawn elsewhere when the last person she expected to interact with, sat down on her other side.

"Hello Jeff-with-a-three." She made a point of keeping her voice low. "To what do I owe the pleasure?"

"Must you people insist on calling me by that ridiculous name?" Jeff rubbed at his temples as he spoke quietly enough that only she could hear him.

"Sorry, it just seemed the best way to honor Kira's memory." Ginger jabbed at his conscience.

Ever since the pyramid job six months ago, she couldn't help but question the overly serious elf's loyalties. According to Alastair, his assistant had been the one to suggest the idea of a heist in the first place. She'd discussed her suspicion with Max months ago, and he agreed. The fact that Nix had been in place within the palace in Reliqua well before Alastair had sent them in could only mean one thing.

The mission had all been a set up from the start.

With the knowledge that it had been J3ff's idea, well, that

only led to one conclusion: he worked for Nix. It made too much sense. Considering that Nix had been one step ahead of them since the beginning, the evil woman had to have a man on the inside of Checkpoint Systems. Everything had gone according to Nix's plan, even before Carver's quest that had started it all a year and a half ago.

Ginger let her hand fall to the armrest she shared with Max. He wasn't sitting close enough to hear anything J3ff was saying, but still, she could feel the tension in his arm next to hers.

Sorry to put you through this.

It must have been taking every bit of restraint he had to keep from reaching for his guns. They had decided it would be best to pretend they hadn't figured out J3ff's true nature. They hadn't even let Alastair know about the theory, the hope being that they could take advantage of his connection to Nix at some point. As long as Alastair didn't let J3ff know that he'd told Ginger about whose idea the heist had been, they might be able to manipulate the spy. Maybe even trick Nix into showing her hand.

"Yes, speaking of Kira's memory." J3ff flicked his eyes to the avatar sitting quietly next to Farn further down the row of seats. "I see her Echo is still stable."

"Should she not be?"

"Simply speaking, no. That thing shouldn't even exist."

"That's a harsh assessment."

"I'm sorry to be harsh, but according to all of our system information, Kira died six months ago." His severe expression softened as he continued. "Having her avatar still roaming about is nothing more than an error. It's Noctem's way of responding to one of your people's inability to let her go. I know Alastair has been avoiding pushing the subject, but he does agree. For whichever one of you is holding her here, the best thing would be to move on."

Ginger sighed. He wasn't wrong, and judging from how much Farn took care of Kira's empty shell, it wasn't hard to figure out who was holding onto her memory. Who could blame her? Losing Kira had hurt everyone, even Ginger. She had stayed by Max's side while he grieved. He had pressed on under the guise of finding his lost friend, but Ginger could see the loss in Max's eyes. The thread of hope keeping him going was growing thinner by the day.

Farn, though, was a different story. Ginger could only imagine how hard losing Kira must have been for the *Shield*. The little fairy had been her first friend in years, not to mention the first person she'd fallen in love with for real. Losing her, only minutes after confessing her feelings, must have been devastating. Despite that, Farn never seemed to consider the possibility that Kira was gone for good. No, to her, she was just missing. The way she spoke, it seemed like they might find Kira any day now, and they could pick up right where they'd left off.

Ginger looked away from the *Shield* and the empty shell beside her before the sight of them broke her heart.

"Letting go is hard." Ginger lowered head. "Some people just need time, even if they need a crutch to get through each day. I'd appreciate you leaving it well enough alone." She turned to look J3ff in the eyes. "Why are you here, anyway? Shouldn't you be over with Alastair?"

His face blanched at her words, making it clear she'd struck a chord with his conscience. "Yes, Alastair wanted me to give you an update on Nix."

"Good, spill it."

"We're doing everything we can to track her now that we know where she is in Noctem, and we think we might have narrowed her location down to a country."

"And?"

"She's in the U.S."

"Thanks for that." Ginger rolled her eyes. "We'll assemble a search party and go door to door."

"I realize that it's not much, but it's a start."

"Just keep at it." Ginger turned back to the stage, making it clear that she was done talking to him.

"Fine, we will." He stood up and slithered back to Alastair, leaving Ginger to shudder at the thought of having to talk to him again. Turning to her other side, she caught Max staring daggers at the elf's back.

"I swear, I will end him."

"Yeah, I know, you're out for vengeance." Ginger elbowed Max in the arm. "Just make sure I can still have you when you're done. I still have plans." She finished with her most charming smile.

Max clearly tried his best to hold onto his intensity but couldn't stop his cheeks from turning red. He coughed and slumped into his seat. "Sure, I'll look forward to that."

Ginger let herself relax beside him, giving her attention back to the twins on the stage who were finally wrapping up their explanation of what to expect of the event. Grindstone faded back into the background while Dalliance smiled wide and clapped his hands together.

"How about we start the bidding with some appetizers?"

The Auction of Souls had officially begun.

CHAPTER ELEVEN

"Just sit still for once." Farn passed Echo another loaf of bread from her Sack of Snacks as Dalliance addressed the room from the stage.

"Before we get to the main event, we're going to start with a round of non-contract items." He immediately held up his hands as if anticipating groans from the audience. "I know, I know, everyone is here for contracts. But do you really want to rush right to the end? I assure you, everything will be far more exciting if we allow a little build up." He leaned forward and placed a hand to his mouth as if telling a secret to the entire theater.

"Besides, each of these non-contract items are unique drops, meaning they are one of a kind and no one else can get them. Some may even rival a contract in power." He continued to speak as the auction's staff wheeled in a table containing an assortment of items.

Farn couldn't help but recognize one of Dalliance's employees on stage, an elf dressed in the formal gear that matched the rest of the auction staff. Luka, also known as Agent Delgado of the Federal Bureau of Investigations.

Why are the Feds here?

Farn hadn't seen the elven woman since the heist a few months back. Luka had flown the getaway craft they used to move the loot, in exchange for help getting an item from Reliqua's vault. Nix had killed her halfway through the job.

Farn tensed up. Last she'd heard, the Feds were pretty scared of what Kira had become. She may have helped them stop an arms dealer from selling something dangerous, but she'd also shown them what her power could do. All the firewalls in the world weren't enough to stop her from getting any information she wanted. It must have been terrifying to have their databases cracked in seconds. It didn't seem to matter that Kira would never mean any harm. As far as the government was concerned, something like her couldn't be allowed to exist.

She must be here tracking Nix to make sure Kira's off the table. The realization reminded Farn how important it was that she find her friend first.

Farn glanced at Echo in her peripheral. The avatar had finished the loaf she'd been given and was now staring blankly at Seven who sat on her other side. The newly minted *Venom* mage seemed to be trying to ignore her, like the fairy's vacant expression made her uncomfortable.

Farn reached over to brush a lock of hair from Echo's face, hoping to give some input into the system so the avatar might behave a little more human. Echo snapped back to life as soon as Farn's fingers came in contact with her skin, leaning into her touch. The fairy gave her hand an affectionate nuzzle. Farn yanked it away, afraid to let herself be pulled into the illusion that the system had created.

"Why don't you go check out the buffet over there?"

The avatar's dull pupils dilated at the mention of food and flicked over to the table. That was all the system needed to send the little error off on a new task of destroying a buffet. Farn watched as the imitation fairy snuck her way across the theater.

"She's a bit odd." Seven leaned into the empty seat that Echo had just vacated.

"Who, Echo?" Farn sunk into her chair. "Sometimes you have to keep her busy or she runs off and gets into trouble."

"Why do you call her Echo, by the way?" Seven gestured to her journal. "Her name shows up as Kirabell in the area search."

"Ah, well…" Farn felt her forehead begin to sweat, not having an answer for the question. Fortunately, Dalliance chose that moment to display the first item.

"Behold the Possessed Hatchet!" Dalliance threw his hand up, brandishing a plain-looking weapon with a slightly curved handle attached to a small ax head. "Dropped by the Hatchet Ghost that resides in the attic of Gracie Manor at the edge of Port Han. This weapon functions like your basic throwable item. Similar to a throwing knife, it can be used by any class. However, since it is larger than a knife which deals a flat fifty points of damage, this fella can dish out twice that against monsters. The damage is also tripled to three hundred points of damage when used against other players." He paused to admire the item. "Shall we start the bidding at a thousand dollars?"

Farn heard Seven sputter as her elbow fell off her armrest.

"A thousand. That's half my mortgage." She turned to Farn. "Is it that good of an item?"

Unsure why the woman had suddenly become so curious, Farn answered her by gesturing at the audience, none of which had raised their number tiles.

"Throwables can't deal critical damage, so they aren't that helpful in combat other than to get a monster's attention so you can pull it away from a group. Three hundred damage against players is good, but not that helpful since you would have to retrieve the weapon afterwards. Battles are chaotic and there isn't always time to go looking for things. Most players consider throwables disposable."

Seven looked disappointed along with the rest of the bidders who started to taunt the auctioneer.

"Wake me when something good comes up." Lord Murph

of House Saint dropped his head back and feigned sleep, his tail swishing beneath his seat.

"Rude." Dalliance crossed his arms and pouted. "Seriously? No one wants a possessed hatchet?" He held out the weapon and tossed it in one hand a few times, catching the handle. Then without warning, he threw to the side so that it flew off stage. A crash came from behind the curtain, followed by a surprised shout.

"Sorry, Grindstone," Dalliance said with a wink at the audience. "No one wanted our possessed hatchet, despite it sounding so cool and spooky."

"Whatever, just move on." Grindstone shouted from off stage.

"Yes, that may be best." Dalliance lowered his head and began walking back to the table of items. On his way, he held out his hand. Suddenly, the hatchet flew back onto the stage, landing firmly in his grip.

"What the…?" Farn clenched every muscle in her virtual body.

"Oh, did I forget to mention that this hatchet always returns to its owner when beckoned? And that it bonds to any player that touches it until abandoned?" Dalliance gave the audience a smirk as bidding tiles were thrust into the air.

"Ey, what?" Lord Murph lurched forward when his Knight elbowed him. He immediately raised his tile.

"That's better." Dalliance smiled wide. "Okay we have one thousand, can I get two?"

Seven fell off her armrest again at the price.

"You know," Farn started, feeling the urge to help the woman. It was clear that Seven had no idea what she was doing, no matter how much she tried to hide it. "For a low-level like yourself, that hatchet would be a huge help starting out. You won't be able to deal much damage to anything for a while."

"No." Seven gave her a puzzled expression as she hid behind the professional demeanor that she seemed to be holding onto. "I don't have a need for anything like that, and

I'm strictly here for my house. I don't think my lady would appreciate me purchasing items for myself with her money."

"I guess that's true." Farn felt a stupid for suggesting it. Obviously that would be a misuse of funds.

"What about Lockheart? Would any of your members benefit from a possessed hatchet? I would think a few thousand dollars would be affordable for a house like yours."

Farn glanced to Ginger, who hadn't placed a bid.

"Sure, but we're here for contracts only. Regular items won't help us with what we have to do."

"And what do you have to do? Maybe my house could help."

Farn tightened her jaw at the question.

That was an awfully suspicious thing to ask. She was starting to wish Seven had taken a seat next to Ginger instead. The *Coin* was much better at dealing with other houses. All Farn was good for lately was killing things. She held up the Death Grip that encased her hand. The contract that had crippled her ability to protect others with its smaller than average barrier. Farn let out a sigh as she realized Seven was still expecting an answer.

"Oh, ah, no. We wouldn't want to drag you or your house into our fight."

"Of course," Seven shied away. "Sorry. I shouldn't pry. Forgot that houses don't always get along. I'm still learning the rules of diplomacy it seems."

"It's okay. We won't start trouble with other houses as long as they don't make trouble for us." Farn eyed the woman, wondering if she would take her words as a reassurance or as a warning.

Seven simply nodded and turned back to the stage just as Dalliance called for final bids on the hatchet.

"Okay, we have fourteen thousand going once. Going twice, and sold, to Lord Tusker of House Boar."

The large burly man pumped his fist in victory.

"Congratulations, you may claim your new item when this

round of bidding is over and we've transferred your funds."
Dalliance placed the hatchet back on the table and tapped a few
commands on his stat-sleeve, probably to abandon it so that it
would stop returning to his hand. A second later, he spun back
around, dangling a heart-shaped pendant from his hand. Silver
filigree covered its surface.

"Our next item has an air of mystery about it. Its description simply names it as a Royal Locket and it grants the wearer
a bonus to health equal to two percent of the player whose
image is placed inside."

Again, no one raised their number tiles to bid. Obviously,
plus two percent health of another player wasn't much to make
note of. Even a high-level player would only grant an extra
couple hundred HP at most.

Although, after considering the possibilities, Farn couldn't
help but think how helpful it would be for Kira. Sure, Echo
couldn't be damaged, but Kira as she was would have benefited
from it significantly. If they placed a photo of Farn inside it…
she tapped the Celtic knot on the underside of her wrist to call
up her stat-sleeve and did the math.

Her current health read 5888 HP out of 5888 HP.

*Two percent of that would still be over twice the fifty hit points that
Kira has. That would bring her up to 167.*

It wasn't much, but it was plenty to save Kira from being
killed by a random fall or accident. Plus, the locket was cute.
Maybe it would make a good present for her when they got her
back from Nix. Farn glanced to Ginger, debating on if she
should speak up.

That was when Dalliance pushed her over the edge.

"No bids?" He dropped the locket into his other hand,
letting its long silver chain coil around it. "I should mention that
it was dropped by the Ghost of Magnus Alderth, in the crypt
beneath Alderth Castle in the Fallen City of Rend."

Farn immediately sat up straight at the mention of Kira's
favorite dungeon. The dungeon that they had somehow
named as House Lockheart's home as part of an ongoing

quest. She reached across Max and swatted Ginger in the shoulder.

"We're getting that."

"Hey, hands to yourself." The *Coin* swatted her right back as Max struggled not to get hit in the crossfire.

"I'm serious, that will be a perfect present for Kira when…" Farn trailed off, seeing the pity in Ginger's eyes.

"I know." The *Coin* placed a hand on top of Farn's. "But we can't afford to spend our money frivolously. We may need it later."

Farn's vision blurred as tears began to well up, catching her off guard and threatening to break through the dam that she'd held in place for months. She nodded. Ginger was right, buying presents for Kira wasn't going to help them find her. It hurt to let the item go, but she settled back into her seat nonetheless, wiping away a tear that nearly escaped.

Seven averted her eyes, clearly trying not to let on that she'd noticed. The shocked expression on her face said otherwise, like she couldn't understand how anyone could be so emotionally invested in a game.

"We have one thousand." Dalliance pointed to a bidder. "I knew we would have some collectors here. Now can I get two?"

Another bid came in, stabbing Farn in the chest like an ice pick. Then another. She glanced to Ginger who just sat with her arms crossed. Fortunately, the bidding only made it to four thousand before the audience's interest waned.

"Okay, we have four going once." Dalliance swung the pendant like a pendulum. "Going twice, and sol–" He stopped mid-word and thrust his finger out at the audience. "We have five thousand. Knew you couldn't resist, milady."

Farn's head jerked to the side, following the line of his finger to where Ginger sat holding up her bidding tile. The *Coin* gave Farn a warm smile and shook her head.

"You're right, Kira would love it. And we have plenty of money."

Farn blinked away a tear, and mouthed the words, "Thank you," to the *Coin*.

"And sold, for five thousand." Dalliance swung the pendant in a circle before tossing it up and catching it his other hand. "Congratulations, Lady Ginger. I'm glad this item will be returning home to those loyal to Rend. There's something fitting about that." He placed the locket back on the table before hefting a large hammer out from under the table. Its surface shone with a mirror-like finish.

"Next, we have Hard Times." Dalliance raised the weapon and slammed it into the ground, causing the entire hammer to ripple as if made of liquid. "If you can't tell, this item is made of mercury, held in solid form by the same enchantment that maintains the plates of hard that most of you use as currency. So essentially, it's worth about twenty thousand if you can reforge it. Or, if you're a *Rage* class, you can just hit things with it. That works too. Let's start the bidding at fifteen thousand considering its raw value."

Farn shook her head at Dartmouth as he and Tusker got into a bidding war that sent the item's price up above its value. Eventually Dartmouth took the prize, though Farn wasn't sure what he would do with it since he wasn't a class that could use it.

Next up was the pelt of a chimera, which seemed to fade from one color to another with a stripe of scales passing through the middle. Larkin seemed interested, though he refrained from bidding.

Farn closed her eyes and put her head back while the rest of the bidding took place, finding the remaining items pretty useless. Mostly they were a bunch of armor sets and weapons. Her head finally shot back up when Dalliance called one of the auction's guards up on stage.

"Ah yes, thank you, my good sir. I needed a *Shield* class to help demonstrate this one." He held up a heavy brass gauntlet to the guard. The guard wasted no time in pulling off his gauntlet and slipping the new one on.

"Perfect." Dalliance held both hands out to the guard as if presenting him to the audience. "I give you The Tower!"

The man readied the gauntlet as the whole wrist snapped open to reveal one of the largest barrier generators that Farn had ever seen. Energy crackled as the shield pulsed to life, covering the guard from head to toe. Its curved plane of light didn't just protect his entire body, but also provided enough cover for a player or two to hide behind him.

Farn couldn't help but lean forward in her seat.

"That's right." Dalliance danced around the guard. "The Tower projects one of the largest barriers in Noctem. Just imagine slamming down this bad boy like a human fortress in the middle of battle while a *Fury*, *Leaf*, or mage unleashed hell from the safety behind you. Even Nightmares will tremble before you."

For an instant, Farn's heart skipped a beat. Then it sank back down. She couldn't use a gauntlet like that. The Death Grip would only corrupt it anyway. She clenched her clawed fist and cursed the contract item again, which had become a regular occurrence.

Technically, the Death Grip wasn't a gauntlet. Instead, it was more of a permanent status effect that altered the stats and abilities of whatever gauntlet she equipped. It didn't matter that her current gauntlet, the White Rose, was listed on her equipment list. Even with something as powerful as The Tower on stage, the Death Grip wasn't going anywhere. It had even turned her white armor and cape an ashen black, making her look like some kind of death knight.

Farn crossed her arms and ground her teeth until Dalliance called the bidding on the item final. She watched as he reclaimed the tower gauntlet from the guard and placed it back on the table with an air of respect. As soon as he was done, he snatched up a small round object.

"Last but not least." Dalliance tossed the oblong shape in the air, catching it and letting it roll down his arm and across his shoulders to his other hand. He stomped one foot as he thrust it out toward the audience. "I present to you, an egg."

Farn squinted at the item; its surface was speckled with dark green scales, mixed with bright orange and red patches. There was something familiar about the colors.

"But this is not just any ordinary egg." Dalliance waggled one finger in the air. "No, this is a scalefang egg, dropped during the Culling event that takes place in Hunter's Canyon."

Max scoffed, drawing Farn's attention. "I hate those things."

"I'm not a fan either." Farn couldn't help but remember all the times she had fought her way through the Culling while farming with Kira. It had always been the best place to get materials for the bone charms that the fairy had relied on to avoid being killed. The scalefangs were over-muscled reptiles that always reminded Farn of a cross between a large dog and a dinosaur. Though the mane of feathers that surrounded their neck was always pretty to look at. Well, provided they weren't trying to eat you.

"Now with this egg, a player can spawn a loyal pet monster, making it the perfect gift for that special *Whip* class player in your life." Dalliance held the egg to his ear and tapped on its surface. "How you doing in there?"

At this point the audience had grown accustomed to his way of presenting, waiting patiently for him to reveal what made the egg special. He didn't disappoint.

"I should mention that this egg in particular was dropped by the boss of the Culling, the ferocious and brutal One-Eye. That's right, this isn't just a scalefang egg, but a dire scalefang egg. It will take some time to reach its full size, but once it does, well, just imagine the possibilities."

"Who knew One-Eye was female?" Max cringed. "Now I feel kinda bad for killing her so many times."

Suddenly, Dalliance pointed a finger toward Farn. "And we have a bid already. How 'bout we call it a thousand?"

She turned to her side, finding Seven with her number tile raised high. The low-level player looked like a kid in school desperately trying to get the teacher's attention to remind them that they forgot to assign homework.

"I thought you weren't bidding?"

"I wasn't, but this isn't for me." Seven lowered her hand only to throw it back up again to beat someone else's bid. "The Lady of my house is a *Whip* class. Her current pet is quite small, and a bit annoying, so she might want something bigger for protection. I know I would."

Farn's eyes widened at the thought of a player commanding a beast the size of the boss that had dropped it. Maybe it would be a good idea to play nice with Seven, considering her employer might become a force to be reckoned with.

The bidding exchanged for a minute or so, but when Dalliance called the sale final, Seven fell back into her seat looking pretty pleased with herself. She was now the proud owner of a dire scalefang egg. The satisfied grin on her face made Farn want to celebrate with her.

Unfortunately, the celebration was short-lived.

A distant shout drew Farn's attention to the back of the theater just as another came from backstage. Suddenly, one of the auction guards appeared in one of the box seats above. He released a gurgled shout as several arrows slammed into his back, sending him over the edge. The guard screamed as he plummeted to the floor, crashing into the theater's seats below.

Farn reached for her sword as players appeared in the box seats, one after another. More poured into the room from the doors in the back. They outnumbered the auction's attendees and guards at least two to one. Max drew his pistols beside her.

They were surrounded.

That was when Tusker, Lord of House Boar stood and turned on his fellow bidders. He gestured to the intruders above who unfurled a banner on either side of the Theater, each bearing the crest of his house.

Tusker drew his weapon and donned a crooked grin.

"It's about damn time."

CHAPTER TWELVE

"Kill them all!" Lord Tusker swept his sword in front of him as the theater flooded with chaos.

Larkin remained seated, ignoring the man and tapping one finger on his armrest.

"This was... unexpected."

All around him players leaped into action, dozens of duels breaking out all at once. Clearly it was a bad idea to bring all of Noctem's ruling houses together, after all. Who could resist trying to wipe them out in one fell swoop?

Apparently not Tusker. Larkin rolled his eyes.

There was nothing productive about what was happening. It wasn't even all that interesting, just another power play like what Berwyn had attempted six months ago.

The madness continued regardless, Tusker's Boars charging in with wild abandon. Guards fell one after another, proving to be no match for the attacking house. It was to be expected; they were only there to earn a bit of money. They weren't security professionals.

Suddenly, a pair of arrows hit the chair beside Larkin as a

third slammed into his shoulder. He calmly checked his health, noting a five percent loss.

"Ah, good to see the new cape's defenses are stable." He pulled the arrow out and examined the fabric he had draped around him. "I was a little worried that the piercing resistance wouldn't take."

He retrieved his player journal and scratched in some notes about the experimental item he wore.

Clients will pay well for something of this caliber. Not to mention how well it would complement some armor types. The cape didn't actually match well with the vest and slacks that Larkin wore underneath, but it did serve to keep his new assistant hidden. He tapped on the lantern that hung from a hook on his belt, debating if he should use it.

That was when a noise pulled him out of his thoughts, the sound of a theater seat creaking behind him.

Larkin let out a sigh and spun just as a dagger came down. He ducked behind his journal, the weapon's tip digging into the leather-bound cover. He fell back against the seat in front of his row with his legs flailing in the air for footing.

His attacker was a *Coin* with a pair of tall fox ears pinned back in aggression. The Boar's crest adorned her cloak. She bared her teeth as she withdrew her dagger for another strike. Just then, a guard, thrown from the balcony, landed a few rows behind. The *Coin* glanced back at the ruckus, taking her eyes off Larkin for an instant. It was all he needed.

I suppose it's time I helped out.

He drew his crafting shears from the sheath at his back and plunged them into her chest. Her attention whipped back to him, a surprised gasp erupting from her mouth. Clearly, she hadn't been expecting him to attack with something so mundane. Sure, the pair of crafting shears were a bit longer and ornate than most, but still, they weren't a weapon.

Understanding washed over her face as her eyes fell to the class emblem on his hand.

"Sorry." Larkin gave her a wink. "You just got unlucky."

Of course, it didn't matter that his shears weren't classified as a weapon. Larkin was a *Rage*, which could apply their damage bonus to anything. Essentially, the whole world was his weapon. His shears were just convenient, and considering that his level had reached Noctem's current level cap of 175, the *Coin* had gotten unlucky indeed.

From where he lay draped over a chair, Larkin let go of his shears and kicked the crafting tool deeper into her chest. She staggered as he righted himself, taking a moment to adjust his cape so that it sat on his shoulders in a way that flattered his slender frame. The *Coin's* body began to shimmer, prompting Larkin to pull his shears from her corpse before it burst into sparkling particles.

Larkin took a breath. His battle wasn't over.

Before the *Coin's* body could dissipate, the cloud of shimmering flakes was cleaved in two by a rusty claymore sweeping through the air to claim him. An enormous woman followed, the ram-like horns of a faunus bracketing her face. The glowing particles remaining from the *Coin's* body swirled around her form as she lunged over a row of chairs.

Larkin brought his shears up to block, feeling the impact of the blow all the way down his arm as she shoved him back. The tattered banner of House Winter Moon hung from her shoulder.

"Nice to meet you, Kashka." Larkin's arm shook under the weight of the woman's sword. He had been keeping up to date on the who's who of Noctem's elites, so how could he miss the First Knight of the Winter Moon? Like really, how could he miss her? She was huge, not to mention probably the second highest level *Rage* class after him.

"I think we have some mutual friends over in Lockheart." Larkin's voce wavered under the strain of holding her back.

Kashka blew a hot breath out her nose. "You can't talk your way out of fights like they can, little man."

"Nonsense, I was just being polite."

A lock of Larkin's light blue hair fell into his face. Apparently, the ribbon he'd tied it back with had come loose and fallen off. It was always doing that in combat. Sure, the red ribbon looked fantastic against the color of his hair, but it wasn't always the most practical.

I hope I can find it later when the dust settles.

Several gunshots barked from somewhere behind him, tearing his attention away from his lost ribbon and back to the fact that he was fighting for his life.

"You know, we may want to focus on the Boars who are attacking the auction rather than fighting each other." Larkin blew the lock of hair out of his face. "Just a suggestion."

"You are the highest level *Rage* I've met." Kashka gave him a savage smile. "I prefer this."

"Ah, so the Winter Moons are a chaotic neutral sort of house, then?" Larkin tilted his head to one side.

She answered by pressing down harder on the pair of crafting shears holding back her claymore. Larkin's leg threatened to buckle as he struggled to keep her from crushing him, even with his level being higher. The faunus must have been huge in the real world to have such physical strength.

It was actually quite impressive.

"Have you ever considered trading in that awful set of leathers for equipment more fitting of a First Knight?" Larkin gestured at the armor she wore, implying that the distressed leather didn't present the best impression. "I could help with that if you wanted. You're an interesting canvas and I could really design something to bring out the qualities of your character that make you stand out."

"You think I have finer qualities." Kashka laughed, letting up the crushing pressure a little.

"Absolutely, you could really shine with the right gear." Larkin pushed his glasses up on his nose with his free hand. "Tell you what, you let me go back to defending this auction, and I'll get to work on something special for you afterward."

Kasha's face softened. Clearly she wasn't someone that had been told she could shine before.

Shame, Larkin thought. He wasn't one to lie, and he certainly wasn't one to offer his services to anyone that he found boring. He really could do a lot for someone so unique.

"What about this duel? I would like to finish it." She pressed down again.

"That's a good question." Larkin was actually a little curious about who would win as well. "I'd be happy to meet you for some friendly PVP at a later date."

"I'd like that." Kashka suddenly pulled her sword away and rested it on her shoulder as she held out her hand. "Give me your contact info."

"Ah, sure." Larkin gripped her hand and shook it, allowing her access to his profile data. "I'll get to work on some designs for you—"

"Goodbye!" Kashka blurted out as if in a hurry, just before running in the opposite direction.

"Well, okay then." Larkin winced sympathetically as she plowed into one of Tusker's Boars. "There's something to be said for understanding your priorities." The huge faunus proceeded to drop her claymore to the floor and pick up another player by their foot, transferring her damage bonus to her captive. Larkin smiled as she beat a pair of Boars to death with their comrade.

"I suppose I should get my priorities in order as well." Larkin turned to Tusker and began stalking toward him. "Can't let anyone get in the way tonight."

As if sensing his intent, a *Blade* class rushed to meet him along with a *Venom* mage and a handful of *Leafs*. They all wore the banner of the Boar. The mage threw up his hand, activating a spell while the archers reached for their quivers. Larkin smirked as a thick plume of green smoke swirled around him.

"Really, poison? You'll have to do better than that." The buttons on his vest carried a heavy resistance to most status effects.

The *Venom's* eyes widened, he must have put a lot into the spell. Throwing out his other hand, he snapped open a second caster and began throwing spell after spell into his quick-cast queue.

Had to taunt him, didn't you? Larkin regretted his words as the mage hit him with several layers of debuffs, wearing his resistance down. The *Leaf* class players surrounding him let loose, sending a dozen arrows into his body. Spikes of virtual pain spread across his skin before being dulled back down. *Damn!* His cape could dampen their attacks, but only for so long.

"Heads up!" shouted a voice from behind, followed by a loud pop.

Larkin dropped to one knee just as a grappling line flew through the space where he'd been. It struck the mage in the arm, and yanked him forward just as someone planted a foot on Larkin's back.

Ginger soared over him, using his body as a spring board and slamming her heel into the mage. The surprised *Venom* fell to the floor with his mouth wide open. She took the opportunity to shove a small bomb into his gaping jaw, its wick sparking.

The Lady of House Lockheart rolled off of the unfortunate player, a burst of crimson light exploding from his face. She sat back up as the group of *Leafs* took aim at her.

"Try not to lose your head!" Max shouted from across the room.

"That's what I should have said." Ginger slapped a hand to her forehead just before scampering out of the way of a few arrows.

"Thank you for the assistance." Larkin gave her a casual salute.

"We did ask you to back us up. Can't have you getting killed." She fired a grappling line into the ceiling and shot up to one of the chandeliers above. "You might want to make use of whatever you have hiding under your cape."

Just then, a player behind Larkin fell to a group of *Blades* nearby. It was one of House Saint's higher ups, Archmage from the look of his robes. The *Blades* swarmed, stabbing the helpless player mercilessly.

"I suppose it's time I tested some of my experiments. Besides, if these Boars are going to behave like monsters, then so should I." Larkin reached his hand into his item bag just as the *Leaf* class players surrounding him let off another volley.

Arrows streaked through the air only to be caught up in the fabric of Larkin's cape as he ripped it from his shoulders with a flourish. A lantern covered in a shroud of black fabric hung at his side.

He let the cape drift to the floor before lifting his crafting shears over his head and opening them as if ready to cut the heavens. Twisting the handles in a practiced motion, he released the pin at the tool's center. The shears split apart with a metallic snap, becoming a pair of twin daggers. Larkin threw his arms out wide as if inviting the Boars to attack.

An arrow struck him in the thigh, cleaving another fifteen percent off his health and bringing him down to less than half. He smirked and reached into his item bag for his latest experiment, a red and black mask bearing two rows of bone white teeth. Positioning the item over his face, Larkin covered his nose and mouth with a demon's grinning visage. Then, pulling a second item from his pouch, he slid a metal cylinder filled with pixie dust between the mask's jaws and pressed a button on the side.

A puff of shimmering dust escaped as he took a deep breath to inhale the restorative particles he'd collected from Kira's echo. Power flooded his lungs, tingling as if every cell in his chest had begun to vibrate. The sensation faded as he checked his health.

Back to full.

Four breaths left, Larkin reminded himself of how much dust remained in the cylinder. He'd had a theory that inhaling the stuff increased its potency, making each use the equivalent of one high-level heal spell. The mask served as Larkin's personal *Breath* mage, as long as he didn't run out of dust cylinders.

He rushed forward, spinning his twin daggers around his fingers for added flair before crossing them in front of his face in defense. Arrows stabbed into his wrists and legs. Larkin ignored them and lunged for the first of the *Leafs*. His shears bit and sliced into the players as he tore through them like a tornado of razors. At close range, the archers were as good as dead.

The Boars' First Knight pushed toward him to protect his comrades, shoving Larkin back with his shield barrier. The Boars' Archmage, a *Cauldron*, joined the fray and dropped a velvet pouch full of ingredients into the glowing circle above his caster.

That could be a problem.

Larkin drew in another deep breath of Echo's dust, getting a rather horrified look from Ginger who was swinging from one chandelier to another above him. For a moment, he questioned if he had taken his experiment too far.

Another of the auction's guards fell from the balcony, followed by a pair of *Coins*, dropping into the fight behind him. The Boars' Archmage smiled. Whatever spell he was brewing was bad.

Larkin sighed.

Well, if I've gone too far already, why stop now?

He slapped his shears back together and reached for the shrouded lantern at his side. Thrusting the object out toward the Boars' Archmage, Larkin tore off the fabric that kept its contents hidden.

"You may want to start running." Larkin narrowed his eyes as his mask twisted his words into a menacing threat.

The Boars, however, did not run. Instead, puzzled looks surrounded him, all staring at the small doll sitting peacefully inside the lantern. Its silver hair and white dress gave it an air of innocence.

Larkin groaned as he tapped on the glass with the tip of his shears.

The doll, a miniature version of Kira, snapped to life, its sparkling eyes locking on the Boars' Archmage. Its face instantly contorted into a mad snarl.

"I really do suggest running." Larkin twirled his shears casually as a rumbling came from the back of the theater. It was a deep and forbidding sound, like a stampede in the distance.

The color slowly drained from each of the Boars' faces as they turned toward the noise, toward the trunks that Larkin had brought with him. He'd said they were full of items to trade, he just didn't mention that he'd intended on trading in lives.

The trunks rattled and shook as Larkin began to laugh.

They really should have run.

CHAPTER THIRTEEN

"What have I unleashed?" Max stood with his pistols hanging limp at his sides as all of Larkin's trunks burst open. A familiar torrent of nightmare fuel erupted into the theater, hundreds of dolls pouring into one porcelain beast.

Max gawked as the crafting-obsessed *Rage* laughed maniacally while vapors of pixie dust leaked from the jaws of his demonic mask. The Boars' Knight and Archmage turned to run as the conglomerate of dolls simply consumed a few of their lower level housemates. A chorus of tiny voices sang the word 'fashion,' sounding like the strings of a thousand violins being plucked out of order as the writhing beast crashed through the theater's furniture. An unlucky *Fury* screamed, the dolls latching onto their foot. They tried to claw their way free, only to be swallowed whole, their hand the last thing to disappear into the terrifying mass.

Max shuddered, wondering if hiring Larkin as backup was a good idea after all.

"If I ever have kids, I am so not buying them dolls." Farn let out an awkward laugh just before ripping the life from a random *Blade* class that got too close to her Death Grip.

"Where's Echo?" Max shouted over the sound of screams and laughter emanating from Larkin's rampage.

"I lost track of her." Farn spun to meet one of Tusker's men, a sword coming down at her. She caught his weapon with her clawed gauntlet. "I sent her over to the buffet table back during the auction, haven't seen her since."

Max put three rounds into the man she fought with. "Well, Echo can't be hurt so I guess we'll just have to find her later and hope she doesn't get into trouble."

The bark of a familiar three-round burst drew his attention to the other end of the theater where Nix took out a pair of players with her M9. He suppressed the urge to shoot her. Instead he fired on a *Leaf* taking aim at her from one of the box seats above. He couldn't let her die, not when he had finally found the evil woman. Keeping her breathing was the only option, so as much as it hurt him, he raised his house ring and gave an order.

"Everyone, listen up. Whatever happens here with Tusker and his Boars, we can't let Nix die. Protect her. Even if it cost your lives." He glanced to Farn as if asking if he was making the right choice.

"I'll keep an eye on her." A pained expression covered the *Shield's* face as she turned toward Nix and drew her sword, clearly ready to protect their enemy at all costs.

A pang of guilt ate away at Max's chest for allowing Farn to take on such a burden. Fortunately, he didn't get much time to think about it as a saber trailing purple mist streaked past his head. Max ducked just in time, using his pistols to block another three attacks as Amelia, the Lady of House Winter Moon, tried to end him.

"What the hell are you doing?"

"Enjoying the situation." The ferocious reynard woman winked at him while simultaneously attempting to skin him alive.

Her saber tore through the air as he ducked again, getting a whiff of the mist that wafted from her weapon. It smelled like rotting fruit, reminding him that it would only take a scratch to kill him.

"Damn it, Amelia. We're allies, remember? We stole all that hard together back in Reliqua."

"How could I forget? I got rich."

"Then why are you attacking me?" He caught her sword with the trigger guards of his guns.

"Mostly for fun." She shrugged as if it should have been obvious. "And we were only allies back during the pyramid job, so that partnership is null and void now."

"I thought we were friends."

"We are!" She sliced a lock of hair off Max's head as he dodged. "But I kill most of my friends a couple times a week. I killed Kashka yesterday."

Max grimaced; there was no negotiating with her. He'd learned that much about Amelia back when they'd fought in Tartarus six months ago. She had destroyed half a city before listening to reason, and besides, she didn't know what they were really up against. How could he expect her to get serious when she thought that Noctem was nothing but a game? Other than Larkin, he hadn't told anyone about Kira's fate or his war with Nix. No, he couldn't expect Amelia to listen.

"Fine!" Max tightened his grip on his guns. "I didn't want to have to kill you, but you leave me no—"

Suddenly, out of nowhere, Larkin's porcelain beast plowed into the woman with a battle cry of, "Fashion!"

Max fell back on his rear in surprise.

"Need some help?" The fashionable *Rage* sheathed his shears and offered a hand to Max.

"Ah, thanks." He tried not to look at the doll wearing Kira's face trapped in the lantern hanging from Larkin's other hand.

Amelia pushed off the stage and cut a swath through the porcelain beast, killing a dozen dolls.

"Looks like my little fiends bit off more than they could chew." Larkin winced as Amelia severed another ten dolls from his pet monstrosity. "We'll catch up later." He flipped his shears out of their sheath and charged into the mess he'd created.

"This is fine, everything's fine," Max whispered to himself just as a voice came from behind him.

"Hey, Max!"

He immediately spun and pistol whipped the source on reflex.

"Wha fa phak?" shrieked a woman dressed in the same uniform as the auction's support staff. It took Max a moment to recognize her as Luka, also known as Agent Delgado, one of the Feds that took part in the pyramid job.

"Oh shit! Sorry!" He dropped his guns to his sides as if he hadn't just cracked her in the nose.

"God damn, Max, look before you maim." The F.B.I. agent in disguise pulled her hands away from her face, leaving a crimson glow to fade from the bridge of her nose.

"Well maybe don't sneak up on people during an all-out brawl." Max fired a few rounds into one of Tusker's men. "What the hell are you doing here?"

"We thought Nix might show up, so I infiltrated the auction staff in case we were right. If there's even a chance that Nix still has access to whatever's left of Kira, then she's far too dangerous to let run free."

"Go capture her then." Max gestured toward Nix with the muzzle of one of his pistols. "I'll wait here."

Luka rolled her eyes. "If we knew how to do that, we would have done so already. It's somehow more frustrating to find her here when we can't out there in the real."

"Tell me about it."

"Is Alastair having any luck on his end?" She snapped open a caster and tossed a heal spell Max's way, reminding him that she was a *Breath* mage. "I get the feeling that he would tell you before saying anything to us."

"He's working on it. Last I heard, he was sure she was in the U.S. That was the best he could come up with so far." Max held out his pistols in an exaggerated shrug.

"Where is…" Luka spun around, clearly searching for the head of Checkpoint Systems. "There he is. Cover me so I can get to him." She pointed toward the back of the theater where Alastair seemed to be arguing with J3ff.

"Ah, okay." Max took up a position next to her, not sure why he was following her orders. Then he paused as Dartmouth ran past them, flailing his arms in the air, leaving his Archmage and Knight to be murdered by Tusker.

"I can't say that's surprising." Luka turned away from the scene as a cloud of shimmering particles rose from behind her. "Whatever, let's go."

Max nodded.

It didn't take long to cross the room. He took out a few more of Tusker's Boars on the way, receiving a couple bad hits in the process. Fortunately Luka was there to drop a well-timed heal on him.

"Thanks." He shot another Boar sneaking up behind her.

"Likewise."

He gave her a smile, grateful to have a healer again. Just the knowledge that someone was there behind him made him feel a little better. It had been a while since he'd had that kind of support. Besides, relying on Larkin's pixie bombs wasn't a sustainable strategy. Max only had a couple of the items left, and with the rate that Larkin was inhaling the rest of their dust supply, he wasn't getting any more.

Together, they reached Alastair and his assistant, who were in the middle of a battle of their own.

"Sir, we have to shut down this madness." Jeff-with-a-three stomped one foot as he spoke.

"Oh, yes, sure we do." Alastair stood with his arms folded like a stubborn child.

"Might I remind you that this is your game, and it wouldn't be possible without investors such as the twins up there. Their money was integral to Checkpoint back when this was all a file on Carver's hard drive."

"Oh, I know, Jeff-with-a-three." Alastair's voice was thick

with sarcasm. "We should help them undermine the very spirit of Noctem right now, and sell contracts off to the highest bidder."

"Sir, you are a Game Master of Carpe Noctem." J3ff stabbed a finger at the GM band around Alastair's arm. "All you would need to do is put a ban on PVP for the duration of the auction. That would fix everything. You could put a stop to this in seconds."

Max's jaw clenched. If they banned PVP, he wouldn't be able to go after Nix. Her escape would be secured. Hell, that was probably why J3ff was insisting on it. He just wanted to keep his real boss safe. Fortunately, Alastair seemed to be avoiding taking such an extreme step.

"If it's that easy, you should have no problem taking care of it yourself."

J3ff broke eye contact with his employer. "I would, but I lack the programing skills to set up a localized ban on PVP. I can only target individual players from the GM console, but you, you know exactly how to implement such a thing."

"Look, J3ff." Alastair shoved his hands in his pockets and flapped his coat open and closed. "I don't like this whole event, and I don't want to use something that heavy-handed to protect it. Even if the twins are our valued investors."

"But if this continues, some of Noctem's rulers may die, and that could throw the game world into chaos just like what followed Berwyn's fall. It has been six months and things are only now just settling back down."

Alastair sighed. "Yes, well, you have me there."

"We won't let that happen." Max stepped into the argument. "We can kill Tusker for you, and it looks like the other Lords are holding their own so far. The rest of Noctem should be safe without a PVP ban."

"Oh, look Jeff, it's Max." Alastair took the opportunity to exit the conversation. "Hello Max. And, oh, Luka is here with you. How nice. How have you been?"

"I'm fine." Luka glanced over her shoulder. "Are you any

closer to pinning down where Nix is connecting to Noctem from?"

"Ah." He raised one finger as if thrilled to have a way out of the conversation that J3ff had been forcing on him. Then he dropped his hand back down as he deflated. "No, sadly we haven't been able to nail down her position yet."

"Damn."

"Sir, please." Jeff-with-a-three held out one hand, pleading to his boss. "You represent Checkpoint."

"Fine, tell you what…" Alastair tore his GM band off and wrapped it around J3ff's arm on top of the overly serious elf's own GM band. "You can represent Checkpoint tonight because, as you have reminded me," he paused to flip up the collar of his coat and adjust his caster, "this is my game, so tonight, I'm going to play it for once. And I feel like stopping Tusker the old-fashioned way."

"But, sir—"

"Come on, Max, let's go kill some Boars."

With that, Alastair marched off toward the chaos.

Max gave Luka a shrug and chambered a round.

"Shall we?"

CHAPTER FOURTEEN

"Why does this keep happening?" Seven weaved to one side to avoid one of the reynards from Thrift, the ones that Nix had referred to as murderous kittens. A fitting description as they tore into an unsuspecting member of House Boar. Lord Murph finished them with a bullet to the chin.

"Eek!" Seven cupped her hands over her mouth to stop herself from drawing attention to herself.

Some help Lockheart was.

The house of sketchy individuals that she had been tasked with getting close to had dispersed the instant the Boars attacked. Their lack of concern irritated her, although part of her couldn't deny that their willingness to defend the auction was admirable.

She jogged in place with her hands still clasped over her mouth, her head on a swivel, looking for a place to hide.

To her left, that enormous faunus from Winter Moon swung her giant sword like a golf club, launching a player into the air with an insane smile on her face. To her right was even worse, a hulking mass of dolls consuming a screaming member of the

House Boar while that crafter, Larkin, stabbed people with his scissors.

Then, she saw it.

Safety!

Sweet inconspicuous safety.

The buffet table still sat near the stage covered with an assortment of food items. Seven took off at a sprint, racing for the only bit of protection she could find. With a little luck, she might be able to ride out the insanity that was going on all around her. She dropped to her knees and slid for home, rolling under the tablecloth with her eyes shut tight.

Safe! She celebrated internally as the sounds of combat surrounded her hidey-hole.

Seven pushed up on her hands and knees and opened her eyes, only to find herself face to toe with a rather delicate foot. Following the slender leg up, she found Echo sitting rather unladylike with her legs out in front of her. The fairy munched on a pastry of some kind obviously claimed from the table above their heads. Seven blew out a sigh.

"I see you abandoned everyone and got to safety." The silent mage answered with a smile but continued to eat as if there was nothing wrong with their situation.

"At least I'm not alone." Seven pulled her legs up to her chest and rested her chin on her knees to keep her head down in the cramped space. "How did things get so far out of hand?"

Echo answered with a nonchalant shrug.

Seven raised her house ring to her mouth, ready to ask for help. Then she lowered it again, questioning if she even should ask. After killing her superior earlier, she wasn't sure how much support she could expect. She shook off her worry and raised her ring again.

"Hello, Leftwitch? My Lady?" She felt stupid calling her boss by her title. "I'm having a slight problem. It seems that one house has staged an attack on the auction. I'm doing what I can to stay hidden, but I was wondering if Cassius might be close to reaching the ship?"

Seven waited, getting a confused look from Echo.

No one answered.

Maybe Leftwitch is on a different line right now?

She dropped her hand to her lap and sighed, not sure what she should do. Then the table cloth beside her flew up.

"Move over, move over!"

Seven took an elbow to the shoulder as the elf, Dartmouth, scurried under the table.

"Alright, alright." She scooted closer to Echo, who didn't take up much space. "Aren't you the Lord of Serpents? Shouldn't you be with your house out there fighting?" Seven shoved a lock of dark blue hair back behind her ear with a huff, dropping her professional persona a bit. She was officially at her wits end.

"I, ah," the cowardly elf stuttered before getting a word out, "no, I'm more of a delegator. I'm sure my Knight and Arch-mage are doing just fine without me." He glanced at the party read out on his wrist for a moment, then cringed.

"Uh huh." Seven narrowed her eyes at the snake.

"Whatever." He leaned forward toward Echo. "Miss Kirabell, might I trouble you for a favor?"

Seven raised an eyebrow at the name Kirabell, wondering again why the rest of the fairy's house called her Echo.

Some kind of nickname maybe?

She shoved the thought aside as Dartmouth continued.

"This event has gotten a little too lively for comfort. Do you think you could teleport me to safety? I would deeply appreciate it."

Echo simply shook her head.

"I suppose not. You wouldn't be able to get back on board, would you?" A slight sneer slithered across Dartmouth's face at her response, as if he thought asking her to abandon the rest of her house was reasonable. He shook his head. "Surely, you must have some sort of plan to survive this."

Echo raised a finger like she had an idea and shoved the rest of her pastry into her mouth. Then with a sudden serious expression, she flipped the hood of her cloak up and pulled it down to hide her face. A second later she was gone, vanishing under the table cloth to enact some sort of plan.

Seven waited with Dartmouth, listening to the sounds of violence outside their hiding place.

Suddenly, Echo rolled back into the safety of the table.

"Any luck?" A hopeful glow filled Dartmouth's eyes.

The fairy answered with an excited nod, before reaching under her cloak and producing a loaf of bread and another pastry. She held them out to Dartmouth, a proud smile evident on her face.

"I don't want a Danish!" The elf slapped the pastry from her hand causing her to shrink back, her dull eyes flicking back and forth between the fallen snack and its murderer. The fairy pulled the loaf of bread back, holding it close like she feared for its safety. Dartmouth let out a sigh. "Sorry, I didn't mean to frighten you. Sometimes I forget how frail your kind are."

The silent fairy narrowed her eyes at him, clearly not accepting his apology. She bit into the loaf of bread, then tore off one end and held it out to Seven.

"And you're a member of the most feared house in Noctem?" Seven shook her head at the girl but accepted the offering and took a bite regardless.

Echo gave her a playful nudge and settled in to eat beside her.

Suddenly, the tablecloth flew up on both sides of the table revealing a pair of players tumbling into the space in unison. The new additions to the cramped space collided with Dartmouth and Seven, both falling over in a pile.

"Oh, hi Seven, wasn't expecting to find you here." A familiar archer waved from where he lay on the floor tangled up with Dartmouth. An equally familiar reynard lay draped over her legs.

"Kegan, Corvin." Seven gave the pair a sarcastic bow and gestured to the table above. "Welcome to the coward's clubhouse. What brings you to my domain?"

"We saw this little one from the box seats and watched her raid the buffet before ducking back under here." Kegan gestured in Echo's direction as he shoved himself free of the indignant Lord of Serpents beside him.

"We thought we should come down check on her." Corvin added while carefully righting himself.

"Nice, food." Kegan snatched the fallen pastry off the floor and mashed it into his face. "The Boars are putting up a fight out there."

Seven wondered again how Lockheart had become so infamous as the archer spoke with his mouth full of floor pastry and spat crumbs all over Dartmouth.

"I'd heard that the Boars have been recruiting aggressively. I guess it was true." Dartmouth brushed off his shoulder and attempted to inch away from Kegan.

"Yeah, they brought a small army." Corvin pulled his legs in tight, clearly trying not to crowd the rest of the table's inhabitants. "But from the looks of it, the Boars have gone with quantity over quality."

"So there's a lot of them, but they aren't skilled fighters or high-level players." Seven felt the analytical side of her mind assert itself to take over the situation.

Dartmouth's shoulders relaxed. "So the rest of the auction's guests should be able to beat them off?"

"Heh, that's what she—" Before Kegan could finish his sentence, an arrow slammed through the table's protective surface directly in front of his face. The elf's eyes crossed as he stared at the tip.

Seven's whole body tensed as everyone ducked their heads a few inches.

"And no, the auction might not be easy to defend." Corvin cupped his hands over his long, furry ears to hold them down, lest he get an unwanted piercing. "The Boars may lack quality fighters, but quantity is still quantity. There's only so long everyone out there can keep up the fight without being overwhelmed."

The group of hidden players fell silent at Corvin's assessment. The quiet didn't last.

"Hey, Seven!" a gruff voice shouted in her ear. She jumped in surprise, whacking her head on the underside of the table.

"Ow ow ow." Seven rubbed at her skull, noting the loss of a few hit points on her stat-sleeve as everyone in her hiding place stared at her like she'd lost her mind. It took a moment for her to recognize the voice as Cassius. She brought her house ring to her mouth.

"What!" she shouted back before remembering she was addressing a superior. "Sorry, um, what's up?"

"I apologize for startling you. Just getting you back for pushing me off the ship."

"Yeah, about that…"

"Heh, don't worry about it. Chalk it up to bad planning on our part. But anyway, I'll be there in about five minutes. I take it you're still alive in there?"

"Yes, sir." Seven nodded even though he couldn't see her.

"Great, make your way out and get to the landing pad. I never got to see where the auction is being held when I was on board earlier, so I'll need you to guide me there. I'll try to put a stop to things when I get inside."

Seven froze, listening to the chaos outside. "But, I'm not sure I can make it to you."

"You killed me, didn't you? You'll be fine."

"But…" Seven started to say, before realizing there wasn't a reasonable argument to give from his perspective. "Damn."

"Everything okay?" Corvin looked her in the eyes.

"My house is sending backup. I have to go meet him on the landing pad. Provided I can make it there."

"Reinforcements? Sounds good, want us to escort you there?" Kegan finished off the pastry that he'd found on the floor.

Seven opened her mouth to say yes on reflex but shut it again. It may not help her mission to get on Lockheart's good side if they found out that she was working with the player that had attacked them earlier.

"Ah, no, you should stay here and help fight the Boars. It sounds like we're going to need everyone to hold them off." It wasn't technically a lie. Seven let out a breath when they didn't argue, only to take it back when realizing that she had to leave the safety of the table.

"Good luck." Kegan pulled a wooden cylinder from his pouch. "If you get into trouble, pull on both ends and smash it at your feet."

"Thank you." Seven took the item, despite not knowing what it was. Then she paused to psych herself up, taking several more deep breaths. "Okay, can't wait here forever." She threw up the table cloth and stood up, coming face to face with one of Tusker's Boars.

"Oh shit!"

Before the word even left her mouth, a chandelier of thousands of tiny crystals crashed into the floor, obliterating the man in front of her. Instinct took over and she dove to the side, away from the crystal hail.

"Sorry!" called a voice from above.

Seven rolled over to find Ginger dangling above her from the chain that once supported chandelier. The Lady of Lockheart gave her an apologetic tilt of her head before firing a grappling line and zipping off to another light fixture. Seven started to push herself off the floor but was knocked back down when a reynard jumped over her. A furry tail swatted her in the face as she landed on her back again.

"My bad!" Nix shouted back as she vaulted up onto the stage. "I thought you were a corpse." The reynard didn't wait for a response before leaping over the table of rare items that had just been auctioned off earlier. She kicked it over with a crash and fired over the side at a player in the viewing boxes above.

Items clattered to the stage, sliding and bouncing off in all directions. The scalefang egg that Seven had purchased rolled to the edge of the raised platform and she lunged on instinct to catch it. The item dropped into her outstretched fingers just as a hatchet embedded itself in the floor next to her.

"Gah!" Seven held her scalefang egg close to her chest for protection. She wasn't sure if the item could break or not, so she tapped the transfer option under the inventory tab of her stat-sleeve. The egg vanished as if it had never been there and she dropped her hand to her side, coming in contact with the hatchet's handle sticking up from the floor. The instant she touched the weapon, a haunting voice echoed through her head.

"Ah, there you are!"

Seven pulled her hand away from the handle like the thing might bite her at any second. The voice didn't stop.

"Now, you have to ask yourself, is this possessed hatchet actually speaking… or is it your imagination?"

Seven stared at the weapon, remembering what Dalliance had said during the auction, that it would bind to whoever touched it until they abandoned it.

Did that mean it was hers?

Her thoughts were interrupted when one of the Tusker's Boars stepped in front of her. Seven scooted away a few inches on her rear until her back hit the stage.

"I believe my Lord won the bid on that fair and square." The player pointed at the hatchet with the point of his sword.

Seven glanced between the sword and the possessed item beside her. Technically the swordsman was right, Tusker had bought the weapon at the auction.

"Well now," the hatchet's ghostly voice spoke in her ear, "it seems that you have been targeted. You could try asking politely for your enemy to let you live." Its words were vague, like it was reading from a script and didn't actually know what was happening.

Probably an NPC, like the ones back in Lucem.

Seven reached for the strange weapon with the intent to hand it over to the swordsman, maybe being polite was the way to go. The hatchet disagreed.

"On second thought, you'll probably be killed. What will you do?"

Seven tensed up, pulling the weapon from the floor boards as it continued.

"Of course, there's always my way…" The hatchet's voice trailed off, making the implications of its suggestion clear.

The swordsman stepped closer, his hand outstretched. "Give it and you might live." The look in his eye told her he was lying.

"Sure, take it!" Seven lobbed the hatchet expecting it to bounce off his armor harmlessly.

It didn't.

The man's scream blended with a haunting laughter that swam through Seven's mind. That was when she realized that she was laughing too. The hatchet had flown straight at his head as if guided by a wire, like the NPC ghost inside was helping her out.

Seven held out her hand, just as Dalliance had done during the auction. She braced as the possessed weapon dislodged itself from the swordsman's skull and twirled back to her hand.

"Big mistake!" The man clutched one hand over a crimson streak that lit up his forehead.

There was no turning back. Seven swept her hand up to open her spell craft menu and cast a pulse that threw him off balance. Then she let the hatchet fly. This time it hit her opponent in the leg, combining with the impact of the pulse to knock him over. Seven didn't hesitate, calling back her weapon only to throw it again and again while he was down.

He didn't get the chance to recover.

Seven's chest heaved as she struggled to comprehend what she had just done, the evidence staring her in the face as the man's body began to shimmer. He was dead, and she had killed him.

All by herself.

There was no happy little chime to signal a level up like there had been when she'd pushed Cassius off the ship. Must not have been a high-level player. Seven watched as the sparkling cloud drifted away.

"Nice job." A voice came from the stage where Nix offered a slow clap.

"Whatever." Seven rolled her eyes and beckoned her hatchet, catching it as she made a break for the door.

Jumping through a curtain, she exploded into a hall and took off at a sprint. She weaved to the side to avoid a player running another through with a sword. Then threw her hatchet at another blocking her path. It struck him in the head, giving her enough time to slip by. Without looking back, she threw her hand behind her to call to the weapon. It had stopped talking now, apparently out of dialogue.

Seven ran through the theater's lobby and kicked open the door to the deck only to find herself staring down the barrel of a gun.

"Ah, hello Piper," she awkwardly greeted the last of Lock-heart's stowaways, while trying to ignore the pistol in her face.

"Seven." The reynard lowered her gun. "What are you doing out here? With everything I've heard happening inside, I thought you'd be—"

"Dead?" Seven finished her sentence.

"Pretty much." Suddenly, the girl's ear pinned back and she shoved Seven to the side to put three bullets in a player that was sneaking up behind her.

Just then, Kegan and Corvin burst through a pair of doors further down, being chased by a full party of Boars. Apparently they had left the safety of the buffet table.

"Do something, Corvin!" Kegan shouted.

"You do something!" Corvin argued back.

"Like what? I'm out of arrows."

Seven reacted without thinking, stepping past Piper to throw her hatchet and cast a pulse. The Boar in the lead took the hits, causing the rest to topple over them in a heap. Seven swiped open her spellcraft menu as she beckoned to her hatchet with her other hand. This time she skipped past the pulse spell and selected the glyph for poison, targeting the Boar in the back. She cast it again on a second target.

Corvin took the opening she had created and spun on his heel. He slid his fingers down the back of his sword and said something that Seven couldn't hear as he sliced through the empty air before him. Her jaw fell open when two translucent currents of air flew from his blade, slashing crimson streaks through the party of Boars.

Piper piled on, firing round after round with careful accuracy. Seven launched her hatchet another few times as the three of them surrounded Tusker's men. It didn't take long to finish them off, and this time, that happy little chime returned to her ear.

Another level.

"Well shit, Seven, where did you get that?" Piper gestured to the hatchet as she reloaded.

"It sort of found me." Seven held it up before tucking it into her belt beneath her robes.

"So where's this backup of yours?" Kegan jogged over.

She froze, realizing that she had ended up right in the situation she was trying to avoid.

"I, ah…"

As if on cue, a transport ship swooped over the deck, not bothering to land. Cassius dropped from the craft, landing in a crouch with his spear held out behind him. At least he didn't wear the helmet this time.

"Hey, that's the guy that attacked us earlier!" Corvin drew his sword.

"It is?" Piper took aim.

"Yeah, just look at his weapon."

Cassius raised his head with a fearsome glare. Seven's heart nearly exploded from her chest as everything fell apart. She was running before she even knew what she was doing.

"Wait wait wait!" She threw herself between them with her arms held up. "He's on our side. This is Cassius, my backup."

"You mean the dude you offed earlier?" Kegan stood with his arms folded, still out of arrows.

"Yes, he's the First Knight of my house."

"That makes no sense." Piper shifted her aim to Seven's chest.

"Ah, yes, yes. That's true. But I didn't know who he was earlier. I didn't recognize Cassius with the helmet on and I had only met him once. I just thought I was in danger, because I've only been logged in for, like, three hours and I don't know anything about anything."

"At least you're honest." Cassius let out a laugh. "In truth, our house, the Silver Tongues, would like to be on good terms with Lockheart."

"Then why did you attack us earlier?" Corvin didn't lower his sword.

"My team stowed away." Cassius shrugged. "You walked in on us. That made you loose ends."

"We were stowaways too." Piper shifted her aim back to Cassius.

"Well I didn't know that at the time. The three of you ran before I had time to think about it."

"So, what you're saying…" Kegan tapped one finger on his chin and casually stepped into the middle of the conflict along-side Seven. "…is that all of us here…" he swept his hand around the group, "…are all just really dumb."

Silence fell across the deck, leaving only the ship's engines to fill the void. Seven's heart raced as she waited for someone to speak.

"Okay, that tracks." Cassius nodded.

"Yeah, we're not the brightest." Corvin sheathed his sword.

"Speak for yourself." Piper holstered her pistol.

Seven released the longest breath of her life and sunk to her knees. "How the hell did I get here?"

"I don't know, but welcome to Noctem." Kegan offered her

a hand back up. "Now that we're all friends here, how 'bout we go back in there and help everybody else make nice too? You know, before Max and the others destroy the place."

Seven took his hand and pulled herself back up.

"Why not?"

CHAPTER FIFTEEN

"Tusker!" Max roared through the Mantle of Death that covered his face like a bandit's mask. Smoke wafted from his pistols as swirls of translucent blades swatted arrows and bullets out of the air around him. He stood atop a mound of broken chairs while the bodies of two players dissipated at his feet.

Alastair stood to his right, a glowing circle of power hovering in the air above his caster. Luka, the federal agent turned *Breath* mage, bracketed Max's other side. She swiped her fingers down the selection column of her spellcraft menu, casting a regenerative spell around Max to stop his *Reaper* subclass from draining his health. Farnsworth held the frontline, her claws glowing with stolen life.

The fighting in the theater slowed as all eyes turned to the conflict at its center.

"You think you can stop me?" Tusker shouted as his Knight and Archmage rushed to his sides. "I have allies all over Noctem ready to seize each city once I've killed their rulers. The empire of the Boar will rise in one fell swoop."

"Not if I have anything to say about it." Alastair swept his hand to the side dramatically. "I made this world, and I'm not about to let you take it."

"That why you're standing alongside the house that stole millions from your company?" Tusker smirked. "A little desperate, if you ask me."

"I'll work with whatever lowlife I have to in order to protect what I've built."

"Hey!" Max glowered at Alastair. "Little harsh there, man."

"Pshaw." The vampiric-looking mage waved away the complaint before whispering a response. "Just keeping up appearances. I can't go about letting everybody know how close we are. Think about the optics."

"That's fair." Max saw his point.

"Yes, anyway." Alastair returned his attention to Tusker and hooked a thumb at Max. "Lockheart's hoodlums might be the scum of Noctem's underbelly, but they're clever, and I have to respect that much. You, on the other hand, well, you're just an opportunist looking to take the world in some poorly-conceived smash and grab."

"Okay, I would hardly call us scum." Max whacked Alastair with one of his pistols.

"Oh relax, I called you clever, didn't I?"

"What's wrong with you two?" Luka stomped one foot. "Get your crap together, we have bigger problems."

"Sorry." Max took aim at the Lord of Boars. "Enough talk, it's time to end this."

"This won't be like last time." Tusker readied his sword.

"That's where you're wrong." Max held his arms wide and narrowed his eyes. "Farn, kill him."

Everyone froze.

"Umm, I can't." The *Shield* looked back at Max awkwardly. "The Death Grip can only instakill a player once. I already used it on him months ago in Torn, when we broadcast that message to Nix."

"Oh shit." Max dropped his pistols to his sides realizing how foolish he looked standing there in all his glory while everyone stared at him. "I forgot that."

"Ah ha!" Tusker pointed at Max with his broadsword. "See, it won't be like last time."

"Okay, yeah, it won't." Max pulled the Mantle of Death down off his face, letting it return to being a plain scarf.

The class emblem on his hand shifted from the *Reaper's* coffin back to his normal *Fury* icon. It didn't make sense to keep the sub-class active since Tusker and his top housemates didn't use guns or bows, and it would do nothing to protect him against magic. It looked cool, but it wasn't worth the continued drain of 30 hit points every 3 seconds.

"Ah, what now, Max?" Alastair fidgeted in place.

Farn flexed her glowing claws. "I could punch him real hard if you like."

"New plan." Max took aim at Tusker and switched his pistols to full-auto. "Unleash hell."

Alastair immediately activated the spell he'd been brewing, firing a pillar of super-heated steam from his hand as Max unloaded both guns. Farn let out a growl and charged in to finish the attack. The Death Grip shone with crimson light as she thrust her fist forward. A thunderous crack struck the air as the impact blew away the lingering steam in an instant, revealing the Boars, all safe behind a massive energy barrier. The blast had only pushed them back a few feet.

Max's mouth dropped open. "What the fu–"

"Nice try." Tusker cut him off.

Farn leaped back to Max. "It's the tower shield from the auction. They must have snatched it during the commotion!"

"That's not all." Tusker laughed as his Archmage stepped out from behind him with his hand placed against a fully-charged overcast sigil. Max gasped. Whatever spell was coming carried one hundred percent of the mage's mana.

Farn raised her gauntlet, its meager barrier blinking into place just as a pulse spell exploded into existence. It didn't matter if it hit her or not, the amplified spell hit them all like a grenade lobbed into their center.

Max's world went white and silence engulfed him as the energy blast overpowered his virtual senses. Everything seemed to slow as his vision returned, his body launched backward into the wall.

Farn, Luka, and Alastair all flew in opposite directions, their forms spiraling through the air. Farn crashed into the theater's seats, bowling through the built-in chairs like a wrecking ball. Luka was more fortunate, her body tearing through the curtains at the back of the stage. Max didn't see where Alastair landed; he was too busy falling to the floor with the wind knocked out of him. It had taken everything he had just to hold onto his guns. He checked his health, finding it down only thirty percent.

"Thank god pulse spells don't carry much damage." Most of it had come from his impact with the wall. As to why Tusker's mage had decided to dump all of his mana into a spell like that was beyond him.

Unless… it was a distraction. Max staggered to his feet, coughing, as Tusker rushed him.

"Shockwave!" the Lord of Boars screamed as he swept his sword through the air. An arc of energy flew from his weapon, hitting the theater seats to create a tsunami of furniture.

Max crossed his arms in front of his face in a feeble attempt to mitigate damage. The wave hit him at full force, slamming him back into the wall.

Tusker didn't give him a chance to recover. The Lord of Boars came at him with a downward chop. It was all Max could do to raise his empty pistols up to block.

"Now you die!" Tusker shouted as Max crossed his guns in front of his face to catch the falling blade.

"Do, you mind, not, spitting at me, when you shout, generic bad guy lines?" Max braced his arms with everything he had as Tusker pressed down, his blade inching closer to Max's face.

"Joke all you want. It won't matter when you're dead."

"What will killing me even do? I'll just respawn."

"It will make me feel better after your house embarrassed me in Torn. Sometimes a Lord has to save face."

"I'm sorry we killed you, okay? It was nothing personal. We just needed to send a message. You have no idea what's really happening in Noctem."

"I know exactly what's happening."

Max clenched his jaw. There was no talking to the guy.

He glanced at his health. Thirty percent left.

There was nothing he could do to hold Tusker back. There was a reason why *Furies* didn't fare well in PVP, after all. Once they were out of ammo, that was it. Max's arms shook, the slides of his own pistols shoved in his face to hold back the attack.

"Where are your jokes now?" Tusker angled his sword so that its edge dug a crimson line into Max's forehead.

"Sure, I got, one more for you," Max relaxed his arms just enough to let his guns rest against the bridge of his nose, close enough to activate his class skills. Tusker's eyes suddenly widened, clearly realizing the threat. It was too late. Max had already whispered a command.

"Last Stand."

The slides of his pistols snapped back into place, ready to fire rounds crafted from his remaining hit points. He didn't have much to work with but, with a little luck, it would be enough. With that, Max dipped to one side, pushing Tusker's blade away with one gun while pumping two shots into the man's gut.

Tusker staggered back, giving Max a chance to check his health.

Twenty percent left.

Tusker covered his vitals with his arms, taking another bullet in the stomach.

Fifteen percent, then ten, then five. Max fired off all but the last of his health.

"Damn it." It wasn't enough.

Tusker lowered his arms, revealing a smug grin. "What's wrong? Finished already?"

Max stood there panting as the Lord of Boars rose to his feet. He struggled to think of a way out, circling back to one regretful thought.

If only Kira was still here.

She always had been. Always. Max shook his head, trying to bury the truth away. Kira was gone. Tusker drew back his sword and readied a thrust. Max let his guns fall to his sides and closed his eyes.

Damn it.

Then, warmth spread across his skin, tingling like pixie dust. Max opened one eye a crack, finding Echo hovering between him and his enemy. She spread her arms wide, as if to say, 'you'll have to go through me first.'

Of course, Max remembered the system was still using their memories of Kira to animate her empty avatar. His thoughts must have pushed Echo into action.

"Get out of the way." Tusker raised his sword to her throat, unaware that there was nothing he could do to hurt the error.

She ignored him and glanced back at Max with a cheerful smile that made his heart ache. He glanced at his health as it ticked back up from the effect of her dust.

"Even now, you're still here for me, aren't you?"

Tusker motioned to grab Echo's arm, but Max moved faster. Pulling the fairy back for protection, he fired another few rounds into the man's chest. Crimson light filled the air.

The Lord of Boars dropped to one knee, supporting himself on his sword just before toppling over. He let out a shocked whisper as light began to sparkle across his body. "My empire… I had it all planned." He vanished a moment later.

Max stepped away from Echo, searching the devastated theater for the rest of his friends and allies. He found Farn digging herself from a pile of broken chairs, while Luka crawled out from under a curtain that had been torn from the stage.

Alastair turned up at the back of the room, electrocuting one of the remaining Boars with a bolt of lightning.

The Boar's Knight and Archmage were still there, standing with a lack of direction, confused at the loss of their lord. Max let out a sigh and gestured to Luka for a heal.

Tusker was dead, but Noctem's rulers were still in danger.

The fight wasn't over yet.

CHAPTER SIXTEEN

Seven marched back toward the theater, following Cassius through the lobby. The three stowaways from Lockheart bracketed her on both sides. To her surprise, the moment made her feel like part of a team. Everyone moved with determination, like they were ready to take on the world. All that was missing was some background music and slow motion.

Even more surprising was that a part of her liked it.

A stray Boar turned in their direction as soon as they entered the theater lobby. Cassius held out one arm in front of her, indicating that he would take care of the obstacle. Without a word, he drew back his spear with one hand and placed his other to his forehead. Whispering the command, "Javelin," he let it fly.

The weapon seemed to shoot from his hand under its own propulsion and the lone Boar was torn from his feet like a rag doll. His body hung limp, pinned to the wall behind him. He hadn't stood a chance. Cassius didn't skip a beat, walking past the dead Boar and ripping his spear free as the body flaked apart.

Seven's shock at how easily Cassius had ended the player

must have been evident on her face, because Corvin leaned over to speak.

"That's a *Rain* class for you."

"*Rain* class?" Seven whispered back.

"Yeah, they use mana to augment their movement and amplify their weapon's impact. It's a class that lacks utility, but they have huge damage potential that's great for one-shotting things. They like to leap into the air and strike from above."

"Ah, so I assume that's why they're called a *Rain*." Seven frowned for a second. "Good to know, I've been calling him a spear guy."

Kegan snorted at the conversation. "And what have you been calling us?"

"Mostly, I've been calling you..." Seven held up one hand and counted her fingers. "Bow elf, sword fox, and angry girl."

Piper crossed her arms and harrumphed, demonstrating the accuracy of her description.

"Maybe you should start learning people's actual classes," Kegan held his journal open to one of its information pages so that she could see a list.

"That's probably a good idea." She deflated, remembering how much she had to learn. "I'll try to look over it the next time I have a chance."

"To get you started..." Kegan gestured to himself. "I'm a *Leaf*, Corvin is a *Blade*, and Piper is a *Fury*." He slipped his journal back into his pouch. "Oh, and you're a *Venom* mage."

"I know what class I am, thank you very much." Seven waved her hatchet at him in a vaguely threatening manner.

"Sorry to interrupt lesson time," Cassius stopped abruptly, causing Seven to bump into the slab of muscle that was his back.

"Omph." She blinked a couple times to clear her vision.

He ignored her. "Does this theater have a balcony?"

"Yeah, we checked it out earlier while we were sneaking around." Corvin pointed to a doorway to the side of the theater's main doors. "There's stairs right in there."

"Perfect." Cassius headed in the direction the reynard had pointed without explanation. In turn, Seven followed without question.

The sounds of battle met her ears as soon as they set foot through the door. The din swelled and grew as they climbed the stairs, ramping up the tension in Seven's chest. She was about to step right back into the chaos she'd run from just moments ago, but this time she wasn't alone.

I can do this. She took a deep breath and followed Cassius through the curtain.

Kegan loosed three arrows as soon as they stepped out onto the balcony, killing two of Tusker's Boars and wounding another. Now that Seven was beginning to understand Noctem's classes, she recognized each of them as *Leaf* classes like Kegan. They had been sniping at the players from the balcony.

The wounded *Leaf* spun around and tore Kegan's arrow from his back. He placed it on his bow and raised it to fire.

Seven reached for her hatchet, but before she could throw it, Corvin sent a Phantom Blade into his chest while Piper finished him off. Whatever their quarrel was about, it didn't stop Corvin and Piper from working well together.

With the snipers dead, Seven ran to the edge to assess the situation below. Her fingers tightened on the railing as her mouth fell open. The theater floor had been completely demolished. Splintered wood was all that was left of the rows of built-in chairs. The buffet table was no more and some of the curtains were on fire. Sure, the fighting had been bad before, but now it was a war zone.

"I was only gone for a few minutes."

"Yeesh, Max might have gone a little too far down there." Kegan stepped up to the railing beside her.

"It looks like most of the Boars are dead and I don't see Tusker." Corvin joined them. "Might be dead too."

Piper took a place on the railing as far from him as possible. "Not that Tusker would be easy to spot in that mosh pit. I don't even see Max." She paused. "Wait, no, there he is, getting punched in the face by Kashka."

Seven searched the scene, finding Max in the grip of that enormous faunus from House Winter Moon. He was saying something, no doubt struggling to talk his way out of being pummeled. It didn't seem to be working. Even worse, Echo had her whole body wrapped around Kashka's arm and it didn't even slow her fist down. Seven snorted a laugh at the sight, quickly covering her mouth. It made her like Max a bit more, knowing that he was in over his head just as much as she was.

She couldn't find Ginger, but the rest of the Lords all seemed to be alive, sans Tusker. The Boar's Archmage and Knight were still in the fight, though. The mage stood directly below with Alastair. They both circled each other with glowing circles hovering near their wrists like they were waiting for a spell to finish brewing before destroying each other. The Knight was on the stage, locked in combat with Farnsworth, while a few other duels went on around them.

On the upside, most of the Boars had been killed already. Granted, that didn't seem to stop the fighting, as each of the Lords just picked new fights with each other. It was as if there was blood in the water and they had fallen into a frenzy.

"How are we going to stop this?"

Seven turned back to Cassius, realizing that he hadn't said anything for a while. To her surprise, he was standing away from the railing at the other end of one of the aisles. She tilted her head at him for a second, just before he started running. He barreled toward her with no sign of slowing, his massive boots shaking the floor with each step. She dove out of the way just as he touched his forehead and roared the word, "Leap!" With that, he sprang into the air and soared over the edge of the balcony.

Seven leaned over the railing, tracking him with her eyes as he cleared the devastated seating area and thrust his lance down into the Boar's Knight on the stage. Farnsworth jumped back and hid behind her gauntlet as the man she had been fighting crumpled under the sudden attack from above. As soon as Cassius' spear hit the floorboards, a shockwave of fire exploded outward in all directions. Anyone unlucky enough to be caught in the blast was thrown at least two dozen feet. Only Farnsworth was left standing, her boots somehow sticking to the floor as she braced behind the Death Grip's small barrier.

Cassius ignored her, twirling his weapon through the dispersing cloud of his victim's body. Finally, he dropped the butt of the spear down beside him.

Then he waited.

The room went silent as his commanding presence overpowered the chaos. Duels simply paused as heads turned to him expectantly. Amelia froze with her saber resting against Larkin's shears as his army of dolls closed in on Klaxon, her Archmage. Dartmouth threw water on a small fire before stopping to stare at the stage. Even Kashka stopped punching Max in the face for a moment, though she still held him off the ground by his collar.

Seven couldn't believe the stillness that had fallen across the theater just from Cassius' presence.

Now that's a Knight.

Cassius opened his mouth to speak. "I am—"

A falling chandelier drowned out his words as it crashed into the floor, landing on the Boar's Archmage that had been circling Alastair. Ginger dangled from the end of the chain above, clearly the culprit of the murder.

With that, the chaos immediately reasserted itself, with every delayed act of violence resuming as if it had never been interrupted. Cassius shook his head and rubbed at the bridge of his nose before slamming the butt of his spear down again to regain the room's attention.

"Stopppp—arggggoooooblaahhhh…"

His booming voice shifted into a scream that trickled off into an embarrassing gurgle. In the same instant, a cloud of crimson light burst from his body and streaked toward

Farnsworth's gauntlet where it was swallowed up by her glowing claws.

Seven's eyes bulged as Cassius' body fell forward, hitting the stage like falling tree. He was dead… again!

"Farn! What the hell?" Seven leaned over the railing. "He was on our side."

"He was?" Farnsworth looked down at her clawed hand for a second, then shoved it behind her back. "Sorry, that one's on me."

Seven slapped a hand to her forehead. *Good lord, these idiots are the people I was terrified of?*

That was when a strange sound echoed in her ear. Instead of the musical chimes that the system usually used, this one almost sounded digital, like an old eight-bit system trying to say the word 'no.'

That was when things got weird.

Slowly, confusion took hold throughout the theater. Seven couldn't put her finger on it, but there was something different. She raised her hand from the railing and rubbed her fingertips together. They felt… off.

Below, Kashka's fist slowed as Max stopped complaining about the repeated battering. They looked at each other awkwardly for a second before she cracked him in the nose again. The *Fury's* head flew back, but the crimson glow that normally represented damage was replaced with a pale blue shimmer.

He wasn't hurt.

Kashka dropped him a second later. From the looks of things, the rest of the theater was making the same discovery. A few players stood, confused, with arrows and swords sticking uselessly from their bodies. Clearly, they should have been dead. Larkin stabbed himself in the thigh to test the situation.

Nothing happened. He didn't even seem to be in pain.

"I see you're all beginning to realize there is no point in continuing this idiocy." A voice echoed across the room.

Seven searched for its source, finding an overly serious elf at the edge of the stage, walking up the stairs. She tried to remember his name, *J3ff?*

"I am here as a representative of Checkpoint Systems, and as such, I am a Game Master." The elf gestured to a band around his arm. "Now, this took me a little time to set up, but I have activated a localized PVP ban that covers the entirety of this airship. It will prevent all players within its range from causing any damage to another. The ban can't be disengaged until the craft lands in the morning. So I apologize, but until then, I'm afraid you will all have to behave like civilized people. Instead of," he swept his hand across the room, "whatever this is."

Seven blew out a sigh of relief.

She was safe.

Finally, she could go about her job without all of this insanity. The elf on the stage may have been condescending, but right now, Seven could have kissed him. She wouldn't, of course, that would be unprofessional, but still, she was grateful.

Seven turned and ran to the nearest flight of stairs, bounding down them two at a time until she reached the theater. Now that she didn't have to hide behind others, she didn't want to miss anything.

"Oh, come on, J3ff!" Alastair's irritated voice whined as soon as Seven reentered the theater. "I had everything under control. We literally just finished off the last of the Boars. They're all dead!"

"Not all of us." A pair of Tusker's men both raised their hands. Neither looked particularly strong.

"Alright, sure," Alastair brushed the two of them aside. "All but two randoms are dead."

"I'm sorry, sir," J3ff took an apologetic tone but held his ground. "But you left me in charge as a representative of Checkpoint Systems, and I did what I thought was appropriate."

"Fine, fine, whatever." Alastair deflated and grumbled under his breath. "Well that came back to bite me."

"So what you're saying," Ginger stepped into the argument. "Is that you intervened in the game to protect an event run by your investors."

"'Cause that sounds a lot like giving preferential treatment to businesses that are willing to pay for it." Max joined in, his knuckles turning white around the grips of his pistols. "And that sounds like a violation of the rules."

"I assure you, it is not." J3ff barely looked at him as he responded.

"He's right, unfortunately." Alastair's shoulders sank. "It's definitely against the spirit of the game, but it isn't against the actual rules. I don't like it, but it is what it is."

Max didn't say anything more, but a low growl emanated from his throat.

"I, for one, can't thank you enough." Dalliance strolled onto the stage and threw an arm around J3ff. "You may well have salvaged this entire night." He turned, steering Alastair's assistant away from the center of the stage where his twin, Grindstone, took their place.

"Now that order has been restored, I must ask for any items that may have been borrowed from our first round of bidding to be returned." Grindstone gestured to the item table that had been kicked over by Nix during the battle. "Currently, we are missing: a tower gauntlet, a scalefang egg, and a possessed hatchet. I saw Tusker's Knight with the gauntlet, but the others are still unaccounted for."

Seven's chest tightened, realizing that she had to give up the hatchet she'd been using. She started to raise her hand, feeling a bit crestfallen.

"Sorry, the egg rolled off the stage, so I grabbed it and stored it so it wouldn't break. I did win the bidding on it, so I thought that was appropriate."

"That's ridiculous." Grindstone gave her a disapproving sneer, like she was some kind of idiot. "That egg is a unique item. No matter how fragile it might seem, it can't break."

"Well, I didn't know that," Seven spat back, with half a

mind to keep the hatchet and pretend she knew nothing about it. Unfortunately, she was still too afraid that she might get in trouble if she got caught. She reluctantly reached into her robe for the weapon and opened her mouth to speak.

"Ow, hey," was all Seven got out as Ginger seemed to trip over herself to elbow her in the side.

"Sorry, clumsy me." The Lady of House Lockheart shot Seven a knowing look and swiped a hand across her neck, giving her the universal sign for 'shut up before you incriminate yourself.'

To Seven's surprise, she felt herself slip the hatchet behind her back as Ginger gave her a lesson in theft.

"I saw Tusker take the hatchet." She raised her hand with confidence. "My guess is, he's respawned back in Torn by now. He did win the bid on it though, so maybe you can bill him for it or something?"

Seven's mouth fell open as Ginger covered for the theft, her forehead breaking out in a cold sweat. She hadn't meant to steal the item, just borrow it. Now, though, her actions were quickly becoming a crime of opportunity. Seven swallowed, unsure what she should do.

That was when Grindstone blew out an aggravated huff. "Well, there's nothing that can be done about that." He pulled out a ledger. "Anyway, if everyone who purchased items during the first round of bidding could approve a transfer of funds, we can get everything handed out to their rightful owners."

Oh no! It was already too late.

That hatchet was an item worth thousands, and she had stolen it. Guilt racked her chest while a strange sense of satisfaction swam through her as she realized that a small part of her wanted to keep the possessed weapon. She felt the corner of her mouth tug upward in a crooked smile that felt entirely foreign.

The rest of the auction's guests met with Grindstone one by one to approve their account transfers. Farnsworth pocketed the locket she'd purchased like a raven snatching up something shiny. The thought reminded her that Ruby hadn't arrived with Cassius like Leftwitch had said he would.

Where is that dumb bird?

She shrugged. It wasn't like she wanted the thing clawing her shoulder all night anyway. It could stay lost for all she cared.

Once the accounts were settled for the first round of bidding, Grindstone addressed the crowd of players standing in the wreckage of the theater.

"Unfortunately, we need to take some time to get this mess cleaned up before continuing the auction. So I'm afraid that we will have to take a break. Please feel free to venture out onto the deck of the ship. We will reconvene in one hour."

With that said, the auction's surviving guests dispersed, leaving Seven with nothing to do. A large part of her wanted to find somewhere quiet to sit and wait, maybe reclaim the professionalism she'd lost. After getting pulled into Lockheart's affairs and stealing hatchets, she felt she was losing her grip on herself. In truth, she wanted nothing to do with them. Especially after Farnsworth had killed Cassius.

Then she remembered her orders.

Leftwitch had wanted Seven to get close to Lockheart. To get close to a house that she had been terrified of for most of the night. Fortunately, the brawl had showed her a bit of who they really were; a bunch of misfits as inept as she was.

She needed to take control of the situation, and with the ban in place, she could afford to be more assertive with them. It wasn't like her to be a pushover anyway. It was time to take charge. She turned toward Ginger and Max, taking a breath to psych herself up, then started jogging to catch up.

Max immediately spun and stomped toward her, sending her heart into her throat as he drew one of his pistols. Seven froze, dead in her tracks, only to watch him blow right past her. Of course, that was when she realized he was stalking toward Nix, who was standing behind her.

"Oh hi, Max." The strange but non-threatening reynard raised her hand to wave as he approached. He responded by unloading his gun directly into her head, sending blue light bursting from the back of her skull. "Very mature." The azure glow faded, leaving her unharmed under the protective ban.

"Yeah, but it made me feel better," he growled through his teeth.

Seven slapped a hand to her face as Max stomped his way back to her and his housemates.

Why me?

CHAPTER SEVENTEEN

After making their way to somewhere secluded, Max leaned back against the railing down on the lower deck where Kegan and his team had boarded earlier that night. He wasn't leaning to rest, though. No, he was trying to get away from the woman jabbing him in the chest with a finger.

"Can you not fight with people every five seconds?" Seven poked him again.

He looked to Ginger for help, but she only smirked at his discomfort. Farn was even less help, fixated on Echo, who was sitting dangerously on the railing. Corvin and Kegan actively avoided the conflict, the *Blade* playing a game on his emulator and the *Leaf* pretending to take a nap despite that being impossible in Noctem. Max didn't bother looking to Piper for help; there was already enough hostility in the situation, and adding her in would only make things worse.

"And you!" Seven swept an accusatory finger to Farn. "Have you ever heard of asking questions before immediately killing someone? Cassius was here to help."

"Ahh—" Farn stammered, clearly feeling bad about her reaction earlier that had deleted Seven's backup.

"In all fairness." Kegan rolled over on the deck. "You did kill him earlier too, Seven."

"I didn't know it was him at the time." She stomped one foot. "And weren't you pretending to nap over there?"

"Yeah, sorry, just talking in my sleep." Kegan rolled back over, emitting a few fake snores to sell the performance.

"It's okay, these things happen." Ginger attempted to placate Seven's melt down.

"Oh yeah, and thanks for making me an accomplice, by the way." The *Venom* mage pulled out the hatchet she'd liberated from the auction and waved it around. "You do realize that taking this was grand theft, right?"

"I didn't see you rushing to give it back." Ginger hit the nail on the head like she usually did. "Pretty sure you wanted to keep it."

"Oh yeah? Then would I do this?" The woman tossed the hatchet over the side of the ship. Max couldn't help but notice a pained look in her eye as she did, like she'd just thrown a cherished family heirloom overboard.

Ginger simply folded her arms and waited. After a few seconds, Seven beckoned the hatchet back, catching it without looking, like she had become used to the weapon.

"That's what I thought." Ginger smirked.

"Okay, fine, I like the hatchet. But I feel terrible about taking it. Honestly, I just want to get through this night without making any more moral sacrifices." Seven turned back to Max and tapped the back of her hatchet against his chest. "So please, can you just not shoot anyone in the face for five damn minutes?"

"I was testing the ban." Max brushed Seven's weapon aside, wondering why the random low-level was even still hanging around them, let alone getting in his way. "None of this matters if we can't fight Nix when the time comes."

"Listen." Seven walked away from the rail and paced across the deck. "Leftwitch would like our houses to be allies here, and I'll do my best to help you out at the auction. But to do that, I need the auction to actually happen! So can't you just forget about whatever ridiculous feud you have with Nix for one night?"

"You don't know what you're talking about." Max fought down the urge to raise his voice as she belittled everything that had happened.

She rolled her eyes. "What could Nix have possibly stolen from you all to warrant this kind of dedication to hunting her down? This is all just a game, for Christ's sake."

"She stole our friend," Max growled through his teeth, becoming increasingly irritated.

"What does that even mean?"

Ginger stepped forward to stop him from blurting out the truth. "We can't trust her–"

"It's fine, no one would believe her anyway." He let out a mirthless laugh. "How could they? I don't even believe it."

"Believe what?" Seven's eyes flicked between him and Ginger for a silent moment.

"I'm going to offer you a choice." Ginger's voice went cold. "You can leave now and go about your life, or stay and have your world shattered."

Seven raised an eyebrow as the corner of her mouth wavered, like she was holding in a laugh. She probably thought Max and the rest of Lockheart were just a bunch of dedicated role-players, acting out an overdramatic fantasy. She crossed her arms stubbornly and held her ground.

That's that then. Max lowered his head.

"Nix hurt Kira," he whispered, the words nearly choking him.

"So? It's a game." Seven dropped her hands to her hips. "You all hurt each other all the time, from what I can tell."

"No." Ginger shook her head. "He doesn't mean in game. Nix kidnapped Kira's body in the real world and the system recorded a death when it happened. We're not sure if she's alive or dead."

"What?" A quiver entered into Seven's voice as she gestured to Echo. "She's sitting right there."

"Have you wondered yet why she doesn't speak?" Max avoided looking at the avatar. "It's because she can't. That's not really her. It's just an echo of who she was, animated by the system from our memories."

"That's not possible, the system can't just—"

"It can, and it does whenever it lacks information. It uses your own memories to fill-in the blanks. That's all Echo is, just a blank being filled in. The lights are on, but nobody is home."

"How is that…" Seven turned to the fairy for confirmation, getting a confused look in return. Suddenly, she clasped her hands over her mouth. "Oh my god, I ate something earlier that tasted familiar. Is that how—"

"Yes." Ginger tapped her head. "The system probably asked your mind to produce a flavor, because it didn't have a way to produce the sensation. It doesn't go digging through your head for just anything, but technically, it has access to everything you know. Noctem uses those memories when it needs to represent something that the system doesn't understand. In our case, it stopped receiving input from Kira but never received a log out, so from there it started using our minds to keep her avatar active. From what Alastair tells us, this isn't uncommon when a player dies in their sleep, although other echoes usually destabilize in a matter of minutes. Apparently, we knew Kira well enough to keep her avatar running."

"We call her Echo because it helps us remember that she's not real." Max crossed his arms.

"But how?" Seven staggered backward. "How could Nix have hurt her?"

"She set us up." Max slammed his fist into the railing. "Nix was working with Neil Carver back before he was fired by Checkpoint. They have been pulling our strings for years. Practically since Noctem's launch."

Ginger took over, recounting the events that led up to the present. The quest that had nearly brought Noctem crashing down and how it bound Kira to a god-like artificial intelligence. She explained the heist six months ago, where they'd helped two federal agents take down an international arms smuggler. Then how Nix had set Kira up and how her sacrifice stopped the sale of a biological threat that could have killed billions.

"After that," Max finished the story. "Nix sent two men to break into Kira's home and take her body. I lived next door and shattered my wrist chasing their van as it drove away. I'll never get full use of my hand back." He made a fist, opening and closing it to remember the pain the action held in the real world. "That's why we need to catch Nix and make her tell us the truth."

All the color drained from Seven's face as she dropped to the deck. She sat there blinking away tears with no words to describe the shock she must have been feeling. Max almost felt bad; there was no going back for her.

"We're sorry to tell you all of this." He crouched down next to her.

"Sorry!" She shoved him so that he fell back. "You're sorry? You just told me that the world almost ended six months ago. That the only reason it didn't was because your friend gave herself to a digital god and may have died for it. Christ, there is a woman on board this very ship, who abducted someone out there in the real world and probably has the resources to do anything she wants out there. I freaking spoke to her and didn't even know. So, no, sorry is not going to cut it."

"I know." He gave her a sympathetic look. "But you did ask."

"Argh!" She threw her hands into the air in frustration. "I'm only here because I needed a job, and my boss told me to get close to you to get information for her show. But Christ! I can't report back with any of this. Leftwitch will think I'm insane, or a liar, or both."

"That's good to know." Ginger sat down beside her. "So Leftwitch asked you to spy on us, huh?"

"Obviously!" Seven stood back up abruptly. "I have to get

out of here. I can't do this. I don't want..." Without finishing her sentence, she bolted toward the railing.

Max jumped up and reached for her, afraid she might throw herself over the side to escape. The *Venom* mage crashed into the railing before he could catch her, leaning over the side. He lowered his hand as she began to dry heave.

"The system won't let you throw up in Noctem." He approached her cautiously, not wanting to freak her out any more than they already had.

"Of course it won't." Seven coughed a few times then hung her head in defeat.

Max and Ginger leaned on the railing next to her, letting her take all the time she needed to get under control. After a few minutes, she'd calmed down for the most part. Kegan and Corvin joined them as if accepting her into their inner circle. When Seven finally opened her mouth to speak, she said the last thing Max expected.

"You should follow the money." Her voice sounded surprisingly rational.

"I'm sorry, what?" He wasn't sure he'd heard her right.

"You want to find Nix out there in the real world, and she has been pulling strings for years. Then I guarantee she has been involved in some way since Noctem's early development. If Alastair took money from the twins running this auction, then there will be other investors to look at. If Nix has the resources you think she does, then I bet she's in there somewhere. There's always a trail."

"I don't even know where to begin with that." Max felt a little stupid at his lack of knowledge on the subject. Hell, he didn't even know how to do his own taxes.

"You should use your connection with Alastair to get access to Checkpoint's records. Money doesn't lie. Trust me, I'm an unemployed accountant." Seven's head jerked up. "Wait a second, you said you never saw Kira's body, right?

Max felt a familiar thread of hope tug at his heart. "That's the detail that we keep coming back to, but it's hard to hold onto the hope sometimes. The system registered her death, and all the servers she was occupying melted. As much as we don't want to face it, there might not be a Kira left to rescue."

"So what? Errors happen all the time with computers. Those readings could be false. Why else would Nix need to steal her body?"

"Finally!" Farn shouted from behind them. Max turned to find the *Shield* standing there pointing at Seven. "Finally, someone agrees. She can't possibly be dead." The *Shield* wore a manic grin on her face. "The sooner you all accept that as fact, the sooner we can focus on getting her back for real. Not just how to get revenge on Nix."

The hope on her face hit Max like a truck. He wanted to believe, he really did, but it had been six months, and all the facts pointed to the worst.

He sighed. "I know, Farn. I want to, it's just—"

"It's just nothing." Her lip quivered. "I'm sick of all your faces whenever we talk about her. You say things like we'll get her back, but none of you really mean it. I can hear the grief in your voices, and I know you've given up." She threw one hand out to one side as if shoving the thought away. "I know you all think that I can't let her go, and that's why Echo is still here. But I'm telling you now, that's all on you. I know this thing isn't real." A tear slid down Farn's cheek as she glanced at the vacant avatar. "No offense."

The fairy blinked and silently mouthed the words, "None taken," while nodding happily.

"Look, I know having even just a little of her still here is comforting." Farn dried her cheek on her shoulder. "But I would love for whichever one of you that's holding onto her memory to release her, because I don't need her."

Her words caught Max off guard, his chest aching at the thought that it might be him clinging to Kira's ghost. He opened his mouth to speak, but didn't know what to say. Farn didn't wait for him to figure it out.

"For you, Kira is a constant that has always been there for

you. And now that she's gone, you put her in the past and mope about what you've lost. But I didn't have decades to be with her, so to me, she's the future. Kira is the first person that I've ever said I love you to and really meant it." Tears fell as she spoke. "I don't want a replacement and I can't give up on her. I have to believe she can be saved. So you all need to shut the hell up and get on board with that, or I'm done here."

Max looked into the frustrated *Shield's* eyes, then dropped his head to the floor, unable to honestly give her what she'd asked for. She immediately spun and stormed off with Echo following her close behind.

"I'll be on the upper deck. Call me when you need me."

Max motioned to go after her.

"Let her go." Ginger placed a hand on his chest. "She's been practically numb for months. I think we forget how hard this has been on her sometimes."

Max sniffed once, then nodded his head. Farn could believe whatever she wanted. What really mattered now was finding Nix. His jaw tightened at the thought of their real enemy and he absentmindedly ran a hand over the grip of the small knife sheathed at his side. It had her name on it.

"Farn will be fine. She's one of the strongest people I know, and we can count on her to be there when it matters." Max turned back to Seven. "You, on the other hand, I have to ask, now that you know what we're up against. What are you going to do?"

Seven closed her eyes and let out a breath. "I don't know."

CHAPTER EIGHTEEN

Farn sunk her face into her hands, leaning her elbows on the countertop of a small bar on the Night Queen's forward deck. The NPC behind it set down a mug of cider in front of her. Its AI must have retained her order from when she'd purchased a drink earlier. She had needed something to do when Piper had used the shift beads to sneak into the auction.

Farn laughed to herself as she placed her hand on the counter to process a transaction. They wouldn't need to sneak anyone in again, not when most of auction's guards were dead. She immediately felt guilty for the thought.

What the hell have I become?

She clasped her unarmored hand around the wrist of her gauntlet, sending just enough stolen life into her claws to make them glow. Back when she had gotten the Death Grip, she'd told herself that she'd never use it.

Then she lost Kira.

After that, Farn had given into the temptation almost immediately, telling herself that if it was to win back the person she loved, then anything was worth it.

Part of her couldn't help but wonder if she'd fallen too far.

Before, she thought only of protecting others, but now, not even an hour ago, she had killed Cassius solely on reflex.

Would Kira even want what she'd become?

A memory rolled through her mind of how upset the fairy had been back when Ripper had used the Death Grip to slowly drain the life from Luka. Kira had blamed herself for breaking the contract system and allowing an item like the Death Grip to be born.

Farn had never dragged out the Death Grip's drain ability for any of the players she'd killed with it. No, she always made it quick, not wanting to cause any of the discomfort she had felt when the instakill ability had been used on her. Still though, there was no honor in using the contract. It was cheating, plain and simple.

"Could you stop that?" Farn grumbled at Echo, who sat on a stool next to her, gently spinning it around like she was bored. "You're driving me nuts."

Echo caught herself with her foot and lowered her head apologetically.

Farn let out a long groan. "I'm sorry. It's not your fault." She took a sip of her cider. "You're not even real. How could it be?"

Echo shrugged.

"Sometimes I just want a break, you know?" Farn glanced to the avatar out of the corner of her eye. "But you're always here, imitating her. Always doing the fun and ridiculous things that she would. Always beside me, the image of everything I hoped for and fantasized about since I met her."

Farn tipped her mug back, if only to give herself an escape for a few seconds.

"It's killing me. Every time you smile or brush up against me, my heart breaks a little. I want so bad for you to be real. To pick you up and hold you…" She trailed off.

"And now I'm talking to an error."

Farn downed the rest of the cider, then slammed the mug on the bar before wandering off to look for a comfortable bench to pass the time. Finding one in a quiet spot on the side of the airship, she dropped into the seat, put her head back, and closed her eyes. A moment later, she felt something warm against her side.

"That's not fair." Farn opened her eyes to find Echo resting her head on her shoulder.

Eventually, she shook her head and wrapped her arm around the fairy, pulling her close and draping her cape over her shoulders. Then finally, she smiled.

"I'm not sure how accurate our memories of her are, or how well the system represents her, but I hope Kira still wants to be this close when we find her."

Farn reached into her pouch and pulled out the locket she'd purchased at the auction, the one that Dalliance had said was dropped from a boss in Rend.

"I can't wait to give this to her." Farn held it up, letting it dangle in front on the fairy to watch the avatar's reaction.

Echo's eyes widened as she mouthed one word, "Home."

"Our home." Farn thought back of their time in Rend, Kira's favorite dungeon.

She opened the pendant and pried out the photo it came with, some kind of royal portrait of Magnus Alderth, the fictional ruler of Rend from back before the city fell. The man smiled in the image as if thinking about the person he intended to give the locket to. Farn wondered what kind of smile she would make in a photo meant to be worn around Kira's neck.

That was when she noticed someone else in the picture, a small form standing at the edge as if captured in the frame by accident. Farn sat up straight without warning, almost knocking Echo off the bench beside her.

She held the image closer, squinting before pulling out her journal and retrieving her inspector from its back cover.

It can't be, Farn thought as she held the glass window over the image and swiped it to enlarge the picture. Her mouth fell open as she recognized the mousy creature near the man's feet. A jerobin, but not just any jerobin. No, it was one she recognized. It was the NPC from the shop where she had bought the rings that she shared with Kira. Farn glanced at Echo's hand, still wearing her half of the item.

At one point the rings had the power to save the fairy from a killing blow in exchange for Farn's life, though now they were nothing more than jewelry, having been used up. Farn thought back, remembering how unique the NPC in the shop had been, a well-dressed old jerobin. His suit was identical to the one in the photo, though less worn than she remembered.

She flipped to her journal's mission log, finding the ongoing quest that she and Kira had activated when they had pledged their house's loyalty to the fallen city.

Reclaiming Rend.

Farn slid her finger down the page to find the first step that they had been stuck on. All it said was 'Locate a survivor of the fall.' She let herself sink back into the bench in shock.

"I've found one."

She clutched the photo in disbelief. The NPC that sold them their rings, at the Arcane Imports shop back in Valain, was the next step. For a moment, she almost ran off to tell the others, but then she remembered everything else. They didn't have time to chase after quests or NPCs. That would have to wait.

Farn sunk back into the bench, letting Echo curl up under her cape.

"I hope she'll be up for a quest when we find her." She stared off into the night. "Because when I do, I'm bringing her home."

She tilted her head to rest her check on the avatar's silver hair.

"...and I'm never letting go."

CHAPTER NINETEEN

Max took one last look at the star-filled sky from the Night Queen's lower deck, then turned back to the hatch that lead up to the auction.

"You coming?" He glanced back to Seven who had been sulking against the rail for the last few minutes. He didn't blame her, not after having their entire situation dumped on her.

"Yes." She avoided making eye contact.

"I'm sensing a 'but' coming." Max pulled open the hatch and stepped aside to let Ginger and the rest of the party through.

"I can't get involved in all this." Seven stepped through the hatch. "It's not that I don't want to help, but I'm an accountant, not a heroine. Things like saving the world and tracking down Nix are more than I'm capable of."

"You've handled yourself well so far." Kegan waved Corvin and Piper on as he hung back to wait for Seven. The *Leaf* seemed to have built a rapport with her since bringing her in.

"That's true, you've survived the night so far." Max nodded in agreement.

"I feel like not getting myself killed yet is setting the bar a bit low." Seven laughed sarcastically. "Honestly, I can't even take care of my real-world responsibilities. I'm trying to be a good royal assistant here, but that's just because I've been struggling to find a decent job for months. I was laid off a while back and my husband broke his hip shortly after."

"Oh damn." Max stopped short.

"He's fine." She waved away his concern. "But he worked for a roofing company and probably won't be able to move the way he used to, so that's over. Plus, we lost our insurance along with my job, so we've gone through our entire savings to pay the medical bills. At this point, we'll default on the mortgage next month." She lowered her head. "I can't let that happen, so I have to prioritize my position with the Silver Tongues. I won't bid against you at the auction, but that's about all I can do. And I won't tell Leftwitch anything about all this."

"That's reasonable." Max couldn't help but sympathize. Until recently, he had struggled to make ends meet for as long as he could remember.

Ginger turned to walk backward. "I think I can speak for everyone here when I say that we understand where you're coming from. If we could have avoided falling into this mess, we would have. Plus, I know what it's like to struggle to get by." She dropped back and slipped her arm around Max's elbow to walk beside him. "Sometimes you just have to focus on the good and keep pushing forward."

That was when Larkin burst into the hallway, his head on a swivel. His face lit up as soon as he saw Max and Ginger.

"There you are! I've been looking all over." He stopped for a second, his vision sweeping across them, settling on their interlocked arms. "Hmm, I thought so."

"Well, you've found us." Max ignored the comment. "You didn't bring your dolls down here, did you?"

"No, just the one." He tapped the lantern hanging from his belt, covered by a black cloth. "The rest are safe and sound back in their trunks."

"How did you do that by the way?" Max had been

wondering how the *Rage* class had commanded the dolls for the last hour.

"I was wondering that too." Ginger chimed in beside him.

"I'm glad you asked." A twinkle of excitement shined in the crafter's eye. "It's the lantern actually. I had originally constructed it to hold will-o-wisps so I could farm in the forest near Sierra. There's a ton of great materials there, but the wisps always swarm if you stay in one spot for too long. The lantern just makes them think you're one of them if you catch one in it. Works the same with the dolls. I just placed one of my favorite ones in here and their algorithm thinks I'm in charge." He held the lantern up to his face and rubbed his cheek against it lovingly. "I feel terrible whenever they get destroyed, though."

"I hadn't pegged you as the sentimental type." Max took a step back, a little disturbed by Larkin's continued nuzzling.

The *Rage* class immediately dropped the lantern to his side. "Of course I'm sentimental. I worked hard designing each of their outfits. I can't have their clothes getting ruined. They are supposed to be for display only."

"Okaaaay..." Max raised one eyebrow, dragging out the word. "That's an odd set of priorities."

"And speaking of odd," Ginger pushed forward. "What is up with that disturbing mask you were wearing during the brawl?"

"Yeah, is it what I think it is?" Max pointed at the man hesitantly, a little afraid of the answer.

"Another great question." Larkin reached into his pouch and pulled out the creepy item. "And yes, it's exactly what you think it is; a pixie dust inhaler. I'm particularly proud of this experiment." He dangled the mask from its neck strap. "I was making a batch of pixie bombs for you when I started wondering if the effect of Echo's dust would be greater if it was ingested. Low and behold, I was right. With this mask, you can increase the potency and number of uses of a fairy's dust."

"But doesn't it feel..." Max cringed. "I don't know, kind of wrong? It's like you're inhaling her magic. That's about a step and a half from drinking her blood."

"So?" Larkin stared at him blankly, inviting an awkward silence to fall across the hallway.

"Okay, then." Ginger shuddered against Max's side.

"Anyway, we should get a move on." Max began walking down the hall again, prompting Larkin to follow along with Seven. "Why were you looking for us, anyway?"

"Oh, yes." Larkin walked at casual pace. "There's a bomb on board the airship." Both Max and Ginger stopped short, nearly falling over when Seven ran into them.

"What do you mean, a bomb?" Max caught himself on the wall.

"Yeah, maybe lead with that next time." Ginger threw her arm out in frustration.

"Of course." Larkin cleared his throat. "I meant to, but you asked interesting questions, and I enjoy explaining my ideas."

"Did someone say bomb?" Corvin's tall ears flicked back as he turned around further down the hall.

"Yes, an explosive." Larkin casually removed his glasses and wiped them on his shirt sleeve. "And a particularly powerful one at that."

"How do you know there's a bomb?" Seven's voice rose an octave.

Larkin breathed on the lens of his glasses and continued to clean them as he turned to Max. "Do you remember how you blew up the pyramid in Reliqua six months ago?"

"Yeah." Max stepped closer, resisting the urge to throttle the man.

"Well, since you had used a couple thousand small explosives packed close together, you pointed out a potential problem in the game. One that could be exploited by others to disrupt Noctem's cities. There was technically nothing stopping anyone from collecting an equally large number of cheap explosives and setting them off in a crowded entertainment district. So, after you showed people the destructive potential, people started buying bombs up by the hundreds."

"And?" Max beckoned at the *Rage* to draw out more.

"And Checkpoint brought down a nerf on all explosive items. Essentially, stopping them from being able to set each other off by proximity. So now, if you set off one in a bag of a hundred, it won't blow up the whole bag." Larkin made a fist and opened it to pantomime a small explosion.

"How is there a bomb on the ship, then?" Max had trouble following the crafter's point.

"Well, with Checkpoint taking that level of destruction away, people started looking for ways to get around the nerf. So when someone came to me and asked me to craft the most powerful explosive in Noctem, I might have obliged."

"Why would you do that?" Ginger's eyes bulged.

"Yeah," Max spoke through his teeth, "why would you do that, Larkin?"

"It was supposed to be impossible, and that sounded like a challenge." The crafter gave a slight shrug. "What could I do?"

"Okay," Max lowered his head, not bothering to point out the flaws in his logic. "But what makes you think that the bomb is on the ship?"

"Because the player who requested the item was that *Rain* class that Farn just killed up in the theater. The one that jumped from the balcony, Cassius."

Max and Ginger slowly turned to Seven at the same time.

"That can't be." The royal assistant to the House of Silver Tongues shook her head. "Leftwitch sent Cassius here to make sure the fighting stopped and that the auction continued without disruption. Why would she do that if she knew there was a bomb on the ship?"

"Or, she knows the bomb is in place to take out all of Noctem's rulers and she wants to make sure they stay there. The auction might just be a convenient trap." Max tapped a finger on his ammunition pouch. "That's what I would do if I wanted to take over Noctem."

"But, why would she send me here if..." Seven's face went white as she trailed off.

Max assumed that the low-level mage had been sent to draw suspicion off the Silver Tongues, but he kept that part to himself. From the expression on her face, it looked like she had come to the same conclusion.

"Wait a second." Max turned back to Larkin. "What makes you so sure that the bomb is on board? Just because it was ordered by that Cass guy doesn't mean the device was intended to be used here. Maybe Leftwitch just wanted to have a bomb to save for a rainy day."

"Well, I'm not completely irresponsible." Larkin straightened the lapel of his vest. "I built in a notification system to ping its location once it was activated. Of course, I didn't tell them that."

"Activated?" A chill ran down Max's spine at the thought that he might be standing on top of the thing without knowing it. "Does it have a timer of some kind?"

"Yes, I provided a variety of detention options. It seems that the one-hour countdown was chosen."

"Damn." Ginger slapped a hand against her thigh. "That means it will go off right in the middle of the auction."

"Is there a chance that the PVP ban will protect us?" Kegan stepped in.

"I don't think so." Larkin mimed punching something. "I put my hand through a window on my way down here and that did damage."

"Why would you do that?" Ginger eyed the crafter.

"Curiosity, mostly. Things like that count as environmental damage and I'm pretty sure the bomb or at least the fall back to the ground does too."

"It doesn't matter if it will or won't hurt us." Max slammed a fist into the wall. "Hell, it doesn't matter if all of Noctem's ruling houses fall. What matters is that we get a contract item that can trap Nix. So we can't let anyone interfere with the auction either. Beyond that, all of Noctem can burn for all I care." He felt Ginger flinch as he spoke but ignored it. "The bottom line is that if this bomb goes off, our chances of getting Nix will be as dead as we are."

"So what can we do?" Seven asked.

Max arched an eyebrow at her. "*We* will need to search the ship and throw the bomb overboard. You, on the other hand, should probably check in with your boss. Because from the looks of things, you're working for the villain."

"Oh god." The *Venom* mage sunk a little. "I'm a henchman."

"Could be a hired goon?" Kegan offered.

"That's not better." She glowered at him.

Max started down the hall. "Either way, you may want to start thinking about finding a new boss."

After parting ways with Seven and the others, Max followed Ginger into the theater to warn the twins. Larkin trailed behind them until they found Grindstone.

"No, put those over there." The business-like elf directed what remained of the auction staff, while Dalliance attempted to adjust the curtains on the stage so that the burned portions were less visible. The cleanup effort seemed to be running behind as some of the other attendees had arrived and were waiting at the sides of the theater.

Max's chest tightened when he saw Nix. She was standing behind Aawil at the other side of the room. They both looked bored.

Ginger stepped forward to get Grindstone's attention. "Excuse me, there is a matter—"

"Not now." He cut her off, shoving a hand in her face.

Max cringed as the *Coin's* eye twitched.

Note to self, don't talk over Ginger.

"I'm sorry, but this can't wait," she started again, a little louder.

"It will have to." Grindstone glanced at the time on his stat-sleeve. "We have to start the auction back up, and we have yet to salvage this auditorium after the destruction that players like you caused." He gestured to one of the fallen chandeliers then immediately went back to what he was doing.

Apparently the elf's nerves were wearing thin.

From the tension visible in Ginger's back, it seemed that her patience was running out as well. Max decided to help, drawing a pistol. For a moment, he started to raise it above his head to fire it in the air. He lowered it back down just as fast, thinking better of it.

Then he offered it to Ginger.

"Ah, thank you, Max." She took the gun by the handle and thrust it upward. The whole theater jumped in unison as she pulled the trigger.

"What!" Grindstone spun back around, ready to lash into them for disrupting him again.

"There's a–" Ginger started to say just as a bit of plaster fell from the ceiling to land on her head. It burst into a cloud of dust that made her cough as she handed Max his gun back.

"There's a bomb on board." Max shoved his pistol back into his holster. "We have an hour to find it before we all explode."

"About forty-five minutes actually." Larkin peeked out from behind him, getting a blank stare from Grindstone.

Max pushed past the elf as he processed the situation and stomped up onto the stage to address the room.

"Okay, listen up, most of you don't like me, and honestly, I don't like most of you either. But it has been brought to my attention that there is a bomb on the ship that can kill all of us."

The crowd of attendees lining the side of the theater all started talking at once, to which Max responded by drawing his gun again and firing it in the air. He made sure to angle it so that nothing would fall on his head.

"Let's get through this fast. Yes, I am sure. And no, the PVP ban won't save us." He beckoned to Larkin who joined him on the stage. "This is the guy that built it, but he did not plant it."

"Hello, hi there, sorry for the inconvenience." The crafter gave an awkward wave. "The device in question uses eighty pounds of refined black powder infused with dragon's breath for added oomph." He jabbed a fist forward to emphasize the explosive's power. "The trick to it was getting that much powder to remain stable–"

"Not the time for explanations." Ginger hoisted herself onto the stage, letting out a lingering cough as she stood and turned toward the crowd. "Look, we're going to need to work together to find it and disarm this thing."

"Yes, yes," Larkin said awkwardly, "disarm it." That was when Max noticed a troubling expression on Larkin's face, like he had just let out a fart but wasn't going to own up to it.

"Umm, Larkin. It can be disarmed, right?"

The crafter fidgeted with the buttons on his vest for a second before looking back up.

"Ah... sort of?"

CHAPTER TWENTY

While Max and Ginger dealt with the bomb situation, Seven skulked away from Kegan and the others, with the intent of checking in with Leftwitch to get the truth. She raised her house ring to her mouth, but said nothing.

Christ, what am I going to say?

Hey Leftwitch, what's up? Are we the baddies?

"Shit." She shook her head.

That was when she realized she just said that last word out loud and was still holding her house ring close to her mouth.

"Having a rough time there, Seven?" Leftwitch's voice responded.

"Shit, crap." A few more uncontrolled words fell from her mouth before she got a grip on herself. "No, no, everything's fine."

"Uh huh." Leftwitch sounded skeptical. "I imagine you're at least having a better night than Cassius has been."

"Yes, sorry, but I didn't kill him this time."

"Well, that's good." Leftwitch chuckled.

"I haven't found Ruby; didn't you send him here with Cassius?"

"Yes, and don't you worry, he's around."

"Okay." Seven didn't like the sound of that.

"How is the mission going? Get any decent items?"

"The auction is taking a break right now, but I did obtain an egg of a dire scalefang. I was thinking since you're a *Whip* class, that you could–"

"I hope you didn't spend too much on that."

"I'm sorry, was that not something I should have purchased?"

"Meh, a scalefang is more of a frontline pet. I'm not really one to get in the thick of things. I use Ruby for reconnaissance and I don't really want to give him up to bond with a new pet." Leftwitch paused. "Although, I suppose I could use a scalefang as a throwaway pet. A dire monster would certainly make for a good distraction if things got hairy. It could probably take out a few players before it dies. Good choice, actually."

"Thank you." Seven's voice wavered, feeling a little sad that the egg that she'd claimed might be used once and then tossed away.

"What about your other mission? Have you made any progress gaining Lockheart's trust and finding anything out?"

Seven's voice got stuck in her throat, unsure of what she should tell the Lady of her House. She settled on a partial truth. "Yes, I believe they trust me."

"Good, try your best to keep it that way. And find out what their little war with this Nix player entails. The world is dying to find that out after they broadcasted their intentions months back. My views would double if I could get that story."

"I understand." Seven held back anything more. Of course, she could have told her everything and become employee of the month, or gotten herself committed. Instead she took a deep breath and asked the question she was dreading. "Is there a bomb on this ship?"

There was a long pause before Leftwitch said anything, just enough time to lower her house ring and swear a few times.

"Let me guess, Larkin built a notification into it?"

"Yes, it pinged him when it activated and he told Max and Ginger. They're organizing a sweep of the ship now."

"And I assume from the fact that you're asking, that they all know that I commissioned the bomb?"

"They do. Larkin recognized Cassius."

"Well damn, that isn't great. Now I'm going to have to spread a few false rumors to keep that hidden."

"Why would you want to blow up the ship?" Seven put her foot down, getting sick of always being the person in the conversation that had no idea what was going on.

"I can't let the auction happen. Just think about how much damage those contract items might cause if they fell into the wrong hands."

"I realize that, but if that's the case, why send me here, and why send Cassius to make sure the auction happens?"

"Plan B."

"What?"

"You're plan B. The bomb is plan A. If I can't stop the auction, then it's up to you to win bids on anything you can to keep the other houses from getting anything too dangerous."

"But that doesn't make sense. You said earlier that Noctem was thrown into chaos when the House of Serpents fell, and they only ruled over three cities. If you blow up the ship and kill all of Noctem's rulers at once, then the damage would be far worse than if they were allowed to get a few contracts."

"Look, Seven. You're new and I apologize for giving you a job that might be more than you can handle." Her words cut deep, scoring a direct hit to Seven's insecurities. "I have a city to run and sometimes that requires me to have several irons in the fire, and I can't be expected to keep everyone in the loop."

"I understand that." Seven backed down.

"Don't worry about the bomb, okay?" Leftwitch's tone softened. "None of that is your problem. The ship will either explode or it won't. If it doesn't, just make sure you get some of the contracts at the auction and report back everything you can on Lockheart. That's your mission, just focus on that."

"What will happen to me if the ship explodes?"

"You'll respawn, no harm no foul, and you'll have performed well on your first job. Sound good?"

Seven wanted to let herself relax. She wanted to tell herself that it was okay to do nothing, but something about knowingly letting herself be blown up made her sick to stomach.

"Sound good?" Leftwitch repeated when Seven took too long to respond.

"Yes, I can do that." She did her best to keep the disappointment out of her voice.

"Good, then keep doing what you have been, and you'll do fine."

"Okay." Seven let her hand fall to her side and slid down one wall to sulk on the floor. "This job sucks."

She remained like that for about ten seconds, then, at a loss for what to do next, she pulled out her player journal and opened it to her character page.

CHARACTER NAME: Royal Assistant Seven
TITLE: Born in Blood
HOUSE: Silver Tongues

LEVEL: 11
RACE: Human
RACIAL TRAIT: Versatile – All stats develop equally.
CLASS: Venom Mage

Upgrade points earned: 55, 0 have been assigned.

STATS
Hit Points - 50
Mana Points - 20

CONSTITUTION: 0
STRENGTH: 0
DEXTERITY 0

DEFENSE: 0
WISDOM: 0
FOCUS: 0
ARCANE: 0
AGILITY: 0
LUCK: 0

PERKS: NONE

SPELLS: 2
Poison
Pulse

She read her title, Born in Blood, a second time, wondering where it had come from. She flipped to her notifications.

You have gained a title.
For successfully defeating an opponent much more powerful than you without assistance from another player, and without setting a single upgrade point, you have unlocked the title Born in Blood. This title has only been obtained 17 times. Due to its rarity, you will be granted a bonus of plus 100% experience until you set your first stat point. Good luck, you masochist.

That must have been from killing Cassius back on the ship's engine wheel. Now that she thought about it, she was the only one that had landed a hit on him. Granted, she wouldn't have been able to kill him if she hadn't pushed him off the ship. Really, it was the ground that finished him off, not her. But, apparently, the game didn't see it that way and saw fit to help her out. The bonus experience explained the multiple level ups.

Seven tried to remember how many players she had killed so far, catching herself off guard when she realized that she wasn't sure. Reading further, she found that she'd also gained access to new spells from leveling up.

You have 1 new primary spell rune and 7 modification runes that may be learned

Primary Rune:
Fragility. Cost to learn: 3 upgrade points. Casting cost: 10 mana.
Description:
Inflict Fragile status on a target, making it weak against specific types of damage.

Modification Runes:
Pierce, Slash, Blunt, Ice, Fire, Spark, Wind. Cost to learn: 1 upgrade point per rune. Casting cost: +5 mana for each modification rune used per spell.
Description:
Apply an attribute to a primary spell rune.

You have 55 unassigned upgrade points. (Warning! You have not assigned any points to any stats. This will hinder your ability to remain alive.)

She stared at the last line for a good thirty seconds. Then she shook her head.

"No way I'm just waiting here to die."

Seven pulled the small, silver pen from its slot in its binding and reached for the page. She held it there, hovering just above her stats.

But what should I do?

She flipped through the book for a help section, finding a tips page. She read over her class description.

Venom Mage: A caster specializing in quick cast spells, designed to cause damage over time and enfeeble targets.

Her mind began to process the numbers. There was something comforting about it. Numbers had never betrayed her.

She skipped over her constitution; it wouldn't matter how many points she dropped into it, she would still probably be killed too easily with her level as low as it was. Nix or whoever else could end her in an instant, making more health pointless. The same went for defense.

Seven skipped over strength and dexterity as well, finding them useless for a mage. She ignored agility and luck too.

That just left wisdom, arcane, and focus.

She flipped back to the tips page. *Okay, my main stat is arcane to increase damage, and my focus will increase my total mana.*

Seven scratched a 33 into her arcane stat, dropping her unassigned upgrade points to 22. She used 3 to learn the Fragility rune and another 1 to learn the Pierce modifier, hoping it was the right choice. She didn't know anyone that could use elemental attacks, but Kegan was fast and seemed like a good shot, so if she could inflict a weakness to piercing, she might enable him to deal more damage.

She assigned her remaining 18 points into focus, bringing her mana pool up to 200. That would get her plenty to cast all the low-level magic she had.

"There, that should do it."

She flipped back to the tips page or anything she might have missed, landing on a list of racial traits. She started to flip past it but stopped, realizing that she hadn't checked them when making her character. She had just selected human because that was what she was and saw no reason to change it.

That was when she remembered that she needed to learn everything she could. If she was going to be fighting other players, she should at least understand their strengths and weaknesses. After all, Noctem was just numbers, and numbers could tell her anything.

She ran her finger down the list, taking in everything.

HUMAN: Versatile
All stats develop equally.

ELF: Control

At creation, choose one stat to receive a bonus for each upgrade point used, and choose two stats to receive a soft-cap.

FAIRY: Fragile
Receive a significant bonus to arcane, wisdom, and focus, however strength and constitution are soft-capped. Physical capabilities are also limited due to character size.

REYNARD: Nine Tails
All nine attributes gain a bonus equal to half your lowest.

FAUNUS: Imbalance
Plus ten percent to all stats for each one that remains zero.

"Wow." Seven hadn't realized what kind of difference each trait made. There was so much more than just having a tail and pointy ears than she'd thought.

The human and elf traits were pretty straight forward, but the rest had a lot of depth. The fairy seemed designed to be a pure magic user, but came with a price. It was no wonder why Echo could barely lift anything. The reynard was interesting too, as it was balanced incredibly well, but really couldn't stand out at any one category. Even more curious was the faunus, since it could get a huge bonus in exchange for a massive weakness. It seemed that along with horns, they could build highly-specialized characters.

Finally, Seven stood up, wishing she had more time to learn. She looked over her character page one last time then shoved her journal back in her pouch. She couldn't help but notice she stood a bit taller, knowing that she had some more tools in her arsenal.

Debating on what to do, she settled on the idea of helping with the bomb sweep. It wasn't like Leftwitch would find out if she ignored her order to do nothing.

Seven looked both ways down the hallway.

"Now where did Kegan and the others go?"

CHAPTER TWENTY-ONE

Corvin tried his best to be stealthy as he followed Kegan down a hallway through the bowels of the Night Queen. Though with his *Blade* class, he didn't have any actual stealth skills to speak of. Then again, considering it wasn't an enemy that he was hiding from, skills wouldn't have helped anyway.

Piper's eyes bored holes into his back like daggers as she stalked her way down the hall behind him. "We should start searching where we ran into Cass and his men back when we snuck aboard."

"Yeah," Corvin tried to keep his response to a minimum. During the night, he'd found that his best course of action was to keep his mouth shut.

"Maybe the reason they attacked us was because they had just planted the bomb and didn't want us finding it," she continued.

"That's a good point." Corvin tried to be supportive.

"Yes. It is," Piper added, an icy cold filling her voice.

Corvin shut his mouth again, still trying to figure out what he had done that was so bad. Sure, he wasn't that experienced at dealing with girls, but he didn't think he was that off base.

It didn't seem fair.

She had to know that there was no way he could have said yes when she confessed to him earlier that night. He had a criminal record already and dating a girl almost four years younger than him was not going to help the situation. It wouldn't have mattered even without his past mistakes; she was still in high school.

Is she really so immature not to see that? He let out a silent sigh and refocused his efforts not to provoke her further.

"Does anyone remember where that lift that we took earlier was? I can't find it on the map." Corvin held his journal sideways.

"We were hiding in a crate at the time, so no." Piper passed by on his left.

"I tried to keep track how many turns we took based on the motion of the crate but I lost track," Corvin added, apologetically.

"Of course you did." Piper continued her assault on him.

He let out a small growl without meaning to.

"What was that?"

"Nothing…"

"It didn't sound like nothing."

"Okay, you know what…" Corvin raised his voice, finally having enough of her attitude.

"Oh, here we go." Kegan cringed and covered his ears.

Corvin pointed a finger in her direction. "All I wanted was to remain friends and let this weirdness just pass by, but you are doing everything you can to make sure this is as uncomfortable as possible. I have been trying to be nice and you have been a jerk all night."

Piper just stood there saying nothing for a few seconds. Corvin started to feel like he had said too much, afraid that she might burst into tears at any second. Finally, she smirked, looking a lot like her mother.

"You really don't get it, do you?"

"Clearly I don't."

She didn't say anything more. Instead, she just shot him.

"Argh! My penis!" Corvin keeled over as Kegan burst out laughing.

"Okay, that's pretty funny." The elf nudged him with his foot. "Thank god the PVP ban is in effect, am I right?"

Corvin shuddered as the pain in his, well, private area faded to a numb throb. His mind had trouble reconciling what had happened. It shouldn't have hurt, even for a second. Not with the ban in place. He looked down at the fading crimson glow, then to his health.

He was down twenty percent.

"Ah, guys…"

Kegan continued to laugh as Corvin tried to get their attention.

"I just took damage."

"Oh, fuck." Piper's eyes went wide. "Sorry, it was supposed to be funny."

"Well it wasn't!" Corvin raised his eyepatch to wipe a tear from his eye.

"It was kind of a low blow." Kegan covered his own crotch sympathetically.

"Whatever." Piper crossed her arms. "He deserved it anyway."

"More importantly…" Corvin pushed himself up to his knees. "What happened to the ban?"

"Maybe it ended?" Kegan assumed.

"Didn't Jeff-with-a-three say it would last until the ship landed?" Piper holstered her pistol.

Corvin took a second to rest. "Or maybe it just doesn't cover the whole ship."

"Well, that is a question that is going to have to wait for later." Kegan bumped his hand into Corvin's ear as if he was trying to get his attention, but not looking where his hand was going.

"Cut it out." Corvin swatted him away as the *Leaf's* finger inadvertently probed his ear canal. Then he saw what the problem was. "Oh."

Three players stood at the end of the hall, the same ones that they faced before on the ship's engine wheel. They must have snuck back on board after Cassius had been dropped off. Another two closed off their escape behind them, bringing the total to five.

They were outnumbered.

"At least we know we're getting close to where they planted the bomb." Kegan shrugged as the faunus in front of the group brought up his gauntlet's barrier.

"They must have heard the gunshot," Corvin whispered.

Piper winced. "I didn't mean to—"

"It's okay." Corvin moved past it. "It doesn't matter now."

"Do you think they know about the ban not affecting us down here?" She glanced down at him.

"They will soon enough," Kegan answered for him.

"Not if we don't attack them." Corvin eyed the men as they slowly approached, the *Shield* player staying in front. Then Corvin threw his hands up above his head. "We give up!"

"Yup, no point in fighting with that damn ban in place." Kegan followed his lead, dropping to his knees and raising his hands.

Corvin shot Piper a look, telling her to do the same. Her tail twitched, in a way that suggested irritation, but she followed suit to continue the bluff.

"Listen, Piper," Corvin lowered his voice until it was barely audible, taking advantage of the enhanced hearing that the reynard race's tall ears gave them. What he said was for her ears only. "We're outnumbered just like we were before. I doubt we're getting out of this. So when I see an opportunity, I'm going to use my basilisk eye and try to make some space. When I do, I want you to run and keep searching for the bomb. Kegan and I will slow them down."

Piper nodded her head almost imperceptibly. He smiled. Even if she was mad at him, he could still count on her.

"Good luck." He held his hand behind his head and slipped a finger under the strap of leather that held his eye-patch on. Then he waited.

The five players from the House of Silver Tongues approached with caution. Corvin took the moment to make a note of their classes; one *Shield*, a faunus; a *Blade* and a *Coin*, two humans; and last, another *Blade* and a *Leaf*, a couple elves.

We have to kill the Shield *first if we're going to stand a chance.*

"Any chance of you guys letting us go?" Kegan raised his eyebrows hopefully.

"No, we're going to throw you off the ship. PVP ban can't protect you from that." The faunus with the gauntlet glowered at them.

"Okay then, should we just follow you to the deck or…?" Kegan trailed off, giving them an annoying smile.

Corvin rolled his eyes as his friend continued to banter. Then, when they were close enough, he made his move. Ripping off his eye patch, he spun around and shoved into the *Leaf* behind him. At the same time, he locked eyes with the *Blade* blocking Piper's escape. The player froze, trapped in place by Corvin's yellow pupil as she dashed forward. Piper weaved past him, then disappeared around a corner.

Kegan jumped to his feet, firing off several arrows to keep the *Shield* from moving forward. It didn't last long. Clearly still under the impression that the ban was in place, the faunus charged forward with reckless abandon, shoving Kegan over.

"Shit! The girl got away." The *Leaf* that Corvin had pushed shoved him back, knocking him to the floor where he held him down with a boot.

"Don't worry about it." The *Shield* kicked Kegan's bow away. "Even if she finds the bomb, she can't move it alone and it can't be disarmed. Let's just get these two overboard." He reached down and grabbed Kegan by his ankles and started dragging him so one of the others could get his hands.

"That some kind of contract ability?" The enemy *Coin*

placed a hand over his comrade's eyes to break Corvin's hold on him.

"Yeah." Corvin glared up at the player from where he lay on the floor.

The *Coin* picked up his eye patch off the floor and tossed it back to him. "Put that back on, and don't try that again."

Two of the Silver Tongues grabbed his hands and feet, like they had Kegan, and hefted him off the floor. Thankfully, none of them had realized the PVP ban's range was limited, otherwise they would have executed them right there. Corvin decided not to struggle for fear of giving away their advantage. No, it was best to wait for another opportunity. Although, with Kegan's bow left behind on the floor, it wasn't looking good. At least they hadn't bothered to take away his sword.

Corvin closed his eyes and let his mind fall back to Piper.

One of them still had a chance.

CHAPTER TWENTY-TWO

"Stupid goddamn Corvin!" Piper stomped her way up a narrow flight of stairs that climbed back and forth toward the Night Queen's upper decks. She checked her map page, making sure she was heading to the right floor, the one where she'd run into the Silver Tongues earlier that night.

She continued to rant as she slid her journal back into her item pouch.

"That jerk just had to go and sacrifice himself for the good of the mission while I'm still mad at him." She stopped midstep and checked his health on the party readout inked onto her wrist. He was still alive, so technically there was still time to save him, even if the idea of it pissed her off. For a moment, she raised her house ring, debating on calling her mother to come rescue him.

Nah. Corvin was right, as much as it pained her to admit it. She lowered her ring and continued up the stairs. The priority had to be finding the bomb and calling the rest of her house down there would only slow them down.

Besides, calling her mom for help was something a kid would do, and she was not a damn child. That was what she'd been telling herself for months, every time she caught herself fantasizing about Corvin. Whether she thought of his avatar or the boy behind it, she always told herself that he wasn't that much older and it wasn't that weird. Honestly, her mom was going after a guy almost a decade younger than she was, and no one seemed to bat an eye.

It wasn't like it was her fault for liking the jerk either. Corvin simply had no right being that cute. Out there in the real world, he was tall, handsome, and had amazing hair that she just wanted to run her hands through. Even worse, he didn't even seem to realize he was hot. He just acted like a sweet nerd that went to college a couple towns over and never stared at her hearing aids.

The help he gave her with her school work had pushed her to the top of her class. If things kept going the way they were, she would be able to take her pick of colleges. She could even go to UMASS along with him. He would be a senior when she started, after all. How could he say no to her then?

She stopped mid-step again and slapped a hand to her forehead.

Don't think like that, Piper. He's an ass. No way you're following him to the same college. You'd basically be stalking him and that's not a good look on anyone.

Finally, she buried the thought and continued on. This time, going over her current mission in her head. A mission to find a bomb set to blow up a virtual ship, so that her mom's boyfriend could capture a woman that had kidnapped his best friend.

"How did my life get screwed up so fast?"

She turned up the next flight of stairs only to stop yet again in mid-step as soon as the landing came into view. At least this time she hadn't stopped because of her thoughts.

No, this time, she had stopped because she had just come face to face with Aawil, Nix's silent but deadly accomplice. The faunus *Coin* was in the middle of eating an apple and standing on the landing that lead to the floor that Piper was heading to.

"Oh shit!"

Piper drew her pistol and fired on reflex, the sound of gunfire reverberating up the stairwell. Aawil threw her half-eaten apple and darted to the side. Chunks of bullet-riddled fruit splattered Piper's cheek as splinters exploded from the wall where Aawil had been a second before.

The faunus hopped onto the banister and leaped up the center of the stairwell to escape the line of fire. Piper's mouth went slack as Aawil shot up several flights in an inhuman display of physical prowess.

Damn...

Piper had heard that the *Coin* was strong, but that kind of vertical leap just wasn't possible, even in game. The only way to jump that high without the help of an ability would be if Aawil's body were that strong in the real world. Her natural prowess would be used as baseline for her character, just like everyone else's. Either way, it was still impossible.

What the hell is she?

Piper didn't bother to ask, instead she fired up the stairwell to keep the faunus pinned down. The last thing she wanted was to let Aawil get anywhere near her. Bullets slammed into the railing above with a crack as wooden shrapnel filled the center of the stairwell.

"Damn it! I am not in the mood, Aawil. Now poke your stupid head out so I can shoot you in the face!"

Aawil decline to accept her polite invitation. Then Piper's pistol locked back, empty. She reached for a new magazine but before she could reload, a pop came from above.

"Shit!"

A grappling line streaked by her face, a metal anchor spike hitting her in the hand. It threw her arm back and pinned her to the floor. Piper fell against the wall. She reached for her gun with her free hand, but she wasn't fast enough to stop what came next.

Aawil drew her dagger and leaped from a perch on the banister above. The *Coin* slipped her thumb through a metal ring at the butt of the knife and twirled the weapon as she soared down to claim Piper's life. The impact took her breath away as the dull blade pushed into her chest.

Damn it!

Even after Corvin had bought her some time, she wasn't able to do anything but die. Piper cursed herself, even though she wasn't surprised. Based on everything she had been told, Aawil was a monster. The only one who had actually beaten the feral *Coin* was Piper's mother. It had been during the heist six months back, and that had only been because they'd lined the halls of Reliqua's palace with explosives.

A low growl rumbled through the *Coin's* throat as she straddled Piper and twisted the dagger in her chest.

It felt… strange, not like any attack she had felt before. Absent was the muted sensation of pain that the system produced for the sake of realism. Instead, there was just an uncomfortable pressure.

Aawil snarled in Piper's face, giving her a long look into her eyes. There was something animalistic and predatory about them. Then, suddenly, her pupils dilated and a more human side took over again. It was like someone had thrown a switch.

The faunus pulled back and looked Piper all over, clearly confused as to why she wasn't dead. Actually, for that matter, why wasn't she? With a critical hit to her chest like that, she should've been sent straight to spawn, but there she was, still breathing with a dagger shoved through her heart.

Piper followed Aawil's eyes down to the wound on her breast, finding the outlines glowing blue. That could only mean one thing…

That little jerk was right.

Apparently, Corvin's guess about the PVP ban having an area of effect was correct. She must have passed back into its range while climbing the stairs.

"I guess there's no point in fighting, huh?" Piper tried her best not to let on that the ban was limited. For all she knew, the difference between life and death might only be a single flight of stairs.

Clearly coming to the same conclusion, Aawil pulled her dagger from her chest.

Piper let out an involuntary gasp. The sensation felt weird, but not painful. It was like something inside her had been out of position and removing the dagger caused it to snap back into place.

Aawil sheathed her knife and stood up, holding her hands out to her sides, empty, as if agreeing that the fight was over. Piper cleared her throat and gestured to the grappling line that still pinned her hand to the floor. The faunus flexed her fingers, triggering the wire to retract.

Piper felt something click within the metal spike in her hand, as if something released its hold. A second later it whipped out of her palm and snapped back to the launcher on Aawil's wrist. Piper wasted no time, scrambling back away from the monstrous woman and standing up. She clasped one hand around the other as the blue glow faded from her skin. It didn't hurt, but she was glad not to have part of her body nailed to the stairs.

"So, we can just go our separate ways." Piper stood with her back against the wall, trying to put as much space between them as possible.

Aawil simply gave her an expressionless nod.

"Okay then." Piper crouched down to pick up her gun without taking her eyes off the *Coin*. Then she took a step up the stairs.

To her dismay, so did Aawil, their shoulder's bumping together as they turned in the same direction in the narrow stairway.

"Ah," Piper looked at the door that lead to the level she intended to search, remembering that Aawil had been standing in front of it when they had stumbled upon each other.

"You're searching for a bomb, aren't you?"

The faunus nodded.

"And you intend to check this floor next."

She nodded again.

"Okay then, I guess we're not going our separate ways." Piper started walking again.

Aawil fell back to let her take the lead but remained behind her up to the door.

"Great, just great." Piper grumbled to herself, not ready for the responsibility of interacting so closely with her mother's enemies.

Nevertheless, the two of them walked in silence. Piper regretted taking the lead as soon as they passed through the door, feeling like she might be attacked from behind at any second. The image of Aawil slitting her throat kept running through her head. She tried her best to forget about it as they checked every room they came across. Fortunately, it didn't take long to find some familiar ground.

"We're close." Piper slowed as they entered a room full of empty crates. "This is where we were smuggled on board. We ran into the Silver Tongues' team right after and they attacked us almost immediately. That ass, ah, I mean Corvin," she corrected, "thinks we walked in on them before they could plant the bomb. That must have been why they came back."

Aawil nodded but raised an eyebrow at the 'ass' comment.

Piper pretended she hadn't said it and pressed on, pushing past the empty crate that she had ridden in earlier.

Beyond the storage room was a wide corridor that led to what could only be described as a kitchen. Various cooking equipment lined the room's wooden shelves and a butcher-block island stood in its center. A small crate, half full of food items, sat on top, while a large old-fashioned stove took up one wall.

Piper hadn't invested anything to raise her cooking skill, so she didn't really recognize much in the way of equipment. She'd helped Corvin farm ingredients for his confectionary skill, which was a subset of cooking, but that was as close to a kitchen as she'd ever gotten. For that matter, she knew even less about cooking in the real world.

The kitchen was spotless, which made sense since it seemed

like most of the ship's food items were delivered ready to serve. It probably would have taken too much to craft everything served aboard the ship in individual batches. Apparently, this space was only used for plating, and from the looks of things, it was specifically for special events like the auction. There must have been a much larger kitchen area that serviced the rest of the ship. That realization brought up a new concern in Piper's mind.

"Why aren't there any people here?" She rested her hand on the butcher-block counter. "On a ship this size, there would normally be at least a few people working to earn some extra money."

Aawil responded by pointing down with one finger.

Piper inched her way around the island, finding a serving tray on the floor. Cheese and crackers littered the area around it. She leaned her head to one side, not sure what the *Coin* was getting at.

Suddenly, Aawil drew her dagger and plunged it through a square of cheese, causing Piper to jump halfway across the room. The faunus pulled the morsel off with her mouth, then tapped one of her horns with the flat of her blade. Then she spoke.

"The serving staff is dead." Aawil chewed and swallowed. "The Silver Tongues killed them just before planting the bomb. That's what I would have done."

"Umm, okay." Piper eyed the suddenly not so silent *Coin*, noting the presence of an accent. It sounded British. Piper stored that thought away for later, returning back to the suggestion that the staff had been murdered.

"That's... probably right. Sending the staff back to spawn would ensure nothing gets discovered here. Especially with all the confusion that killing them would cause for the twins running the auction topside. I doubt they would think to come down here and go looking for trouble."

Aawil nodded.

"And you do talk after all, apparently?" Piper added.

Aawil raised her hand, holding her thumb and pointer close together as if to say, 'a little.'

Piper didn't press the subject, opting to find the bomb as soon as possible. Though, after taking in the room, there wasn't anything that resembled an explosive, not that she really knew what one would look like.

"This thing can't be that hard to find." Piper leaned on the counter. "Larkin said it was eighty pounds of black powder. That doesn't sound small."

Aawil stalked her way around the room for a moment, stopping near a rack of serving platters. It looked a little crooked against the wall. Piper stepped closer to see if she could help shove it to the side. Before she could approach, the *Coin* simply reached out and pulled the rack forward like it weighed nothing, sending the entire thing crashing to the ground.

Piper cringed as she waited for a plate to stop spinning on the floor. Then she took a look at what was behind the shelf.

"I can't argue with results." She sighed, standing in front of a pantry door.

With little effort, Aawil dragged the fallen shelf away from the door then gestured for Piper to go first.

"Thanks." Piper reached for the handle and pulled it open. She immediately wished she hadn't.

A chest sat between the shelves of basic ingredients with a wooden cylinder protruding from the lid. Through a window on its front, numbers flicked up and down on little tabs like the display of a vintage cash register.

They counted down.

Piper took one step inside before she realized that the bomb wasn't the only thing in the pantry that meant to do her harm. She swallowed and reached for her pistol as a pair of beady eyes locked with hers from behind the chest.

Then, there was only screaming.

CHAPTER TWENTY-THREE

Corvin swung back and forth gently, like he was lying in a hammock. Although, considering he was being carried by two players that intended to throw him and Kegan off the ship to their deaths, he was far from feeling relaxed.

"Hey Corvin?" Kegan sounded entirely too casual while dangling from the two players leading the way.

"Yeah?"

"What did you say to Piper earlier when she asked you out?"

Corvin rolled his eyes. "Is now really the best time to talk about this?"

"Nothing better to do." Kegan attempted a shrug but couldn't quite make the gesture work while being carried. "So spill it. What did you say to piss her off so bad?"

"I already told you." Corvin's forehead started to sweat, realizing that five enemy players were listening in on his girl troubles.

"Yeah, you said you turned her down. But what exactly did you say?"

"Why didn't you say yes?" The *Blade* class walking beside them jabbed Corvin in the side with the tip of his sword's sheath. "Her avatar's pretty cute. She ugly out there in the real or something?"

"Oww." Corvin wiggled to move away from the man's weapon. "No, god, I'm not that shallow. She's underage."

One of the players carrying him laughed. "How underage we talking here?"

"Wow, so that guy's a creep." Kegan cringed.

"Shut up." The creep swatted at him with his sword. Kegan bent his body to the side to avoid him in that way that cats did when they didn't want to be petted.

"But seriously, Corv. What did you actually say to her?"

"Okay, fine." Corvin tried to avoid the eyes of the enemy players that were now staring at him expectantly. "All I said was that I was flattered and she was a great girl. I'm sure one day, when she grows up, she'll make someone very happy, but right now she's still just a kid, and I can't see her that way."

"Oh, now it makes sense." Kegan sucked air in through his teeth. "That's… pretty much the last thing you should have said."

Even some of the players carrying them agreed.

"What should I have said, then?" Corvin's scalp started to itch as he felt even more self-conscious.

"Ha, well not that." Kegan made everything worse by not taking things seriously.

"She is still a kid. What should I have done, lied to her?"

"No, and you're not wrong, she is too young for an adult relationship." Kegan paused. "But here's the problem. You're only twenty. I'm in my forties, so that's like nothin'. I love ya, man, but you're not much more adult than she is, in the grand scheme of things."

"I'm not a kid." Corvin spat back.

"Hurts, huh?" Kegan closed his eyes and let himself swing back and forth. "Nothing worse than having your friends not take you seriously. Now imagine it coming from the first person you've had feelings for."

Corvin's mouth fell open. He was right. A bead of sweat rolled down his face from embarrassment.

"Damn it. I screwed up."

"Oh my god." The *Blade* class that had poked Corvin with his sword moved to the front of the group. "Are we almost to the engine room? I don't know how much more of this crap I can take."

"No kidding," the other *Blade* in the group responded. "We can't throw these two to their deaths fast enough."

"I just can't believe they're from House Lockheart." The faunus holding Kegan's arms spoke up. "Aren't these guys supposed to be badasses?"

"That's the rumor," replied the *Leaf* holding Corvin's feet.

"Don't worry, the engine room is just up this lift," the enemy *Coin* added as they entered a room the next room. "We won't have to listen to them much longer."

The lift must have been the one that they had been smuggled to the upper decks on earlier. Seeing the space now, without being stuffed in a crate, it was just a dimly lit room with access to the lift. There weren't even any doors on to keep someone from falling down the shaft.

That was when Kegan opened his mouth again.

"So back to the topic of your inexperience, Corv. How many women have you slept with?"

"Wha…?" The question hit Corvin like a freight train. "I, ah," he stammered, knowing full well the answer was a great big zero. His whole body proceeded to heat up worse than before. Even his palms began to sweat.

Suddenly, the player holding his wrists adjusted his grip, having trouble holding on as Corvin's body became increasingly moist. Corvin's eye widened as he realized what Kegan was doing. He was a genius. A complete jerk, but a genius nonetheless. Kegan wasn't trying to make him uncomfortable, he just wanted to make him sweat.

"I'm sorry for this," Kegan apologized for what was about to come next. "But I assume from your stammering that you're still a virg—"

A fist cut off his words as the faunus carrying him grabbed both his wrists in one hand, then cracked Kegan in the face with his gauntlet. "Will you please shut up!"

With that, they all froze as a crimson glow faded from Kegan's jaw. Each of member the Silver Tongues team stared at him as a wave of realization swept across their faces.

"Yeah, the ban isn't working down here." Kegan smiled before adding. "Now!"

Corvin wasted no time, kicking one foot forward and twisting his body. His wrists immediately slipped free. He spun in the air, getting his feet under him so that he could land on all fours. The maneuver would have been impressive if it hadn't left him exposed. A kick to the ribs sent him back to the floor.

At least he'd caused a good diversion for his partner.

Kegan used the chaos to his advantage, yanking his feet toward his chest to pull the player holding his legs off balance. He immediately kicked the man in the stomach. The move freed Kegan's feet and launched him back into the faunus that held his wrists. The burly player stumbled back, losing his grip and bumping into the unsuspecting *Blade* class behind him. The player screamed as the impact sent him falling into the open lift shaft.

Yeah, that's definitely a safety hazard. Corvin pushed himself up and scrambled to draw his weapon. Before he could get it free, the remaining *Blade* class attacked, the elf plunging his sword through his shoulder. It cleaved away thirty percent of his health and pinned him to the floor face down. Corvin did the math based on the damage, figuring the *Blade's* level at around ninety.

Damn! Corvin glanced back to check on his friend.

Kegan wasn't faring any better. There were too many of them. He tried to pull an arrow from his quiver to at least do some stabbing, but all he managed to do was scatter them across the floor. The faunus grabbed him by the shirt with his gauntlet to hoist him up, then slammed him back to the floor. The burly *Shield* dropped down, placing his knee on Kegan's chest to keep him from getting up again.

Kegan struggled to get away, his head hanging inside the lift shaft. He snatched a loose arrow from the floor and stabbed it into the *Shield's* thigh. The heavy faunus didn't even flinch. He only glanced at his health and continued to hold him down.

"Nice try, but that only took ten percent." The faunus flicked his eyes to the *Coin* standing nearby, then over to the button beside the lift shaft. "Call the elevator. Gonna shut this one up for good."

The *Coin* slapped a hand on the call button, then stood by to wait. From the look on Kegan's face, Corvin assumed the lift wasn't far away. There was no time to worry about his friend, though; he had his own problems. He was still pinned to the floor and the enemy *Leaf* was reaching for an arrow.

"Can't send your pal to respawn alone, now can we?" The *Leaf* drew back his bow and took aim at Corvin's head. "Good luck with the girl troubles, though."

Corvin started to push himself off the floor, shoving his shoulder further up the sword that held him down. Another kick to the ribs put him back down. Again, there were too many of them.

Suddenly, out of nowhere, a pulse spell slapped the *Leaf* in the face, disrupting his aim and causing him to release the arrow. It slammed into the floor beside Corvin's head. As to where the spell had come from, he had no idea.

It didn't matter, Kegan was already out of luck.

From the corner of his eye, Corvin watched in horror as the lift came into view at the top of the open shaft. It was a slab of solid stone covered in levitation runes. It slowed as it reached their level, lowering itself toward Kegan's head.

Another spell materialized out of nowhere, a plume of gray smoke swirling around the *Shield* holding Kegan down. As soon as it reached the faunus' head, a blue glyph appeared, hanging over him for a second before fading away. From his time as a *Venom* mage, Corvin recognized the spell and shouted as loud as he could.

"He's fragile against piercing damage!"

Kegan responded in an instant, ripping the arrow from the *Shield's* thigh and stabbing it back in repeatedly. With the fragile debuff adding twice the damage, the faunus couldn't afford to stay there. He let go, giving Kegan just enough time to roll away from the slab of stone that was about to take his head off.

Corvin used the commotion to his advantage, kicking at the *Blade* that had him pinned. Another ten percent of his health slipped away as the sword pulled free of his shoulder. He rolled over and scurried back across the floor like a crab. Drawing his sword, Corvin finally caught his breath and stood up.

Kegan did the same, grabbing a handful of arrows off the ground and facing off against the faunus. Judging by the faded coloring of the class emblem on his hand, the *Shield* was close to death after the repeated stabbing.

That was when a spellcraft menu illuminated a hooded form standing at the edge of the dimly lit space. Corvin blinked once at the figure's low-level gear. It was obviously Seven.

She swiped her hand through the glyphs in the air and cast another fragility spell on the *Blade* Corvin was facing.

Without a lot of options, Kegan grabbed the *Coin* by one of the straps on his leather chest piece and yanked the player off balance. Using a bit of leverage, he swung him into the lift while holding onto the player so that the momentum sent him slamming into the floor buttons on the inside of the shaft. The player bounced off the wall, and fell to the stone plate. The surprise on his face was evident as the slab began to rise.

"That'll keep him busy for a minute." Kegan brushed his hands together.

The faunus, still near death, retrieved a health vial from his pouch. A well-timed pulse spell from Seven swatted it from his grip. It splattered on the wood-paneled wall behind him. He brought up his gauntlet and ducked behind it. A protective construct of energy blossomed in front of him.

Kegan let out an annoyed growl. There wasn't much he could do to get around the barrier, or even fight back against the others without his bow.

The rest was up to Corvin.

"Little help!" His back hit the wall as the elven *Blade* shoved forward. At the same time, the *Leaf* got his bow back up. The player took aim at Corvin, then, he smirked and turned to aim at Seven.

"Duck!" His eye bulged as the *Leaf* fired. With Seven's level deficiency, a single attack was all it would take to put her down. She weaved to the left but it was too late, the arrow hit her side with a sound like tearing cloth and her body fell to the floor.

"Shit!" Corvin cursed as he waited for her body to dissipate. His heart rose a second later when it didn't. The arrow must have only hit her robe.

Like an ambush predator, she flipped back over and tossed something into the air. A hatchet spiraled past the enemy *Leaf*, shaving off a lock of his hair as it flew through the space.

"Ha, you missed!" He drew another arrow from his quiver.

Seven said nothing, probably trying to keep her voice hidden from her housemates. Corvin spoke for her.

"She wasn't aiming at you."

The *Leaf* cocked his head to the side, then turned to find the faunus behind him drop to his knees, a hatchet protruding from the side of his head. He must have been close enough to death for the blow to finish him off. Suddenly, the small hand ax uprooted itself from his body and flew back across the room to land in Seven's outstretched hand.

Corvin couldn't help but be impressed. For that matter, even the enemies in the room took a moment to stare. It was short lived.

Kegan let out a ridiculous yell as he charged the other *Leaf*, a pair of arrows in his hands as weapons. He tackled the player to the floor, knocking his bow out of hands to level the playing field.

Corvin pushed his opponent away, getting enough room to move without the wall against his back. Hoping to draw the enemy *Blade* away from Seven, he jumped backward over Kegan toward the lift. The player gave chase, hopping over Kegan to keep Corvin in front of him.

That was when the elevator returned behind him, passenger included.

A loud pop, followed by a quick poke of simulated pain reminded Corvin of where the Silver Tongues' *Coin* was. He didn't have to turn around to know that he had just been shot with a grappling hook. His shoulder yanked backward with a dull throb as the *Coin* reeled him in toward the elevator.

The elf he was currently fighting didn't let up either, as he took a swipe at his chest. It was all Corvin could do to leap away and let the *Coin's* line reel him in. Allowing the momentum to take him, he flipped his sword back and tried to drive it through the enemy behind him waiting in the lift. No luck. He stabbed the wood paneling on the elevator shaft's wall with a thunk as the *Coin* weaved out of the way. Corvin yanked back, struggling for an instant before his sword came free of the wood.

He brought the weapon up just in time to deflect the *Blade* class barreling toward him. The *Coin* didn't let up either, forcing Corvin to pull his scabbard off his belt to block a dagger coming from the other side. He ducked as both enemies swung for his head, then he leaped to escape the lift.

Again, no such luck.

The *Coin* yanked back on the grappling line that was still hooked in his shoulder. Falling, Corvin pivoted on his heel, just enough to flip himself around and slash at the player's legs. The *Coin* let out a yelp and fell forward, landing part way out of the lift. Corvin wasn't going to let the opportunity pass by. He rolled over to hold the man down and threw his scabbard at the buttons on the inside of the lift shaft.

Panic surged through his captive's eyes as the slab of stone began to rise again. The *Coin* let out a sudden scream that was cut short by a horrible crunch as they passed the next floor. A burst of shimmering particles flooded the lift to keep the player's brutal death from being too graphic. Corvin gave a silent thanks to the developers for that detail. He was sure he didn't want to see what sort of mess that would have been. Fortunately, there was no time to stop and think about it. There was still one more enemy in the lift.

The elf drew back his sword and Corvin flipped himself back to his feet to dodge. It was the best he could do in the cramped space. He tried to ignore the feeling of vertigo caused by the lift's open walls, the wood paneling moving down as the stone plate rose within it.

Finally, he struck back, his sword meeting his opponent's in a clash of steel that echoed up the shaft above them. With so little room to work, the fight devolved into a brawl, Corvin using anything he could to land a hit. He cracked the elf in the head with the butt of his sword, receiving a kick to the gut in return. On instinct, he reached for the wall for support, its moving surface throwing him right back down to the stone slab under his feet.

He swiped at his enemy's feet, scraping the opposite wall with the tip of his sword. It stuck into the wood for an instant, before getting caught between the wall and the slab of stone. The combination of the two surfaces moving opposite each other, ripped the weapon's handle for Corvin's hand and flung it into the air. It bounced off the other wall and ricocheted around the shaft.

The elf across from him let out a squeal as the airborne katana flew at his head. He raised his sword to block, but the angle was bad and he took a slash to his wrist that forced him to drop his weapon. It clattered to the floor along with Corvin's.

Using the distraction to his advantage, Corvin rolled and snatched his sword off the stone. He thrust upward and drove a critical attack home, the hilt of his katana coming to rest against his opponent's chest.

The fight was over.

Then… it wasn't.

Corvin held still, waiting for the player's body to go limp and dissipate. The elf seemed to be doing the same, both of them standing there awkwardly as floors passed one after another. Finally coming to the realization that something was off, Corvin glanced down at where his sword was buried in the player's chest. He let out a shocked gasp as the wound glowed a pale blue rather than crimson to indicate damage.

Corvin flicked his eyes up the lift shaft. They must have passed back into the PVP ban's area of effect.

Oh no.

He looked back to his enemy at a loss for words just as the lift slowed to a stop at whatever level Corvin had randomly selected. A hallway ten floors up from where they started came into view, along with a confused-looking Dartmouth standing there as if waiting for the lift. The three of them stared at each other in silence for a moment.

"Umm," The Lord of Serpents' eyes shifted from Corvin to the player he was currently impaling, then back again. "I'll wait for the next one."

Corvin firmed up his grip on his sword and caught ahold of his opponent's shirt with his free hand to make sure he couldn't get away. Then he gave Dartmouth a conspiratorial eyebrow pump.

"Think you could maybe send the lift back down?"

"What floor?" Dartmouth leaned into the elevator shaft to look at the buttons on the inside of the wall.

"Just ten levels down." Corvin requested, hoping he had counted right.

Dartmouth tapped a button and leaned back out as the stone slab began moving again.

The impaled elf that Corvin held captive started struggling, clearly realizing what would happen if the lift brought them out of the PVP ban's area of effect.

"Oh no you don't." Corvin tightened his grip on the man's shirt as he fought to get free.

The elf punched him in the throat, loosening his grip. He couldn't hold on forever, but he hoped he could last long enough to get out of the ban's radius. The only question was, how many levels down would they have to go?

Suddenly, his captive stopped struggling to escape and grabbed a firm hold on Corvin's vest. A headbutt came next, flooding his vision with stars. Corvin tried to hold on, but a well-placed foot against his chest forced them apart as the elf kicked with everything he had.

Corvin flew back expecting to hit the wall off the shaft. Instead, he fell straight out of the lift, landing on the floor of a hallway outside. Hitting the carpet with a thud, he coughed and pushed himself back up.

Oh no, he thought, remembering that he'd sent the lift back down to where Kegan was. Last he'd seen, his friend had been wrestling with another *Leaf* below, each of them trying to stab one another with a handful of loose arrows.

Corvin threw himself to the side of the lift shaft, staring down at the elf riding the stone plate down. The player smirked back up at him. It was obvious there was no way to make it down in time. Seven had to be out of mana, and Kegan wouldn't last long unarmed. They needed help.

Corvin paused to think. Maybe there was a way down...

The lift came to a stop five floors below.

Five floors.

He checked his health.

Nope. Jumping would kill him. Then he asked himself an important question. WWMDD? What would Max Damage do? This led him to a new thought.

If I can stop myself halfway... then maybe.

Corvin glanced at his sword, then walked a dozen feet away

from the opening of the shaft. He tightened his grip on the weapon's handle, then he took a running leap.

I regret my choices!

He fell two levels before slamming into the wall of the lift shaft, his sword burying its tip into the wood paneling. The impact broke his fall for an instant, but he lost his grip and fell the rest of the way down.

I hope I did my math right.

Simulated pain shot up Corvin's legs as he hit the stone slab, his sword still stuck in the wall of the shaft three levels up. The system did its work, dulling the pain down to an annoying tingle. He sprang up without bothering to check his health. He wasn't dead, that was good enough.

The enemy *Blade* had just stepped out of the lift with his sword raised to strike down Kegan, who was panting on the floor. His partner must have finished off the player he'd been wrestling with, and from the look of him, it hadn't been easy.

Before the *Blade* was able to put an end to his friend, Corvin grabbed the player by the collar and yanked him back. Unarmed, Corvin used every ounce of strength in his virtual body with the hope of throwing the elf into the lift again. The act knocked him off balance and he fell back down to the stone slab. He flailed his arms on the way down, accidentally slapping the floor buttons on the inside of the shaft.

The lift began to rise again, Corvin's head dangling just off the edge of the stone platform. He rolled, ducking at the last second.

The elf recovered and pushed himself off the moving wall to raise his sword high above his head. Corvin lay defenseless on the lift plate. In desperation, he ripped off his eye patch and locked eyes with his opponent.

The elf froze, mid swing.

"You're going to have to blink eventually." The player fought against Corvin's hold, only succeeding at grinning down at him from where he stood at the back of the lift. "How long do you think can hold me?"

"That's not the question you should be asking." Corvin relaxed, not bothering to get up.

"No, then what is?" the grinning elf spat, clearly thinking he'd won.

"Where's my sword?" Corvin grinned right back at him just as the lift reached the floor where his weapon waited, still stuck in the wall of the lift.

The elevator rose toward the katana at full speed, the sword's edge gleaming above the last remaining member of the Silver Tongues' team. Steel cut down to the lift, snapping in half when the plate hit it. The broken sword clattered to stone beside Corvin as a confused look fell across the elf's face. A crimson glow illuminated his forehead, tracing a line down the center of his body.

Corvin turned away as the player simply peeled apart, dispersing into a cloud of shimmering particles. He placed his eyepatch back on his head, he glanced at his health. Only 74 HP out of 2720 remained. He let out an awkward laugh.

"That's cutting it close. Maybe jumping down a lift shaft wasn't the best plan."

He grabbed his broken weapon from the stone and shoved himself up, waiting for the elevator to reach the floor it was heading to. Corvin hit the button to bring him back to his friends and examined his katana's severed edge on the way down. He'd never snapped a sword before. Lost one, sure, but then he could just wait a few minutes and it would just reappear back in his inventory to be retrieved. A broken weapon, though, he wasn't sure. What was he supposed to do now?

Oh well, it was getting to be time for a new sword anyway.

A short wait later, the lift came to a stop.

That was when a hatchet flew at his head. He raised his broken sword on reflex, sending the weapon off at an angle.

"Sorry!" Seven pulled her hood down as soon as he staggered out of the lift alone.

"No harm done." He picked up the hatchet and handed it to her so she didn't have to beckon it back.

"You've looked better." Kegan panted, clearly having had just as much trouble with his fight.

"You're not looking much better."

"That's true." Kegan glanced around the hall, noting the absence of enemies. "We might be getting too good at murdering."

"I'm not sure how I feel about that." Corvin let out a sigh. "Let's just hope Piper is having more luck than us."

CHAPTER TWENTY-FOUR

"Oi, what the fuck!" Aawil scrambled backward, falling back against the counter of the island that sat at the center of the kitchen. Talons slashed at her face as wings beat against her head.

Piper struggled to hold in a laugh as the fearsome Aawil flailed around the room with a large black and red raven clinging to her horns.

"I guess that explains where Ruby has been."

The overgrown avian alternated between screeching directly in Aawil's ear and pecking her in the eye.

"Shoot it, shoot it, shoot it." The monstrous woman knocked over everything in sight trying to shake the bird free.

Piper shrugged, then pulled her pistol and unloaded it indiscriminately in Ruby's direction, peppering both the bird and Aawil with bullets. If it weren't for the PVP ban, she might have even killed her. Sadly, she was not that lucky and had to settle for just the feathered hindrance.

Ruby squawked and fell to the floor as blue light exploded from Aawil's head, her face becoming collateral damage. She stood there, breathing heavy as the glow faded from her skin.

"Not a fan of birds, huh?" Piper blew on the muzzle of her pistol.

"No! I am not. They're loud and spread diseases. I got salmonella from them fourteen times." Aawil stood there huffing for a second, clearly unaware that getting sick fourteen times from birds was an oddly large number. A moment of silence passed, then Ruby sprang back up from the floor and reattached himself to her horns.

"Interesting." Piper stood watching as the *Coin* struggled. "At least we know the PVP ban applies to pets as well as players."

"No one cares." Aawil cried, an apparent fear of birds clearly overriding her commitment to playing her role as a strong silent killer. Eventually she let out a growl and tried to bite the bird back. Ruby screeched as the faunus got a mouthful of feathers. The *Coin* took advantage of the opening to tear the bird from her face and wrap her fingers around its head.

Piper winced as a loud snap came from the pet's neck and Aawil threw the thing to the floor. The *Coin* made a break for the other side of the kitchen's island where she took up a defensive position, mostly hiding behind Piper. A moment later, Ruby was back up, his head twisting back into place as he staggered back toward the pantry.

"He must be under orders to keep people away from the bomb." Piper ducked down below the counter, kneeling in a pile of broken crackers and cheese. Glancing down at the mess, she got an idea.

"Want a cracker?" she shouted as she scooped up a handful and threw it at the bird. Buttery bits bounced off the large pet's face and wings, causing him to squawk and flap. Other than that, he ignored the assault.

"Okay, maybe that wasn't a good idea." Piper wished Corvin was there to help. They made a good team, even if he was an ass. They would have had that bomb dealt with by now. Instead, she was stuck with Aawil, an enemy of her house who was more than likely a killer out there in the real world.

Well, you work with what you have.

Piper peaked around the side of the counter.

"Is it still there?" Aawil bumped into her back, knocking her forward.

Ruby hopped from side to side, spreading his impressive wingspan as if trying to block the pantry door. He looked straight at Piper and squawked.

"Yeah, it's not going anywhere."

"It's going to have to go somewhere." Aawil peered over the top over the counter into the pantry. "That timer only has ten minutes left on it and we can't defuse a bomb with that thing clawing at our faces."

"Maybe we can trap it in something." Piper scanned the room from where she sat on the floor. There were a few large stewing pots on a shelf nearby. She gestured to them with her head.

Aawil nodded and grabbed the largest one, about the size of turkey fryer.

"That should work." Piper grabbed the lid and held it like a shield. "Okay, you go around the other side of the island and try to sneak up on it. I'll go at it from the front and try to herd it in?"

Aawil crawled off without another word and Piper got into position, standing up and stepping into the open.

"Hi there, Ruby." She crept forward. "Easy now, I'm not going to make any sudden movements. So just stay right there."

That was when Aawil let out a howl and charged the bird from behind.

"So much for no sudden moves." Piper ran forward, her improvised shield held in front. Ruby squawked and launched into the air as Piper and Aawil crashed into each other. The difference in strength was clear as the *Coin* bowled her over. It was like being hit by a truck.

The pot crashed to the floor as Ruby fluttered back down to land on the faunus' horns. The resulting scream from both of them was earsplitting. Piper wished she had a way to block out the noise.

Wait, that's it!

She grabbed the stewing pot and hoisted it up. Then, she simply dropped it back down on Aawil's head, stuffing Ruby inside.

At least that's quieter. She nodded to herself as muffled complaints and screeching spilled from the opening of the pot that rested on Aawil's shoulders.

"Hold him in there a sec!" Piper drew her pistol and placed its muzzle against the pot's side at an angle. "And probably cover your ears."

The gun barked as the pot rang like a bell, Aawil dropping to the floor with dazed expression. Piper slammed the pot to the ground before Ruby had a chance to escape and threw her body over the top. The pot rocked as the overgrown avian fought to get out.

"Damn, this thing is stronger than it looks." Piper struggled to hold on.

Aawil shook off her confusion and leapt to help, having no problem keeping the pot down with her monstrous strength. Piper took the opportunity to break away and check on the bomb.

"Shit." She raised her house ring and called for help. "Found the bomb, time is running out." There was a moment of silence before her mother's voice responded.

"Oh, thank god. You're amazing, sweetie."

Piper rolled her eyes. "Yeah, I know, but we have eight minutes on the clock. How do I disarm this thing?"

"Hang on, let me get Larkin." A moment went by before Ginger spoke again. "Okay, I have him right here, but this part is going to be hard. Is Corvin with you? You're going to need another pair of hands."

"Sorry," Corvin's voice came across the house line. He sounded out of breath. "We got separated. I see you on the map, but I'm not going to make it to you in time."

"It's fine, I'm not alone." Piper glanced to her temporary

frenemy sitting on the floor with her arms and legs wrapped around a pot. "I'm with Aawil."

"What?" Max's voice shouted over the line.

"Are you safe?" Ginger added.

"Yeah, I'm fine. We tried to kill each other for a bit but we're in the ban, so really there's no point to that. We're kind of cooperating for now. Common goals and all."

"That's less than ideal." Ginger paused as if talking to someone else. "Wait, really? Why would you make a bomb like that?" There was another pause before she continued. "Okay, Piper, it looks like Aawil is the perfect choice to help here."

"Sure. Let me get her freed up then." Piper ignored her mother's suspicious wording. "We had a bit of a problem with a bird."

"A what?" Ginger asked.

"Never mind, not important. Just give me a minute here." Piper lowered her house ring and turned to Aawil.

"Looks like we need two sets on hands to disarm this thing."

"Mine are right full right now." Aawil leaned on the pot.

"We're running out of time so we're going to have to put that thing somewhere else." Piper glanced around for a moment, then she smiled. "How about here?" She opened the door of the old-fashioned oven sitting against one wall and gestured to it.

Aawil nodded with a wide grin, then proceeded to push the pot across the floor to force the bird inside closer. Piper slid the lid underneath to hold Ruby inside while they reoriented the container to face the open stove. Then, as fast as she could, she pulled the lid away and banged it on the bottom of the pot.

The oversized bird flapped out of the frying pan and into the fire, Aawil slamming the door shut behind it. Piper wedged the pot's lid into the oven's handle to keep it closed. A steady stream of muffled squawking expressed Ruby's opinion of the situation as feathers beat against the window on the front of the oven. Aawil reached forward and turned a knob on top to high. A flickering glow illuminated the window.

"Let's see if the ban can stop that." The faunus brushed a stray lock of hair behind her horns.

"Was that really necessary?" Piper peeked through the window to see the poor bird glowing blue in the fire, in a state of continuous undeath.

"Quite so." Aawil turned away toward the pantry. "Now let's see about this bomb."

CHAPTER TWENTY-FIVE

"Okay, tell me what to do." Piper swallowed as she looked down at the wooden cylinder protruding from the top of the large chest. A timer counted off the seconds. "We have six minutes."

"That should be enough time," her mother assured her over Lockheart's house line. "From what Larkin says, the bomb is not complex but it is delicate, so you're going to have to be careful. Start by removing the cover."

"Okay." Piper slipped behind the chest and examined the cylinder sticking out from the lid. The surface was polished to a flawless shine with several metal pins securing it to the top of the chest. Each one had a round head at its end.

"You're going to need something to pry those pins out with."

Piper looked around, then held her hand out to Aawil. "Let me borrow your dagger, I need something to work these out with."

The *Coin* eyed her skeptically, but handed the weapon over without argument.

"Thanks." Piper took the dagger, and wedged its edge under the first of the pins. "Okay, I'm prying them out now."

"Wait!" Ginger shouted.

"What?" Piper's hand slipped and the dagger nicked the wood.

"Before you touch anything, have Aawil hold the chest still so it can't move. Apparently, the trigger mechanism is extremely sensitive to moment. If you jostle the cylinder, it could go off right there."

"Wait, what?" A bead of sweat began to roll down Piper's forehead. "You can't be serious."

"I am. Honestly, we have been lucky so far. If the ship had listed to the side even slightly tonight, we could have been killed."

"What the hell? Why would they bring something like this on an airship?" Piper complained, before relaying the instructions to hold the chest still to Aawil.

"Yeah, I've already yelled at Larkin about this. He never explained how sensitive it was to his client, so they didn't know. Fortunately, the timer can be stopped easily once you have the cover off. So get to it. Chop chop. We don't have all night."

"Alright, alright. Jeez, Mom, give me a minute." Piper lowered her house ring and reached again for the first pin, her hand shaking from the pressure.

One wrong move and everything we've worked toward goes up in smoke. Her hand immediately slipped.

"Oh god." She winced for a second, half expecting to explode. "I don't know if I can do this." She wiped sweat from her hairline as her whole body started to run hot.

"You don't have a choice." Aawil tightened her grip around the cylinder to keep it steady.

"Shit, okay, I need a distraction." Piper reached back to the metal pin she'd started on. "Say something to take my mind off what I'm doing."

"In case you haven't noticed, I don't talk much."

"That's perfect, tell me why." Piper's hand began to shake less as she worked the dagger under the head of the pin.

"Why what?"

"Why you don't talk when you clearly can."

Aawil tilted her head to one side. "If you worked for Nix, you wouldn't say much either. I'm not stupid, but with everything she has going on, it's hard to keep track of what is sensitive information and what isn't. Keeping my mouth shut stops me from saying anything I shouldn't."

"That actually makes a lot of sense." Piper pried the first pin out, dropping it to the floor with a metallic ping. "So why do you work for Nix?"

"I'm not telling you that."

"Why not? I think it's a reasonable question. How do you justify working for the bad guy?"

"She's not that bad–"

"She killed one of my friends." Piper hoped that Aawil might say something that would deny Kira's death.

"I…" Aawil went silent, falling back to her default.

"Don't clam up on me now, I need the distraction." Piper wedged the dagger under another pin.

"Nix does some bad things." The *Coin* spoke slower, as if choosing her words carefully. "But she doesn't enjoy them, and sometimes it's necessary. Plus, I trust her."

"Why?"

"She saved me." Aawil looked her dead in the eyes. "When one of Nix's men found me, I was in a bad place, being used by some bad people. I was a tool to hurt others with no say in my future. Nix got me out of that life."

"So, you, what? Just hurt people for her now?" Piper dropped another pin to the floor.

"Sometimes." Aawil deflated. "It's what I'm good at."

"Okay, I'm not sure if I want to know more about that." Piper decided to change the subject. "What's with the accent?"

"What?"

"You British or something?"

Aawil tilted her head back and forth. "No, I was born in America, I'm not sure what state though; I was too young then.

I grew up in London, though. That's where Nix's people found me. I was twelve."

"You were twelve and working for bad people?"

Aawil nodded. "There are a lot of uses for someone as strong as I am."

Piper's hand froze halfway through prying up a pin. It was pretty obvious what those uses were. "So that isn't a system glitch then, you're actually that strong out there in the real?"

"The world is a much stranger place than you think." Aawil sighed and looked away. "You don't know how lucky you are. The best thing for you would be to forget all about Nix and what she did to your friend. Just go back to your life before it's too late." Aawil shook her head. "Maybe you never had a chance to begin with. I have seen the file Nix has on you."

"There's a file on me?"

"There's a file on everyone. Yours is… comprehensive."

Piper's mouth went dry. She had never considered that she might have gotten in too deep. All she had ever done was help out occasionally; she didn't think she was important enough to be on Nix's radar.

"What happens when it's too late?" Piper's voice cracked a little. "If I don't get out of this?"

Aawil frowned in a way that seemed sympathetic. "I think I've told you more than I should have, so you better be close to getting those pins out."

"Whatever." She tried to make like the question wasn't killing her. "I'm almost done now. How are we on time?"

Aawil checked the window on the front of the cylinder. "Three minutes."

As soon as the last pin was out, Piper relayed the information to her mother.

"You're making great time." Ginger's voice sounded over the line. "Now you're going to have to carefully lift the cover off the device."

Piper stood and signaled to Aawil to get ready. The wooden cylinder stuck for a moment but the *Coin* was able to twist it free. It slid up without much effort after that. They both let out a gasp at what was underneath.

A second cylinder. This one made of glass with a domed top. A panel bearing the outline of a hand adorned the front, along with an elegant clockwork timer. Tabs of numbered paper flipped up and down, marking off the seconds with a construct of gears.

A small marble sat inside the glass enclosure, precariously placed on a metal plate. Veins of glowing embers snaked across its surface. Beneath it, a bed of black powder waited. The function was clear; when the timer hit zero, the plate would drop the burning marble to ignite the chest full of powder.

Piper held her breath, realizing why she had been told to be so careful when removing the cover. The marble seemed to rest in a tiny indent at the center of the plate, but even a slight bump would be enough to knock it off.

"Wow," Aawil breathed the word while looking over the device. "I've seen bombs before, but this is a work of art."

Piper took a second to appreciate the design, trying to ignore the fact that it could kill her. Then she raised her house ring and reported in.

"Okay, Mom. We have the cover off, and two minutes to go. How do I disarm it?"

"That's where this gets a little… problematic," her mother answered back, sending a wave of frustration tingling down Piper's spine.

"What does that mean?"

"Technically, the device can't be disarmed."

"What?" Piper nearly slapped her hand down on the chest, but refrained to keep from being, well, exploded.

"Larkin designed the bomb to be almost impossible to move or disarm. But there is still a way to deal with it."

"And what would that be?" Piper spoke through gritted teeth.

"It's actually really simple. The timer can be paused, but first before I tell you how, I have to remind you that Aawil can't hear what I say on the house line. So I have a question, and I need you to respond as if I'm not asking you anything." Ginger paused as if giving her a chance to prepare a lie. "Is Aawil in front of the chest right now?"

"Okay," Piper glanced down at the back of the chest finding two sturdy handles. She looked to the *Coin* on the other side. "Is there a handle on the front where you are?" She made a point to keep her house ring near her mouth so her mother could hear too.

Aawil nodded as Ginger responded. "Perfect, now all you have to do is get her to place her hand on the panel on the front. That will stop the timer."

"That's it?"

"That's it. Just make sure Aawil is the one to touch it, not you."

Piper leaned to the side and gave the faunus her most casual expression. "Apparently, all we have to do is place a hand on that plate on the front and the timer will stop."

Aawil furrowed her brow for a second then raised her right hand and placed it against the outline traced on the plate.

"You mean this one?" Her face fell a second later as a buzzer sounded and the numbers on the timer were replaced by a row of red skulls. "What just happened?"

"Mom–" Piper stared to ask but was cut off before she could get another word out.

"Don't let Aawil move!"

"Hold still!" Piper reached forward to keep the faunus from pulling her hand away.

"Why?" The *Coin's* voice wavered.

"Yeah, Ma, what happened?" Piper asked.

"You just activated a deadman's trigger. The timer is no longer active so we have as much time as we need, but it will explode fifteen seconds after Aawil removes her hand. It cannot be stopped after that. It's like I said, there's no way to disarm it. This is the best we could do to buy time."

"Bad news, Aawil." Piper let herself fall back onto her rear, and placed a hand on her forehead. "If you take your hand off, we'll only have fifteen seconds to live. We just activated a dead-man's switch."

The *Coin* let out a sigh. "And you expect me to keep my hand on here all night?"

"That is a valid point." Piper raised her ring. "What if Aawil's hand slips?"

"Don't worry, Corvin and Kegan will be there in a few minutes, along with Seven. Just sit tight until then."

"And what are they going to do?"

"They're going to help you move the bomb."

"I thought that was impossible?"

"No, I said it was near impossible."

"Oh, 'cause that's better." Piper rolled her eyes.

"It will be fine," her mother assured her. "With all of you there, you should be able to hold it steady enough to keep the marble from falling off its plate. Then all we have to do is place the chest in one of the Night Queen's lifeboats and drop it off the ship. It'll explode out of range as it falls. Everything will be fine. Trust me."

"Awesome." Piper dropped her hand to her side. "We have to wait a few minutes. The rest of my house will be here to help us throw this thing overboard."

"So this would be a bad time to have an itch on my nose?" Aawil aggressively scratched her face with her left hand. "It's like it knows that I can't move my other hand and just gets worse."

"Well, try to hold out."

"Right then, talk to me." Aawil locked eyes with her. "It's my turn to be distracted."

"Sure." Piper waved a have in the air. "Tell me what you and Nix are planning."

"No, you had your time. Now you can answer my questions."

"Fine." Piper sunk back against the pantry shelves. "What do you want to know?"

Aawil leaned her head to the side. "What are you mad at the boy for?"

"What?"

"That *Blade* class, the handsome reynard with the black tail."

"Corvin?" Piper folded her arms and pinned her ears back. "I'm not mad at him. Why would you even care?"

"I fought him on the roof of the palace in Reliqua. He was a good fighter."

"So?"

"So, before we got into it, he was talking to that *Leaf* he hangs out with about a girl that fancied him. Someone underage."

"What the hell?" Piper grabbed a sack of crackers off a shelf and threw some into her mouth. "Even the bad guys know about me getting rejected. How has this become my life?"

"So, I take it he wasn't interested?"

"No, the asshole called me a kid and tried to tell me he valued me too much as a friend. Like that's going to make it better. Like he's doing me a favor. Like I'm just some child with a crush." Piper spat cracker crumbs from her mouth as she vented her frustrations to a stranger. "Am I wrong here?"

"Maybe, maybe not." Aawil crinkled her nose as if it still itched.

"What the hell is that supposed to mean?"

"It means, I get it." Aawil blew out a long sigh. "You're sixteen and that fox boy is cute. I was your age once and I was dealing with a bit more than boys. It's hard to be the youngest person in the room and have everyone treat you like you don't know anything."

"Tell me about it."

"The worst part is that they're right."

"Yeah..." Pipers face fell. "Wait, what?"

"You're sixteen." Aawil's shoulders sunk. "I certainly didn't know anything when I was your age. I may have thought I did, but the harsh reality is that the world is very small when you're that young. Your problems seem insurmountable, but they only get bigger and more complex the older you get."

"I'm not a child." Piper narrowed her eyes at the *Coin*.

"Yes, you are." Aawil's eyes softened. "And that's fine. There's nothing wrong with being young and lacking experience. That's life, you learn and grow over time. And as you do, you'll gain a whole new set of problems. That doesn't make you weak or daft. It just makes you normal. Don't rush your life away."

"What do you know?" Piper leaned her head back to rest against the shelving. "You're just a henchwoman who removes problems for criminals."

"True. But I'm a henchwoman that's been where you are. You can listen to me or not."

"I'm going to go with not."

Just as she began to sulk, Corvin burst into the kitchen.

"Piper, you in here?"

She immediately rolled her eyes. "We're in the pantry!"

He skidded into the doorway with Kegan right behind him. They both froze as soon as they saw Aawil sitting there with her hand on the deadman's switch.

"Ahhhhh." Corvin's jaw hung slack like an idiot.

"Did you find them?" That *Venom* mage from the Silver Tongues appeared behind them. "Oh." Her face dropped at the scene as well.

"Hello there, Aawil." Kegan pushed to the front and approached. "Last time I saw you, I was falling off the roof of the palace in Reliqua."

The *Coin* nodded, apparently returning to her silent persona for the sake of anonymity. Piper couldn't help but wonder why she had spoken so much to her. *Probably because she knows that no one takes me seriously.*

"So how does this thing work?" Kegan tapped his foot against the chest, causing both Aawil and Piper to suck in a breath.

"What the hell! This thing's motion sensitive!" Piper stabbed a finger in the direction off the burning marble within the cylinder.

"Oh, sorry." The elf held up both hands in surrender.

"Mom says we have to move it up to the ship's deck and throw it overboard."

"And we'll have to do it together so that the marble doesn't fall." Corvin crept past Aawil to reach the side of the chest.

Piper simply tapped the tip of her nose in confirmation.

"No sense staring at it." Kegan slapped his hands together and crouched down, gesturing for Seven to help on Piper's side.

Aawil shifted her position so she could grab a hold of one of the handles without removing her hand from the trigger plate. Corvin got ready as well.

"Okay," Piper curled her hands around the handles. "Everyone ready?" A circle of nods answered. "We lift on three."

"Wait, wait, wait." Kegan let go. "Lift on three, or lift just after three."

"Seriously?" Seven gave him a healthy dose of side-eye.

"We lift on three." Piper counted off on her fingers to demonstrate the timing. "So get ready, 'cause this is happening."

Everyone in the pantry tensed up, and on three, hoisted the eighty-pound chest off the floor. Aawil was slightly faster than the rest, her inhuman strength having no problem with the weight, even with only one hand.

The marble titled.

"No no no." Piper struggled to level out the chest while the rest of the group did the same, creating a wave of motion.

The marble rolled against the lip of the plate, rocking back and forth as it circled round and round. Each movement threatened to ruin everything. Everyone, including Aawil, blew out a sigh of relief when marble finally settled back to where it started.

"Let's not do that again." Piper glanced around the group.

Aawil mouthed the word 'sorry,' reminding Piper of Echo. She ignored the apology and signaled for them to get moving.

The marble rocked a little, but remained in place as they inched their way out of the cramped space of the pantry. Piper glanced at Corvin as they made their way out of the kitchen and into the hall. He met her eyes for an instant.

"Umm." He immediately looked away. "There's a lift just down here. It's not too far."

For a moment she almost snapped at him, but when she opened her mouth, all that came out was an awkward, "Oh, okay." She cringed at her response, catching Aawil shaking her head from across the chest.

That was when Kegan cleared his throat and flicked his eyes to Piper as soon as Corvin looked his way. The annoyingly handsome boy's face flushed and his ears drooped. Then Kegan cleared his throat again. This went on for a few more seconds, until Corvin opened his mouth.

"I'm sorry, Piper."

"What?" Her face went blank as the words caught her off guard.

"For calling you a kid earlier."

She blew out an annoyed sigh. "Yeah, that sucked."

He winced but continued regardless. "I'm not much of an adult either, so I shouldn't have said that. I just panicked and didn't know what to say when you asked me out."

"So we're doing this now?" Piper raised an eyebrow. "Just talking about you rejecting me in front of a henchwoman, a stranger..." She gestured to Kegan with her head. "And this guy."

"Sorry." Corvin lowered his head.

"I think everyone knows already," Kegan defended. "You haven't really been subtle."

"I guess I deserve that." Piper lowered her head for a moment before finally speaking again. "You weren't wrong, Corv. Sometimes it's hard to remember that we're not all the same age when everyone's avatars are so young. I am technically still a kid in comparison. I probably shouldn't have put you in that position. I was being unrealistic, so I'm sorry for being a jerk all night."

This time Corvin's face went blank, clearly not expecting an apology in return. "Oh, it's okay. I'm sorry that I couldn't give you the answer you wanted."

"'Cause that would be illegal." Kegan added, getting a glower from Piper.

She growled as they boarded the lift to take them to the upper decks. "Laws are dumb."

"You should see the tax laws." Seven let out a laugh at her own joke when it failed to get a chuckle. "Sorry, accountant humor. But in all seriousness, sometimes laws keep you from making mistakes."

"Still." Piper made a point to maintain eye contact with Corvin. "I still like you. I understand that I'm not an option for you, and there's no chance of you saying yes. But I want my feelings to be clear. At least that way I can move on."

"That's fair." Corvin braced like he was about to rip off a Band-Aid. "Can we go back to being friends?"

"I guess—"

"Oh, thank god." Kegan interrupted. "Now you kids can put this all behind you and get back to normal. Seriously, you two have no idea how difficult tonight has been for me."

"Kids?" Piper and Corvin said in unison along with a glower.

"What? I'm over forty. I can call you babies whatever I want."

"That's true." Piper smirked. "You are wicked old."

That was when the lift came to a stop on the top level. Max and Ginger stood at the entrance of the lift shaft in a small room with a door to the main deck.

"And speaking of old." Piper gestured toward her mother with her head, getting a dirty look in response.

"Wow." Max leaned against the wall of the lift bay. "That is one hell of a bomb." A flash of anger swept across his face when he noticed Aawil, but washed away just as fast. He seemed to be making an effort to hold in his feelings, like he didn't want to tip his hand.

"Yes, it is an impressive bomb." Piper's mother approached the chest with a covetous twinkle in her eyes. "I'm actually pretty jealous. Kind of want to blow something up with it now."

Behind them, Echo mimed an explosion, pulling her arms in close to her chest and then throwing them out and jumping. The word 'boom' was clearly mouthed. Afterward, she sunk to the floor like a fading cloud of smoke, making jazz hands the whole way down.

"Anyway." Ginger ignored the imitation fairy and gestured to the bomb. "We can toss this thing overboard nearby, just need to carry it another hundred feet or so across the deck." She immediately spun on her heel and began walking toward a door. "Just this way."

Piper shrugged, and pushed her improvised bomb squad to follow her mother. She gasped as soon as she stepped into the open air of the Night Queen's main deck. A crowd, made up of the auction's attendees, had gathered in front of the lift bay. Grindstone stood in the middle, fidgeting in place while Dalliance ran around.

"Give them room, give them room." The elf pranced back and forth, making sure there was a clear path to the side of the ship. "We don't all want to explode, now do we?"

"You're doing great, Aawil!" Nix thrust out a thumbs up from one side then leaned to a random player standing nearby. "The faunus is with me."

Piper noticed Max's jaw tighten.

The crowd began to follow them as they moved toward the side of the ship, ramping up the tension.

Aawil turned her head. "You all are making me nervous." She glared daggers at the onlookers. "Clear out."

Dalliance froze like he had just been scolded for peeing on the carpet. "Yes, yes." He turned and began shooing the crowd back toward the theater. Only Nix remained, though she kept her distance, watching for a minute longer before turning back with the others.

Eventually, they reached the ship's railing where a row of lifeboats hung over the side in case of a water landing. Max opened an entry gate and hopped onboard to help load the chest into a stable position. Once it was safely stowed, everyone but Aawil and Piper jumped back aboard the Night Queen.

For a moment, Piper wondered if she could get to safety and release the lifeboat while Aawil was still touching the bomb. Sure, the faunus hadn't tried to kill her in a while, but that didn't mean that she wouldn't at the first opportunity.

"Okay, so now we just drop it?" She raised an eyebrow at her mother.

"Yes… sort of."

"What do you mean sort of?" Piper narrowed her eyes.

"Well, remember when I said there was a fifteen second delay on the deadman's switch?" Ginger clicked her tongue. "That was a bit of a lie. It will go off the instant Aawil's hand leaves that plate."

Aawil narrowed her eyes in response while Max took over.

"So unless you want to blow up the ship, stop the auction, and kill Nix, you're going to have to keep your hand right where it is until this here chest is out of range."

"Sorry," Ginger added along with a smug smile.

Aawil sat motionless on the lifeboat for a few seconds, silently staring at Ginger before finally shaking her head and breaking her silence. "You suck. I can't believe you're going to blow me up again."

"Yeah, it's probably getting old, huh?" Ginger placed her hands together in an apologetic gesture that somehow seemed sarcastic. "But I thank you for helping my daughter to defuse this difficult situation. I'd say you'll be missed, but… well, you know."

"She didn't need help." Aawil shook her head. "Your daughter, I mean. She's far more capable than you know."

Piper stopped for a second, wondering what that could

mean. Then she nodded to her enemy and awkwardly backed up toward the Night Queen's deck.

"True, she makes me proud every day." Ginger held out a hand to help Piper off the lifeboat.

"But, you still suck." Aawil turned to Piper, then added, "Your mum sucks, you know?"

"Sometimes." She laughed and gave her mother a warm smile. "But she's my mom."

"And?" Ginger leaned closer.

"And I guess I love her." Piper grumbled.

"That's right." Ginger reached for the lever to release the lifeboat. "Now let's throw this henchwoman, ah, I mean bomb, overboard."

Aawil rolled her eyes. "You really do suc—"

Max pulled the lever before she could finish, getting a questioning look from the rest of the group.

"What?"

Piper leaned over the edge, waiting for the inevitable explosion. The rest of her house joined her, each waiting in silence longer than what seemed. "Maybe it was a dud?"

"No, Larkin cares too much about his craft." Ginger gripped the railing just as the ground below ignited in a burst of light and flame a few hundred feet wide, enough to rip the lifeboat in half. "Ah, there it is. And wow, that was larger than I expected. Pretty glad that didn't go off up here."

"Aawil must have kept her hand on the plate the whole way down." Piper watched the ground burn, surprised by the henchwoman's dedication. She could have just let go after a few seconds rather than waiting until she hit the ground.

"That's that, then." Max pushed off from the rail. "Now we can get back to the auction and get what we came here for."

Piper watched him walk away. Her mother gave her a smile before joining him. Kegan and Seven followed close behind.

"Come on." Piper glanced to Corvin before joining the rest of her house. "They'll need backup."

CHAPTER TWENTY-SIX

"You ready for this?" Max pulled Ginger close behind the curtain of the theater's box seats, his heart beating faster.

"I've been waiting all night." She pressed in close and kissed him on the cheek before pulling away to stare up into his eyes.

"Can you two not?" Piper spoke up from behind them.

"Yeah, that's plenty of canoodling." Kegan folded his arms. "You're making Corvin uncomfortable."

"What? No, they aren't." The reynard remained surprisingly calm. "My parents have always been affectionate with each other. It's not anything to feel weird about."

"Ha!" Farn pointed at them. "Corvin just compared you two to his parents."

Echo laughed silently by her side.

"Deal with it." Max held Ginger's hand. "I'm in a good mood. We just got Aawil out of the picture. And the auction is about to start. Things are starting to look up."

"Plus, I like kissing." Ginger grinned at her daughter, giving her a wink. Piper shuddered as Max turned around and pulled open the curtain.

"I have a good feeling about this."

The lights in what was left of the theater dimmed, plunging the wreckage of the seating area below into darkness, as if it had never happened. Then Ginger's bidding tile began to glow. The same light could be seen from the rest of the balcony seats spread out around the walls of the theater. The lords of Noctem's top houses stood waiting, one in each box, almost the entirety of the world's rulers. Nix leaned against the railing directly across the room.

For a moment, Max felt the urge to gloat. However, the small weight of the silver knife on his belt reminded him of what he still had to do. Before he had time to think about it further, a spotlight shined down on the stage.

Dalliance stood at its center.

"Hey hey hey!" The elf threw his hands out wide. "After all of the surprises tonight has thrown our way, we have pulled through, with only minimal casualties. I apologize for separating you all into the box seats. But we have no more seats available down here and, let's be honest, after tonight, I don't trust any of you to be anywhere near each other." He clicked his heels together. "But that is neither here nor there, because right now, it is finally the time you have all been waiting for. The very reason you all have joined us here on the fabulous Night Queen. So, without further ado, I am proud to present to you... the Auction of Souls!"

As the last word left his mouth, the entire stage lit up, revealing several tables, each with a single ornate box sitting on top. Max leaned forward. Ginger did the same beside him. Dalliance strutted his way across the stage to the first table.

"It seems only fitting that our first contract item up for bids should come from the first of Noctem's Nightmares, Rasputin, the embodiment of destruction. The boss that taught our world fear."

Max felt a chill run down his body at the memory of his own fight against the Nightmare. It had been his and Kira's first, and in all their years of gaming, they had never faced a challenge like it. Rasputin had really put them through their paces but, in the end, it made them stronger. Max had learned to dual wield back then, for the simple fact that they needed more damage. He smiled. Those were good times.

Dalliance reached into the box on the first table and pulled off the lid to reveal a single white arrow resting on a velvet pillow. He took it gently in his hands and raised for the bidders to see.

"The Star Burst." Dalliance remained silent to let the name sink in. "This arrow can be charged by any mage by sacrificing a portion of their mana pool, to create a miniature star when fired. The size of the star is limited only by the amount of mana supplied, equaling one inch in diameter for every single point of mana sacrificed. And by sacrifice, I mean the amount will be permanently subtracted from the mage's mana pool, decreasing their total capacity."

The room went silent as each of the lords contemplated what that would mean. Even Max caught himself doing the math.

A high-level mage could have anywhere between 1000 to close to 3000. At one inch per mana point, that could potentially create a star 250 feet wide. That could destroy an airship or part of a palace easily, even guarantee an assassination. From the looks on the faces of the Lords across the room, they were all coming to the same conclusion. Granted, they would be nerfing one of their mages down to the point of uselessness in the process. They would practically need to start over with a new class at that point. Not to mention that the arrow would need a skilled archer to use it.

The bidding started at ten thousand dollars and immediately jumped up to thirty thousand.

"That's tempting." Ginger leaned back to the *Leaf*. "Right, Kegan?"

"Meh." The elf shrugged. "It's powerful, but it feels like more trouble than it's worth. Probably let someone else have it."

"He's right." Max nodded. "Plus, we might need the money later for something that will work against Nix. Not counting what we've set aside for Piper and Drakes' college funds and what we've spent already, we have a little over seven million to work with here. I can't imagine spending that much, but you never know."

"Damn, when you say that number out loud it's hard to wrap my mind around it." Ginger's eyes widened.

"You sent money aside for me?" Piper leaned forward.

"Of course we did." Ginger gave her daughter a squeeze. "I paid off the house too."

"And don't think we've forgotten about your tuition, Corvin." Max leaned back to him. "Your next semester is on us."

"What?" The reynard's ears stood straight up in surprise.

"We're not going to leave you out." Max slapped him on the back.

"Yeah, we couldn't have done any of this without you." Ginger added.

"I don't know what to say." Corvin lowered his head.

Kegan cleared his throat. "I think 'thanks' is probably the word you're looking for."

"Oh, ah, thanks." He shoved his hands into his pockets as the last bid on the Star Burst was called out.

"And sold, for one hundred sixty thousand." Dalliance placed the arrow back in its box and closed the lid. "You may claim your contract after the auction, once we confirm your transaction. Although, I trust that you're good for it." Dalliance smiled up at the top bidder.

Alastair, of all people, lowered a glowing auction tile and gave a slight bow down at the stage.

"He must be trying to keep the more dangerous items out of the wrong hands." Ginger gave the head of Checkpoint Systems an approving nod.

"Good." Max rested his hands on the railing. "I don't think I like the idea of something like that being out there."

Dalliance approached the next box, this time revealing a strange metal spike that seemed to have a number of articulated points running down its length. Everyone in the balconies leaned forward with puzzled expressions. Well, everyone but Ginger who immediately grabbed Max's arm with excitement.

"What is it?" He stared down at the contract as Dalliance held it high.

"From Dorian, the Nightmare of Temptation, we have a piece of equipment exclusively for the *Coin* class. It is, appropriately, named Yoink." As the word left his mouth, the item snapped open with a metallic clink to resemble a simple claw similar to one that might be found in one of those prize machines at an arcade. The item then snapped back together into a triangular spike.

"That's right, this little guy here is a one of a kind grappling hook." Dalliance tossed it in his hand a few times. "Except it isn't just for swinging around, oh no no no. This handy little tool is also for grabbing. That's right, with this equipped to your wrist launcher, you may steal an object from range. No need to get in close when you see something you want, no sir. You can just fire it in the direction of what you covet and it will do the rest.

"See something shiny? Yoink! Want to disarm an enemy? Yoink. Feel like you want something more than the person that has it? Well then, you guessed it, yoink. Of course, it can't transfer the ownership of equipped gear if you manage to claim something that doesn't belong to you, but it can at least stop something from being used against you for a moment. Also, it does take quite a bit of practice and timing to use successfully, but still, what *Coin* could resist this little fella?"

Max felt Ginger squeeze his arm tighter. "You're gonna bid on that, aren't you?"

Ginger responded with an excited nod. "I'm going to steal so much crap with that. I'll even take things I don't need."

"Okay, calm down. Just don't spend too much on it." Max smiled and placed a hand on her back.

"Shall we start the bidding a little higher? Say, fifty thousand?" Dalliance shot a wry smile up toward Max's balcony as if he knew there was an interest.

Ginger immediately raised her bidding tile high above her head. Unfortunately, so did Lord Murph a few boxes over. His Knight was a *Coin*, come to think of it. Seven raised her tile as well, but dropped her hand back down the moment she noticed Ginger bidding.

"We have 50, now 60." Dalliance pointed at up at each of them. "Can I get 80?"

Ginger raised her tile higher.

"That's 80, can I get 100–"

Lord Murph raised his tile before Dalliance had finished his sentence. Ginger didn't let up. Bidding again and again, to stay in the lead.

Max watched as her breathing increased and her skin flushed. There was something endearing about her enthusiasm that made him glad she'd made the first move six months ago. If she hadn't, he would have let his chance slip by. Sure, nothing had happened between them since then, but with everything going on, that wasn't a surprise. He just wished he wasn't so awkward around her.

"And sold! For one hundred ninety thousand." Dalliance clutched the contract item to his chest. "Thank you, Lady Ginger, may you steal many shiny things."

Ginger smiled wide, clearly feeling the joys of a shopping high. Then suddenly, her face fell. "Oh god, that cost more than my house!" She turned to Max. "I spent almost two hundred thousand dollars on a grappling hook, am I insane?" She grabbed his shirt. "Why did you let me do that?"

"Gah." Max pulled back. "What did you want me to do?"

"Talk some sense into me." She shook him. "You know I can't be trusted."

Dalliance didn't give her any more time to dwell on her buyer's remorse as he headed for the next box and pulled out a pretty badass coat. "The Nightfall." He swept it around himself and draped it across his shoulders.

Max smiled. It looked like something out of an old hack and slash game he'd played, the kind of coat a demon hunter would wear. It came down to mid-thigh and hung open in a way that felt aggressively casual. The garment looked light enough to move freely in, but also heavy enough to provide some protection. If Max hadn't been there for other reasons, he might have been tempted.

Dalliance twirled in place before pulling up the large hood that hung over his shoulders. The instant he did, a wave of darkness swept across the fabric's surface. He stepped back into a shadow, disappearing into the darkness only to reenter the spotlight a moment later.

"With this contract, you will be immune to any and all darkness-based attacks as well as blend into the shadows, which are plentiful here in Noctem." He held out his hands as if framing a picture. "Imagine yourself, stalking through high-level areas, nearly invisible. You pass by players and monsters alike without so much as raising an eyebrow."

He was right. Max could hardly keep track of him as he passed in and out of the shadows on the stage.

"And I'll add that its stats aren't half bad either." Dalliance looked back at the audience over one shoulder as he pulled down the hood. "Plus, the hood will protect your head from taking a critical."

"I should have waited and bid on that, it would look amazing with your scarf and shoulder holsters, Max." Ginger looked like she might drool for a moment before collapsing against the balcony railing. "Stupid Yoink, grappling hook. Now I can't justify spending any more money."

"It's okay, I forgive you." Max rubbed her back as the bidding progressed. He groaned as soon as it finished, with Nix claiming victory. He would prefer the coat to have gone to anyone else. Not to mention it would make his job of catching her more difficult.

Ginger buried her face in her hands for a moment before raising her head again. "Take a note, Max."

"Okay."

"Remind me to steal that coat from Nix."

"Okay, I'll add that to the to do list." Max just hoped they would get the chance.

Ginger recovered from her depression just as Dalliance pulled an orange feather from the next box. It glowed with a flickering light that burned from within.

"Next up is the Quill of Rebirth." Dalliance fanned himself with it. "The Darkness gave this contract after a fight with the Nightmare Orpheus, the embodiment of regret. Its use is actually quite straight forward, in that you can use this quill to edit your journal's character page, allowing you to rebuild your avatar. Maybe you wish you had chosen a different race, or want to try a new class, or maybe you just want to have different color eyes. Well, you can do that all of that and more."

"What's the point of that?" Max furrowed his brow. "You can already change your class and start over at any time."

"I did that a year ago." Corvin stepped forward to look at the item. "Plus, the game lets you redesign your appearance once every two years to stay in line with your current age if you choose to. That's how I got taller."

"And you could just make a new character if you wanted to try a new race." Max continued.

"I know what you're all thinking." Dalliance held up one hand. "You're wondering what the point of this contract is if you can already do all that. Well, obviously it has an advantage." He blew the feather into the air to let it flutter back down. "That's right, with this little quill, you can do all that without restarting back at level one. Instead, it will keep your current level and allow you to redistribute any upgrade points that you may have used."

"Okay, that would do it." Max couldn't help but think of Kira. If she had a contract like that, she could change to a race that wasn't so frail. Then he shook his head. She would never use it. The little mage had always liked being a fairy.

"We'll start the bidding again at fifty thousand, since it

worked out well last time." Dalliance offered the quill up to the bidders. "Do I have fifty?"

Nearly everyone raised their hands, and why wouldn't they? The contract was essentially a full character respec. That would be useful for any house to have in their vault. The bidding went back and forth for a while but finally ended at just under one hundred eighty thousand. Seven stood proud in the balcony next to theirs, her house being one contract item richer. Max smiled; the low-level mage was starting to fit in with the rest of the auction's attendees.

The next item up for bids was a ring, nothing too fancy. It just allowed the user to stay underwater without needing to breathe. It would've been nice back during the fight with the Deep, but it wasn't really a necessity. It went for forty thousand to Dartmouth.

After that was a pendant hanging from a braided leather cord. Dalliance announced it as the Heart of Ember. It made its wearer immune to fire while simultaneously applying a massive flame attribute to any weapon held. It was actually pretty badass, but again, it wasn't a priority. Max was glad to see it go to Seven as well, who was gathering every contract she could for Leftwitch like a good employee.

Dalliance threw open the next box.

"That's it!" Max lurched forward as soon as he saw what was inside. "That must be what then note on their invitation was referring to."

"The Duelist's Manacles." Dalliance held up a long silver chain with a wicked-looking cuff dangling from each end. "From the Nightmare Monte Cristo, this contract is essentially a portable Thunderdome. Once it connects two players, the manacles won't open for one hour, or until one of them is dead, whichever comes first. During this hour, neither player may log out or teleport. If you demand satisfaction, this is the way to get it."

Dalliance swung the chain back and forth for a moment,

making a point to make eye contact with Max before opening the bidding.

"Can I get fifty?"

Ginger raised her tile before Max had time to say anything.

Nix did the same.

"I don't care how much we have to spend, we are leaving with that contract." Max practically growled his words.

Ginger bid again.

Nix followed suit.

"That contract must be a threat to her." Ginger raised her tile.

"Good, that confirms the theory that she can't overpower a contract."

"Can I get 200 thousand?" Dalliance skipped ahead, clearly noticing the level of interest in the contract.

"200." Lord Promethium from House Iron Forge joined in. Max shot him an annoyed glare.

"300." Nix called out with her tile held high.

"500!" Ginger didn't hold back.

Promethium lowered his hand, the bidding apparently becoming too rich for his house.

"Wow. That's a new high." Dalliance pulled the chain taught. "I can't say this was the item that I expected to go—"

"One million!" Nix cut him off mid-sentence as everyone in the room's jaws hit the floor.

"Two million!" Ginger answered her in kind.

The theater erupted in gasps and whispers. It was clear no one expected anything to go for more than a few hundred thousand. The room immediately went silent when Nix raised her hand.

"Four million."

Dalliance let out a sputter and nearly dropped the contract item. A bead of sweat rolled down Max's forehead as he realized that Nix might have more resources than he thought.

"We might not stand a chance."

"No, she's flexing." Ginger shook her head. "She's trying to intimidate us. Why else would she go up that much at once?"

Dalliance turned to look up at Lockheart's balcony for a response.

"I definitely regret buying that grappling hook now." Ginger whispered under her breath before raising her hand again. "Five million." Finally, her mouth curled up into a smug expression of casual defiance aimed at Nix.

Max's heart raced as everything came down to money. They still had a couple million more, but that was it. Then, Nix lowered her tile.

"You win." She threw her hands out to her sides. "Good luck catching me."

Max nearly collapsed to his knees, barely holding himself up on the railing. Ginger did the same, her chest heaving. He understood how she felt. Hell, he'd never been so stressed in his life.

From there on out, the bidding was uneventful. Nothing particularly dangerous came up, and most of the houses present took home one or two contracts each. With no contracts left to bid on, Dalliance closed out the auction.

"Thank you all so much for attending what we hope will be the first of many Auctions of Souls. Please give us a brief recess while we confirm everyone's account information. We will send out a ping to each of your bidding tiles when your contracts are ready to pick up." He took a final bow then turned to meet his twin Grindstone back on the floor.

Max leaned on the side of the balcony and wrapped his hand around the dagger sheathed at his side. It felt heavy.

"We're almost there."

"What about the PVP ban?" Ginger leaned beside him.

"I'm hoping a certain someone can help us out with that." Max let his gaze settle on Alistair. "After all, it is his game."

CHAPTER TWENTY-SEVEN

"That wasn't so bad." Alastair dropped into a chair to wait for a notification that he could pick up the contract he'd won. "Aside from that Star Burst arrow, there wasn't much to be afraid of."

"Yes," Jeff-with-a-three remained standing to survey the activity below. "It's almost as if you have been worried over nothing."

"Still—"

"Excuse me." Larkin entered through the curtain behind him without warning.

"Oh, hello, Larkin." Alistair hopped up from his seat. "How is the shop treating you? What was it called, Fashion Souls?"

"Yes, the shop has worked out quite well. In fact, that's why I'm here." Larkin looked Alastair up and down. "If you have any free time in the near future, I would like you to stop by if at all possible. I have some designs that would fit well with your rather unique persona."

"Oh, that would be excellent, I've been meaning to visit for quite some time." Alastair gestured to the crimson eyeliner he wore. "It's not exactly easy to find gear that matches this."

"Exactly." Larkin reached out and clasped Alastair's hand in both of his, to shake it tightly. "After all, you are the head of Checkpoint Systems, you must take your appearance seriously." Larkin's smile faded, leaving only serious frown as he gave Alastair's hand a final squeeze. "It is of the upmost importance."

"Yes, of course." Alastair pulled his hand away, feeling something in his palm, possibly a scrap of paper.

"Excellent, then I'll see you sometime this week." Larkin's smile returned as he slipped back out into the hall.

For a moment, Alastair motioned to look at whatever Larkin had passed him, but stopped just short. Something didn't add up.

Why would he go through the effort of being secretive when it was only myself and J3ff here? Alastair wondered before coming to the obvious conclusion, that whatever it was, was only meant for him. He shoved the paper into his pocket and unfolded it inside. It was about the size of a page torn from a standard player journal.

Alastair checked over his shoulder, finding J3ff preoccupied with his own journal. Seeing the coast was clear he slipped the page out and glanced down.

Alastair,
Not safe to talk in the open. Jeff-with-a-three is an enemy working for Nix. 90% sure about this. He's using the PVP ban to keep her safe. Shut it down. Counting on you.
-Max

Alastair's blood ran cold.
How… How could that be?
J3ff had been one of his first employees, back before Checkpoint's first investors, when the Somno system was still a mess of wires and data. How could Nix have flipped him? Or worse, what if he had worked for her from the beginning?

J3ff had never been friendly, but he was a professional who had proved himself time and time again.
I trusted him.

The thought sent a jolt of terror down Alastair's spine.

Oh no!

I trusted him!

J3ff knew everything. Had access to everything. If Max was right about him, then Alastair had allowed a breach in security larger than any he could fathom. Nix could have access to Checkpoint's entire system, and if Carver was working with her, then there was no limit to what they could do.

Alastair's hand shook. If Nix could infiltrate the top level of his company, then how many other operatives did she have within his walls? She could even be in Checkpoint's headquarters herself and he would never know. His stomach lurched.

He was currently sleeping in the building.

Alastair shook his head. No, Nix didn't have a reason to hurt him, especially if she had gone through the trouble of placing an operative so close to him. Harming him now would be counterproductive, as long as he didn't let on that he was suspicious.

Damn, who the hell was Nix? How could one person have done all this? More importantly, *why* did she do all this?

What did she even want?

Alastair took a deep breath, then swallowed down the fear that rolled through his gut, calling back some of his resolve. Max and Ginger were already handling the problem. Finding Nix in the real world was the priority, and they already had a way. They just needed his help, and by god, he was going to give it to them.

"I'm going for a walk on the deck." He hopped out of his chair as if nothing was wrong.

"Alright." J3ff continued to watch over the theater below. "I'll message you when the twins are ready to release our contract."

"You'll do no such thing." Alastair shoved his hands in his coat pockets. "We are aboard the Night Queen, one of Noctem's most impressive airships. You'll join me and take in the sights; I'll not have you holed up in here when there's something like this all around you." He gestured out to his sides. "Honestly, you help run an entire fantasy world, the least you can do is go on an occasional walk."

"Very well." J3ff sighed. At least he understood that arguing would get him nowhere.

"Perfect." Alastair made his way to the hall and held the balcony's curtain to one side to let J3ff pass through first. "Now get out."

The overly serious elf seemed to suppress an eye roll as he acquiesced. They walked in silence the entire way to the deck before Alastair finally found the right words.

"How did everything get so out of hand?"

"Pardon?"

"This whole thing with Nix and Lockheart." Alastair blew out a long sigh. "We have some kind of criminal running around in our game, abducting players and manipulating events. If you had told me that a game that I created would have this sort of problem, I might not have moved forward with it."

"Yes, you would have." J3ff countered without hesitation.

"I'm sorry?"

"You are ambitious and seldom let fear hold you back." The elf continued walking in front without looking back. "It's a big reason why Checkpoint has been as successful as it has been."

"I suppose so. Though, I'm not sure those traits are really virtuous."

"It's not about virtue." J3ff finally looked back. "The world doesn't need virtue. It needs progress. And that's what you do."

"Yes, but at what cost? Kira is likely dead. And if she isn't, could she even still be called human after what Nix did to her?" Alastair shuddered, remembering how she had spoken to him just before her disappearance, her voice coming from the tiny speaker of his smart watch in the real world. It had been as if there wasn't a device in existence that she couldn't access.

"I think it's best not to dwell on those we've lost." J3ff stopped by the ship's railing and stared off into the sky. "I realize how responsible you feel about what happened to Kira, but this system gives so much back to the world. Sometimes sacrifices have to be made to move forward."

"That's horrible." Alastair's throat tightened.

"That's progress." J3ff swept a hand out toward the stars. "Progress isn't always kind. The question is, what do you think Kira would want you to do?"

"She'd want us to stop Nix."

"Would she?" The elf lowered his head. "Kira never seemed the vindictive type."

"Yes, well," Alastair glowered at his assistant's back. "Either way, we have to do something about Nix. Not that we can do anything right now with the PVP ban of yours in the way."

"I would deactivate it if I could." J3ff offered nothing more than a shrug. "Unfortunately, I don't know my way around the GM system as well as you. I could only set it up as a permanent effect. I'll have to clear my system and reinstall everything to clear it off my character."

"What?" Alastair's eyes widened. "Did you set the ban up using your avatar as its center point?"

"Yes. I couldn't set it to a specific system coordinate since the ship would just fly away from it. Instead, I set it as a radius around my location.

"Why didn't you say so?" Alastair groaned. "Just log out so the effect goes away."

"I would, but I accidentally set it to latch onto the closest user if my connection is interrupted."

Alastair deflated, assuming that there was nothing accidental about it. Clearly J3ff just wanted to make sure Max couldn't go after Nix. If that wasn't confirmation that his assistant worked for her, he didn't know what was.

"That is problematic." Alastair glanced over the side of the ship at the world below, noting the lights of a village.

"Agreed. So, as you can see, we're stuck at the moment." The elf leaned on the railing. "We'll just have to find a way to deal with Nix without fighting her."

"Yes, about that." Alastair suppressed a wry smile that threatened to creep across his face. "There might a way to get around the ban."

"And what's that?"

"Oh, I think it's pretty obvious." A wave of smug satisfaction filled him from top to bottom as the overly serious elf froze. It was already too late. Alastair was already moving.

He dropped down to grab the elf's ankles before leaping back up and lifting his unsuspecting assistant's legs up to tip him over the rail.

"Sorry about this."

"Wait, what are you–" J3ff caught one hand on the side so that he fell against the ship's hull, his feet dangling over the ground below. "You can't…"

"Oh, I can." Alastair pried one of the elf's fingers free. "This is the only way, just try not to hit anyone down there when you land. That would be bad for our public image."

"Stop, I can find another–"

Alastair sucked his teeth. "Sorry, no time, bye now."

The elf's face was priceless, consumed by complete and utter shock as Alastair pried his last finger from the rail. He fell into the night, leaving Alastair alone. He didn't even scream.

With a bit of luck, J3ff would hit the ground close enough to another player so that the ban would latch onto someone in the village down below instead of anyone on the ship.

Alastair leaned on the railing and let out a maniacal laugh, indulging in the ridiculous video game villain persona he played. He settled down a minute later, letting out a depressed sigh and staring down at Noctem's surface below.

"So long… Jeff-with-a-three. See you at work tomorrow."

CHAPTER TWENTY-EIGHT

"Looks like Alastair came through." Ginger snapped her journal shut after reading a short message from Checkpoint's CEO. "He actually pushed J3ff off the ship."

"Wow." Max gave an approving nod.

"He did what?" Seven slipped into Lockheart's box from the hallway outside.

Echo brushed her hands together as if saying, problem solved.

"He does call himself Alastair Coldblood." Farnsworth shrugged, then pulled the balcony curtain closed so that they could talk without being seen. "I guess pushing your assistant from an aircraft is par for the course."

"Just as long as he didn't let on that we know where J3ff's loyalties lie. We might need to use him to deliver some misinformation." Ginger ran her finger down the blade of her dagger to check for herself the status of the ban. The split second of pain told her that it was gone. The system immediately dulled the sensation down to the familiar numbness that had become synonymous with damage. She noted the loss of a couple hit points on her status readout.

"Okay then." Kegan slipped his hands around the bow he wore slung across his shoulder.

"Now how do we catch Nix?" Corvin tightened his grip around the handle of his broken sword. "What's to stop her from running away now?"

"She won't." Max closed his eyes. "She thinks she's safe. Or at least she will until J3ff gets back online. I assume he won't message her directly, since that would be traceable. But I'm sure he has a way to let her know the ban is down. By my guess, we have fifteen minutes."

"We'll have to make our move when she goes to pick up that shadow coat she bought from the twins." Piper motioned toward the hall. "Kegan, Corvin, and I can wait at the theater's exits and slow her down so that you can get those duelist cuffs and catch up."

"Good thinking." Ginger gave her daughter a smile, a little impressed by what her children had brought to the table. Even Drake had helped out by following the Night Queen in the Cloudbreaker, just out of visual range. She still didn't want them getting too involved, but she couldn't deny how capable they were, and against Nix, they needed all the help they could get. "Why don't you three head out now and get in position? We'll get down there as soon as the twins are ready for us."

Piper nodded and slipped out of the room. Kegan and Corvin followed close behind.

"Is there anything I can do?" Seven stepped closer.

"Yes, actually." Max pointed in her direction. "You spoke to Nix earlier, right?"

"I did."

"Do it again. Stall her long enough for us to get our contract before she can get hers."

"I can handle that. Getting in the way is pretty much my specialty right now."

"Good." Max closed his eyes again and leaned against the wall. "Then the rest is up to me."

Ginger couldn't help but notice he was acting strange. He

had been ever since they fought the Deep, since he got that contract. It was like he was avoiding eye contact with everyone, especially her. She couldn't shake the feeling that he was hiding something.

"Max?" she asked quietly.

"Yeah?" He kept his eyes closed.

"Once we have Nix trapped, what comes next?"

"I use the contract I got from the Deep to get her talking."

Ginger placed a hand on his chest. "But how does it work? You've been… vague about it."

Finally, Max let out a sigh as his mouth curled down into a frown.

"It's called Vendetta."

He drew the small knife from the sheath on his belt. Its silver edge gleamed in the dim light of the theater box. Ginger caught herself holding her breath at the sight of it, like she could somehow sense how dangerous it was. Max flipped the knife over and pressed the tip into his thumb.

Seven clasped both hands over her mouth in shock as a bead of blood rose up to rest on his skin.

"That's what I was afraid of." Ginger lowered her head. "It causes real pain doesn't it?"

Max nodded, finally looking her in the eyes as his welled up. "It ignores the system's sensory input that dulls the sensation of pain when we get hurt."

"Oh my god." Seven stepped back until she ran into the wall. "You're going to torture her."

"Only if she doesn't tell me what I want to know."

"Why would Checkpoint put something like that in a game?" Seven shook her head.

"They didn't." Ginger's heart sank as she realized where the item came from. "The contract system is broken. The game doesn't generate contracts, it asks the user's subconscious what they want instead. That's why they're so powerful and unpredictable."

Echo stepped closer to Farn, as if trying to hide behind her. The look on the avatar's face said it all.

That knife shouldn't exist.

Ginger turned away from the man she'd wanted for the last few months. No, it had been longer than that. Maybe since they'd met.

"How could you?" Her tone wavered.

"How could I what?" His words came out sharp.

"Create something like that." Ginger struggled not to raise her voice. "How could you ask the system for something so cruel?"

"I can't control what my subconscious does." Max pushed off the wall. "It's not like I want to do this."

"Then don't." She fought back a tear. "We'll find another way. One that won't cost us our souls."

"There is no other way." Max swept away the possibility with one hand. "How else can we catch someone who has been ten moves ahead of us every step of the way?"

"That doesn't mean we should sink to her level." Ginger looked to Farn to back her up. "You can't be alright with this."

"I don't like any of this." The *Shield* dropped her eyes to the floor, standing silent for a heavy pause. "But I want Kira back."

Echo immediately pulled away from Farn, her face pained like she'd been slapped. The avatar shook her empty head, as if she didn't want to believe what she was hearing. Ginger understood full well what the fairy's actions meant, that none of them believed that Kira would be okay with the plan.

"But you said that Kira was your future. That she was everything you wanted." Ginger pleaded with the *Shield*. "What good is getting her back if you can't look her in the eye?"

"What good is being able to look Kira in the eye if we can't save her?"

With that, Echo stomped a bare foot on the carpet and stormed out of the room. Seven motioned to go after her.

"Let her go." Farn ignored the outburst. "She's not real."

Seven hesitated before chasing after the avatar anyway. She

probably just wanted a reason to get out of the room. Ginger couldn't blame her.

She flicked her eyes back to Max. "We aren't monsters. I know we act like we're this infamous house of ruthless fighters, but that's all it is, an act. We're just a bunch of players. Just people that are in over their heads."

"That's why I have to do this."

"But at what cost?"

"It doesn't matter what the cost is."

"It does if we lose you in the process." Ginger's throat ached with every word. "Why don't you see that?"

"Because it was my fault!" Max turned away, his eyes welling up.

"What was?"

A long moment passed by before he spoke again.

"I froze." His whole body deflated as he sunk back against the wall. "Back when Nix's goons stole Kira's body. I saw them, and I froze."

"You can't blame yourself for tha—"

"It was one minute." He rubbed at his forehead. "I called 911, then I waited for one minute before finally going next door. When I got there, they were already gone. Kira's body along with them." Max raised his head, giving Ginger a look at the pain in his eyes. "I told myself that I had to wait for help to arrive, but I know that was just me justifying the fact that I was scared."

"Of course you were scared." Ginger knelt down and placed a hand on his knee. "Anyone would be."

"But I'm not just anyone." He swallowed. "I've gone up against everything from Nightmares to arms dealers. I'm Max freaking Damage, and I did nothing while my best friend was stolen or worse."

"What would you have even done?" Ginger squeezed his leg.

"I don't know, they had guns, I could have gotten one away from them and—"

"And what, killed them both?"

"I don't know." Max lowered his head. "But that's why I have to do this. I can't let Nix win. And I can't afford to hold back." He looked up and met Ginger's eyes. "I can't just keep playing games. I have to grow up."

"Did you ever consider that some of us like who you are now? That I might not want to be with whatever you intend to become?"

"I..." His face went blank for a second. "Sometimes there is a price to pay. Kira paid it when she gave herself to the system. I have to be prepared to do the same."

"I understand how you feel. And I won't get in your way." Ginger lowered her head so he couldn't see the tears filling her eyes. "But I'm not going be with someone who hurts people to get what they want."

She stood up and walked toward the hall, looking back for only a second.

"I'll be downstairs waiting. There's still time to change your mind."

CHAPTER TWENTY-NINE

This game is insane! Seven stormed away from Lockheart's box.

Kidnapped players, artificial intelligences, federal agents, and super villains. She could handle finding out about all that.

But torture? That was just too much.

How was she supposed to go and interact with Nix knowing what Max intended to do to her? How could she become an accomplice to that? Nix may be a bad person who wouldn't think twice about hurting any of them, but still, torture was extreme. At least, too extreme for an accountant to have anything to do with.

To make matters worse, all the rulers of this insane game were at each other's throats. Not to mention her own house was morally gray at best, what with planting bombs aboard the ship and trying to blow the whole auction to hell.

"How's it going?"

Seven suppressed the urge to jump as the disembodied voice of Leftwitch reached across her house line. She was almost getting used to the interruptions.

"Everything's fine." Seven stopped in her tracks.

"Really? Because I couldn't help but notice that the Night Queen isn't laying in a pile of burning scrap right now."

"About that." Seven glanced back and forth. "Lockheart found the bomb and threw it off—"

"I see." There was a long pause that left Seven sweating. "You wouldn't happen to know about another low-level *Venom* mage that helped them fight my team, now would you?"

"That was me." Seven decided to go with honesty. There was less to keep track of that way. Besides, Leftwitch had almost certainly assumed it already.

"Was it now?"

"I realize how that looks, but I was following your orders."

"How so?"

"You instructed me to befriend Lockheart's members and gain their trust. I did that in the most efficient way possible. Besides that, my only other responsibility was to bid on some contracts at the auction, which I did. The bomb, as you said, had nothing to do with my presence here." Seven winced as Leftwitch said nothing for another few seconds.

Finally, the lady of her house let out a chuckle. "Well, efficiency is why I hired you. Were you able to find out anything about Lockheart's feud with this Nix character? That's what the world is wanting to know."

"She stole something from them. They want it back." Seven left her answer as vague as possible, not entirely sure where her loyalties were after discovering what Max intended to do.

"What did Nix take?"

"Something important enough to make their fight personal. I'll write up a report with everything I can find out after tonight."

"That would be very helpful. What about the auction? Were you able to obtain any of the more dangerous items?"

"There was only one up for bids that could be considered a threat. It was won by Alastair Coldblood. He seemed to be here for the same reason as us. To keep things out of the wrong hands. I bid on the contract as well but he didn't seem like he was going to let anyone else have it."

"I suppose that is to be expected." Leftwitch sounded disappointed. "What were you able to get beyond that, then?"

"I won two." Seven couldn't help but feel a little proud of her performance. "Both seemed like they would be helpful to our house. The first was a pendant that gives immunity to fire damage and adds a flame element to an equipped weapon."

"Oh, that does sound helpful. I could really use something like that in case I ever end up in a tight spot, adding a flame element to my whip is pretty strong, and would look pretty impressive."

"Yes." Seven nodded to herself. "The second contract is a little different, as it's a single use item that allows for a player to completely respec their character. They can change their race, appearance, and class, as well as redistribute their upgrade points."

"That's a great buy. With that I could respec our Archmage into one of the more powerful races like a fairy. As far as I know, Lockheart is the only house that has one at high level. They're too much of a pain to level, being so fragile. But I wouldn't mind having a glass cannon in my arsenal if they can skip over the grind to get there."

"I'm glad you approve."

"I more than approve." Leftwitch let out a victorious laugh. "You did a great job. I couldn't be happier."

"Thank you, my Lady." Seven bowed halfway before remembering her employer couldn't see her.

"Now you just have to pay and claim our prizes. Did you end up needing to use any of the hard that I sent you with?"

Seven slapped her hand to her item bag, feeling for the silver box that she'd almost forgotten about. *Thank god.* It was still there.

"No, I only spent two hundred ninety five thousand of the three hundred that you deposited in the account, so I shouldn't need to open the box you gave me."

"Excellent. Just return it to me when you get back to Lucem then."

"I will—"

Suddenly, the auction tile in Seven's pocket vibrated, signaling that the twins were ready to process her purchases and hand over the Silver Tongues' contracts. She nearly fumbled the piece of wood as she took it out from her robe.

Oh no!

I never stalled Nix.

Seven broke off into a run down the hall toward the stairs, realizing she had completely dropped the ball. She still wasn't sure if she even wanted to help Max, but she wasn't about to completely abandon her mission. At the very least she could maintain a good relationship with Ginger if she at least tried to help.

"I'll have to report back later, I just received a page to pick up our contracts."

"You should get going then."

"Already on my way."

"That's my assistant, always on top of things. I think you'll have a bright future here in Noctem."

"Thank you, and I'm glad to be of service." Seven lowered her house ring and sprinted down the stairs.

She held her head up high. The night hadn't gone according to plan and Lockheart hadn't turned out to be the allies she thought they were, but she was still a royal assistant. There would be a place for her in the Silver Tongues as long as she performed her duties. Leftwitch seemed to value her professionalism too. She might have tried to blow up the Night Queen, but at least her motive was altruistic. All she wanted was to keep dangerous contracts away from people that might use them for personal gain. There was something admirable in that.

Seven raced into the theater, nearly tripping over a broken chair on her way in, forgetting the destruction that had been wrought upon the room earlier. She stumbled forward, hopping on one foot into the arms of another player.

"Ompf," she heard herself utter as she looked up to find Nix holding her up.

"That was a close one there."

"What..." Seven's body locked up.

"Nice to see you too." Nix pushed her back to a stable position.

"What..." Seven repeated, sounding like a complete idiot.

"I take it from your intimidated expression that your new friends over in House Lockheart have told you some pretty scary things about me."

Unsure of what to say, Seven simply nodded.

"Don't worry, I'm not as bad as they must have made me out to be." Nix gave her a warm smile without a trace of hostility.

"Oh, okay." Seven got a grip on herself. "That makes sense. I'm sure there's two sides to every story."

"Exactly." Nix started walking toward a table that the twins had set up to take care of the transactions.

"So there may have been a misunderstanding between you and them?" Seven walked just behind her.

"Hmm." Nix stopped for a second, her fluffy ears twitching. "No, in this situation I definitely did all the things they think I did."

"What?" Seven stopped dead in her tracks.

"Well, I am a villain." The reynard laughed as if she had no shame whatsoever. "I'm not as bad as they make me out to be, sure, but I'm definitely still a bad guy by most people's standards." She hopped once and looked back. "But don't worry, Karen, I don't have any interest in you."

"What did you call me?" Seven's heart leaped into her throat at the sound of her real name.

"Please, Karen, I've had all night. That more than enough time to look into you." Nix shrugged. "I had to; you were an unknown variable. I couldn't just ignore you. That would be irresponsible."

Seven's feet simply stopped responding, leaving her standing stock still in the middle of the ruined theater.

"Oh, don't be like that." Nix hopped closer and took her hand. "I don't mean you any harm. It's like I said. I'm not that bad." She winked. "In fact, I could even help you out."

Seven's lip trembled as she allowed the reynard to drag her toward the twins' table.

"If you would be willing to fill me in on whatever Max has planned, I could be persuaded to help you out." Nix tilted her head to one side. "Maybe I could make sure that your husband's medical bills are covered. It was a broken hip, right? He's awfully young for something like that. A frisbee golf accident, huh?" She frowned. "If only people could be better educated of the dangers of frisbee golf-related injuries."

"You can't..." The room started to spin as Seven's breathing sped up.

"I can." Nix made an effort to help her stay standing. "Look, Max is not a complex man, so it's not hard to guess what he has up his sleeve. I just want to be sure. That's all I'm asking. In return, I can change your life. Imagine, no more money troubles. No need to bow down to Leftwitch for her table scraps."

"I..." Seven regained her composure, if only a little. "I don't know."

She wasn't lying. She really didn't know what to say. Nix was offering her salvation from the financial hell she had been trapped in for months. At the same time, the offer told Seven everything she needed to know about Nix. The woman was cunning and dangerous but, most of all, cruel. To dangle an offer like that in front of her, knowing the situation she was in, was heartless.

Max, on the other hand, might be just as bad. Maybe he wasn't always that way. She was sure he was good once, but losing his friend had twisted him into something else. No, Nix had shaped him into what he was by taking away someone he cared for.

It was an impossible choice. She owed Max nothing, but still, she felt for him as well as the rest of House Lockheart. They weren't evil, just damaged. Nix, on the other hand… was something else entirely.

"What will you do if I say no?" Seven's voice quivered as she spoke.

"Nothing." Nix sighed. "Like I said, I have no interest in you."

"Then I refuse." Seven answered without hesitation, surprising herself more than Nix who seemed to be expecting the response.

"You know…" The reynard stepped forward and handed Grindstone her auction tile. "All you people with your damn integrity really make it hard for a villain to get things done. But I guess I have to respect that."

Seven stood dumbfounded as Nix gave Grindstone approval for a final account transfer and claimed her Nightfall coat. The reynard draped the garment over one arm and gave Seven a somber smile.

"I like you, Karen. The world needs people like you as much as it does people like me." The reynard patted her on the arm and walked away as if parting ways with a friend. "Remember that."

Seven watched her throw her new coat on and blur into the shadows of a doorway just as Max entered through it. She passed right by him without him noticing.

Damn. So much for stalling her.

Seven wasn't sure if she should feel guilty. Maybe it was just as well that Max missed her. She absentmindedly handed her auction tile to Grindstone, watching Max stalk his way toward the table to claim his contract.

"I'm sorry, your account balance is short."

"Wait, what?" Seven's head snapped back to Grindstone.

"Your balance is a thousand shy." He placed both of her contracts on the table in front of her. "I can give you one of your contracts now, but not both. Although I would be happy to hold the other until you can get me the rest."

"That's impossible, I was told there was 300 thousand in the account." Seven shook off the encounter with Nix and planted a finger down at a ledger that he had laying open on the table.

"I'm not sure what to tell you, there's only 294 thousand in there now." Grindstone began to close his ledger.

"Wait, okay. I have extra funds for emergencies. Will you accept hard instead?" Seven dug the silver box out of her item bag, ignoring the red flags that went off in her head. The question of how Leftwitch could possibly be wrong about her account balance, or why she might have withdrawn the money faded into the background of her primary mission.

"There should be 20 thousand in hard in this box." Seven handed the item over to Grindstone. "Just dump it out."

"That's not a problem." The elf flipped open the lid without hesitation, tipping it upside down. Nothing came out. He flipped the box over and peered inside. "There doesn't seem to be anything inside…"

His words trailed off as his lips and hands began to tremble. He closed the box, only to have it snap back open, releasing a force that knocked him backward. Even Seven was pushed away as a plume of black smoke erupted from the box.

Seven fell back as a strange manifestation poured up to the ceiling and swirled above her. She looked down at the box it had come from, wondering just what Leftwitch had hidden inside it. She glanced up at catching a glimpse of something in the smoke for an instant. A shape, something otherworldly. A shape of something unknown.

Before she could stare at the cloud any longer, she felt a strange tingling run down the length of her forearm. She looked to her stat-sleeve as a health bar trailed down her skin.

Grindstone's stare traveled from his own arm, then to the box as it crumbled to dust. "Oh my god, that's why it's been missing. It's been trapped in that box." His eyes snapped back to Seven. "How could you have brought it here?"

"Brought what?" Seven struggled to understand what was happening.

"Brought that." He thrust one finger down to point at her stat-sleeve as a few words appeared just above the massive health bar.

Nightmare: The Void.

CHAPTER THIRTY

"What in the actual fuck is that?"

Max lowered his head as a plume of black smoke burst from Grindstone's table and swirled around the ceiling. Then he noticed the lengthy health bar that traveled down his arm.

"A Nightmare? Now?"

"Don't look at it!" Alastair shouted from somewhere behind Max. "It's the Void, it will target anyone who stares into it."

The rest of the room's occupants immediately averted their eyes as the lighting in the room dimmed. The dark cloud spread itself wide to fill the ceiling. Max dropped his gaze to the floor as flashes of light came from above, casting ghastly shadows across the theater. The simple fear of the unknown screamed at him, daring him look up.

"Just ignore it, the Void will give up and move on." Alastair crept up to Max's side, being careful not to look up.

"Where did it come from?" Max tightened his grip on the handles of his guns.

"Someone must have moved the Nightmare from its dungeon and brought it here."

"Could this night get any worse?" Max shook his head.

"Oh, I'd say it's about to." Alastair kept his eye on the floor. "The Void was designed to be fought by a party of six. Once the boss finds everyone out on the main deck…" Alastair shuddered. "I don't really want to think about what will happen then. And this is just phase one."

Almost as soon as he finished speaking, the lights in the room returned to normal. Max glanced up to catch the Void trailing off through the balcony curtains above.

"We need to barricade the doors." Alastair reached for a broken chair. "We can't let Noctem's rulers fall victim to the Void."

"Whatever. Right now, I'm getting my contract and finding Nix." Max headed toward Grindstone.

"Wait, don't you want to know how to fight this thing?" Alastair began to chase after him.

"Not my problem." He pushed his way through the crowd gathered around Grindstone's table and left Alastair behind to fend for himself. Making his way to the front of the crowd, Max ignored one conflict and walked right into another.

"You can't just keep my items." Seven instead, sounding like she was going to ask to speak to the manager at any moment.

"Excuse me, you just doomed this entire ship." Grindstone stabbed his finger down on his table into what looked like a pile of metallic dust.

"I don't even know what a Nightmare is. I can't help it if there was one hiding my belongings."

"Like I'm going to believe that." Grindstone flicked the pile of dust at her.

"Look, I need these contracts." Seven lowered her voice as if looking for sympathy. "Christ, this is my first night working for my house. If I come back empty-handed, I won't have a job."

"That's not my problem."

Max winced as Grindstone used the same words he had a moment earlier. He wondered if he had sounded like a jerk too.

It was easy enough to put together what had happened.

Seven's house must have used her to smuggle the Void aboard the ship to release if things didn't go their way. It made sense, considering they already tried to blow up the ship once tonight. Although, from what he could tell, Seven hadn't been in on the plan.

Max's heart went out to the woman. Her situation reminded him of his own, being manipulated and toyed with. Her house had been pulling her strings all night, just like Nix had pulled his for years. He shook off the thought. There wasn't time to be feeling sorry for her or himself. He had things to do.

"Give her the damn contracts and quit slowing down the line." Max shoved up beside Seven while cutting everyone else in the process.

"Absolutely not. She still owes one thousand." Grindstone simply folded his arms.

"That's nothing, just take it from my account." Max slammed his hand down on the table.

"But she has doomed this auction."

"Let me rephrase that." Max drew one of his pistols and aimed it at the elf. "Give her the shit she bought."

Seven's body went rigid, clearly unsure what to do.

"You wouldn't dare." Grindstone blanched and took a step back.

"Try me." Max gestured a small circle with the muzzle of his gun to imply that they should move things along. "And while you're at it, give me my shit too. There's no need to drag this out."

"Fine." The elf sneered with as much disdain as he could muster. "But I want you both gone."

"Sure, like I'm gonna hang around here anyway."

Grindstone grabbed Seven's two purchases, making a point to place them on the table in front of her as hard as he could. Afterward, he did the same with the Duelist's Manacles that Max had bought.

"Here is your... shit, as you put it." Grindstone's face suddenly shifted back to something more professional. "Thank you for choosing the Auction of Souls." He paused for effect before adding, "Now get out!"

Max grabbed the manacles from the table and coiled the twelve feet of chain that connected them around one arm. He had no idea how he was going to get one end around Nix's wrist. Hell, he had no idea how he was going to find her.

"Thank you for honoring our transaction. Sorry for any trouble that I may have caused." Seven gave a polite bow, before turning toward the nearest doorway.

Max did the same just as Grindstone called out to them.

"And consider the both of you banned from all future auctions."

Seven turned back, looking like she'd been punched in the gut. Max turned to say something rude, but stopped. Grindstone wasn't worth it. He shook his head and kept walking.

"Don't worry about him, he'll get over it." Max sped up his pace to leave Seven behind.

"Wait."

"What now?" Max looked back.

"Why did you help me just now?" A frown tugged at the corners of Seven's mouth, as if she suspected him of wanting something in return.

"You were taking too long, I had to speed things along."

"Oh." Seven began to turn away.

"I felt bad, okay?" Max blurted out the truth, surprising himself as much as her.

"You're not as cold as you pretend to be." Seven's face softened as she stepped closer.

Max looked away and shrugged.

"Nix picked up her coat right before you got here. She left through that door. If you go now, you might be able to catch up to her." Seven pointed to the other side of the theater.

"Thank you." Max let his attitude fall away and gave her an honest smile.

"You're welcome." Seven returned the gesture. "I hope you find your friend."

"Me too." He started for the door. "I hope you find your place in Noctem."

"Me too." She sighed as he left her behind.

Max let his resolve fall back into place as he snapped one cuff of the Duelist's Manacles around his wrist. He passed by Alastair, who was enlisting the help of anyone who would listen to aid him in sealing off the theater. Max didn't look back as they barricaded the doors behind him.

Screams bled through the lobby doors from the main deck. Apparently, the Void had already been busy.

Max kept walking.

"Don't you dare die on me, Nix… I'm on my way."

CHAPTER THIRTY-ONE

Where the hell are you, Echo? Farn looked both ways down the hallway. It didn't really matter what happened to the avatar, but still, it didn't sit well with her to leave her alone. Not with a Nightmare on the loose. Maybe it was the *Shield* class in her, urging her to protect others out of habit.

She glanced at the Void's health bar on her wrist, then back down the hall. Echo was nowhere to be found.

Who she did find, however, was Seven. The low-level mage was pacing in the hallway outside the theater.

"Why aren't you inside?" Farn jogged up to her.

"I got kicked out. Grindstone apparently doesn't like it if your house hides a Nightmare in your possessions."

"Oh, this was you then?" Farn gestured to the bar on her forearm.

"Sort of." The woman gave an awkward shrug just as a plume of black smoke flooded into the hallway behind her.

"Hit the deck!" Farn shoved her to the floor as the Nightmare surged down the hall toward them. Seven huddled close and screamed as it passed by overhead. Farn did her best to cover them with the Death Grip's energy barrier. Pins and needles lit up her shoulder as a tendril of smoke grazed her.

"I don't want to die!" Seven screamed.

Without any options, Farn screamed too. Then, to her surprise, the dark plume simply blew past them as if it had somewhere else to be. Farn raised her head just in time to see someone step into the hallway from the theater's lobby. It was Kashka, Winter Moon's Knight. She leveled her eyes on the shape and readied her claymore as the Nightmare raced toward her.

"Come on!" The burly woman called a challenge just before the smoke passed through her body like a ghost. Her face went blank in an instant, as if her soul had been ripped from her body. She only stood for a moment before collapsing to the floor.

"She never stood a chance." Farn released Seven from her protective hold as they both stared at the corpse of House Winter Moon's First Knight.

"Why would my house want that thing on the loose here?" Seven pushed herself up.

"I can't imagine they have good intentions." Farn got up as well. "You might want to get Leftwitch on the line and find out."

"I know, I was looking for a safe place to do that when you..." Seven suddenly trailed off, her eyes staring past Farn's shoulder.

"I'm not going to like what's behind me, am I?"

Seven raised a finger to point. "Aren't player corpses supposed to disappear after death?"

Farn turned to find Kashka's body still on the floor where it had fallen. It twitched. Then a hand slapped down on the floor to push itself up. Her eyes snapped open, each socket filled with an inky black orb. It was like staring into... a void.

"They say that when you look into the void, it looks back at you." Farn swallowed as black liquid poured from Kashka's eyes, spreading across her body until it was covered from head to toe with glossy wet ink.

"Oh!" Seven suddenly dropped her eyes to the floor. "Don't look at it. Alastair said it only targets you if you stare at it."

"So it would be bad if I've been making solid eye contact with Kashka since she got up?" Farn took a step back as the oily form hefted its claymore off the floor. "Never mind, don't answer that."

"Can you do your... Death Grip... thing?"

"Maybe." Farn stretched her clawed hand out toward Kashka. "Sorry 'bout this."

Nothing happened.

Farn let out a sigh.

"And apparently Kashka doesn't count as a player anymore." She dropped her gauntlet to her side in defeat.

Kashka's corpse started moving toward her, leaving slippery black footprints on the floor.

"On to option two then." Farn took a second to limber up.

"What's option two?" Seven continued to look away from the hulking form.

"We run." Farn immediately turned tail and bolted.

"Is there more to this plan?" Seven followed without skipping a beat.

"It's kind of a developing situation." Farn glanced back to see Kashka break into a sprint, spattering ink across the hall. "Of course she's a fast zombie, why wouldn't she be?"

"I am so going to have a talk with my boss." Seven picked up her pace.

"Yeah, probably do that now." Farn reached out and shoved the mage down a corridor that forked to the left.

"Whoa! Hey!" Seven stumbled across the carpet as Farn left her behind. Kashka blew past her as well, ignoring the mage all together.

Oh, thank god. Farn had hoped the void creature was targeting her and not Seven. Pushing her out of the way seemed like the only thing that made sense. At least that way one of them would be safe.

Now she could focus on what was important, that being not getting murdered by an enormous void woman.

Farn pressed down the hall, taking a turn back toward the theater lobby where Kashka had come from. Maybe she could make it out to the main deck from there, and find a way to lose the tail. On her way, she made some assumptions on what Void Kashka's stats might be. They were probably the same as when she was alive. If that was true, well, the math didn't look good.

The only thing that might level the playing field was the Death Grip's charge attack. Farn grimaced. She only had one life stored in it from when she'd killed Cassius earlier. Just one shot.

I'm going to have to make it count.

Farn took a hard left into the lobby, catching the wall with her claws to fling herself into the room. Kashka stayed close on her heels. Makeshift barricades sealed off the theater, ensuring that no one would be walking in on them.

Just you and me here. It's now or never.

Farn touched a fist into her chest plate to activate her Sure-Foot ability and fed Cassius's life to her gauntlet. The Death Grip's claws heated up until they glowed an angry red. As soon as they were full, she stopped dead and spun.

"Quit following me!" she growled as she planted her feet and shoved her armored fist into Kashka's chest.

The void creature acted fast, bringing up its claymore to block. The Death Grip didn't care. A crack of thunder ripped through the air with a blast of heat and wind that threw every-thing away from the epicenter. Queue lines made of velvet ropes and brass stands were launched across the lobby as the world seemed to slow.

Then it sped up.

The blast ripped the inky form's boots from the floor and threw it twenty feet into a concession counter. The thing crashed into the shelves of bottles, falling down behind the counter, leaving a smear of black fluid on the wall. Farn had only slid back a few inches thanks to her Sure-Foot buff keeping her glued to the floor. Still, even with that, she stood there heaving with her fist held out as the red glow faded from her claws. Shattered crystals trickled down around her from the chandeliers above.

"And stay dead." Farn panted in the sudden silence that filled the lobby.

A quiet moment went by. Then a hand reached from behind the counter to slap down onto its surface.

"You have to be kidding me." Farn didn't even wait for Kashka to climb up before making a break for the ship's deck. She stopped short as soon as she made it outside.

The Night Queen was under siege.

Plumes of smoke trailed across the deck, claiming the lives of any passenger unable to avert their eyes. All who fell simply got back up, pouring black fluid from their eyes as they set out to systematically murder whoever looked at them. Whatever type of boss fight the Void was supposed to be, it had a devastating first wave. The fact that it had been triggered aboard a heavily-populated airship seemed to ramp up the impact. If it only involved a single party, things wouldn't have been so bad. Now though, the numbers were off the charts.

All across the deck Farn witnessed players running for their lives. Most of them only there to enjoy a relaxing night cruise. They probably didn't even know what was happening, having been thrown into a boss fight without warning. From the look of the chaos, most lacked skills for a high-level encounter, let alone a Nightmare.

To her left, a pair of low-level mages ran by, one of them swiping at their spell craft menu. Farn winced as they repeatedly tried to set up a teleport spell to escape the chaos. If a Nightmare was here, then that would mean that the whole map would be designated a battleground. Fast travel was probably off the table.

"Hurry up!" shouted one of the players.

"I am, but my glyphs are grayed out!" cried the other.

That answers that, Farn nodded to herself.

"What about Flight?" One mage motioned toward the ship's side. "We can jump and try for the ground."

"That's grayed out too!" The other mage frantically swiped at the air as a plume of smoke snaked toward them. Farn dashed for the pair, shoving them out of the way just in time.

"Someone triggered a Nightmare." She scanned the deck for threats. "Your escape spells won't work. The only way out now is a transport ship."

"You're... you're the Death Grip!" One of the players started to panic as they stared at her clawed hand.

"Maybe we should just let ourselves die," the other player whimpered.

Their words cut through Farn's heart, reminding her of the time she had let herself die to save Kira and Max back when they had first met. The little fairy had hated it and attempted to give her the silent treatment for giving up so easily. Farn wasn't about to let her down again.

"Now isn't the time to give up." She grabbed them both by the shirt. Their faces lit up as if she was their savior.

I wasn't that inspiring, was I? Farn questioned as she realized they weren't even looking at her. Spinning around, uncertainty filled her mind as a transport ship flew in to land on the Night Queen's platform.

"We're saved." One of the players pushed past her. "We might be able to make it."

Maybe. The platform was perched atop the front of the ship, standing several floors above the main deck as the bow of the ship curved up. If they ran for the stairs, they might be able to make it, but that raised the question, was the ship even there to help?

A number of surviving players that were closer to the craft seemed to have the same idea, rushing up the stairs toward safety. The two mages that she'd rescued started running as well.

"Wait!" Farn reached out to them. "There's no way that ship can hold everyone."

Almost as soon as the words left her mouth, Cassius appeared at the edge of the landing platform. He lunged into the air and slammed his spear down, sending a half dozen players flying off the edge. They fell all the way down to the main deck with awful crunches.

Note to self, Cassius is not here to help.

The two mages stopped short, immediately turning back to Farn as if they had lost all hope. She wasn't sure what to say; it wasn't like she could actually help them. To make matters worse, that was when Kashka stumbled out from the theater's lobby. The creature's claymore was missing, probably still somewhere behind the concessions counter, but that didn't stop its black eyes from locking on Farn.

"Head into the theater." Farn pointed to the doors behind the void creature. "That thing is after me, just sneak by and get inside. Nearly every ruler in Noctem is barricaded in there. If anywhere on the ship is going to be well protected, it's going to be there. Just be ready to help protect them."

One of the mages started moving while the other took a step toward Farn.

"Thank you."

"You're welcome." She gave them a nod and gestured for them to leave. Then she brought her attention to Kashka. "Okay, I don't seem to have a choice here, so let's do this."

Farn pushed off into a run, letting out her most ferocious roar as she rushed the abomination. Void Kashka responded in kind, arms outstretched to grab her. Farn met her, ducking low at the last second and slashing at the threat's flank. She ducked past and made a break for it, hoping that she could lose the stalker if she could make it around the theater.

A plume of smoke blocked her path, rushing toward her between the outer wall of the theater and the ship's railing.

"Crap!" Farn dropped to her knees and tried to slide underneath the cloud of death. Ducking her head, she evaded by mere inches, only to have Kashka catch up while she was distracted.

A wet, meaty hand clamped down around the back of her neck and tore her off the deck. She swiped her sword behind her, feeling it catch something as it was suddenly ripped from her grip. She heard it clatter to the deck a second later. She had swung it right into the creature's waiting hand.

Farn tried to kick herself free but was tossed from one hand to the other and slammed into the outer wall of the theater. Her feet dangled off the ground as Kashka tightened her hand around Farn's throat, smearing oily fluid on her skin.

She kicked her captor in the stomach but got no reaction, doing no more than chip damage. Farn struggled to breathe but couldn't get any air with Kashka's hand closed around her windpipe. She wasn't actually taking damage, but that didn't matter. If she wasn't able to take in a breath in the next couple minutes, the system would register her as suffocating and claim twenty percent of her health every ten seconds. Death would take her either way.

Out of desperation, Farn scanned the deck for an unfortunate soul that might be within range of her Death Grip. If she could charge another attack, she could at least blast herself free. She immediately hated herself for even thinking it.

What kind of monster have I become? I'm a Knight for crying out loud! Murdering innocent bystanders shouldn't be my first reaction.

That was when she remembered something important.

I am a Knight, damn it! I need to start thinking like one.

She glanced at her stat-sleeve, catching the flashing icon of her Sure-Foot buff. It was running out of time, but still active. She pulled her knees up and placed her boots flat against the wall she was held against. Gravity shifted around her body, reorienting itself to give her solid footing against the wall. Farn pushed against Kasha, getting her legs under her in a stable crouch. With the last bit of air in her virtual lungs, she choked out one final threat.

"Let's... see if... you can fly."

Then she kicked off the wall with all of her strength. Slamming her shoulder into Kashka's chest, she launched them both into the railing just a few feet away. The creature hit the barrier and tipped backward, fumbling its grip on Farn's neck.

"Ha!" Farn caught the rail with her claws and held on for dear life as they both went over the side. The night sky spun around her as she swung down and hit the hull of the ship. She looked down as the stars cleared from her vision. "Have a nice fall—oh crap, no!"

Her final taunt was ruined when Kashka's meaty fingers clamped around her ankle, the hulking abomination putting all of its weight on Farn's grip. She threw her other hand up to grab the rail, clinging to a desperate hope that she might find the strength to pull herself up.

Her mind flashed back to her first night fighting alongside Kira and the others, back to when she'd learned of a hidden stat that all players had.

Willpower.

It was the amount of influence that a user's mind could impose upon the system. On rare occasions, it could even defy the limits of the game.

Farn pushed all her belief she had in herself into her chest and held it, forging her will into a single point of light to sustain her. Then she climbed. Her clawed hand pulled her body up the side of the ship, bringing her chin to the rail's edge just enough to see back onto the deck. Then she realized that the idea of her overpowering the system was ridiculous.

Who did she think she was?

She wasn't Kira, who had sacrificed herself to save the world.

She wasn't even Max, who had gone toe to toe with Nix.

No, she was just Farn, a woman who had lost the first person she'd loved in years. The best her willpower could do was keep her chin above the railing, and even with that, she was slipping.

Oh well, I tried.

Then her heart skipped a beat as a familiar avatar ran across the deck with their arms flailing in the air, mouth open in a silent scream.

Echo was right in front of her.

"Hey!" Farn coughed out over the railing as she struggled to hold on.

Echo skidded to a stop and dropped her arms to her sides as if the flailing had just been for comedic effect. She pointed to herself, and mouthed the word, "Me?"

"Of course you." Farn beckoned the fairy with her eyes. "Come help me."

The fairy hesitated a moment as if still scared of Farn for her willingness to torture. A second later she shook her head and materialized her wings to dart to Farn's aid. Grabbing her wrist, Echo pulled as hard as her pixie hands could... which was pretty much useless.

"No, no, Echo, stop that." Farn blinked twice at the attempt. "You're not strong enough to pull me up."

Echo immediately held up one finger as if she had a brilliant idea in her empty little head. She spun around and hopped backward, planting her rear down on the railing beside Farn's claws. The fairy materialized her wings and fluttered like her life depended on it.

A shower of shining pixie dust poured straight into Farn's face.

"Ack, hey, stop that."

It wasn't that the feeling was unpleasant, but it wasn't helping and the dust made her nostrils tingle every time she breathed. Of course, speaking only made it worse as it just got in her mouth too. A fizzy sensation danced across her tongue along with a taste like honey. Echo stopped and peeked back over her shoulder.

"Sorry," Farn closed her eyes. "The Void has a block on flight magic, you're not going to help me that way."

The fairy hopped off the railing. "I have to poo!"

"Have to poo?" Farn repeated, realizing that she had obviously not read the avatar's lips correctly.

Echo, confirmed this by shaking her head and trying again. "I love you!"

Farn felt her face flush, not sure why the system had chosen a response like that for the fairy.

"Okay, I know you think you love me but—"

Echo stomped one foot and shook her head. "What can I do? What can I do? What can I do?" She finished with her fists balled up and panting from the outburst.

"Oh, what can you do?" Farn would have laughed if the situation hadn't already been so grim.

Echo nodded her head in an exaggerated manner. "Yes. Finally. What can I do?"

Farn thought for a moment, before responding. "Nothing, there's nothing you can do, but you can get help. I'll try to hang on, just find someone and bring them back."

Echo nodded and started running, only to stop and spin back around. She glanced both ways for an instant, then out of nowhere, pushed a silver lock of hair out of her face and lowered her lips to Farn's.

For a moment, Farn panicked. The kiss wasn't real and Echo wasn't really the person she loved. Despite that, her body responded on instinct, and the need Farn had been struggling to ignore took over. The fairy's mouth was soft and warm, like Farn had imagined in a thousand different fantasies. She was gentle and passionate at once. Farn wanted so bad for it to be real.

Echo pulled away, avoiding eye contact. "Just in case."

Without another word, she materialized her wings and darted off into the chaos off the ship's deck.

Farn closed her eyes, trying to forget how real the kiss had been, and how much she needed it to be. It was overwhelming. She knew it was only the system trying to animate Kira's avatar using her memories to make her as realistic as possible. She knew Echo wasn't really Kira, but still, she felt like she was.

Farn could still taste the pixie dust on her tongue. She shook her head. There was no replacing her. Echo wasn't real.

Stupid game system. Why is it so cruel?

She closed her eyes as her arm began shaking. The kiss had actually made her forget she was one slip away from death. Farn hadn't even felt the dead weight that still clung to her ankle. It was as if her will had overruled the system to give her that one moment of imagined happiness.

In reality, she had passed her limit long ago. Her strength left her all at once and her chin slipped past the rail as she began to lose her grip.

"I guess… this is as far as I go."

That was when a familiar voice came from just above her.

"Jeez, Farn, don't give up that easily."

Farn's arm stopped shaking the instant the cruel yet casual tone met her ears. Then the rage set in.

"I'll kill you!"

"Is that any way to talk to an old friend?" Nix slowly peeked her head over the rail. "Would it help if I said I was sorry?"

Farn didn't answer, instead she tightened her grip on the rail with one hand and thrust out her claws toward her enemy's face.

"What are you going to do with that?" Nix placed an elbow down on the railing and sunk her chin into her hand.

"I could drain you," Farn growled her words, "slow."

"You could, but you won't." The reynard's ears twitched. "I'm pretty sure you want me alive. Can't trap me if I'm dead. To be honest, I was considering throwing myself off the ship to get away."

"Then why don't you?" Farn stretched her claws almost close enough to scratch her face.

"I still have work do here." Her Cheshire grin faded into something more somber.

"Enough!" Farn couldn't stop her eyes from welling up. "Just give her back."

All Nix did was let out a sigh, as if there wasn't a Kira left to return. The thought was too much for Farn to bear, and just like that, her hand slipped. She closed her eyes as she fell, not wanting Nix to be the last thing she saw.

That was when someone caught her wrist.

"Shit! No." Nix threw half her body over the side holding onto the rail with one hand while she struggled to stop Farn from falling. "Are you crazy?"

Farn reached out on reflex, digging her claws into the reynard's flesh. Nix winced as crimson puncture marks lit up her skin.

"Hold on, damn it." Nix's eyes widened with panic. "This isn't how the night ends."

"And how does it end?" Farn shouted as her hand slipped, shredding through the woman's wrist.

"It doesn't matter." Nix let out a grunt of exertion. "Just grab onto the stupid railing." Farn reached out and sank her claws into the wood. Nix pulled her hand back as soon as Farn was stable. "Look, I'd pull you up, but that would probably be hazardous to my health. However, that doesn't mean I will just let you fall."

"Why?" Farn locked eyes with the woman.

"Because I don't want to." Nix looked away just before pulling her pistol and putting a round into the forehead of Kashka's ink-covered face below. It felt like ten tons had been cut away from her Farn's foot as the dead weight clinging to her vanished into the night. She struggled to pull herself up with both arms shaking.

"You can do it." Nix turned away from the rail, disappearing from view. "Just don't give up."

Confusion engulfed Farn's mind as she frantically pulled herself up. She couldn't lose her grip now. She was so close. A hand reached out to help as Ginger's face came into view.

"Easy, now, I got you." She pulled with everything she had to drag Farn's armored body over the railing to safety. Finally, she collapsed to her hands and knees on solid ground.

Echo stood behind Ginger, gesturing to the help she'd

brought like a magician finishing a trick. The fairy looked away as Farn made eye contact, her face burning red. Apparently, the system wasn't over the kiss yet either.

"What were you doing hanging over the side?" Ginger helped her to her feet. "There's void monsters everywhere, you know?"

"Yeah, I figured that part out." Farn glowered at her before letting a smile take over. "I had one hanging from my foot up until a moment ago."

"Oh, I'm glad you were able to kick it free then."

"I wasn't." Farn shook her head. "Nix shot it."

"You saw Nix?" Ginger's body went rigid.

"I think…" Fan stopped to go over what had just happened in her mind. "I think she saved me."

"That doesn't make sense." Ginger stepped closer. "Why would she do that?"

Farn just stared off in the direction that Nix had gone.

"I don't know."

CHAPTER THIRTY-TWO

"Please don't eat me, please don't eat me." Seven stumbled across the carpet after being pushed by Farn. Her first thought was that the Lockheart's Death Knight had shoved her as a way of slowing down the void monster. That way she could get away while it was busy killing her.

Seven turned around, finding the hall empty. There was no sign of either of them. Kashka must have been targeting Farn all along.

"Did Farnsworth just protect me?"

The thought threw her for a loop. The only members of Lockheart that she felt comfortable with were Kegan and the rest of the JV-team. As far as Max and Farn were concerned, she was still a little wary. Now, though, she was starting to reshape her opinion of them. They had both helped her in the span of fifteen minutes.

"Could they really be the good guys?"

That was when her thoughts traveled back to her house and the Nightmare that Leftwitch had unleashed upon the ship.

"Maybe I should worry about myself first."

She started off toward the lower deck to avoid the fighting

that was sure to follow Void's appearance. As she walked, she raised her house ring.

"What just happened?"

Leftwitch responded immediately, like she'd be sitting there waiting.

"You opened the box, huh?"

"Yes, I opened the box. The account balance changed, so I was short." Seven wasn't sure what had gone wrong.

That was when Leftwitch started laughing.

Her outburst went on uncomfortably long, tinged by an arrogance that made Seven's skin crawl. It felt like the woman was laughing at her. Eventually her employer settled down.

"Finally." A few last chuckles trailed off. "Finally. I can't even explain how glad I was that you mentioned the amount of money you spent. I was able to pull some of the funds out of the account to make sure you'd open the box."

"You wanted this to happen?"

"Of course, I didn't have Cassius race all over Noctem to find and capture that Nightmare for nothing. I even blew a contract to do it."

"But I just got banned from all future auctions for bringing that thing on board."

"Oh." Leftwitch paused. "I guess that makes sense."

"No, it doesn't. None of this makes sense." Seven fought back the urge to raise her voice. "Grindstone said that I've doomed this whole ship. Why would you want that?"

"Look, Seven," Leftwitch sighed. "Obviously I haven't been completely honest with you."

"That's an understatement."

"But what's important is that you have carried out your role perfectly. Without you, the auction would have simply ended and everyone would have gone their separate ways. I couldn't let that happen."

"So, what? I was just some kind of Trojan horse?"

Leftwitch laughed. "That's a great way to put it."

"But what happened to trying to keep the peace? Isn't that why you wanted me to purchase contracts?"

"Hmmm. Yes and no." Leftwitch sounded smug. "I just wanted to get some contracts for myself and keep them from being used against me."

"And you got that, so why release a Nightmare on the ship?"

"Same reason I planted a bomb. To kill all of Noctem's rulers."

"So it was all about world domination then?"

"Oh god no." Leftwitch scoffed. "I have enough work to do running Lucem, the last thing I want is another city to deal with."

"Then why bother?"

"Simple. Viewers."

"I don't…" Seven's mind hit a wall, not understanding what killing Noctem's leaders had to do with Leftwitch's night show.

"Look, Seven, you're an accountant. You of all people should understand how much money the Late Nite show makes off ad revenue and sponsors. I just need a way to increase viewership."

"So everything tonight has been about money?"

"What else?" Leftwitch spoke as if it should have been obvious. "Back when the House of Serpents fell six months ago, the resulting power vacuum threw half of Noctem into chaos. No one knew what was going to happen, and they needed someone to tell them. My online views went up by the millions for months. Just imagine what would happen if all of Noctem's rulers were killed at once."

"It would be a free for all." Seven's voice came out as a whisper.

"Exactly." Leftwitch sounded undeniably proud of the situation she'd created.

"That's horrible." Seven made her way towards the lift where Corvin had fought a few of her housemates earlier.

"Is it though? This is all just a game. Whatever happens in here doesn't really matter."

If it had been a few hours earlier, Seven would have agreed, but now, the statement made her heart ache. Lockheart was fighting to stop whatever Nix was up to, the F.B.I. was running operations in Noctem, and an innocent player was missing. There was so much more going on in the virtual world than she'd ever imagined.

It all mattered.

Seven hesitated, wondering if any of Noctem's secrets had anything to do with her. She still had a mortgage and debts to pay. Did she even have the option to care about what happened?

Seven balled up her fist, hating herself for being so blind to her own employer's actions.

She wanted to care about everything.

"Why didn't you at least tell me any of this?"

"Would you have been able to go through with it without giving yourself away?" Leftwitch asked matter of factly.

Seven didn't answer.

"That's what I thought. And that's what made you so important. Why did you think I hired someone with no experience in Noctem? I needed a player that could get this done without realizing what they were doing. I needed someone oblivious to Noctem's ways, because the best cover is one that you believe is true."

"You used me." Seven's blood began to boil.

"You're an employee. I gave you an assignment. It may have been unorthodox, but you will be paid well for your time. I'm sorry that you feel used, but this is business and if you don't like it, you can always quit."

Seven closed her eyes and released a sigh. She knew what that meant. Leftwitch was putting her in her place and reminding her that she didn't have a choice. What made it worse was that Leftwitch was right.

A wave of exhaustion swept over Seven's body, like a part of her had died inside. No, it wasn't just dying, she was killing it. She slammed her fist into buttons on the inside of the lift shaft, snuffing out the ember that had been flickering inside her all night. Then, finally, she dropped her fist to her side and turned her back on Noctem.

"So what do I do now?"

"Nothing." Leftwitch sounded pleased with herself. "You've accomplished everything I sent you there to do. All that's left is to come home."

"How?" Seven couldn't help but frown. "I'm currently trapped on a doomed airship thanks to the Nightmare we set loose."

"I think Van Halen said it best." Leftwitch paused for effect. "Might as well jump."

"Jump?"

"Yes."

"But I'll die."

"Oh, definitely."

"But—"

"Oh, don't be a baby. You're going to get killed by something on that ship. Might as well go out on your own terms. You'll just respawn back here in Lucem. You can give me the contracts that you're carrying and enjoy a nice bonus for a job well done."

Seven staggered as she made her way to the lower deck of the ship. The sound of people fighting for their lives drifted down to her. She pushed it out of her mind and resigned herself to her fate.

"Okay, I'll meet you in Lucem as soon as I can."

"Good, I'll see you then." Leftwitch went silent, like she had gotten what she wanted and didn't have time to continue holding her hand.

Seven pushed herself forward, dragging her feet. The sounds above made her want to cry. She felt ashamed for the part she'd played so far, as well as for what she was about to do.

Holding up her hands to the sides of her head, she blotted out the sounds of combat. Then she took a deep breath and kept walking, trying her best to ignore the voice inside her screaming for her to stop. None of it was her problem, she was just doing her job, and that job would take care of her from now on.

That was all that mattered.

Seven reached the side of the ship. There wasn't much point in stalling. She was just a pawn, and her time was up.

She let out one last defeated sigh, then climbed up onto the rail.

CHAPTER THIRTY-THREE

Max stepped out onto the deck of the Night Queen, one pistol held at his side while a coil of silver chain dangled from his other hand. He closed his eyes and took in a breath, drinking in the madness of the fighting that surrounded him. The sounds of battle engulfed him as he opened his eyes and focused on his singular goal: Nix.

Where are you?

He stalked forward into the chaos, scanning the deck for his target. Making a point to keep his eyes moving, he never lingered on any point for longer than a second. The void creatures that littered the deck seemed to ignore him for the moment, too busy slaughtering the rest of the players on the deck.

A mage beside him died as two ink-covered corpses fell upon them with daggers in their hands, each dripping with black fluid. The mage pleaded for help as Max passed by. He ignored them, not wanting to waste the time or ammunition to come to their aid.

It was all just a game. It wasn't like they were really dying. The mage's calls for help were cut off with a sudden croak.

Players across the deck met the same fate one after another while they ran for cover. As they fell, more victims came running up from the lower levels in search of a way off the ship. The result kept the battle flowing in a continuous wave of death. Max just hoped that Nix hadn't been caught in its wake.

That was when he saw it, a dark blur passing in and out of the shadows, running up the stairs toward the ship's landing pad where a transport had set down a moment before.

Oh no you don't.

Max took off at a sprint, weaving through the deck, even shoving players out of the way. He hit the stairs to the landing pad in record time. The blur was almost at the top. He had to slow her down.

"Nix!" he shouted at the top of his lungs as he took aim at where he thought her legs would be. The shadow turned, and for an instant, a pair of eyes and furry ears came into view.

He squeezed the trigger and a muzzle flash lit up the deck, reflecting in a dozen glossy, black eyes. A spurt of crimson light flew from the shadow's lower half.

"Gotcha!" Max raced up the stairs as Nix stumbled into view near one of the Night Queen's many hanging lanterns. She spun around as she fell and pulled her gun to return fire. A three round burst poured down the stairs. The railing beside Max exploded into wooden fragments. He ducked to the side for an instant before throwing himself up the stairs in pursuit.

"Where do you think you're going?" Max reached the level she was on.

"Away from you, for starters!" Nix shouted back, limping for a moment before the damage to her leg faded away. He leveled his gun at her head, getting a smirk from her in return. "Haven't we been through this already tonight? You can't shoot me."

"I don't intend to." Max stepped closer dangling the silver chain and manacle from his wrist. Nix blanched, her eyes flicking to the contract item in his hand then back to his face.

"Hold on a sec. We can talk about this, can't we?" She

shoved her pistol behind her back like she hadn't just shot at him a moment before.

Max didn't stop.

"I thought not." She nodded to herself before shooting him in the leg right where he'd hit her. "Fair's fair." She waved and jumped up to grab one of the ropes that held the canopy of lanterns that stretched across the deck. She fired several rounds, hitting the connecting points with precision to send many of the lanterns crashing to the deck as she swung down on a loose rope.

"Damn it!" Max limped after her.

She hadn't been heading for the landing pad to escape. No, she was trying to take out some of the ship's lighting to make it easier to move around in the shadows. Nix laughed the whole way down to the deck where she plowed into a group of void creatures. They swarmed around her.

Damn it, she must have made eye contact with some of them.

Acting fast, Max threw one end of the chain he carried over the only rope remaining and leaped off the stairway. He took aim as he slid down, executing two enemies before he dropped to the deck and rolled to a stop.

"Hey there." Nix was right there waiting with her gun drawn. The weapon barked, sounding like an explosion at close range.

A streak of pain tore through Max's cheek as a burst of smoke and flame lit up his vision. Silence took over, filling his ears as a subtle ringing that grew to a defining whine. Max fell to his side and placed one hand against his cheek, glancing at his health.

Only five percent down?

Had he dodged somehow? He thought about activating his *Reaper* sub-class but shook his head. The defense that it provided only worked at range. It would be useless up close where he needed to be.

Nix adjusted her aim, ignoring three players, dripping with darkness, that closed in behind her. She fired again, blowing a hole on the deck beside Max's head as he rolled. The scent of gunpowder and sawdust filled the air.

Max pushed up to one knee and took aim at Nix. She winced in anticipation, still wearing the smirk that reminded him that he couldn't pull the trigger. His jaw tightened. He had to do something.

Shit!

Max retargeted and put a round in one of the void creatures behind her. Nix fired back, the bullet slamming into his arm and knocking him over.

Down thirty percent heath.

He hit the deck with a grunt and rolled to get her back in his sights. That was when a black form grabbed her by the hair and pulled her head back. A second brought a blade to her throat, ready to end her.

Max responded in an instant, firing two rounds. Crimson light exploded from the possessed players' eyes. That was when Max noticed something unsettling.

Nix's smile never faded.

Even when surrounded by enemies with a knife at her throat, her confidence was unshakable. She wasn't even trying to fight back. It was as if she didn't care, or she knew he wouldn't let her die.

Nix glanced up, making eye contact with another few players on purpose, to pull their aggro her way. Then she gestured to Max as if to say, "Get on with it."

His eyes widened as he realized she was using the enemies as distractions. Max needed to stay close. He needed to get his contract locked around her wrist. She put another bullet in the deck beside him, forcing him back.

There was no way to reach her, not with the constant need to protect her distracting him from trapping her. Not while she could focus all of her attention on him.

"Quit using yourself as a hostage, damn it!" He placed his gun against the temple of one of the players lumbering toward her and fired, blowing the darkness from their skull.

"What can I say?" She shrugged as if trying to be as annoying as possible. "I trust you."

Max pulled his scarf up over his mouth to activate his subclass. He held his breath and the spectral swords of death blurred into the air around him as the emblem on his hand shifted from the *Fury's* icon to the *Reaper's* coffin.

His health began to tick down every three seconds.

- 30 HP

- 30 HP

Nix fired a round in his direction, only to have it deflected by a translucent blade.

"If you're not going to let me get close, I'll fight you at range." Max swung one end of the Duelist's Manacles in a circle. "You'll slip up eventually."

"Oh really? How long can you keep that sub-class active?" Nix weaved between the dark forms that used to be players. "Think you'll have enough time?" She pulled up her hood and stepped back into a shadow, vanishing into the darkness.

Max darted for the stairs and climbed two levels to get a better view of the deck. Nix couldn't have gone far. He just had to think like her. With his *Reaper* class active, she couldn't touch him at range. Unfortunately, that helped her just as much as it did him. They were in the same boat, both unable to win without closing the gap.

They were at a standoff.

Or were they...?

Max immediately raised his house ring.

"Okay, I know not everyone is on board with this, but Nix is on the main deck and I need help."

Silence answered back.

"Damn." His heart sank. "I guess Ginger was serious about not helping." That probably meant that she was serious about not staying with him too. He had been hoping she might forgive him, but it was pretty clear that their relationship had ended before it even had a chance. A pang of guilt echoed through his chest as he slammed a fist into the side of the stairway.

Nix had ruined everything.

That was when Farn's voice reached him over the line.

"I heard the gunshots, I'm already on my way."

Max placed a hand over his chest, grateful that he still had a friend that understood what they had to do. That was when a strange pop came from one side of the deck. His heart skipped a beat as Ginger emerged from the fighting. Max ducked to the side just as a grappling line flew past his head.

What the hell is she shooting at? For a second he thought it might have been him. Then she raised her house ring to her mouth and spoke a single word.

"Yoink."

Max spun around to see the claw-like joints of Ginger's new thief tool as it held onto a shadow behind him. Suddenly the grappling line retracted, pulling the hood of Nix's coat down, leaving her standing stunned only three feet away.

"Oh, fu..." Her voice trailed off as she raised her gun in defense.

"Too late!" Max slapped her weapon away with his own and swung the chain coiled around his other wrist up.

All the color drained from Nix's face as his new contract snapped around her wrist.

CHAPTER THIRTY-FOUR

"You're not going anywhere." Max shoved Nix back against the wall of the platform.

"Yes, but you are." She planted a foot against his chest and pushed, sending him into the railing behind him. She lunged forward and forced him over.

The ship tumbled end over end as he fell, the twelve feet of chain between them pulling tight just above the deck. Nix let out a howl of protest as his weight almost yanked her over as well. She immediately pulled her gun and unloaded it at him. Sparks flew as spectral blades swept into existence to deflect it all.

"Nice try." Max righted himself and planted his feet against the wall as if he was rappelling down. He pulled back on the chain with all of his strength, ripping Nix off her feet and over the side.

She let gravity take her and thrust an elbow down, ready to drive it into his gut. Rolling at the last second, Max dodged and Nix hit the deck with a sickening crack. Her arm lit up crimson as she hobbled back to her feet and limped away.

Max pulled the chain tight to halt her progress. She

continued to run, yanking him forward in a desperate attempt to escape. Max grinned. There was nowhere to run.

He gave her some slack, letting her go for a dozen feet before stopping her short. She fell and reloaded, firing back at him uselessly. The blades of his *Reaper* sub-class canceled everything out as he stalked toward her. Her eyes widened, then she turned her weapon on herself, shoving the muzzle to the side of her head.

Max shot her in the hand, sending her gun flying. It fell to the deck, where it was kicked away by one of the many players still fighting for their lives. Nix pushed herself back up, spinning in a frantic attempt to make eye contact with the closest pair of black eyes she could find.

Max simply reloaded and shot any creature that noticed. Nix kept moving until she reached the side of the ship near one of the Night Queen's massive wings. Without hesitation, she climbed up on the rail and threw herself over. Max braced himself to hold her weight. There was no way he was letting her take him over the side with her.

He stepped forward, letting each link of the chain slip over the edge, sounding like a saw as it chipped away at the wood. Approaching the side, he made sure to look as smug as he could.

"Where do you think you're going?" He peered over the edge, letting her dangle from the chain. Crimson lines spread across his skin as the manacle bit into his wrist. He ignored the pain.

For once, Nix didn't have a comeback. Instead she just hung there, looking like a deer in headlights. Max dragged the chain to one side along the railing until Nix hung over the ship's wing. Then he climbed up over the railing and down the rungs of a ladder that ran down the side.

Nix scuttled away as soon as he lowered her to the wing's surface. She scurried up the inclined surface, using handholds built into the wing. Max let her go, watching her struggle, waiting for her to run out of room.

He reached for his knife. It was time to make her talk.

"Wait!" Ginger climbed down the side of the ship behind him.

"You don't have to be here for this." Max didn't look back.

"Yes, I do. We can still find another way." She fired her grappling line into the wing for stability as she inched her way up behind him.

"You know there isn't one." Max continued climbing after Nix.

"Damn it, Max! We have her, we can figure something else out."

"There's no time. The Void will probably kill everyone aboard the ship. If we don't make her talk now, we may not get another chance."

"Then we stop it."

"Stop what?"

"The Void. That's what we do, right? Fight Nightmares?"

"That's not our problem."

"The hell it isn't, just look down there." Ginger threw a hand back toward the deck of the ship, their position on the wing giving Max a clear view of the scene.

Most of the players on the deck were already dead. Those that remained were searching for safety wherever they could, many attempting to enter the theater. They banged on the doors to no avail. All they were able to do was draw the horde to the lobby doors. It was only a matter of time until the creatures made it inside to where Noctem's rulers hid.

"You know as well as I do what will happen if those things make it inside and kill everyone. Everything will fall apart. It's not just this ship on the line, but all of Noctem." Ginger lowered her hand to her side before looking up to Max.

"It's just a game, it doesn't matter if a few lords fall. More will just take their place eventually." Max looked away from the deck, shutting the thought out of his mind.

"That's right, it is a game. One that you used to care about." She stomped one foot. "I mean, you risked everything to save it twice over. You loved this game. And I loved that about you. I miss that. I miss going on adventures with you." She let out a frustrated growl. "I miss you, damn it."

"I know." Max softened his voice. "I miss all that too. But things can't just go back to the way they were. Nix stole that from us when she took Kira."

"I know, but I don't want to lose you to her as well. I didn't help you catch her just so you could torture her."

That was when Nix started laughing.

"Torture me? Really? That's your plan? How the hell do you plan on doing that here?"

Max gripped the silver dagger and held it so she could get a good look at it. "This is a contract item; it bypasses the system's pain management."

Nix suddenly shut her mouth.

"Please, Max! Don't do this." Ginger shouted from behind him. "This isn't you."

"I have to."

"I don't want to lose you." Ginger's voice cracked, almost becoming a sob. "We have something good, and I want to see where it goes. But I can't if you go through with this."

Max turned around to see the wind blowing through her hair, carrying a tear off into the night sky.

"What about Kira?" Max pulled his scarf down so she could see his face.

"I could ask you the same thing." She wiped away her tears and bared her teeth. "Kira wouldn't want this and you know it."

"She's right," a voice called from the deck. Farn began climbing down the ship to the wing. "I thought I was okay with this. I thought that as long as I got Kira back then that was all that mattered." The *Shield* stepped onto the wing as Echo floated down behind her. "I thought I could handle it if Kira never looked at me the same again. That I could handle losing her as long as she was alive.

"But I need more than that." Farn anchored herself to one

of the indents on the wing and pulled Echo close to keep her from falling. "I need to be a part of her life. I need her to look at me the same as before."

"Be realistic, Farn." Max held out his hand toward her. "Do you think Nix will just give her back to us? No harm done?"

"I don't know. But—"

"But nothing. We don't even know if Kira's still alive." Farn flinched as Max spoke the biggest fear that had been gnawing away at him for months.

"I can't." Farn's eyes welled up. "I can't give up."

"That's right, we can't give up. We have to know for sure." Max turned away from Farn. "And you don't have to help. I'll do this alone if I have to."

He took a step toward Nix, his hand trembling as he forced himself forward.

"Max, please." Nix seemed to shrink, looking smaller than she had before. "I'm begging you not to do this. You know as well as I do that you don't have the stomach to torture someone. You're not a monster."

"But you are."

"That's right. If the situation was reversed, I wouldn't even hesitate." Nix sat up straight like she thought she could talk her way out of it. "But it isn't too late for you."

"You're just trying to save yourself."

"No, I mean it. You're not like me."

"Enough." Max readied his knife and climbed closer, keeping the chain between them taut.

Nix lowered her head in defeat.

Max's heart raced. There was no turning back. It was already too late. He was going to get answers even if he had to sell his soul to get them. He owed that much to his friend.

After all, it was his fault she was gone.

That was when the last person he expected to get in his way planted themselves between him and his captive.

Max's breath froze in his throat as her whispered her name.

"Kira?"

CHAPTER THIRTY-FIVE

"Get out of my way, Echo."

Max couldn't help but growl at the avatar blocking his path. Pixie dust drifted into the night as the wind blew through her silver hair. For a second, he actually thought she'd been real, somehow appearing before him in the nick of time so he wouldn't have to go through with his plan. The brief moment of hope slipped away the instant he looked into her dull, lifeless eyes.

His heart ached like it was being crushed in a vice.

Echo threw both arms out to her sides as wide as she could, the same way that she had earlier that night to protect Max from Tusker. Now, though, she was facing the other way with a surprised Nix behind her.

The system was cruel, choosing now of all times to represent Kira so accurately. Max knew his friend would never have gone along with what he intended to do. Kira didn't have it in her to torture anyone, not even Nix.

"Move! I'm not going to ask again. You're not even real. You don't get a say in this."

Echo stomped one foot and shook her head, making it clear

that she wasn't budging.

"Fine. Be that way. You're not strong enough to stop me." Max reached forward to push her out of the way.

Echo slapped his hand away. Max flinched, pulling back for an instant. It hadn't hurt, but he hadn't expected her to be so forceful. Echo immediately threw herself against him, taking advantage of the moment of hesitation. She shoved with all her might to hold him back. It wasn't enough.

It never would be.

She couldn't stop him.

The little mage pounded on his chest with tears in her eyes. Max's insides twisted at the sight. He refocused his sights on Nix to remind him who he was fighting. No, that wasn't it. He just didn't want to look Echo in the face, even if she wasn't real.

"Max, please!" Ginger shouted from behind.

"You have to stop." Farn's voice piled on. "Echo is proof. Even you know Kira would never let you do this."

"She isn't real! It could be any of us making her get in my way." Max caught both of Echo's wrists to put an end to her useless rebellion. "The system uses all of us to control her. It listens to your minds as much as it does mine."

"No, Max. I don't think it does." Farn stepped closer. "I already told you. Kira is my future. Echo is just a representation of the past. I've moved on, and I have hope. I don't need a reminder of her to keep me fighting."

"So what? You think it's me that's holding her here. That I can't let go?"

"I've suspected it for a while now, but it wasn't until the fight with Tusker that I was sure. Echo practically flew to your defense in the space of a heartbeat."

Max froze, remembering the moment. He had only thought about Kira for a second, but Echo had responded to his mind in an instant. His knees started to shake.

Could it be me?

Max shut his eyes tight, letting the thought wash over him.

Maybe?

Echo settled down, her fists no longer struggling against his grip. They both held still until he snapped his eyes back open.

"It doesn't matter." Max threw the fairy to the side, forcing her to materialize her wings to keep from falling off the wing. "I have to do this." He pushed forward, tightening his grip on the knife until his knuckles turned white. His heart raced and stomach churned.

Ginger and Farn cried out but their words couldn't reach him over the sound of his own frantic breathing.

Suddenly, a burst of shining dust nearly blinded him, covering his skin in a gentle warmth. Echo's wings hummed as something soft flew past him. Max reached for the chain connecting him and Nix to make sure they were still tethered. He couldn't lose her. Not now.

Wind swept the pixie dust away, leaving Max staring down at Echo and Nix together. The mindless avatar trembled with her body draped over Nix's to cover as much of her as she could. The villain underneath sat stunned, clearly at a loss for words. Echo turned her head to look up at Max, her dusty blue eyes glistening.

Max froze, the sight of her almost too much for him to bear.

"Please…" He reached down, unsure what he intended to do.

She shrank away from his touch, holding onto Nix tighter. Pain streaked through his chest like an iron spike as the truth hit him all at once. His legs buckled, dropping him to his knees. He almost fell over but caught himself with his hands. The knife scraped against the wing's surface. It sounded like a voice sobbing.

"Why?" He sniffed. "Why can't you just let me save you? It was my fault. I have to bring you back." He lowered his head. "I need to bring you back. I can't do any of this alone."

That was when a hand touched his chin to pull him back up.

"It wasn't your fault." Echo mouthed the words, crouched

in front of him. "So maybe stop being selfish and pretending to be something you're not."

Her silent words cut into him like a scalpel, slicing away at everything weighing him down. She was right. He wasn't even sure why he was doing it anymore. Kira might not even be alive, and torturing Nix wasn't going to bring her back. Even worse, it was a disgusting way to honor her memory.

"Why do you all have to be right all the time?" Max exhaled, letting out as much tension as he could before breathing back in. "I can't do it."

"You jerk, you scared the hell out of me." Ginger rushed to him, dropping to her knees and throwing her arms around him.

"I knew it." Farn joined them.

Echo looked at the three of them, then shrugged and leaped into the mix, nuzzling against him and Farn.

"Okay, okay." Max let her be. "I'm sorry I went off the deep end there. We'll find another way."

"Good." Ginger tugged on the silver chain that hung from his wrist. "So what do we do about this?"

Max glanced down at the confused reynard still sitting a few feet away as the sudden group hug drifted apart. Nix stared up at the bizarre scene like a cat seeing snow for the first time.

Then she started laughing. It was the sort of awkward chuckle used to cover for something embarrassing.

"What's so funny?" Max stared down at her.

Nix settled down. "I don't think I've ever been so glad to be wrong before."

"What are you wrong about?" He eyed her carefully, watching for any sudden movements.

"About you."

"What's that supposed to mean?"

"I thought you'd go through with it." She looked away. "Who would have thought Kira's echo could talk you down off that ledge? Seriously, that damn fairy isn't even here and she's still screwing up my plans. Honestly, if I had known she was going to make everything so difficult, I would have just found someone else."

"Your plans?" Ginger furrowed her brow. "You mean you wanted Max to torture you?"

"A bit." Nix shrugged.

"Are you insane?" Ginger threw up her hands. "Why would you want to be tortured?"

Nix tilted her head from side to side as if debating on telling the truth. Then she looked up to meet Max's eyes. "I wanted to see how far you would fall."

"That's disgusting." Farn covered her mouth with her hands.

"What kind of person does that?" Max couldn't believe what he was hearing. Somehow, she was worse than he imagined. "Haven't you taken enough from us? Now you want to tear me down to your level on top of it all."

"No," Nix scoffed. "I would never torture someone. It's pretty much the worst interrogation technique you can use. Just gets you bad info. Anyone that tells you otherwise is stupid." She rolled her eyes as if Max had been an idiot for thinking it might work. "And no, I'm not trying to hurt you. That's just an unfortunate side effect."

"Then why?" Max held out both hands, pleading for answers.

"I just wanted to see you do it." She tapped the side of her right eye.

"Oh god." Ginger sucked in a breath. "She's recording."

Max froze, along with Farn and Ginger.

Nix gave a smug nod. "Yup, have been recording everything I've seen all night. And until now, it was going according to plan. All that was left was to get a video of me at your mercy, begging for you to stop."

"Who would you show that to?" Max avoided looking into her twisted eyes.

"No point in hiding things now." A Cheshire grin slithered across her face. "She's alive."

Max's heart skipped a beat, grabbing onto the last thread of hope that he had been clinging to for months. Ginger squeezed his hand tight. They were the words they had fought to hear.

"Kira's alive?" Farn lunged past him.

"Of course she's alive." Nix blew out a ridiculous raspberry. "She's no good to me dead."

"Give her back!" The *Shield* bent down and grabbed her by the shoulders, shaking the reynard for all she was worth.

"No." Nix narrowed her eyes.

"Why?" Farn let her go and collapsed to the wing, her claws scratching the surface.

"Because I'm not done with her yet." Nix rolled her eyes.

Max shook off the shock and confusion. "What do you need her for?"

"She's the key." Nix lowered her voice to a whisper so it was barely audible over the wind.

"The key to what?" Max crouched down beside Farn.

"Everything." Nix's ears pricked up. "Kira is the first of her kind. A human-AI hybrid with the ability to overpower any system in the world. She's incredible."

"And that's why you're recording everything tonight?" Ginger placed a hand on Max's shoulder as she stared down at Nix. "It was some kind of attempt to manipulate her."

"Pretty much." Nix let out a long sigh, sounding like a leaky tire before turning away. "Kira has been… uncooperative."

"That sounds about right." Max laughed. "What, did you think you could just kidnap her and she would fall in line?"

"I had hoped so, but obviously she doesn't trust me and nothing has worked to motivate her. She just keeps fighting." Nix's ears drooped, suddenly looking exhausted. "She can be annoying when she wants to. There are so many puns."

Max couldn't stop a goofy smile from taking over. Just the knowledge that his best friend was alive and doing everything she could to irritate Nix was enough to make his heart soar.

"And so you thought that showing her a recording of me hurting you would, what? Convince her to behave?"

"I did." Nix sat up straight. "I need her full cooperation without fighting me every step of the way, so forcing her or threatening the people she cares about is out of the question."

"So you got creative?"

"I thought that if I showed her how far you had fallen after losing her, Kira might realize how much you all needed her back. All she has to do is help me, and I'd let her go. Plus watching me get tortured by her friends in her name would probably get me some sympathy." She frowned. "So thanks for being a good guy and ruining my plan."

"Would you really let her go if she gave you what you want?" Max let a few links of silver chain slip through his fingers.

"I'm not sure." Nix gave him a surprisingly warm smile. "The Feds know about her and they're scared. After what she did back in Reliqua during the heist, I don't think they would allow her to exist. Right now, the safest place for her might be with me."

"So we're back to square one then." Max stood up. "You still have our friend and have no intention of letting her go."

"It seems that way."

"You know we're still going to come after you." Max rested his hand on the butts of his guns. "Somehow we'll find you out there and come knocking."

"I expect nothing less." Nix laughed.

Ginger stepped forward. "Laugh all you want, because we might find you faster than you expect." She glanced back to Max and gave him a wink.

"Good luck with that." Nix raised her hand, jingling the chain that hung from the manacle on her wrist. "What do you plan to do about this? Doesn't one of us have to die to unlock these?"

"Ahh..." Max trailed off realizing he didn't really have a plan.

"Last I checked, there was a Nightmare attacking this ship, so you all have your work cut out for you." Nix pressed a finger gun to the side of her head and mime shooting herself. "Probably just blow my head off and get on with things then?"

"Okay." Max drew his pistol and shoved it in the reynard's face. Her ears went back and she closed her eyes in preparation. A moment went by before Max took his finger off the trigger. "Actually, I have a better idea."

"And that is?" Nix cracked one eye open.

"There are quite a few of those void creatures down there." He hooked a thumb over his shoulder at the crowd of inky forms scrambling to get into the theater back on the deck. "And you and I have fought beside each other before. I'm not quite ready to let you out of my sight yet. So how about we go do some good while you're here?" He pulled on the chain, forcing her to stand up.

"Fine," she groaned.

"Are you serious?" Farn gave him a sideways glance.

"I am." Max started heading back down the wing, dragging Nix behind him.

"It is literally the least she can do." Ginger took his other hand. "Don't love her being chained to my boyfriend, though."

"Does that mean I haven't screwed up my chance?" Max smiled at her, but found her looking away. "Umm, you okay?"

Ginger didn't respond, instead she stared down at something near the bottom of the ship.

"Is that...?" Farn caught up to them, taking a moment to gawk at the scene as well.

Max squinted down at the observation deck below. It looked like a person standing on the railing, ready to jump to their death.

"Is that Seven?"

CHAPTER THIRTY-SIX

Seven stood on the railing on the Night Queen's lower deck, clinging to a lamp post while a lantern swung back and forth in the breeze. She didn't mean to hesitate. It only gave her time to think. Now, after standing there for what seemed like forever while a battle raged on the deck above, she found herself unable to move.

The view below was incredible. She stared out over the world and let it take her breath away. Sure, she had seen Noctem before, but she hadn't really paid attention.

The lights of a city shone in the distance as a mountain range cut through the horizon with rivers flowing toward an ocean on one side. Below, the glow of camp fires flickered like tiny sparks in Noctem's eternal night. She could swear she could smell the smoke riding the wind up to meet her.

It was beautiful.

Finally, she shook her head and stepped one foot into the emptiness.

Stop hesitating.

It will be over soon.

Just jump, and put all this insanity behind you.

She leaned forward, her hand gripping the light post tighter, as if rebelling against the rest of her body. Then, with one final exertion of her will, she let go.

"The hell are you doing?" a familiar voice shouted from directly above her.

Seven's hand shot behind her, catching the lamp post and pulling herself back until she could wrap her entire body around the pole. Her eyes widened as a confused-looking Ginger swung into view on a grappling line.

"Are you out of your mind?" The *Coin* flew past her in a wide arc that eventually brought her back to hang precariously in the emptiness. "Get down from there."

"I can't." Seven shook her head. "Leftwitch told me to jump so I can respawn back in Lucem."

"Why the hell would she tell you to kill yourself?"

"She wants the contracts I bought. Jumping is the fastest way back."

"Okay, sure, but you can give them to her later." Ginger reached out awkwardly to get one foot on the rail and pulled herself in. "We have a Nightmare to fight up there, and we need all the help we can get. That includes low-level *Venom* mages. So get down from that railing and help us put Void back in its box."

"You can't be serious! I haven't even fought a regular boss, let alone a Nightmare."

"So what? I've fought plenty of Nightmares before." Ginger finally got a foot over the rail and dropped down to the deck behind Seven. She stumbled a bit, just as a black shape that vaguely resembled a player fell from above to pass through the space where she had been hanging. Ginger cringed. "Okay, maybe I haven't fought a Nightmare quite like this."

"You don't get it." Seven's voice cracked. "I did this."

"What's that supposed to mean?"

"I didn't know, but I brought the Nightmare here. Leftwitch wants to kill the rulers of Noctem and throw the world into chaos."

"Why would she want that?"

"To get more viewers?"

Ginger rolled her eyes. "That's the dumbest thing I've heard all night."

"I know, I don't like it either, but I have to do this." Seven loosened her grip on the lamp post. "Leftwitch is still my boss. If I don't jump, I could lose my job. I don't have a choice."

"What if you did?" Ginger's mouth curled into a wry smile.

"What?" Seven pulled herself closer to the post.

"Quit!"

"Are you even listening? I can't quit."

"Yes, you can." Ginger reached into her coat and pulled out a small box, retrieving a silver ring from inside. "You can quit and come and work for me." She thrust the ring up toward Seven. "Something you said earlier got me thinking."

"What?" Seven stared down at the ring, a small heart with a keyhole sitting at its center.

"Follow the money." Ginger stepped closer. "You said that if we wanted to find Nix out in the real world, then we should follow the money. Now I don't know anything about accounting, but I could certainly use someone that does."

"Are you offering me a job?" Seven furrowed her brow.

"How does Head Accountant of House Lockheart sound?"

Seven's mouth fell open, not sure what she should even say. Lockheart was at the center of a conflict that she didn't understand. Not to mention they were a bunch of morally gray misfits in way over their heads. Joining them could be dangerous.

She stood on the rail, teetering on the edge with her back to the world below. Behind her was a sure thing. Her place as Royal Assistant Seven was a done deal. She didn't like it, but it was work and that was all she needed. In front of her... well, that was insanity.

"What kind of pay would there be?" Seven had to run the numbers anyway.

"Ahh." Ginger's face went blank as she stood there, still holding up a ring. Clearly, she hadn't expected a negotiation.

"Whatever the Silver Tongues were paying you, on a one-year contract position."

"Contract position?" Seven didn't like the sound of that.

"It is what it is. We're not made of money, so unless we pull off another heist, there's a limit to our coffers. I can keep you employed for one year. In that time, you can find something else."

Seven frowned. It was true, Lockheart didn't really have a source of income other than theft, so expecting more would have been unreasonable. Still, she had to look out for herself and her husband.

"What about benefits?"

"Benefits?"

"Health insurance."

"I don't know, we'll give you a stipend or something and you can get your own." Ginger reached up for Seven's hand. "Now get down here."

"But what about Max's plan to torture Nix? You shouldn't even need me if he can make her talk."

"That fizzled." Ginger raised both hands in an exaggerated shrug. "Max isn't as heartless as he tries to make people think he is. He wasn't able to go through with it. But we were able to find out that Kira is alive and we're taking that as a win. So how about it? You want to join the winning team?"

Every instinct in Seven's body told her to refuse, to jump and take the sure thing. That was why it surprised her when she reached out and took Ginger's hand.

"Welcome aboard." The *Coin* placed her new house ring in Seven's palm.

"Thank you." Seven started to remove her old one, just as Cassius's voice rang out over the Silver Tongues' chat line.

"Hey Seven, if you haven't killed yourself yet, I could use another hand up here on the ship's bridge. Need to make sure the Night Queen goes down in flames, in case Void can't get the job done."

Seven's cheeks warmed as a ridiculous smile spread across

her face. The spark inside her that she thought was dead began to grow.

"I can't do that."

"Why not?" Cassius sounded annoyed.

"Because I quit."

"You what?"

"You can't quit." Leftwitch suddenly joined in, sputtering like she had just spit a drink from her mouth. "You still have my contract items—"

Seven pulled the Silver Tongues' ring off her finger and tossed it over the side. Then she slipped on her new one, feeling it resize around her finger to a perfect fit.

"You know…" Ginger gave Seven a conspiratorial wink. "You do still have a couple contracts, and in Noctem, possession is ten tenths of the law."

Seven thought about it for a second, surprised at herself for not feeling guilty. Normally, taking something that didn't belong to her wouldn't have even crossed her mind, especially anything that had cost hundreds of thousands of dollars. She reached in her pouch and pulled out the rebirth quill that had the ability to respec her character.

"Feel like making a change?" Ginger raised an eyebrow.

"You go on ahead. Right before I tossed my ring, I heard Cassius on the house line. He's on the bridge and plans to crash the ship." Seven ran her finger down the feather. "I'll catch up after I do some math here."

"Okay." Ginger hopped up onto the rail and fired her grappling hook. "Don't take too long. I *am* paying you now." Then she shot up toward the main deck.

Seven watched her new boss until she was out of sight. Then, without any further hesitation, she took out her journal and opened it to her character page.

She already knew what changes to make. Seven scratched out her race and class. They had both been chosen to help her appear professional, but now… well, Lockheart just didn't seem like the type of house that dressed for business.

Seven wrote in her new choices, pushing the math to its limit. Her meager fifty-five upgrade points weren't going to go far and she needed to make the most of them.

After making some adjustments, she got to her name.

Royal Assistant Seven.

She started scratching it out, but stopped when she got to the last word, Seven. Everyone had been calling her that all night, so it seemed odd to change it now. Instead, she wrote in a new word before it and stopped to admire her choice. Seven laughed to herself at the name, feeling embarrassed and excited at the same time. It was ridiculous, but so were all the choices she'd made in the last few minutes.

She brushed a lock of blue hair from her face, the color having been an accidental choice made during character creation. Seven scratched her hair color out and changed that too, because, why not?

As soon as she was finished, she snapped her journal shut, making the changes permanent. The quill in her hand burst into flames the instant she did.

The fire spread to her hand, sending a twinge of fear through her body. She tried to shake it off but it only climbed her arm further. When it reached her shoulder, she realized the flames didn't hurt. She closed her eyes and let the fire consume her. It burned away the Royal Assistant that she was, leaving someone new standing in her place.

Someone... magnificent.

Seven smiled and pushed a few locks of fiery red hair back behind her new pair of horns. Then, she set off toward the bridge.

Cassius was going to wish he'd stayed in Lucem.

CHAPTER THIRTY-SEVEN

"Hold the doors!" Alastair dropped a velvet sack of spell ingredients into his caster's circle of power. The theater's doors bowed inward despite the barricade, threatening to give way at any second. The dark hands of the fallen reached in through the cracks in between, their fingers dripping with black fluid.

"We should open the doors and use them as a choke point," shouted Lord Promethium of House Iron Forge, in opposition to Alastair's suggestion.

"There's not enough of us for that." Alastair kicked over Grindstone's table and shoved it up against the main doors before they gave way.

"Every Lady for themselves." Amelia ran forward, pushing Lord Murph out of the way.

"Why do I even try?" Alastair rubbed at the bridge off his nose as everyone in the theater went about and did their own thing.

"Do you have any idea where Nix went?" Luka pressed up against his side. The Federal agent posing as a *Breath* mage dropped a few heals into her quick-caster queue. "We can't lose her."

"Excuse me, but there is a Nightmare loose on this ship." Alastair stuffed an empty ingredient pouch back into his coat and pressed his back up against the table. "Nix is a few lines down on my list of priorities at the moment. If we don't stop this madness, then there won't be anyone left to catch her. Not to mention the ruling lords of Noctem are about to be torn apart by void monsters." Just then, Lady Amelia cut down the Archmage of another house. "If they don't kill each other, that is."

"Point taken." The elven woman threw her back up against the table alongside him, holding it to the door. "Any idea how to beat these things?" She gestured with her head to a dripping hand clawing through the door a few inches from her hair.

"About that…" He glanced to his side, making eye contact with her. "We're doomed."

"What?"

"The Void wasn't meant to be fought here." Alastair moved his foot to the side to brace himself against the door. "It's a Nightmare, not a raid boss. It's meant to be fought by a standard party of six. When it hits phase two, things are going to get much worse."

"How so?"

"Now that Carver is gone, we've had to develop the newer Nightmares on our own, but we tried to keep them consistent with the old ones."

"So there's more to this one? Some kind of trick?"

"In the sense that this whole fight is a trick question, then yes. You win by thinking outside the box."

"Great, then let's do that."

"Not that simple. The point is to roll the dice and embrace the unknown. Everyone has to look into the Void right at the start to win."

"But you told us not to!" Luka screwed up her eyes.

"Indeed, because looking at it would have randomly killed half of us. I couldn't roll those odds with so many of Noctem's rulers in the room, as well as myself and the rest of Lockheart."

"That doesn't make any sense. Why would that be any different for a party of six if it will kill half of them?"

"Because phase two will begin once we destroy the monsters created by the Void, then the real boss will attack. At which point it will base its health off the number of players it killed in phase one, as well as scale its attack power off the number of players that survive. It's a balancing act. Exactly half of your party has to die for it to be a fair fight."

"Oh shit." Luka's eye's widened. "And it probably killed most of the players on this ship already."

"Like I said, the fight was never meant for more than a party of six." Alastair nodded halfheartedly. "When the Void spawns in its final form in phase two, it will be larger, deadlier, and have so much health it will be practically unkillable."

Suddenly the door behind them began to give way, forcing the table at their backs into the theater.

"Get clear." Larkin's army of dolls swarmed into the doors, barely giving Alastair and Luka a chance to get out of the way. Their tiny bodies wedged through the cracks, pushing back against the enemies outside in one unified mass.

"Much appreciated." Alastair leaned over to catch his breath and glanced at the glowing circle hovering above his caster that indicated that his spell was still brewing.

"Don't thank me yet. They won't hold them for long. A horde of dolls won't do much against a horde of whatever those things are." Larkin flinched as a slimy hand reached between the doors and crushed the body of one of his minions, its stylish outfit smeared with black ink. "Damn, I had just made that dress."

Larkin's face grew pained as one doll after another fell victim to the horde outside. Alastair felt for the crafter. After all, he understood what it was like to care about the things that he'd created.

Suddenly, a sound drew his attention to the balcony. Alastair froze in horror as a dark form leaned over the railing above and slammed into the floor behind Larkin. It twitched once, then reached out and grabbed the leg of the distracted *Rage* class.

"Look out." Luka fired off a pulse spell to slap the monster's hand away.

"They must have found the stairs in the lobby." Alastair raised his head to the balconies where several of Void's monstrosities staggered toward the edges. When they reached the railings, they simply threw themselves over and crashed into the theater floor. A few died on impact, while others got right back up.

"We can't stay here!" Luka backed up to Larkin.

"We can't go out there either." Alastair gestured to the doors that surround them, each pushed to their breaking point by the victims of phase one.

The theater fell into chaos, reminding Alastair of earlier that night when Tusker's Boars had attacked. The Lords of Noctem's most powerful houses all fell back. At the same time, they each seemed to be staying away from each other, like they feared that one house might take advantage of the situation.

Alastair gasped at the stupidity around him.

They're spreading themselves too thin. We need to fight together.

"Fall back to the stage!" He beckoned Luka and Larkin to follow as he raced back to the high ground. He hoped the rest of Noctem's lords might follow suit. Unfortunately, the only taker was Dartmouth.

"This is your game." The Lord of Serpents climbed up onto the stage and huddled behind him. "You have to do something about this. You have to protect me."

"I don't have to do anything, Dartmouth." Alastair glanced at his caster to check his spell's brew status. "You're not even one of Noctem's rulers. It doesn't matter if you die here."

"True." Dartmouth looked at the floor. "But my house is on the brink of mutiny. I haven't exactly lived up to my predecessor's legacy. If I don't survive this, my Lordship will be in jeopardy."

"Then find a new house." Luka climbed up onto the stage.

"I can't do that!" Dartmouth stomped one foot. "I've gone public with my real-world identity. Think of the humiliation. No prominent employer will want to hire a dethroned Lord, and I shan't have this tarnish my reputation or hurt my future opportunities."

"I understand completely." Larkin leaped up to the stage. "Commoners, am I right? So beneath us."

"Exactly." Dartmouth inched closer to the crafting-obsessed *Rage*, not catching the man's mocking tone.

"Let me help you out," Larkin grabbed his caster. "Believe it or not, you are a *Venom* mage, and this elegant bracelet can be used to cast offensive magic."

"I know that." Dartmouth pulled his hand away.

"Oh good." Larkin placed his hands together in a thankful gesture just before narrowing his eyes. "Then start casting."

"Agreed." Alastair pushed the elf toward the edge of the stage.

A sudden crash came from the back of the theater as one of the main doors burst open. The horde from the main deck poured in, crushing the tiny bodies of Larkin's dolls underfoot.

"Get to the high ground!" Alastair shouted over the chaos, trying to convince anyone that might listen to work together.

"Go down fighting!" Lady Amelia rushed into the horde, ignoring him entirely.

"No!" Alastair reached out in her direction then dropped his hand to his side. It was already too late. Her saber cut a swath into the center of the mass of bodies, only to have the rest surround her. Enemies piled on after that.

It didn't take long for the Lady of House Winter Moon to emerge again, a familiar inky darkness pouring from her eyes.

"That's not good." Dartmouth took a step back behind Alastair.

"Indeed, with her dead, the throne of Reliqua will be up for grabs until she gets back online."

"Who cares about Reliqua? I'm talking about that." Dartmouth stabbed a finger past Alastair's shoulder, pointing at the dead woman's saber.

"Oh…" Alastair's mouth fell open as he watched a purple mist flow from the sword. "What was Amelia's contract weapon called again?"

"Corpse Maker!" Dartmouth shrieked in his ear. "One scratch is enough to kill. How do you not know that?"

"Sorry, I usually have an assistant that keeps track of that stuff." Alastair rubbed at his ear. "But I sort of pushed him off the ship earlier."

Luka shot him a questioning glance.

"Don't ask, it was a whole thing." He shrugged off her gaze just as the glowing circle hovering over his caster shrunk into a single point of energy. "Finally, my spell is ready."

"What is it?" Luka swiped open her spell-craft menu and set up a buff for his arcane stat.

"Desolation." Alastair threw out his hand to target the doors of the theater, making sure Amelia would be caught in the blast radius. "Clear the floor if you want to live. This spell doesn't have an indoor voice."

"Really wish we had a *Shield* here." Luka ducked behind Larkin, who ducked behind Dartmouth, who was already hiding behind Alastair.

"Me too." He stretched out his fingers as power surged through his skin. "Me too."

Ribbons of light swirled into existence, streaking through the air into the center of the doorway. Then they exploded. The blast hit the air like a thousand cannons firing at once, the concussive force throwing Alastair back into the three players hiding behind him. Bodies flew through the air, some landing on the balconies above. Fire climbed up the doorway as smoke filled the lobby beyond.

"Did you get Amelia?" Dartmouth asked from somewhere nearby.

Alastair searched the devastation. "I don't see her."

"How many enemies did you get?" Luka pushed Dartmouth off of her.

"Not enough." Larkin pointed to the flaming doorway as dozens of forms began walking through the smoke; there was no end to them.

"Well, I tried." Alastair rolled over to push himself up.

With nowhere left to run, what remained of Noctem's rulers finally climbed up to the stage. Behind one curtain, Dalliance and Grindstone helped each other to collect a few books.

"Oh good, the lawyers are still alive." Alastair looked out over the theater as more dark abominations sauntered in. "Probably not for much longer though."

Klaxon, House Winter Moon's Archmage, had survived as well. Though the only remaining rulers were Alastair, Promethium of Iron Forge and Murph of House Saint.

"We can't let it end here." Luka cast an area effect heal across the stage.

"You're right." Larkin held up the lantern that had held his favorite doll. Half of it was smashed beyond recognition with a tiny arm hanging limp. He pulled a scrap of white fabric free from the twisted metal scrap and folded it neatly. "I'm not going out looking like this." He gestured to his vest, the front spattered with black fluid.

"I can't argue with that." Alastair swiped open his spell-craft menu and dropped a few Crystal Shard spells into his queue. He rose up as tall as he could, bracketed by a crafting-obsessed *Rage* and an elven federal agent. It was time for a final stand. "As Max would say, it's all or nothing."

The horde trickled in through the smoke, their black eyes trained on the stage. Alastair reached out and took aim, ready to take at least a few down with him.

A burst of crimson light exploded from his target's head.

Alastair froze, looking at his hand. "Was that me?"

Suddenly, gunfire erupted from the lobby beyond as muzzle flashes lit up the smoke. Somehow, they seemed to come from multiple angles at once. Bullets mowed down the enemies blocking the exit.

An excited chill gripped Alastair's spine as a line of text appeared on his stat-sleeve.

You have received a party invitation from MaxDamage24

"Yes!" He slapped the accept option as the silhouettes of two players appeared through the smoke, dropping enemies one after another in their wake. "The cavalry's here!"

His stat-sleeve redrew itself to show the health readout of his new party leader, MaxDamage24, alongside his own.

Farnsworth's name appeared next.

It didn't stop there.

Alastair's whole body froze as a third name appeared.

Nix.

CHAPTER THIRTY-EIGHT

"Oh, hell no!" Ginger swung across the main deck, tucking her feet up as far as she could. She reeled some wire into her wrist launcher as the hands of the fallen reached for her legs. One grazed her boot, but she kicked it away. The momentum spun her around and she took the opportunity to taunt the horde below.

"Nice try–!"

Of course, that was when she slammed into the glass front of the theater's lobby, sounding like a bird crashing into her kitchen window.

"Balls…"

Ginger shook the stars from her field of vision and reeled in a few more feet of wire to make sure she was out of reach. Then she groaned at her reflection in the glass.

I swear, Max is rubbing off on me. Can't believe I just tried to wise ass a bunch of monsters. The thought made her smile, bringing back a feeling that she was afraid she'd lost. Lately, thinking of Max had only made her sad. There had been so much pain in his eyes that things hadn't felt the same. Now, though, knowing that Kira was alive, it was like a dark cloud had lifted from them. Not to mention he hadn't tortured anyone.

That would have been a relationship killer.

Maybe now we can finally move forward?

Eventually, she pushed every thought of her love life out of her head and focused on what was important. That being the fact that no one had seen her slam into a window like her goon of a boyfriend.

Then, as if on cue, a smug voice came from above.

"How you doing down there?"

Ginger pressed her face against the glass in defeat before forcing a smile and looking up.

"Hello, dear."

Piper stood on a walkway above, laughing at her mother's expense. Corvin stood beside her, clearly suppressing a chuckle of his own.

"What are you hanging around here for?" Kegan leaned on his elbows on the railing.

"No time for puns up there, we need to get to the bridge." Ginger shot them a serious look, hoping to guilt them into forgetting what they'd seen. "I just heard from Seven. Cassius is up there and he aims to bring the ship down." She pulled her legs up and pushed off the window until she was practically standing on the glass. "So how about you all quit laughing?"

The three of them promptly shut their mouths.

"That's better." Ginger began stepping up the window to the walkway that circled the roof of the theater. *At least there are no enemies up here.*

"Where's Max?" Corvin helped her up and over the railing.

"He and Nix are attempting to rescue the lords down in the theater." She reeled in the rest of her grappling line, her new Yoink claw snapped into place at the end, ready to be fired again.

"Nix is with him?" Corvin arched an eyebrow.

"Yeah." Ginger took a breath. "A lot happened. All that matters is that we know Kira is alive."

"She is?" The three of them responded in unison as a visible wave of relief washed across their faces.

"That's what Nix said."

"Can we trust her?" Piper held breath.

"Her story tracks. Seems she's having trouble getting Kira to behave. And was recording us to find some footage that she could use to manipulate her." Ginger left out the part about Max trying to torture the woman. It wasn't exactly information she wanted to share with her daughter.

"Has Nix tried bribing Kira with food?" Kegan smiled, looking more relaxed than he had in months.

"Who knows. Either way, Nix is Max's problem at the moment, and we have our own to worry about." Ginger started toward a narrow flight of stairs that led up to the bridge. "Let's go show the Silver Tongues what House Lockheart is made—"

Her sentence was cut off as a bullet ricocheted off the railing in front of her.

"Never mind, they brought a *Fury* this time." She scrambled back to the others around a corner.

"Two, actually." Piper peeked around the side at a pair of gunmen. "And they brought that damn bird, Ruby."

The sound of angry cawing could be heard over the gunfire.

"And a *Shield*." Kegan loosed an arrow up the stairs only to have it blocked by a faunus. He frowned, then shouted up at the group. "Hey, you with the horns. Didn't we kill you a couple hours ago?"

"Maybe." A gruff voice responded. "Did that *Blade* kid apologize to that girl he shot down yet?"

Ginger slowly turned her head to Corvin. "What is he talking about?"

"Yeah! What the hell, you ass?" Piper gave him a good slap on the stomach. "Even those assholes know about me?"

"Wren, language." Ginger scolded her daughter, using her real name for impact.

"Sorry. Even those asshats know?" Piper repeated, slapping Corvin in the gut again.

"Gah!" The *Blade* keeled over. "Hey, Kegan brought it up while we were captured. So this one's not on me."

"I guess asshat is slightly better." Ginger covered her face with one hand. Her daughter was becoming more like her every day, which was probably not something she should encourage.

"Well, did he apologize?" The faunus up the stairs didn't let up.

"Yes, I did, and also, shut up!" Corvin drew his broken sword and motioned toward the stairs.

"Easy now," Kegan grabbed him by the shoulder. "They'll just shoot you and you'll still be embarrassed when you respawn."

Corvin let out a weak groan.

"He's right," Ginger peeked up the stairs. "We need a *Shield* of our own. We aren't getting up there without protection—oh what the hell?" Ginger fell backward on her rear as a massive black and red bird flew around the corner, its talons ready to attack. It went straight for her daughter.

Piper toppled over beside her, shielding her face with hands. "I'm sorry I roasted you earlier!"

"Way to antagonize it, dear." Ginger covered her head as well, getting swatted in the face with the bird's impressive wingspan.

"Both of you, quit flailing," Kegan shouted at them. "I need a clear shot—"

His sentence was cut short by a loud roar as a set of razor-sharp jaws the size of Ginger's head snapped shut only a foot from her nose. Ruby's squawking came to an abrupt stop as feathers showered down around her. Ginger reached for her daughter, who clung to her in return. They both let out a scream directly into the reptilian face of a wolf-sized scalefang.

The four-legged lizard lowered its head, breathing heavily enough to displace Ginger's hair as its mane of bright feathers tickled her ear. Her mind locked up for a second. An airship was the last place she would expect to run into the monster.

Then she remembered the first round of the auction and the item that Seven had purchased for Leftwitch.

The scalefang egg.

Ginger reached up and placed a hand on the beast's cheek. "And what's your name, fella?"

"His name's Flint." A rather professional voice came from behind the beast.

Ginger slid her body to one side to get a look at the source. Then she gasped. "Seven?"

"The new and improved," responded a tall faunus, standing just behind the scalefang. A pair of horns atop her head, curling back, more like a demon's than a ram. Her medium length hair was pushed back between them, each lock the color of dying embers. The simple tunic and canvas pants of a low-level melee player covered her body. A whip hung from a wide leather belt at her waist, marking her new class. She bowed and swept her hand in front of her to show Lockheart's house ring on her finger. "Ready and reporting for duty, m'lady."

"Why a faunus?" Kegan pointed a finger at her horns. "And why a *Whip* class?"

"The numbers worked." Seven held out her stat-sleeve.

Hit Points: 1234 of 1234
Skill Points: 2 of 2

"The faunus racial trait gives a ten percent bonus to all attributes times the number of stats that equal zero. I leveled twice on my way up here by throwing my hatchet at enemies from somewhere safe. That gave me a total of sixty five upgrade points to spend after my respec. I put twenty two in health and the rest into defense. Plus, I purchased one skill to summon a pet."

"Okay?" Ginger got up off the ground, not quite sure what the newly-minted faunus was thinking with a build like that.

"I can't hurt a fly, but I can take a hit. And so can this guy." Seven patted Flint on his muscular neck. "Thanks to the faunus race bonus and having seven stats that equal zero, I have a higher defense than some mid-level players. If I've done the math right, I should be able to take a few good hits as long as they aren't critical. I'll just have to rely on my hatchet's default damage for now, since I can't deal any of my own."

"So you're a tank?" Ginger arched an eyebrow.

"It's what Lockheart lacks right now." Seven sounded like a school teacher giving a lesson. "With Farnsworth's Death Grip limiting her shielding capabilities, you need someone to absorb damage." She patted Flint again. "Now you have two."

"Nice job." Ginger was impressed at how the faunus had worked the system to balance out their house. "I'm starting to pity Leftwitch for losing you."

"Plus, we're fireproof." Seven touched the pendant hanging from her neck, releasing a wave of heat from her body as her eyes began to glow orange. Embers flickered through her hair as if smoldering. The same effect was applied to Flint beside her.

"Okay, now I'm just glad you're on our side." Ginger couldn't stop herself from grinning as she invited the faunus into her party. That was when Kegan burst out laughing.

"Oh my god, did you actually name yourself that?" The elf held up his party readout to show her name. The words Magnificent Seven hung over her health bar. "Who do you think you are, Max?"

"No." Seven blushed and looked away. "I just thought I should fit in." She fidgeted with her hatchet. "Lockheart is infamous. All of you seemed larger than life before I met you. I know I'm not on the same level, but still—"

"Stop that." Ginger held up a hand to cut her off. "You have been logged in for one night, you have somehow survived multiple attacks, killed players a hundred levels higher than yourself, and defected to one of the most badass houses in all of Noctem. Not to mention you've stolen a rare pet, a possessed hatchet, and two contracts." Ginger placed both hands on her hips. "By tomorrow, your name will be plastered all over the internet, whether you want it to be or not. Just be glad you didn't give yourself a name that makes you sound like a stripper, like I did."

Piper snorted a laugh at her expense.

"I mean really, what kind of a name is GingerSnaps? What was I thinking?" Ginger held out her hand to Seven. "My point is, it's too late now, you're already one of us. So let's go murder your old housemates."

"Alright." Seven let out a polite laugh. "Flint and I will take the lead, just be ready to follow up. We can only take a few hits."

Ginger stepped aside and glanced to the others. They each nodded back. Well, all except Kegan, who was stuffing loose feathers into his item bag from when Flint had devoured Ruby.

"What? I can make arrows with these." He stuffed in another handful. "Not going to let you steal them and try to sell them back to me."

"I would never do such a thing." Ginger spun back to the stairs and got into position. "Ready?"

"Okay." Seven crouched down and took a breath as if hesitating.

"You have this." Ginger placed a hand on her shoulder.

"Thank you, my lady." Seven pushed off and bolted up the stairs, covering her face with her wrists to avoid taking a critical. Guns barked above, sending streaks of crimson across her body.

Ginger checked her health, watching it plummet down to one third remaining. She wasn't going to make it. Then, just before taking another hit, Seven dropped down and whistled.

Flint jumped clear over her and continued the charge, only taking one hit before plowing into the energy barrier protecting the trio at the top of the stairs.

Seven sprang back up and let her hatchet fly. It slammed into the shoulder of one of the *Furies* while the other struggled to line up a critical shot on Flint.

"Ah, what the hell?" the *Shield* class complained as the scale-fang chewed on his arm, causing no more discomfort than drooling on him.

Piper opened fire as Ginger leaped off the side of the stairs. She spun in the air, her coat billowing around her. With a pop, Yoink's metal claw flew from her wrist to grab hold of a rail above the three enemies. She reeled in the line and swung up and over, landing behind them. Ginger wasted no time, drawing her dagger and backstabbing one of the *Furies* before he could put a bullet in Flint.

The other gunman shrieked as Seven's hatchet pulled itself free from his shoulder and flew back to her hand. For a second, relief washed over his face, then a pair of arrows slammed into his chest. He fell over the rail, followed by a trail of shimmering particles that marked his death.

Ginger pulled her dagger free of her victim just as Corvin buried his broken sword into the man's gut. He was dead before he hit the ground, leaving only the *Shield* class remaining.

The player kicked Flint away, clearly confused why being bitten hadn't caused any damage. Kegan drew back his bow and held it with the arrow head just inches from the *Shield's* face.

"We meet again–" he started just as Seven nudged his elbow. He let go of the bow string on reflex, putting the arrow through his target's eye at point blank range. "Gah!" He recoiled in horror at what he'd just done before turning to Seven.

"What? We don't have a lot of time for banter." She avoided looking at the *Shield's* body until it began to dissipate.

Ginger stared at the fiery faunus along with the others.

"I was trying to be efficient," she explained, somehow acclimating herself to her new role a bit too fast.

"Umm, sorry to interrupt." Corvin pointed off into the distance. "But are those mountains getting closer?"

"Yes, yes they are." Ginger stared out at the horizon. "We're heading right for them."

"At our current speed and flight path…" Seven went silent for a second before adding, "We'll hit them in five minutes."

"Thanks, but I'd rather not know." Kegan pulled a health vial from his pouch and handed it to Seven.

"Sorry." She downed it and instructed Flint to sit to recover his own health.

"Well, let's get up there." Ginger pointed up to the large panoramic windows of the bridge above. They raced up the next flight of stairs to the entry hatch, only to find it locked. "Or not."

"Is there another way in?" Piper holstered her pistol.

"Not unless we can fly." Kegan pointed to the windows that covered the roof of the bridge.

"Maybe we can." Ginger fired her grappling line up and over, feeling it catch on something. "That'll work, I think I can take one of you up with me and come back down for someone else. We can smash our way in once we're all up there." She held out her arms as if waiting for a hug. "Who wants to go first?"

Everyone took a step back. Everyone except Seven.

"What, hey?"

"Thanks for volunteering." Ginger wrapped her arms around the faunus and retracted the line. Seven let out a small shriek and grabbed on tight as her feet left the ground. "Maybe don't look down, huh?"

Seven didn't argue, burying her face in Ginger's shoulder as they swung out over the deck. The wire made a high-pitched twang as it dragged across the windows above.

"How much weight can the line hold?" Seven tightened her grip.

"No idea. But the launcher is only rated for one, and it's retracting slow." Ginger clenched her fist to tell the mechanism to speed up, though even with that the wire could only manage a few inches per second. This left their bodies being dragged up the main window of the bridge at a snail's pace, the glass squeaking the whole way.

Ginger looked in, finding Cassius and two other players watching as they slid up the window. She made eye contact with the Knight of the Silver Tongues, who just stared back at her. In an attempt to make the moment less awkward, she mouthed a threat through the window.

"We're coming for you."

Cassius responded by leaning his head to one side and holding a hand to his ear like he didn't understand. Ginger repeated herself only to have Cassius respond by mouthing what looked like, 'What? I can't hear you.'

'Never mind.' Ginger rolled her eyes, getting an idea of what things must have been like for Noctem's system trying to control Echo.

Finally, the grappling line brought them to the top of the bridge. Ginger let out a nervous laugh as she realized that the claw at the end was precariously hooked on the metal trim that connected the windows together. It probably wasn't a good idea to try to make another trip. She attempted to fire her grappling line anyway, getting nothing but a high-pitched grinding from the overwhelmed launcher.

Damn, we're going to have to go with just the two of us. Ginger leaned to the side, looking for the rest of her team down on the stairs.

"I can't come back for you. I'll try to get the door unlocked from inside."

Piper gave a thumbs up.

"Okay, you ready?" Ginger produced one of her favorite explosive items from a hidden pocket in her coat.

"What? No." Seven crouched on the glass. "What about the others?"

"No time." Ginger snapped her fingers against the fuse and tossed the bomb to the window a few feet away. "This is happening. Just try to keep Cassius busy."

"Wait!" Panic flooded Seven's face. "I'm not…"

A small explosion went off, sending cracks spider webbing across the window they stood on. Then, nothing happened.

"…ready?" Seven finished her sentence, clearly expecting the glass to have broken. "Oh, thank god."

"Ha ha, little early for thanks." Ginger stomped her foot to force gravity to take over.

Thousands of glittering fragments surrounded them as they fell through the window and into the bridge. Seven landed on a raised platform meant for the captain while Ginger fell to the stairs leading down to the rest of the bridge. She tumbled end over end, rolling to a stop at the base of the ship's wheel near the front of the bridge. One look at the steering mechanism told her it was a lost cause, having been smashed beyond repair. All that was left was a metal rod with a slot sticking out where the steering wheel should have been.

"I probably should have expected that." Ginger let out a groan just as a *Blade* class appeared above her, ready to run her through. She placed a solid kick to his undercarriage and rolled away. With a shove, she pushed herself off the floor boards and raced up the stairs toward the captain's platform above.

She froze as soon as she reached the top.

The crack of a whip shattered the air, followed by a jet of fire as Seven stood facing off against her former housemate. Flames climbed her weapon in one hand while a hatchet gleamed in the other. Her horns glowed red, and embers drifted from her hair.

Ginger wasn't the only one struck speechless by the woman's improved form, Cassius stood staring as well, before finally opening his mouth.

"Who the hell are you?"

"Seriously?" Seven's whole body deflated. "It's me."

"The noob?" Recognition fell across Cassius's face before settling into a disappointed frown. "So you've thrown in with this lot?"

"I have."

"It's not too late. You can still return one of those contracts you stole and help me kill this one." Cassius pointed his spear at Ginger.

"Hey, quit trying to steal my new employee." Ginger argued back.

Seven let out a sigh. "Unfortunately, I have already made up my mind and it would be unprofessional of me to go back now."

"And it wasn't unprofessional to betray us?" Cassius held up his house ring.

"Well, you did try to blow me up, made me smuggle a Nightmare on board, and told me to kill myself." She waved her hatchet back and forth as if ticking off each misdeed. "I feel justified in saying that I am glad to be out of that kind of work environment. So as far as I'm concerned, I will be keeping the contracts I have gained as a well-deserved severance package."

"So you're a thief as well as a traitor." Cassius narrowed his eyes. "Seems like you've found a house that you fit in with, then."

"I think so." Seven took a stance that looked like someone trying their best to imitate a fighter's pose from the movies.

"Fine, then. You're still a noob; a couple contract items won't change that." Cassius rotated his spear around and tapped the base on the floor. The four blades that made up the head of the weapon snapped open to reveal a hollow tube. A small flame flickered to life at the opening. "Let me show you what a player that has earned a contract can do."

Seven braced as he leveled the weapon at her. Then, without warning, he swung it back to aim at Ginger instead, giving her no time to dodge. All she could do was bring up her coat to shield her face to avoid a critical.

Fire erupted from the spear like an explosion, detonating so close to Ginger that it launched her backward into the front window. The sound of glass breaking met her ears as all the air rushed out of her lungs. Through the fragments of shattered window, she caught a glimpse of Seven bracing as Cassius turned his weapon on her. A jet of fire engulfed the newest member of House Lockheart.

You're on your own, Seven, Ginger thought as she flew further from the scene.

Good luck.

CHAPTER THIRTY-NINE

"Listen up!" Max fired another round into a nearby enemy. "Everyone in this room that has not yet become one of Void's minions is going to come with me."

"Yeah! Come with us if you want to live." Nix whipped the silver chain attached to her wrist over the head of a void creature and snapped it back to knock them over.

"Gah, warn me if you're going to do that." Max glowered at the reynard that he had intended to torture up until a few minutes ago. "You almost pulled my arm off."

"Sorry, forgot." Her ears drooped back, looking sheepish.

Farn and Echo just shook their heads at them both.

"What on Earth is going on?" Alastair jumped off the stage with Luka and Larkin following behind. "Why are you working with her?"

"We have a temporary agreement." Max pulled the man close to whisper in his ear, "Kira's alive."

"Is this true?" Alastair looked to Farn for confirmation.

"It seems that way." The *Shield* couldn't help but smile.

"Well then, lead the way." Alastair pulled away, clearly suppressing a smile of his own.

"Don't you even think about running." Luka pushed forward and grabbed Nix by the arm.

"You mind?" The reynard raised her other hand and jangled the chain attached to her wrist. "I'm not going anywhere at the moment. And the situation hasn't changed. You still can't find me out there."

"You…" Luka's face contorted into a severe frown as she ran out of words.

"I know it's frustrating." Max sent the mage a party invite. "But right now, we need to work together."

"Where are Ginger and the others?" Larkin added himself into the party as well.

Echo pointed up as if that was an answer.

"They're heading to the bridge to stop the Silver Tongues from crashing this death trap," Max added as he took out another three enemies, then reloaded. "Which is why we are going to get these people out of here."

"Aren't you heroic." Larkin reached out to adjust Max's scarf so that it hung straight. "There, now you look the part."

"Good luck getting the rest of the survivors to work together." Alastair swept a hand out to the pair of remaining lords, Murph and Promethium, as well as Klaxon, Dalliance, Grindstone, and Dartmouth. "I mean really, it has been like herding cats in here."

"Huh." Max noted that none of them were moving toward the doors like he had suggested a moment before. "Looks like they just need some motivation."

"Okay, everyone, I get it!" Max stomped his way up onto a pile of debris, standing as tall as he could while Farn kept the enemies at bay. "I get that none of you trust each other and would probably stab each other in the back first chance you got. But right now, let me introduce you to someone," He pointed with the muzzle of one of his guns to the reynard chained to his wrist. "This is Nix."

"Hi." The reynard wagged her tail and waved.

"And I hate her." Max ignored her friendly demeanor. "I

know she doesn't look like a monster, but I assure you all, she is a liar, a fake, and she's hurt people that I care about." Max let that sink in. "Yet here we are, working together to save your selfish asses. So, I have to ask, if I can fight alongside this piece of crap–"

"Hey–"

"Then what the hell is wrong with all of you?" He thrust one gun down toward the floor. "Put your differences aside and get down here."

The group stood, scattered across the stage. Many exchanged glances, followed by a few shrugs. Then they started moving.

"About damn time." Max turned back to the theater doors.

"Yeah!" Nix chimed in.

"Shut up, Nix." Max glowered down at her, getting an annoyingly playful grin in return. He turned away from her, half expecting a bullet in the back.

None came.

A part of him was starting to believe it wouldn't. Hell, she could have shot him a dozen times over already.

So why hadn't she?

Max hadn't really kept her alive because he needed her help. If anything, having her bound to his wrist was a hindrance, so why had he brought her along?

The short answer was trust.

He needed to know she was telling the truth. He had to be sure that Kira being alive wasn't a lie. Turning his back on his enemy seemed like the best test. If she shot him and ran, then everything was a lie, but if she helped him through to the end then, maybe, Kira was safe.

Max brushed an ember off his shoulder and stared down at the group that had gathered below him to place their trust in him.

"Get ready," Max stepped down from his makeshift stage and led everyone toward the lobby. "The Silver Tongues have left a transport on the landing pad at the front of the ship. It's not big but it's enough to get a few lords to safety. The rest of us will stay behind and fight the Void once you're clear."

Max didn't wait for confirmation before marching toward the theater's flaming doors. As he walked, he raised both pistols vertical in front of his face and whispered, "Custom Rounds, Frost."

Ice crystals spread across the grips of his guns, chilling his fingers to the bone. He ignored it and flicked both weapons to full-auto. Nix followed behind, holding up a coil of silver chain so it didn't drag on the ground between them.

Max pushed on through the flames without waiting for the villain.

She can keep up.

He raised his weapons and fired in both directions. The heat of the fire faded away, replaced by a cold chill as blue light exploded from his guns. Ice formed around the door on his wake to carve a path through the lobby. Nix took it upon herself to deal with any enemies that stood in their way.

"We don't have to make it far." Max turned back to the others. "Just across the deck and up those stairs."

"That might be easier said than done." Farn peered out through the lobby's glass doors.

Max stepped to her side and peeked out from the side, finding the deck more crowded than he remembered it being on the way in. With all of the ship's passengers dead, the creatures that filled the deck didn't seem to care about making eye contact anymore. Instead, they just went for whoever was closest.

"Looks like we have some work to do." Nix reloaded her M9. "You ready to show off?"

"Just don't slow me down." Max pulled a handful up magazines from his pouch and handed them to Luka. "You're on ammo duty."

"What?" The federal agent stared at him blankly.

"Just stay close and keep me loaded."

Nix did the same, handing a few magazines to Larkin.

"Alastair." Max turned to the *Cauldron* mage. "Get a spell

brewing, but don't use it unless you have to. Save it for the Void if you can."

"Alright." The CEO of Checkpoint Systems nodded and pulled a black pouch from his coat.

"Everyone else, get ready to fight." Max reloaded.

Lord Murph did the same, snapping a fresh magazine into a gun with an extended barrel. He was joined by Lord Promethium, who swiped open a spell-craft menu and readied a few debuffs for the horde outside. Klaxon didn't hold out either, dumping a pouch of ingredients into his caster's circle of power. Even Dalliance and Grindstone pulled weapons from their inventories.

Then there was Dartmouth, who hid behind everyone else. Max rolled his eyes at the elf before placing his hand firmly against the door.

"Stay close and move fast."

He was shooting before even setting foot on the deck. Nix followed suit, her pistol blazing into the night. They sprinted forward, dropping low to sweep their tether across the floor boards. The silver chain caught the feet of a dozen of Void's minions. They fell like bowling pins, becoming easy pickings for Farn following behind them.

Activating her Feral Edge, Farn drew power from the Death Grip's shield generator to increase her sword's damage. The blade snapped open down its length to release a flow of energy from within, forming a massive glowing blade nearly twice as long. It crackled with an aura of rage that hadn't been there before she'd gotten the Death Grip. With it in hand, she tore apart the enemies in her path.

Max pulled the chain attached to his wrist free from the pile of bodies and yanked hard, reeling Nix in. She pushed off him, using him as an anchor point to swing out across the deck and kick an enemy with enough force to send them flying into several more. They were lucky that the void creatures didn't use magic or ranged weapons.

Hell, they didn't even try to block.

"Keep moving!" Max pushed his pistol against the chin of an enemy in his path and fired. A blast of crimson light exploded into the air. "We're almost to the stairs."

Just then, a scream echoed across the deck from the rear of their group. Max stopped cold and spun, catching Grindstone being dragged off by a pair of slimy forms wielding daggers. Dalliance was next, a crimson streak of light cutting across his chest as a sword slammed into the deck at his feet.

There was nothing Max could do.

"Don't worry about them." Alastair kept running for the stairs. "They were lawyers!"

Max didn't argue, making use of the distraction that the pair of fallen elves provided. A moment later he reached the stairs with Nix still at his side.

"Let's go." She bolted up the first few steps.

"Wait!" Max yanked back on the chain. "There's not much resistance up there, we should cover the rear while the Lords make their escape."

"Good call," Nix held onto their chain with one hand to make sure no one tripped over it.

"Go with them, Farn. Just in case." Max gestured to the *Shield* with his head.

"On it." She plowed up the stairs to clear a path for the others.

Dartmouth was first to follow, shoving Nix out of the way as he ran by. Larkin stayed behind to help her back up. Luka hung back as well, taking up a position next to Max. The rest pushed onward, each running up the stairs in an organized line. A few grabby hands reached out as they went, but Nix was able to put them back down. She stepped up the first flight and pressed her back against Max's.

"You worry about the rear. I'll keep them safe as they climb up."

Max nodded and took aim as the entire deck swarmed toward them. The slides of both guns locked back empty in seconds. He tapped the mag release buttons and dropped the spent magazines to his feet.

"Now, Luka." He twisted the weapons toward her and the mage slapped in another pair. "Perfect." He unloaded them again, feeling the elf beside him fall into rhythm, sliding in another pair as soon as he called for it.

"Two left," she called out.

"Same." Larkin added just as he slid a new mag into Nix's M9.

"Start moving." Max pushed his back against Nix, forcing her up toward the landing pad. "We'll have to use the stairs as a choke point."

That was when the sound of engines starting came from above.

"Sounds like the lords are on their way home." Max put another round between a pair of black eyes.

"Then why do they sound so pissed?" Nix pointed up the stairs where Alastair and Noctem's other rulers were shouting in the direction of the landing pad. Curse words filled the air like bullets, as well as some actual bullets from Lord Murph.

"We gotta move." Max shoved Nix up a few stairs before turning and rushing up behind her. Larkin and Luka ran close at their heels. Max stopped short as soon as he reached the top.

Everyone was still standing outside the transport ship, yet the door was shut and the engines were running. That was when Max noticed they were one lord short.

Dartmouth.

"The bastard said there wasn't enough room and locked us out." Lord Murph reloaded and turned back toward the stairs.

Max stalked to the front of the aircraft and pointed a gun at the cockpit.

"Get the hell out of there, or I'll make you get out."

Dartmouth glanced out at him but quickly returned his attention to the controls.

"This is your last chance." Max pointed his other pistol at the spoiled brat in the cockpit. Dartmouth simply ducked out of view. Max groaned and holstered his guns. "New plan, climb on top of the ship, you don't have to have to be inside to get away."

"That's insane." Lord Promethium glanced back to the stairs like he might make a break for it.

"Don' have ta tell me twice." Lord Murph ignored him and ran toward the ship.

"Wait!" Nix threw a loop of chain around the lord's neck.

"Hurk! What's your bloody problem?" He fell backwards on his ass.

"That." Nix pointed to the cockpit as the transport ship began to lift off.

"Oh no." Max covered his mouth, catching a dark shape approaching just behind Dartmouth's shoulder. The Silver Tongues must have left someone behind to guard the ship, only to have them taken by the Void.

The transport climbed a dozen feet overhead, then lurched to one side and dropped out of the sky. Max ran to the edge of the platform just as the craft crashed into the deck in an explosion of fire and slag.

"Anyone else have any ideas?" Nix shrugged.

"No, and also, we're doomed." Alastair pointed back to the stairs as the horde that climbed into view.

"Just keep fighting." Max pulled his guns and opened fire with his last pair of magazines. "How many more could there be?"

"We can't kill all of them!" Alastair took a step back. "If we do, it will trigger phase two of the fight. And we're not equipped for that."

"What choice do we have?" Max fired until his guns locked back empty. "We're out of options here."

Nix holstered her weapon, ready to take on the horde hand to hand. Larkin snapped his crafting shears apart, prepared to charge. Luka dropped every heal she could into her quick-cast queue, ready for one last stand.

"I'm going to cast Desolation!" Alastair outstretched his

hand. "Be ready to rush them afterwards. And don't get blown off the ship by the blast."

Max crouched down and braced for impact while simultaneously getting ready to run into the madness. That was when a voice reached out over Lockheart's house line.

"Looks like you all could use a lift?"

"Wait!" Max grabbed Alastair's wrist.

"What?" The *Cauldron* turned around, an annoyed expression on his face just as the Cloudbreaker rose up from behind the landing platform. Ginger's son, Drake, sat at the controls.

"I was getting a little bored following the ship out there, so I flew closer. Pretty glad I did. You should probably give me a more important job next time." He gave Max a smug wave as he pulled in to land.

"Yes, yes, you saved the day, now get the door open." Max kicked a void creature away from the ship as it touched down.

The door slid open and Max leaped in to grab some ammo from the stash he kept aboard. He reloaded and turned his weapons to the door to lay down some cover fire. Players piled in all at once. Three lords, a villain, a crafter, a federal agent, and one empty-headed avatar climbed aboard. It was a full boat. Farn climbed in last, slamming the door on one last grabby hand.

Drake leaned back over the pilot seat as they lifted off the deck.

"I take it things have not gone as planned?"

CHAPTER FORTY

No! Seven watched her new boss fly into the window of the bridge. At the same moment Cassius shoved the dangerous end of his spear in her face, forcing her to catch it with one hand. She had to do something.

She couldn't survive on her own.

A brief glimpse of her stat-sleeve showed Ginger's health just before Cassius unleashed a torrent of flames in her face. Fire consumed her world and Seven retreated into the only thing that still made sense.

Math.

Numbers never lied or tried to manipulate her. They could always be trusted. Seven's mind sped up as the glass around Ginger shattered in slow motion; there had to be a way to save her.

Ginger's hit points had been 1985 out of 3168. The resourceful *Coin* had blocked a critical hit but still lost thirty percent. On top of that, with the distance she had to fall to the deck, her body would hit terminal velocity before landing.

Seven wasn't sure how the game calculated fall damage, but she did remember how a player had died earlier when Kegan had pushed them down an elevator shaft. If that distance had been enough kill, then so was the distance to the deck.

If Ginger had a functioning grappling hook, she could save herself, but with the mechanism out of commission there was no way to stop her fall.

Seven was out of options.

Or was she?

It might have been a glitch in Seven's overheated brain, brought on by the flame thrower pouring fire into her face, or maybe she was just losing her mind. Either way, one detail climbed to the surface.

Ginger still had more than three hundred hit points…

Seven reacted without thinking further, throwing her hatchet at her employer.

"Catch!"

The familiar sound of the weapon sinking into flesh met her ears just as Ginger passed through the window. Seven immediately thrust out her hand to call the possessed hatchet back.

"Why aren't you dead?" Cassius twisted a ring on the shaft of his spear, increasing the jet of fire pouring into Seven's face.

"Because she's fireproof, you ass!" Ginger plowed into the man as Seven felt the handle of her hatchet slap back into her hand where it belonged.

Cassius and Ginger toppled to the floor, a deep gash of glowing crimson light decorating Ginger's chest. She rubbed at the wound as it faded away.

"I can't believe you just axed me to pull me back to the bridge." Ginger drew her dagger. "I don't know if I should be horrified or grateful."

"Does that mean I get a raise?" Seven fell to one knee, panting as the floor around her burned.

"We can talk about it later." The *Coin* got back to her feet and drew her dagger. "Right now, keep him busy while I get to the door to let the others in."

Seven did as her boss ordered, stepping toward Cassius. The man slammed the butt of his spear down to hoist himself up.

Seven didn't give him time to recover, cracking her whip a few feet before him. The flaming leather cord snapped back, releasing a plume of fire in his direction. He might have wielded a weapon of flame, but unlike her, he could still be burned. Granted, her attacks couldn't hurt him with her stats entirely focused on survival.

But he didn't know that.

Plus, having flaming a whip cracked in your face was probably pretty distracting.

She kept at it, being careful to avoid making contact to keep up the illusion. The sound of her whip shattered the air as Cassius stepped back. Seven glanced over her shoulder to catch Ginger shoving another one of her bombs down the pants of one of her former housemates.

Shock filled the man's face as the Lady of Lockheart booted him down the stairs. A muffled bang came from below followed by a squeal of panic.

That was horrifyingly inappropriate. Seven looked away, pretending that she hadn't seen it happen.

She cracked her whip again, its flames fanned by a cold wind blowing from the broken window. Cassius continued to stay back. It wouldn't last forever. Eventually he would figure out she wasn't a threat and rush her.

Wait, that's not right. Seven hesitated. *He doesn't have to kill me. He just has to keep us busy.*

The hairs on the back of Seven's neck stood up as she realized how much time had already passed. She immediately made the mistake of glancing out the broken window. Mountains filled the view.

They were almost there.

Seven spun on her heel and bolted for the platform's railing.

"Hey, get back here." Cassius' boots hit the floor after her.

Options flooded her mind, none of them good. She could jump the railing, and try to steer the ship away. That would, of course, require her to know what she was doing. Not to mention Cassius would be on her in a second to stop her.

Next, she could make a break for the door and unlock it to let in the Kegan and the others who were still waiting outside. Steering the ship could be their problem. Then again, Cassius was still a problem. She couldn't let him run free to get in their way.

She hit the rail, the decision hanging in her mind as Ginger came into view, locked in a duel with another *Coin*. She must have killed the other player in her way.

That was when a third option presented itself.

Seven simply threw her hatchet down at Ginger's opponent. The now-familiar thunk of a blade hitting bone met her ears as the weapon slammed into his head, dealing its default of three hundred damage.

"Get to the door." Seven shouted just as the head of a spear plunged into her back. Pain exploded through her chest for an instant before being replaced by an uncomfortable numbness. Half her health was stripped away as she fell forward into the railing.

"You're not stab proof, are you?" Cassius yanked his weapon free as Seven gasped for air. She rolled over and reached out just as the spear came down again. It sunk into her palm, igniting her skin with a glowing X of damage. With her back against the floor, she caught the shaft of the weapon with her other hand and held on, thankful for the system as it dulled the sensation to something manageable. Cassius didn't let up, pressing down so the spear inched closer to Seven's throat.

That was when a bullet struck the railing above her. The wood exploded into Cassius' face, giving Seven enough time to look for the source. Piper and Corvin stood below, sending a wave of relief through her mind. Ginger had made it to the door. Seven was saved.

Then she remembered her place in the list of priorities.

"Don't worry about me." Seven tightened her grip on the spear scraping her neck. "Stop the ship!"

Corvin wasted no time turning to the destroyed steering

mechanism and jamming his broken sword into the slot at the end of the metal rod that stuck out.

"Give me a hand," he called to Piper, who tore her aim away from Cassius and leaped to his side. Together, they gripped the handle of his sword, struggling for the leverage needed to turn what was left of the ship's wheel.

"It's not enough." Seven lowered her head back, hanging it off the captain's platform so she could see out the main window. The freezing wind blew through her smoldering hair as the upside-down mountains grew closer, the ship barely turning. "We need to pull up."

"I'm on it!" Kegan sprang onto the scene, throwing himself onto the largest lever he could find. "Is this doing anything?"

"That's the throttle!" Ginger ran to the other side of the steering wheel. "Pull it, we might slow down." She grabbed onto another lever about the same size and yanked it back.

"That's it." Seven watched as the view began to shift, ever so slowly. That was when Cassius shoved his spear down with everything he had. Seven jerked her body to one side, taking the blow to her shoulder and losing another third of her health.

"How are you still alive?" Frustration flooded Cassius' face. "You're not even close to mid-level."

"I planned well," Seven spat back. Then she put her lips together and whistled.

"What the—hey!" Cassius spun around as the jaws of a rather well-behaved monster clamped around his leg.

"That a boy, Flint." Seven rolled away and pulled herself up on the railing. The wind fanned the flames that still licked at the floor around her.

"Where the hell did you get…" Cassius trailed off as he stopped fighting against Flint and held up his stat-sleeve. "Why doesn't this hurt?" Suddenly, his jaw dropped and he turned back to Seven, an awkward laugh trickling from his mouth. "I don't believe it, you put every stat point you had into defense."

"No." Seven froze as her secret was discovered. "I put some into health too."

"That's the dumbest thing I have ever heard." Cassius' mouth closed into a solid grimace as he stepped forward, dragging poor Flint along with him. The scalefang's claws scraped across the floor, trying to hold the man back.

Seven threw out her hand to beckon her hatchet.

"Oh no you don't." Cassius slugged her in the gut; the possessed weapon flew past her grip.

Seven fell against the railing again, gasping for air and wondering why he had used his fist and not his spear. Then he grabbed her by the hair and she realized he wasn't trying to kill her. At least, not any more.

Forcing her to her knees, he shoved her chin into the railing so she could watch as the Night Queen headed for the mountains. At the controls below, the rest of her new house struggled to hold onto the damaged mechanisms, the frozen wind blasting them harder the closer they got. Their voices cried out together.

"We have this, damn it!" Ginger shouted into the sky. "Don't let up."

"Couldn't if I wanted to." Kegan braced his foot on the console beside him. "My hands are frozen to the stick."

"Keep pushing." Corvin gripped the broken blade lodged in the steering column, his hands lighting up with damage. Piper threw her shoulder into the handle of the sword, forcing the ship to turn, even if it was only a little.

Seven couldn't believe her eyes as the members of House Lockheart stood in defiance of all logic. The mountains filled the view, the sky barely visible as shattered glass blew through the air like snowflakes in a blizzard.

They were insane.

Even with all that effort and hope, the massive ship had barely begun to turn.

"Doesn't look like your new friends made it in time." Cassius held her down against the rail. "I hope you're happy with your choice."

"At least they don't lie to me just to get more viewers." Seven pulled her hand up to brace against the rail, inadvertently bringing her house ring close to her mouth. "Look at them, Cassius."

Seven's eyes widened as her words echoed across the house line, realizing that everyone could hear her. She smiled down at her friends and continued.

"I was terrified of everyone in Lockheart earlier tonight. All I'd known of them was a few news articles and a video recording. I thought they were a bunch of thieves and villains. Now, though, I see they're just a group of friends stuck in a bad situation and fighting to protect what they care about."

Cassius pulled her hair.

"Look at them!" Seven held her head still in defiance, keeping her friends in her view. "That band of misfits cares about this game, not just about making money off it. Right now, they're each standing their ground in the face of impossible odds. So you can insult and laugh at us all you want. Even if we fail, I will still be proud to be one of them."

A moment of silence went by. The wind whipping through the bridge as the mountains grew closer and closer. Then a familiar voice answered back over the line.

"That was some speech."

A transport ship drifted in from the side of the window, coming to a stop, hovering in front. Seven smiled when she saw who was standing on top.

"I suggest you unhand my new housemate." Max aimed his guns at Cassius. Nix did the same beside him.

Cassius yanked Seven off the rail and pulled her close like a human shield. Flint still chewed at his leg.

"How long were you waiting to make that entrance?" Ginger interrupted the moment.

"Not long," Max shrugged. "I wanted to have the ship to float up from below but there wasn't time."

"Hey, Ma!" A player waved to Ginger from inside the cockpit window.

"Hi Drake." She nodded back, still holding onto the

controls. "You made it just in time. Now fly down to the hull and start pushing with everything the Cloudbreaker has."

"Aye aye." He saluted his mother and pushed the craft's nose into the broken window to offload the passengers riding on top.

Max and Nix ran along the top of the small ship and leaped through the window as Farnsworth and Echo climbed from a hatch on top. They jumped through the window, joining everyone on the bridge. The transport ship pulled away as soon as they were on board and flew off to one side. A moment later, the whole ship rumbled and leaned to the right as if something had slammed into its side.

Max and Nix dashed up the stairs to the captain's platform, taking aim at Cassius as Farn and Echo ran up the stairs on their side. The view of the mountains behind them began to shift.

"Nowhere to run, Cass." Max tilted his head to look past him. "Is that a scalefang eating your leg?"

"That's Flint." Seven stood taller, feeling a bit proud of her pet. "He's mine."

"Nice horns." Farn added as she drew her sword.

"Thanks, they're new—"

"Quiet!" Cassius pulled her hair back and placed his spear against her throat. "Nobody move."

Nix let out a snort laugh combination. "You do realize she will just respawn, so we can literally just shoot through her."

Seven's eyes widened at the thought, wondering if the villainous reynard would actually do it.

"Nah, that wouldn't be right." Max let his aim falter. "Not after everything she's been through tonight."

A chorus of sudden cheers rang out from below the captain's platform as the mountains began to fall out of view.

"We're gonna make it!" Kegan shouted.

Turbulence rocked the ship a second later, accompanied by the loudest rumbling that Seven had ever heard. It sounded like a stampede running the length of the ship.

"We're not gonna make it!" Kegan changed his mind.

The ship lurched to one side, nearly throwing Seven off her feet as the mountaintop scraped the hull. If it hadn't been for Cassius holding her up, she would have tumbled face first into the floor. Farnsworth slammed a fist against her chest plate to activate an ability, then grabbed onto Echo's dress before she rolled away.

Max grabbed ahold of the railing while Nix tumbled across the platform, getting wrapped up in the silver chain that tethered them together.

"Too late!" Cassius cried in Seven's ear. "We're going down."

Then, it all stopped.

Silence fell over the bridge as a strange calm filled the air.

"Did we...?" Nix raised her head from the floor, one ear hanging down as if confused. "Did we make it?"

"Oh my god," Seven stared out at the clear sky ahead of them. "I think—"

"We made it!" Ginger squealed from below along with her daughter.

"I knew we would the whole time." Kegan's voice joined in.

Seven elbowed Cassius in the stomach. "What was that about being too late?" He didn't respond, other than to pull her hair a little harder, clearly frustrated to be out of options.

Max kept a gun on the man and raised his house ring to his mouth. "Drake, my ship better be in one piece."

That was when the small transport craft blew past the window.

"Yes and no." Drake's voice answered over the line. "The Cloudbreaker's had it. I have to set her down." Almost as soon as he finished the sentence, the craft slid onto the deck below until it came to a stop near the edge of one side. "Sorry, Ma, I'll protect the lords as long as I can."

"You did good, Drake, don't worry." Ginger stepped up the stairs onto the captain's platform. "Just keep the doors shut and we'll be down to help with the Void as soon as we finish with things up here." Her eyes fell upon Cassius as she spoke.

The rest of the group closed in as well, weapons at the ready.

"You might as well let me go now." Seven started to push the tip of Cassius' spear away.

"Gladly," the man growled as Seven felt a boot slam into her back.

She flew forward into Max before falling to the floor and getting tangled up in the chain beside Nix. Seven rolled over just in time to watch Cassius slap Flint away with the shaft of his weapon.

Then he rushed her.

Seven braced for impact, remembering how little health she had left. Another hit would finish her. Except the attack never came. Instead, he leaped clear over her using the same jump ability she'd seen him use before. He soared through the window toward the deck. Everyone ran to the rail as he landed in a burst of fire that somehow broke his fall.

"Where the hell does he think he's going?" Max holstered his pistols.

"He's after the lords." Ginger started down the stairs.

"No, he isn't." Farn sheathed her sword.

Seven squinted at the deck, seeing nothing but a spark of fire in the dark where Cassius had landed. That was when it burst into a geyser of flame.

"He's using that flame thrower again."

"Oh no," Piper covered her mouth. "He's killing Void's minions."

"Damn, if he kills enough of them…" Max looked back at the others. "Alastair said the Nightmare's next phase would trigger."

"You all go, we'll stay and steer the ship." Kegan went back to the controls along with Piper and Corvin.

Everyone else started running, their boots flying down the stairs in a race to the deck. They had to stop him. Seven brought up the rear, watching as the jet of fire swept across the deck, igniting the dark forms that were once players one after another.

They weren't even halfway down before the air went still.

Seven froze as a wall of black clouds swam up from beneath the ship, blotting out the moon and stars. The Void engulfed the Night Queen.

They were too late.

Phase two had begun.

CHAPTER FORTY-ONE

Thunder rumbled through the night, while bolts of emerald lightning lit up the clouds that surrounded the Night Queen's burning deck.

"That's not good." Goosebumps reached across Max's skin as silhouettes of something otherworldly flashed from within the gloom on all sides. He hesitated on the stairs leading to the deck.

"Bwahaha!" Farn exploded in inappropriate laughter. "Sorry, it's not funny, we're just screwed and that was what came out."

"Hey wait, don't you all eat Nightmares for breakfast?" Nix slowed down behind him.

"Not this one, we don't." Max tightened his grip on the rail. "According to Alastair, Void's spawn is all wrong and the fight is broken. It isn't supposed to be aboard this ship so its stats are all imbalanced because of all the passengers it killed."

"What are the values based on?" Seven came to a stop at the rear of the group.

"Oh, nothing much. Just its health is equal to the combined

total hit points belonging to the players it already killed, and its attack values are based on the amount that survived."

Seven's eyes bulged, clearly running the numbers.

"Don't even think about telling me the math." Max covered his ears.

"We don't need to know," Echo mouthed beside him.

"What about Nix?" Farn's claws scraped against the railing. "Can't you control the system, like Kira?"

"No way." The villain laughed. "I ain't wasting that ability on you all."

Max squinted at her.

"What?" Nix folded her arms. "I'm not Kira. I can't use that power like she can. It hurts like hell and isn't exactly healthy for me, so no thank you."

"That's disappointing." Max deflated.

"Plus, we still have that ass to deal with." Ginger pointed her dagger down at the deck at Cassius who was making a break toward the fallen Cloudbreaker.

"Agreed." Max started moving again. "We deal with him firs—" He skidded to a stop as a gigantic clawed hand reached from the clouds above and snatched Cassius off the deck.

"What the…" Max stared at the demonic arm coming from the clouds. It was the size of a building. "I guess Alastair wasn't exaggerating when he said Void would be big."

Cassius let out a victorious laugh, having accomplished his goal of ensuring the demise of Noctem's remaining lords. His voice was cut off by the sound of cracking bones. Crimson streaks lit up his entire body as pieces of shimmering chunks fell from the monstrous hand. They burst into clouds of sparkling particles as soon as they hit the deck.

"Oh, god." Seven froze. "How do I tank against that?"

Flint growled at the sky as the clawed hand returned to the clouds.

"We'll do what we can." Farn gave her an encouraging smile.

"Good, great, whatever." Nix ran forward, tugging Max down the stairs by the chain. "Let's get on with it."

"Hey, you're not in charge." He yanked her back just as a ninety-foot-long tentacle slammed into the deck in the space where she'd been.

"Gah!" She fell back on her tail and scooted away until her back bumped into his feet at the bottom of the stairs. "Alright, I'm fine with that. You give the orders, I follow." The tentacle retracted back into the gloom around the ship.

"Wait a sec, tentacles and big demon hands coming from the Void." Ginger slapped a hand to her face. "Are we fighting Cthulhu?"

The slender arm of a human woman reached from the side to grab onto the ship. Following that, a crab-like claw snapped onto the hull from the other side. Another tentacle coiled around the stairs that lead back up to the bridge.

"Okay, I guess it's not Cthulhu." Ginger nodded.

"Good, Lovecraft was pretty racist." Nix stood back up.

"Like you're an angel?" Farn activated the Death Grip's energy shield and got ready to block what she could.

"Well I'm not racist." Nix defended.

"No one cares, Nix." Max got back to the matter at hand. "If it's not Cthulhu, what the hell is it?"

"Hey, Drake?" Ginger spoke into her house ring.

"Yeah?"

"Ask Alastair what this thing looks like."

"Dude, what's this thing look like?" Drake asked, clearly still holding his ring to his mouth despite talking to someone beside him that wasn't on the line. "Okay, he says it's not anything."

"What the hell does that mean?" Max shouted at his hand.

"It's like a mix of mismatched creatures all shoved together. He says it's meant to be mysterious. There's stuff floating around in the clouds that won't even attack, they're just there for effect."

"Awesome." Max raised a pistol. "So where can I shoot it?"

"Anywhere…"

"Good."

"…but you'll never do enough damage."

"Okay, does it have a weak point?"

"It has an eye that takes crit-damage."

"Okay then." Max turned back to the others. "You heard him; we look for an eye."

"Oh, but don't look at it." Drake added.

Max blew out a sigh. "And why not?"

"Al says looking at it will kill you and make you into more of those void things."

"Of course it does." Max lowered his gun.

"Good, great, whatever." Nix started running onto the deck. "Let's start shooting then."

"I hate to say she's right…" Max let his nemesis drag him along. "But what else can we do?"

The others spread out, each focusing on the limbs holding onto the ship. Farn and Ginger hacked away at the feminine hand while Seven threw her hatchet at the crab claw. Even Flint chewed on whatever he could reach, for all the good it did.

The deck still burned with the flames from Cassius's contract ability. Embers danced through the smoke that wafted through the air, filling Max's nose with the scent of burnt monsters. He stood back to back with Nix, remembering the last time they had fought alongside each other. It had been months ago, down in the catacombs beneath Reliqua, before he knew what she was.

They had made a good team back then.

It seemed like a lifetime ago.

"I'm still going to come after you when this is over." He kicked a coil of chain away from his foot.

"I know." Her ears drooped. "You could join me, you know."

Suddenly, a barbed stinger pushed through the clouds above.

"No thanks." Max dodged to one side as an enormous scorpion tail slammed into the deck. "I've had enough of you pulling my strings."

"Fair enough." Nix launched herself toward him using the chain, coiling it around herself like a dancer. "You wouldn't be able to handle working for me anyway."

"Why's that?" He fired half a magazine into the tail's stinger, spattering a viscous venom across the deck. It smelled acidic.

"That's easy. You're a hero." Nix emptied her gun into the tail as it pulled away.

Max scoffed. "Not quite. I'm just a guy doing my best."

"We'll see." She leveled her eyes at him, her irritating smile fading. "I may be a villain, sure, but that just makes it easier to spot someone like you. And there will come a time when you will have to play the hand that you've been dealt."

"The hell do you know?" Max started to turn away.

"I know Kira will need you." She got his attention again.

"What?"

"Look, I didn't just pick her because she was special. Sure, yeah, she fit the mold I needed, but there are hundreds more like her. I could have chosen any of them, but I didn't."

"Why not?" Max couldn't help his voice from cracking, afraid of the answer.

"Because she had you." Nix jabbed him in the chest with one finger. "I knew how hard Carver's quest was and that's nothing compared to what's waiting for her. Kira is powerful, but she isn't a hero. She needs someone to follow. Someone to make sure she survives. That's why I picked her, because she has someone like you to stand beside."

"I'm not—"

"Too bad." Nix reloaded. "I won't be here to pull people's strings forever." She spun away and fired at a scaled form that slithered through the clouds. "I hope you do hunt me down out there. All that'll mean is I was right."

Max stood with his pistols dangling limply at his sides, unsure what to make of her words. The pressure was almost too much, not to mention the guilt that he may have unwittingly placed Kira in danger by simply being her friend.

That was when Echo shoved him out of the way.

Max crashed into Nix, sending them both toppling into the deck as the demonic fist that had crushed Cassius came down again. The mindless avatar must have flown straight at him with all her strength to be able to push him out of the way. The clawed hand closed its fingers around the fairy, squeezing until her body glowed red.

Echo let out a silent scream, unable to die. The system still didn't register her as a player, leaving her squirming in the grip of the Nightmare.

"No!" Max aimed his gun up at the enormous hand but Nix caught his wrist.

"Better her than us. She's keeping that hand busy."

Max ignored her, firing at the fist until it let go.

"Echo isn't real." Nix grabbed him by the shirt. "That thing is not your friend. It's just an error. You need to stop worrying about it and let her go."

"I know that." Max's chest ached. He knew that he was the one dwelling on the memory of her. It hadn't been Farn or anyone else.

Just him.

So why couldn't he let her go?

Oh yeah…

It was his fault.

Suddenly, Nix let go of his shirt and looked behind him. "Eye…"

"What?" Max spun around as the clouds opened.

The darkness swirled into a vortex, revealing a domed shape covered in gray flesh. It pulsed with a familiar motion, like something rotating underneath. The repulsive mass hung a few dozen feet off the side of the ship. A long seam ran down its center, about the size of a car. Max swallowed as the fleshy mass opened diagonally across its surface, a translucent membrane sliding apart in the opposite direction, leaving a blank eyeball staring back at them. It twitched around for an instant before a black pupil rolled down to face him.

"Don't look." Nix averted her eyes and fired in the direction of the ghastly monstrosity.

Max did the same, holding both his guns sideways, watching the boss' health bar running down the side of his forearm. Bullets hit with a revolting squelch, though only half their shots found their mark. Max counted them off as the enormous health bar lost a few slivers of damage.

"This isn't working," Max noted as the horrible squelch turned into a muted thud. He looked up, finding the eye closed as the clouds swirled back over it.

"We missed half our shots by not looking." Nix reloaded.

"And the ones that hit only dealt a hair's worth of damage." Max added.

"We can't do this." Nix's shoulders sank. "Can we?"

Max didn't answer, not knowing what to say.

Then a smug voice answered for him. "Not alone you can't."

Max turned back toward the fallen Cloudbreaker to find Alastair dropping a pouch full of ingredients into his caster's circle of power. He handed a second pouch to Klaxon, who appeared behind him.

"What the hell, Alastair?" Max threw his arms up. "You're a lord, get back in the Cloudbreaker where it's safe."

"Oh pshaw. Nowhere's safe on this ship. Might as well help out." He cracked his knuckles and waited for his spell to brew. "I'm sure my guards back in Valain can defend my throne if I die. It's not like it hasn't happened before several, ah, dozen times."

"Plus everyone was getting antsy in the ship." Drake jogged out from the direction of the fallen craft.

"Yes, I'm not one for hiding." Lord Murph followed.

"Agreed," added Lord Promethium.

Larkin jogged past Max, pulling his respirator mask up over

his mouth. "I shall be getting some much-needed revenge for my little fashion models."

"He means the creepy dolls he brought on board." Luka followed close behind, swiping open her spell-craft menu. "And I'm not letting Nix out of my sight, I don't care if it matters or not."

"Suit yourself." Nix gave the federal agent a wink.

"There, it's settled." Alastair took up a position behind Max. "If we have to fight the Void out of its dungeon like this, then we might as well treat it like a raid boss and throw everything we have at it."

"Exactly what we were thinking." Kegan stepped off the stairs that led to the bridge along with Piper and Corvin.

Max's eye began to twitch. "Kegan, who's flying the ship?"

"Fly it where?" The *Leaf* gestured to the clouds surrounding them. "We have no idea where we're facing."

"What about the mountains we just narrowly missed?"

"I don't know."

Corvin peeked out from behind him. "We think they're back that way." He pointed in the direction they came from.

"Emphasis on the *we think* part," Piper added as she walked up to her brother and gave him a fist bump. "Way to crash the Cloudbreaker, you had one job tonight."

"Eh." Drake responded halfheartedly.

"Good, great, why not?" Max stole Nix's line. "Everyone get ready. And don't look at the eye."

"Oh, you mean that one?" Kegan pointed with his bow to one side, then immediately dropped his gaze to the deck.

Max glanced over his shoulder, catching the disgusting eyeball staring at his back.

"Crap, yeah." He looked away and raised his guns. "Everyone open fire!"

The night exploded in muzzle flashes as Piper and Lord Murph joined the firing squad next to Max and Nix.

"Ammo!" Max shouted just as Ginger dashed through his field of view.

The beautiful *Coin* reached into his pouch and grabbed a fresh pair of magazines from his belt. She placed a kiss on his check as she slid them into his guns.

"Nice to have you back."

Corvin followed suit, doing the same for Piper, minus the kiss. Larkin took care of Nix and Luka attended to Lord Murph. Kegan simply loosed a handful of arrows. A sound like a scream, heard from underwater, echoed through the sky as the giant clawed hand slammed into the deck as if swatting at a swarm of bees.

Max leaped out of the way, making sure to dodge in the same direction as Nix so that they didn't hinder each other's moment with the silver chain that connected them. Void's hand appeared from above to reach for them.

"Oh no you don't!" Alastair activated the spell he'd been brewing.

Purple light streaked across the deck just below the massive hand, forming a sigil that pulled the limb down. Max recognized the spell from when it had been used on him months ago, Gravity Well. Void's hand fought against the incantation, pulling back up to the sky. The spell wasn't strong enough.

"Now." Alastair shouted.

Klaxon rushed forward and unleashed a second gravity spell on top of the first. The clawed hand fell to the deck the instant the spell activated, unable to attack.

"Make this one count!" Klaxon growled. "I put one hundred percent of my mana in this spell."

Void let out another distant howl in protest as the sound of Max's bullets changed back to a muffled thud like before.

"Hold!" Max stopped firing. "The eye is closed."

The melee fighters turned toward the hand still trapped on the deck and ripped into it with everything they had. Max checked his stat-sleeve and nearly fell to his knees.

Ninety percent.

The Nightmare still had ninety percent of its health left.

They had barely even scratched it.

As if rubbing it in, one of Void's tentacles swept across the deck, connecting with Luka's side. She screamed as the impact launched her into the air.

"No!" Max didn't even have time to react before the mage flew over the side. Her body vanished into the clouds with a flash of lighting silhouetting her for an instant. Then she was gone.

"My spell's done." Alastair dropped his hand to his side.

"I'll hold it as long as I can." Klaxon stepped forward just as the demonic hand broke free of the sigil. A moment later the *Cauldron* mage was in its grasp. "I'm done here, don't you dare lose–" Klaxon's words were silenced with the crunching of bones.

There wasn't even time to process anything before Larkin dropped one half of his crafting shears.

"Everyone, the eye is back." His voice sounded odd.

Max turned to face him. The crafter's eyes filled with the same inky black as the players before, except this time it was slower. The crafter's face went blank.

"I will take my leave now, if that's alright. Can't let myself become another monster to fight." Larkin didn't hesitate before plunging the other half of his shears into his heart. "I should check on my shop anyway." The black faded from his eyes the instant his health hit zero, then he fell. His body flaked apart as shining particles drifted from where he lay.

"Well, it was a good try everyone." Alastair clapped his hands together. "It was exciting while it lasted."

"I'm going to miss my throne." Lord Murph lowered his head.

"As will I." Lord Promethium nodded in acceptance.

"I'm sorry, everyone." Max's whole body grew heavy as thunder rolled through the sky. "We tried."

"Yeah, we did." Ginger added. "No shame in that."

"None at all." Seven stroked the feathered mane of her pet. "I have to say, I did not expect this night to end like this, but I can't say I regret it."

The others added their sentiments as well, leaving them waiting for the next attack. Max let out his longest sigh of the night, just before something slapped him in the back.

It was a little weak to have been the Nightmare.

He turned to find Echo staring up at him. The avatar slapped him in the chest. Then proceeded to unleash a flurry of flailing limbs in his direction. It was so bad that Farn had to pull the imitation mage off of him.

"Easy, now." The *Shield* threw the fairy over her shoulder to wait for the system to calm her down.

"What the hell was that about?" Max brushed himself off.

"We don't give up!" Echo frantically mouthed her words. "We don't quit. You don't quit."

Max rolled his eyes, not even sure if he should bother arguing. Then someone else spoke up.

"Well, fuck."

"What?" Max turned back to Nix.

The villain groaned and rubbed her face. "You all can't just give up, okay? The error over there is right."

"Seriously?" Max threw his hand out to the sky. "What would you have me do here, pull a contract out of my ass and one-shot this thing?"

"No, I…" Nix trailed off before starting again. "Actually, yes."

"What?" Max growled at the reynard as her tail started wagging.

"Everyone!" Nix spun to face the rest of Max's house. "Keep Void busy. I need a moment with Max."

"How about no." Ginger argued just as Void's tentacle took a swing at her.

"Yeah, like that, just keep it busy." Nix yanked on her end of the chain in an attempt to drag Max off to the side. "Quit fighting me here, I have a plan."

"Fine." Max let the shifty reynard have her way. Until he heard her next sentence.

"Give me the knife."

"What? No!" Max clutched the silver contract item that he had intended to torture her with earlier.

"Yes." Nix held out her hand.

"How about no way in hell." Max gripped the knife tighter.

"Look, Max." She stared him straight in the eye. "You were in a bad place when you created that, and I don't think you should keep it."

"What?"

"I doubt you even want it at this point."

"You're right, I don't. But I'm not giving it to you."

"I don't want to use it." She placed her hand on top of his as he held onto the small blade. "Noctem is a wonderful place full of amazing things, so something like this shouldn't exist here. It's ugly and hateful, like the real world. Like where I come from." She squeezed his hand. "I want to destroy it."

"You can do that?"

"I can if you help me."

Max felt his grip loosen. "How?"

"My power, the one I share with Kira, isn't enough to reach inside your mind to destroy something stored within it." She stepped closer. "But I can lend that power to you. You just have to let me."

"I thought that power hurt you."

"It does, but destroying something like this is worth it." She looked away. "Plus we can kill two birds with one stone. So why not?"

"What do I have to do?"

"Just focus on what you want to happen."

"How will destroying it help us against the Void?" Max pulled the knife from his belt and held it in his hand.

"Destroying it won't, but changing it will." She placed her hand on the knife in his palm, her skin surprisingly warm against his own. "A contract can't technically be destroyed, only used or traded. So we just have to exchange it for something else."

"How do we exchange it?"

"You remember." She closed her eyes. "You think back to a powerful contract that you've already used. You must have had something at some point that can help now. It's still there inside your memories. Once you have something in mind, just focus on it and I will tell my power to follow your will. We'll trade this knife as payment and send it back where it came from."

Max hesitated for a moment before remembering that the rest of his friends that were still keeping the Nightmare busy.

"Okay, do it."

"That's all I wanted to hear." Nix winced, then snapped her eyes open, showing him the same violet color that he had seen looking back at him through Kira's eyes before she was stolen away. Except Nix's looked painful, filled with flecks of blue and red like stained glass. "Focus, Max."

"Right, yeah." Max took a breath and thought back to his most powerful contract. He'd had a few over the years, but there was really only one choice. "I got it."

"Good." Nix tightened her hand around his. "I'm making the trade."

Max felt a strange sensation as the system reached inside his mind. Then it was gone.

Nix let out a yelp and fell forward against him, pressing her forehead into his chest with her eyes shut tight. Her body heaved, like she couldn't get enough air. A couple points of damage were shaved off from how tight she held his hand. She gripped his shirt with her other hand, coiling her fingers into the fabric to hold herself upright.

"Are you...?"

"Shhh." She buried her face against him. "Too loud."

"That power," Max lowered his voice to a whisper. "It's doing more than just hurting you?"

She nodded, her tall ears brushing against his chin.

"It's killing you, isn't it?"

Finally, she pulled away from him as her eyes faded back to their usual blue. "Carver doesn't think I'll see another year. But I've proved him wrong before."

"Why?" Max's hand trembled.

"Why, what?"

"Why even use that power?"

"Because this…" She raised their hands together as Max felt something cold in his palm. "This is worth it. The world is won one victory at a time. So why not start here?" She pulled her hand away, leaving him holding a new contract item.

Well, not new. Just… returned.

Max ran his finger over the tiny object, remembering how it had felt the last time he had held it.

Somehow, the bullet felt heavier.

CHAPTER FORTY-TWO

Contract Name: Silver Bullet
Type: consumable
Ownership: unbound
Usage: one-time only
Basic enchantment: none
Advanced enchantment: One-Shot
Ability description: this bullet can kill any enemy in one hit, as long as that hit deals critical damage. Range, limited.

Max ejected the magazine from one of his pistols and snapped the silver bullet in on top before shoving it back into the gun. It felt... different... like a weight had settled across his shoulders.

"Listen up!" Max called to the rest of his friends. "Nix and I just destroyed my knife."

"Good." Ginger shouted while dodging a tentacle.

"I know, I'm glad it's gone too." He held up his pistol. "In exchange for destroying the contract, I've gotten back the silver bullet that I lost when we fought Death back in Rend a year and a half ago, during Carver's quest."

Recognition swept across the faces of each member of his house. All except Seven, who hadn't been with them in the beginning.

"I'm sorry, what bullet?" The horned woman raised her hand.

"It kills anything in one hit." Ginger caught her up to speed.

"Nice, you gonna miss again?" Kegan joked.

"No." Max lowered his gun. "But as you know, I have to land a critical or it won't work."

"How are you going to do that without being able to look at your target?" Alastair called out while dropping another pouch full of ingredients into his caster's circle.

"I..." Max's mouth dropped open. "I don't know."

Everyone let out a groan.

"What? I was excited to get a second chance here." Max defended. "I hadn't thought that far ahead yet."

A half-eaten loaf of bread hit him in the chest.

"Farn, did you give Echo food in the middle of a fight?"

"I did, yes." Farn handed the avatar a second loaf since she'd thrown the last one.

Echo took a bite, then threw that one as well. It bounced off Max's head.

"Thank you, Echo. Your comments have been noted." Max held up his hands. "Now does anyone have any ideas?"

The team went back to dodging attacks from all directions.

"You could simply look at it?" Lord Promethium suggested. "We saw how long it took for Larkin to die; he even had time to kill himself before succumbing to the Nightmare. Surely you would be able to take a shot in that time."

"No. You need to walk away from this." Nix stepped forward. "I'll look."

"What?" Max spun to her.

"Simple, I tell you where to shoot, you pull the trigger." She shrugged. "I'm the only other *Fury* here as deadly as you. Would you rather it be someone else?"

Max stood there looking dumb, not sure how to answer the

question. She ignored him and started shrugging out of her Nightfall coat, only to stop when she realized she couldn't get it off with the chain connecting them together. Eventually, she just transferred it into her inventory to dematerialize it before taking it back out again. Then she dropped it onto Max's shoulders.

"You can use this to hide yourself from the Void." She helped him slip his untethered arm into the garment. "There, it suits you."

"You're giving me your contract?"

"Don't make a thing of it."

"I'm not, but…" Max searched for the words. "We're not friends, here."

"I know, you still hate me and all that." The strange villain gave him a playful punch in the arm. "I just don't care. A lot of people hate me; you're not the first." She pulled the hood up to activate the garment's stealth ability. Black fog swam around the edge of Max's vision as Nix stepped away. "There, now the Void should leave you alone. Plus you look pretty cool."

So many emotions stirred in Max's head. His hatred for the woman struggled with trying to understand her actions. "What will you do if you turn into one Void's minions before I kill it?"

Nix answered by pulling her pistol and placing it to the side of her own head. "I don't intend to let that happen."

"So that's your plan to escape." Max frowned and shook the manacle around his wrist.

"Did you really think this would end any other way?" She gave him a smug grin. "I won't let anyone take me, be it a Nightmare or you."

"You better not be lying about Kira." Max said, realizing he couldn't stop the woman.

"There are some things that even I wouldn't lie about."

"Fine." Max turned away from her and raised his gun. "Everyone get ready. Let's take this thing down in one hit."

"That's the take charge Max I chose." Nix leaned in to whisper in his ear. "Remember that."

Her words sent a chill down his spine before taking root in

the core of his being, a feeling of dread building inside. He shook it off and got ready.

The others did their best to keep the Void's various limbs busy while Nix scanned their surroundings beside him. Then, finally, the moment came.

"It's the eye!" Kegan shouted from behind.

Max spun around just in time to see the enormous eyelid open. He raised his pistol and looked to Nix.

"Shit! The hand's back!" He yanked on the chain between them just as the clawed fist reached for her. It missed by mere inches as she fell toward him.

"I got this!" Farn dashed in to throw herself against a few massive fingers.

"Me too." Seven's whip snapped around the Nightmare's clawed thumb to keep it from crushing the *Shield* standing in its grip. Even Echo swooped in to wrap herself around the thing's pinky. She wasn't particularly helpful but that didn't stop the avatar from trying.

Max stepped out of the shadows and pulled Nix to her feet.

"You ready?" Max raised his gun back to where he thought the eye would be.

"As I'll ever be." She placed the muzzle of her gun against her head and stepped behind him. Max closed his eyes and imagined the Void's eye before him until he heard her voice.

"Raise your gun three inches." Her words were slow as if fighting to stay in control. He did as she instructed. "Too far, drop it just a hair and move to the left one inch."

The sound of Farn and Seven struggling nearby nearly distracted him, but he blocked it out. They could handle themselves. Max adjusted his aim and waited for confirmation.

"How's this?"

"That's it, take the shot!" Nix shouted, her voice laced with a dark tinge that hadn't been there before.

Max didn't hesitate, taking in one deep breath of smoky air and drowning out the chaos around him.

His pistol kicked back, tearing the night sky in two. He

snapped his eyes open in time to catch a glimpse into the infinite darkness of the void just before the eye shattered like glass. The silver bullet seemed to crack the fabric of the world itself. A blast of light, then dark, then nothing.

A shockwave of displaced air hit, blasting the clouds from the sky to leave behind a field of stars. Then a second shot rang out from behind him.

Max flinched, remembering what the sound meant. An instant later, the manacle around his wrist snapped open, the silver chain falling to the deck. He turned around to find Nix gone.

He stared at the empty space, unsure how to feel. All he knew was that everything had just become more complicated. Finally, he reached back and slipped his other arm into the coat that Nix had left him and turned away. He was immediately met by Ginger, who threw her arms around him.

"You did it!"

Before he could respond, she grabbed the collar of his coat and pulled him in for a kiss. He felt her melt against him like the first time their lips met. He kissed her back, letting her know how much he missed her. It felt like coming home, like everything would be alright.

"Ahem." Alastair cleared his throat.

Max and Ginger ignored him, forcing him to clear his throat a few more times, each louder than the last.

"Now I wish I'd stayed in the Cloudbreaker." Drake commented.

"Tell me about it." Piper added.

Finally, Ginger pulled away. "I have waited months for a real kiss with this guy, so deal with it."

"Ahh, guys?" Corvin raised his hand, standing by the ship's rail.

The rest of the team ignored him as several celebratory cheers went out from the last surviving lords.

"Guys?" He tried again.

Max glanced toward him amidst a round of hugs, high fives,

and fist bumps. The reynard's ears stood straight up as an irritated look fell across Corvin's face. Finally, he shouted.

"Brace for impact!"

Max's jaw dropped as he remembered that they had no pilot. He scanned the area, finding nothing but Ginger to hold on to. She apparently had done the same, wrapping her arms around him and burying her head into his shoulder as the ship suddenly slowed to a crawl.

Everyone fell over, toppling across the deck like a pile of Larkin's dolls. A sound like white noise drowned out their cries as a wall of water surged into the air over the Night Queen's bow. The wave crashed down onto the deck, soaking everyone on board.

"Oh, that's cold." Ginger huddled closer to Max as the ship slowed to a stop.

"What the hell did we hit?" Max pushed himself up, taking care to help the lady of his house to her feet as well.

"Is this a bad time to ask if the Night Queen can float?" Kegan hung his head over the rail. "'Cause we just made an emergency water landing."

"There is a giant hole in the bottom for the engine wheel, so I doubt it." Seven sat up with the help of Flint, who happily licked at her hand.

Everyone looked at Max for what to do next, which led to an awkward silence. Eventually he pointed to the side of the ship.

"To the lifeboats!"

Without a word, Lord Murph shoved Lord Promethium out of the way and made a beeline for the water crafts. Lord Promethium simply picked himself up and brushed himself off. He then inclined his head in thanks to Max and Ginger before turning toward the lifeboats as well.

"Well, this night could have gone a lot worse." Alastair shoved his hands in his pockets. "I'm glad to have finally been able to fight alongside you all."

"Hey!" Ginger slapped Max in the chest. "We just beat a Nightmare, so what happened to the contract?"

"Oh, yes," Alastair furrowed his brow. "That is weird. The system has never had to pick from this many players before; it usually only has to keep track of six. It might be having trouble."

That was when the familiar voice of the darkness grated across Max's ears. Everyone else cringed as it chose a name.

"MaxDamage24, make your offer."

"I'm not sure I want to." Max stopped and stared up at the sky. "Not after the last one it gave me. I don't even have anything to offer."

Suddenly, Echo placed a hand on his arm.

"Yes, you do," the avatar mouthed.

"And what's that?" Max stared at the imitation of his best friend.

Echo simply held her hands out to her sides as if presenting herself as an option. Her dress, still wet from the crash landing, clung to her skin as salt water dripped from her hair. A sudden ache swelled in his chest. Kira had always liked the water.

"No." He shook his head.

She nodded hers in defiance as the sound of waves swelled around the ship.

"I am only here because of guilt. Because you regret not being able to save me." Her silent words told him what he already knew, like the system was merely voicing his inner feelings back to him. "Let me go."

"What if I don't find you?"

"Then you move on."

"I don't want to move on."

"I know." She smiled up at him. "No one does. But you won't be able to go forward if you're always looking back."

"She's right." Farn joined the joined the fairy, standing at her side. "We don't need a reminder of what we lost. We need to keep her in our hearts and wait until we find her."

Echo let out a silent laugh.

"Yeah, I know, I'm embarrassing and I don't care." Farn pulled the fairy into a tight embrace.

"Okay, I get it." Max struggled to keep his eyes from welling up. "I'll make my offer."

Farn let the avatar go and placed a small kiss on her cheek. "We'll find you. I promise."

Echo nodded, then kissed her back, standing on her toes to reach her cheek. Afterward she stepped away and raised her head as if to say, I'm ready.

Max reached out and tousled the fairy's hair, getting a punch in the arm in return. He laughed, and opened his mouth to make an offer to the darkness. "I offer–"

"Wait wait wait!" Echo suddenly flailed her arms.

"What?" Max glared down at her.

She reached down and unbuckled her item bag, letting it fall to the deck. Picking it back up, she shoved it into Ginger's arms.

"Hold my stuff, and don't lose it."

"I will keep it safer than the last time I held onto your things." The *Coin* hugged the pouch close to her chest.

Next, Echo twisted the ring Farn had given Kira back during their first mission off her finger. It didn't do anything special anymore, but the system must have understood its sentimental value. She placed it in Farn's hand.

"I'm going to want that back."

"I'll look forward to giving it to you again." The *Shield* smiled as a tear rolled down her cheek.

"You ready now?" Max glowered down at her.

Echo held up one finger as if there was more. She then hopped to one side and ducked behind Farn. The *Shield* started to turn around but Echo stopped her with one hand. The fairy stayed there for a moment, occasionally leaning to one side or there other. Max looked to Alastair who was standing behind her, only to see him blush and look away into the horizon like there was something more interesting in the distance.

Echo hopped back out and held her hands out to Max as if

hiding something between them. He reached out to take whatever it was and she placed a piece of cloth in his hands.

"I'm going to want those back too." She gave him a wink.

Max looked down and unfolded the piece of fabric before immediately wishing he hadn't.

"Oh, hell." He tossed the item to the deck, the pair of bright white underwear landing at his feet. A sparking heart with a keyhole stared up at him. The custom garment contained a backup supply of mana for anyone who wore them, so of course Kira would want them back. "Gah, they were warm." Max promptly wiped his hands on the sides of his new coat.

Echo let out a silent laugh at his expense.

"Yeah, yeah, very funny." Max crossed his arms.

Echo grinned back at him and twirled her hips back and forth so her dress swayed around her as if enjoying some kind of freedom.

"Like hell I'm carrying those around 'til we find you." Max refused to pick the garment back up.

"Okay, yeah, soooo… yeeeaaah." Farn awkwardly bent down and picked them up, letting out a somewhat inappropriate chuckle before shoving Echo's underwear into her item bag.

"Classy, Farn." Ginger placed a hand across her face and shook her head. "Real classy."

"What? Echo said she's going to want them back." Farn rolled her eyes. "Don't judge me."

Max blew out a sigh and moved on, not really wanting to explore the topic any more than Farn already had.

"Now are you ready?"

Echo nodded happily and waited. Max held up his arms so she could tap the back of her hand against his.

"See you soon." He gave her a sad smile, then made his offer. "I offer my regrets."

"Accepted!" The voice of the darkness rolled through sky.

Echo's small form gave him a grateful bow as she began to

shimmer. She raised her head, her silver hair sparkling in the light of the moon. Then, little by little, she drifted away into the wind. Her smile was the last thing he saw.

"We will find you." Max fought back tears as Ginger leaned against his side.

"We will." She held him tight. "I already have a plan."

Farn sniffed, letting her tears fall freely.

Alastair placed a hand on her shoulder. "We'll get her back in no time."

"Thanks." Farn placed her hand on his. "I know we will."

"And you can give her that ring again." Corvin gave her a warm smile.

"And her underwear," Kegan added.

"Kegan?" Alastair threw an arm around the *Leaf.*

"Yeah?"

"Shut up."

"Oh."

Max dropped his hands to his sides, noticing something new hanging from his belt right where the evil knife had been. Except this time it wasn't a weapon. No, instead it was a small, silver flask, wrapped in a decorative leather strap.

"Huh." Max pulled it free from his belt and unscrewed the top to smell the contents. The familiar scent of fermented apples filled his nose. He took a sip, remembering the taste from the many nights that he'd spent with everyone in the Hanging Frederick back in Valain. They hadn't been there since they had lost Kira. Until now, Max wasn't aware of how much he missed it. After a long drink from the flask pulled it away and wiped his mouth.

"It's cider." He couldn't help but smile.

Ginger immediately grabbed the flask and tipped it back, pulling it away just as fast. "Oh, damn." She let out a wild laugh before taking a second drink. "It's rum for me. Good rum at that." She handed it to Farn. "You try."

Farn took a moment to wipe the mouth of the flask on her cape before taking a sip. Her eyes widened, then she tipped it back further, taking several large gulps before stopping to breath. "That is the best water I have ever had."

"Water?" Max raised an eyebrow.

"Yes, I like water." She took another mouthful then poured some of the crystal-clear liquid out on the deck.

"That's boring." Ginger took it back, watching as the contents flowing from the flask turn back to rum as soon as she held the item again. She immediately passed it to Max.

"Oh, that's cool." He watched the liquid turn to cider, unable to stop smiling at how ridiculous the item was. "It's a flask that contains your favorite drink."

"And it doesn't seem to run out." Ginger added.

"I know, right?" Max kept pouring cider on the deck.

"That is neat and all," Alastair cleared his throat again. "But this ship is still sinking. So, you know." He finished by turning and walking toward the lifeboats.

Max put an end to the infinite stream of cider pooling around his boots and placed the flask back on his belt. "Kira is going to love this."

"Ten bucks says it gives her soda." Ginger wrapped her arm around his and started walking.

"It definitely will, she loves sweet stuff." Farn followed.

Max leaned into Ginger as they began walking toward the lifeboats, feeling like, for the first time in months, everything might be okay. Even after everything Nix had said might be heading his way, for now, he could move forward. He slowed as soon as he saw Drake heading in the same direction.

"Where do you think you're going?"

Ginger's son pointed a finger toward the side of the ship. "Ah, the umm, lifeboats."

"Oh no you don't. You crashed my ship," Max pointed at the Cloudbreaker where it lay. "It's not beyond saving, so you're going to have to stay and wait for it to auto-repair enough to fly."

"What? It could be at the bottom of the ocean by then."

"Probably keep the hatch closed then." Max kept walking.

Piper let out a laugh at her brother.

Ginger smiled back at her daughter. "Oh, Piper dear, go help your brother, would you?"

"What?" She stopped laughing.

"Good luck." Max waved behind him as he continued walking. "And don't worry, I have a feeling everything will work out fine."

LOGS

Checkpoint Systems Message Boards: One night after the Auction of Souls

Topic: I might be cursed

ChronicTheHedgehog69: Okay so I won a ticket to ride the Night Queen and happened to be there last night when the shit hit the fan and I mean really hit the fan like it went everywhere.

I'm starting to think that I might be cursed.

First I get killed during that whole thing with the dragons a year and a half ago and now someone spawns a freaking Nightmare on a ship that I happen to be riding on.

PinochioNipples: Tell me about it. I was there too when the Void popped out of that auction thing they had going on. All I remember was looking at some kind of cloud for a few seconds before being sent back to spawn. From what I heard from a friend I went with, my body turned into a monster and went around murdering fools. My boyfriend is still not speaking to me after I apparently stabbed him with a katana.

I don't even know where my body found a katana.

I'm a mage. ¯_(ツ)_/¯

HelveticaNue: What was the auction for?

PinochioNipples: It was some kind of thing for the super high level Houses. Like rulers of Noctem level. I don't know what was up for bidding, but it was called the Auction of Souls, so, that's creepy.

ChronicTheHedgehog69: That's messed up.

EMPIREriot: I know, what kind of overdramatic name is that. It sounds like something out of a bad fantasy book.

Grindstone: Hello everyone. I trust your evening is going well. I happened to have searched the name of my auction and thought I should respond here.

First, I will start by saying that the auction in question was meant to be an upscale event for the rulers of Noctem. The items up for sale were a mixture of rare finds and unbound contracts, hence the name.

Second, I will say that the Nightmare was smuggled abroad the Night Queen by a member of the House of Silver Tongues as part of a misguided assassination attempt on the rest of Noctem's rulers. It was one of many attempts perpetrated through the night.

And lastly, I will say that we have decided not to hold another event like this. To be honest, Noctem's rulers as well as a number of other lords and ladies in attendance, are animals. I would not trust them with my take out order let alone an entire city.

That is all I have to say about the subject.

I_NO_IM_GOOD: Okay so that last guy is full of crap. The Lady of the Silver Tongues was nowhere near the Night Queen. And from what I hear, House Lockheart was at the Auction. So you do that math there. It's no surprise that the Night Queen ended up in the ocean.

Grindstone: Clearly this person is a plant working for the Silver Tongues to help cover their tracks and spread misinformation. Although, I will add that while House Lockheart was in attendance they were not the root cause of the airships demise.

I_NO_IM_GOOD: Not lying. Lockheart did it.

ChronicTheHedgehog69: I heard it was House Boar and that's why they just lost their throne.

TheUnseen: I heard it was Winter Moon, they just got over-thrown too on the same night. I'm just glad those were the only two cities to change leadership. I don't want a repeat of what happened back when the Serpents fell.

Grindstone: You are free to believe what you want, even if you are wrong.

ChronicTheHedgehog69: Don't you tell us what to think we know better than to trust anything on the internet.

Message sent one day after the Auction of Souls

To: MaxDamage24
From: GingerSnaps
Subject: Can we talk?
Hey Wyatt,

A lot of stuff has happened and I know things aren't exactly back to normal. But I was wondering if you might okay with not seeing each other online for a couple days. I kind of want to talk first. In person.

I know that expecting you to fly up to Massachusetts just to talk is sort of unreasonable, but still, I really want to see the real you.

Plus, you can get out of Florida for a few days, and that's always good.

P.S. Florida sucks.

Bye love!

-Marisa

Checkpoint Systems Message Boards: Two nights after the Auction of Souls

Topic: How many players has the new Death Grip killed so far?

TheNoctemTimes: I'm just curious if her body count is anything like the old Death Grip.

Hoover: Yes Farnsworth is a friggin monster. I was the guy recording when she killed Tusker in Torn months back. Still gives me nightmares.

JustaSlimegirl: I heard she killed Cassius of the Silver Tongues without a second thought aboard the Night Queen.

TheNoctemTimes: She doesn't seem to drag out her kills though like the old Death Grip did. That's what made me curious. I was wondering if she might be a kinder gentler sort of Death Grip.

Skellingham: I ran into her with a friend of mine aboard the Night Queen the other day when Void attacked. She actually helped us. Protected us and told us to head to the theater where the auction thing was happening. The lords inside helped us stay alive for a bit. It kinda fell apart eventually and monsters started pouring in from the balconies so we died anyway, but that doesn't change the fact that she tried.

My thoughts, the new Death Grip is a good person.

TheNoctemTimes: That's not as good a headline as I was hoping for but it is an interesting take. Maybe House Lockheart isn't as scary as everyone makes them out to be.

Aawil: Tell that to someone that hasn't been blown up by them... twice.

◆ ◆

- Lucem Bounty Board -
WANTED: MagnificentSeven
Reward: 3 plates of hard to whoever executes her.

Post Comments:

BullShifters: Dang, 3 plates of hard, that's, like, $1000 bucks! What in hell did she do to piss off the Silver Tongues?

TheWhiteSuit: I don't know but I could get in on that action.

HelveticaNue: Wait, the MagnificentSeven is one person? What kind of confusing name is that?

Puddin: Apparently she was one of the Silver Tongues' Royal Assistants, but betrayed them and stole two contract items from Leftwitch. Pretty savage if you ask me.

I_NO_IM_GOOD: That's awful, what kind of person steals from their own house? I hope she gets executed several times over. From what I understand the bounty is standing, so it can be claimed multiple times. And she's still a low level so it's easy pickings. I'd hate to be her right about now.

BullShifters: Just found out she swapped teams over to ol'Lockheart and tamed a dire scalefang as a pet.

TheWhiteSuit: Yeah, no thanks. I don't want any of that noise. Not looking to make enemies of Lockheart.

Puddin: That is BAD... ASS. Wish I could join up with them.

Message sent two days after the auction

To: MagnificentSeven
From: GingerSnaps
Subject: Time to start earning your keep.

I've attached a link to a job posting. We have a mutual friend that can pull some strings to get you in.

I think you can figure out the rest.

Good luck you magnificent accountant. :)

Sincerely, your boss, Ginger

EPILOGUE

Karen Write sat in an extravagant conference room across from a man in a plain gray suit. She tried her best not to sweat as she finished up her second interview.

"Well, everything looks good and your references all had wonderful things to say. Musk, Gates, very nice comments all around. Especially Mr. Jobs. Wait, isn't he dead?"

Karen suppressed a full body cringe.

Really, Ginger? Could you have at least come up with fake references that are actually alive? I knew I should have gone with my normal resume.

"Ah, yes, sorry, different Mr. Jobs, ah, not the dead one." She winced at her own lie.

"Oh yes, that makes sense." The man across the table shuffled a stack of resumes. "When would you be able to start?"

"Immediately." She settled back in her chair not wanting to seem too desperate. "I don't like to waste time."

"That's what I like to hear from an accountant." He closed a folder on the table. "And would you need any help relocating to be near our headquarters?"

"I should be fine." She gave him her most professional

smile. "I have some good friends that should be able to help me move."

"Perfect." He stood up and walked her to the door, holding out his hand to shake. "I look forward to working with you."

"As do I." She shook his hand with just the right amount of pressure then stepped out into the hall.

Karen smoothed out a wrinkle in her suit pants and walked away, her heels clicking on the floor at an even pace. Tapping the button for the elevator, she remarked to herself that at least it had doors, unlike the lift aboard the Night Queen. She checked her watch as she waited. Not that she wasn't already aware of the time. She just wanted to look busy. Eventually, the elevator doors opened and she stepped inside.

Karen waited the right amount of time to make sure there were no other passengers waiting before pressing the close door button. As soon as she was alone, she took a breath.

Then she did a little dance.

"Yes yes yes yes yes!" She twirled in a circle. "I have a real job!"

She still couldn't believe how her life had turned around. Sure, she had to move to a new state, but that wasn't a problem, especially with her new salary on top of what Lockheart was paying her.

Karen took one more victory lap around the spacious elevator, then settled back to the center of the box and straightened her blazer just as the doors opened.

She promptly walked out into the massive lobby, only stopping for a moment to pull out her phone and send a quick message in House Lockheart's text channel. All it said was two words.

I'm in.

She started for the door, but stopped again to take one long look up at the building that she would be working in from now on. Beautiful fabric banners hung past several floors on either side of the two-story company logo adorning the wall. She smiled as she read it.

Checkpoint Systems.

From one of the balconies, she caught a familiar face looking down. It was odd seeing the Death Grip out of her armor. The woman nodded.

Karen returned the gesture without being obvious before making for the door. It was all falling into place.

Nix couldn't hide forever.

All they had to do was follow the money.

◆ ◆

Wyatt stood nervously on the porch of a house in Haverhill, Massachusetts. He wore a plain backpack full of clothes and toiletries and held a bouquet of gas station flowers in his sweaty hand.

"Hi Marisa, so glad I came up. What would you like to talk about?" Wyatt rehearsed a greeting, feeling a bead of sweat form on his bald head.

"I knew I should have worn a hat." He wished they could have just met online; at least he had hair when logged in as Max. He flexed his bad hand as he remembered what it felt like online where his wrist didn't hurt.

Oh well, she wanted to talk in person, and that was good enough for him. Plus, he wanted to see her too.

Finally he reached up to knock on the door, only to stop just before touching. Of course, that was when the door flew open.

"You've been out here for fifteen minutes already." Marisa stood in the doorway staring at him. "If you don't knock, it makes things awkward."

"Sorry." Wyatt couldn't help but smile, he had forgotten how short she was. "I, ah, got you these flowers."

"Oh, thanks." She took one unimpressed glance at the bouquet. "They're... flowers."

"Yeah, by definition they are." He held out a small plastic

box. "Oh, and I got you these mints. I wanted to get you candy or something, but the gas station didn't have anything nice. So, yeah, mints."

"They're open already." She stared at the offering without taking the container.

"Yeah, yeah, they are. I've been on a plane all day, I was afraid my breath was bad, so I had one. Or a few." He reached forward and placed the plastic container in her hand as if feeding an animal at the zoo, equally afraid of being bitten as well as scaring her off.

She popped a couple mints into her mouth and bit them while continuing to stare at him.

"Okay, here we go then." He took a breath. "So I know that I've been a jerk, obsessed with Nix for the last few months. And I'll admit that I went down a dark path for a little while there. For that, I'm sorry. But if there is one thing I know, it's that things would have been much worse without you." He calmed down, feeling better for having said what he had flown all the way there for.

"I know." She bit her bottom lip. "That's not why I asked you up here."

"Sure, sure, then, whatever you want to talk about is good too."

"That was a lie, I don't really want to talk." She leaned against the side of the door frame.

Wyatt froze for a second. "I'm not sure—"

"The kids are spending the night at friends' houses." She immediately smiled, looking a little guilty.

"Ah, okay." Wyatt processed that information, then coughed. "Oh."

"Yeah."

"So no awkward talk, then?"

"Oh, things are definitely going to get awkward, we just won't be talking." She gave him a wink, suddenly resembling Ginger a bit more.

"I see."

"Yes."

They both stood there for a moment, staring at each other like a couple idiots.

Then she leaned forward and kissed him, standing on her toes and holding onto the door frame for balance. Wyatt slid his arms around her to hold her up while he kissed her back as gently as he could.

Finally, she pulled away and looped her hands around the straps of his backpack. "Want to go upstairs? I think I've waited long enough."

Wyatt answered her with another kiss as he stepped into the house.

Marisa kicked the door shut behind him.

Nix shot up straight in a dark room. She had been aboard the Night Queen a moment before.

Hadn't she?

The last thing she remembered was shooting herself.

Pain echoed through her head, reverberating off the inside of her skull in unending agony. She clutched her temples and keeled over to wait for the room to stop spinning. When it settled down, she brought one leg down to the floor and tried to stand, only to collapse to the cold tile of a room that wasn't her own.

The lights came on as soon as she fell, motion sensors picking up her sudden movements. She scooted back against an adjustable hospital bed. Pulling herself up, she took in the room, finding herself in Carver's lab, several floors below her office and the apartment where she normally slept.

At least she knew where she was.

She looked down at the loose medical robe tied around her body. Further down, a droplet of red spattered on the floor followed by another. Nix touched her nose, pulling away a finger covered with blood.

Not again…

Nix wiped her face on her sleeve and started moving just before being hit with another wave of pain, this time accompanied by nausea. She collapsed near the door. It flew open a second later.

"Damn, you're bleeding again." Neil Carver dropped to his knees beside her and placed his hand on her back. "Come on, let's get you back to bed."

"No!" Nix pushed him away and crawled toward the server tower at the center of the lab. "I have to talk to her."

"You are in no condition to talk to anyone. You haven't uttered a word in weeks."

"Weeks?" That didn't sound right. It had only been minutes since the fight with Void.

"Yes, weeks." He struggled to keep her from getting up. "You've been in and out of consciousness ever since that ill-fated plan of yours. Why you decided to invoke that power is beyond me. You might not have woken up at all."

"Then it's even more important to talk to her." Nix shoved him back.

"Then it will have to wait until there isn't blood pouring from your nose."

"I don't have the time." Nix looked at him dead in the eyes, crying for the first time in what seemed like years. "She has to cooperate." Nix fell forward to rest her head on the cold tile, her blood and tears mixing on the floor into a pink mess.

"Fine. I will set up a version of the sphere for you to visit her, but don't push yourself." Carver stood up and walked to the server tower and typed several commands into a keyboard. When he was finished, he grabbed a magnetic cable made specifically for the connection port implanted into Nix's skull. "I have the recording you made of her friends loaded. Were you able to get what you needed on it?"

"No." Nix lay there, her head hurting too much to do anything else.

"Then what is the point?" Carver crouched down to look her in the eyes. "She hasn't listened to you yet, what makes now any different?"

"Because this time you're going to remove all of her limitations. Let her use all of the power you gave her."

"That's insane." Carver brushed a lock of bloody hair from her cheek. "Do you have any idea what that would mean? You would be throwing yourself at the mercy of a god."

"I know."

"She could erase every memory in your head and trap you in there with her. She could stretch a second into months if she wanted to." Carver clutched the connection cable in his hand. "She could destroy you."

"Do you really think she would do any of that?" Nix let out a laugh and rolled her head to the side so she could see him better. "This is Kira we're talking about. The most she'll do is resort to sarcasm and name calling."

"I know, she isn't dangerous." He sunk down beside her. "But she will have access to everything. Your entire mind will be laid bare for her."

"I know. That's why I need you to do this. I need her to understand why I need her." Nix reached for the cable. "And for that, I need her to see everything. I don't have time to try to convince or manipulate her. All I can do now is be honest."

Carver sat motionless beside her for a long moment. "So it's all or nothing, then? Everything we've worked for, simply placed on the scales to be weighed by a fairy."

"How do you like our odds?" Nix smiled at him through the blinding pain.

He shrugged. "I'm not sure. She's always been unpredictable."

"Time to roll the dice, then." Nix took the cable from his hand and let it snap into place at the base of her skull.

Carver stood up and went back to the console to add a few commands, before letting his finger hover over the enter key.

"Are you sure?"

Nix gave him a weak thumbs up.

"Hit it."

ABOUT D. PETRIE

D. Petrie discovered a love of stories and nerd culture at an early age. From there, life was all about comics, video games, and books. It's not surprising that all that would lead to writing. He currently lives north of Boston with the love of his life and their two adopted cats. He streams on twitch every Thursday night.

Connect with D. Petrie:
TavernToldTales.com
Patreon.com/DavidPetrie
Facebook.com/WordsByDavidPetrie
Facebook.com/groups/TavernToldTales
Twitter.com/TavernToldTales

ABOUT MOUNTAINDALE PRESS

Dakota and Danielle Krout, a husband and wife team, strive to create as well as publish excellent fantasy and science fiction novels. Self-publishing *The Divine Dungeon: Dungeon Born* in 2016 transformed their careers from Dakota's military and programming background and Danielle's Ph.D. in pharmacology to President and CEO, respectively, of a small press. Their goal is to share their success with other authors and provide captivating fiction to readers with the purpose of solidifying Mountaindale Press as the place 'Where Fantasy Transforms Reality.'

Connect with Mountaindale Press:
MountaindalePress.com
Facebook.com/MountaindalePress
Twitter.com/_Mountaindale
Instagram.com/MountaindalePress

MOUNTAINDALE PRESS TITLES

GameLit and LitRPG

The Completionist Chronicles,
Cooking with Disaster,
The Divine Dungeon,
Full Murderhobo, and
Year of the Sword by Dakota Krout

A Touch of Power by Jay Boyce

Red Mage and
Farming Livia by Xander Boyce

Ether Collapse and
Ether Flows by Ryan DeBruyn

Unbound by Nicoli Gonnella

Threads of Fate by Michael Head

Lion's Lineage by Rohan Hublikar and Dakota Krout

Wolfman Warlock by James Hunter and Dakota Krout

Axe Druid,
Mephisto's Magic Online, and
High Table Hijinks by Christopher Johns

Dragon Core Chronicles by Lars Machmüller

Pixel Dust and
Necrotic Apocalypse by D. Petrie

Viceroy's Pride and
Tower of Somnus by Cale Plamann

Henchman by Carl Stubblefield

Artorian's Archives by Dennis Vanderkerken and Dakota Krout

APPENDIX

CHARACTER STATS

MaxDamage24

TITLE: Pale Rider
HOUSE: Lockheart
LEVEL: 147
RACE: Human
TRAIT: Versatile – All stats develop equally.
CLASS: Fury
SUB CLASS: Reaper (-30 HP every 3 seconds while active)

STATS
Hit Points: 3584
Skill Points: 400
CONSTITUTION: 112
STRENGTH: 64

DEXTERITY: 196
DEFENSE: 102
WISDOM: 0
FOCUS: 0
ARCANE: 0
AGILITY: 23
LUCK: 38

ACTIVE SKILLS

SLOT 1: Custom Rounds, level 6 – Convert a magazine to a different type of ammunition. May be used once per magazine.

SLOT 2: Last Stand – Fire an empty pistol by creating bullets from your hit points. Duration lasts until death or reloading.

SLOT 3: Heavy Metal – Drastically decreases range and increases recoil enough to damage the wielder and make firearms difficult to handle but grants +75% damage.

REAPER SLOT 1: Unbreakable Defense – Summon the blades of Death to deflect all incoming physical damage (ranged only). Activate by holding one's breath, lasts as long as breath is held.

PERKS

SLOT 1: Dual Wield – Allows a second pistol to be equipped. -5% damage output for each missed shot with an off-hand weapon for a maximum damage penalty of -40%. Penalty lasts until both weapons have been reloaded.

SLOT 2: Last Chance – The last round fired from a magazine deals +50% damage, increasing the likelihood of finishing an enemy before needing to reload.

SLOT 3: Quick Draw – Any shot fired within two seconds of a weapon being drawn from a holster will gain +25% damage.

Kirabell

TITLE: Archmage
HOUSE: Lockheart
LEVEL: ERROR
RACE: Fairy
TRAIT: ERROR
CLASS: ERROR

STATS

Hit Points: ERROR
Mana Points: ERROR
CONSTITUTION: ERROR (-75% racial penalty = 1 total)
STRENGTH: ERROR (-75% racial penalty = 0 total)
DEXTERITY: ERROR
DEFENSE: ERROR
WISDOM: ERROR (+25% racial bonus = 177 total)
FOCUS: ERROR (+25% racial bonus = 191 total)
ARCANE: ERROR (+25% racial bonus = 0 total)
AGILITY: ERROR
LUCK: ERROR

ACTIVE SKILLS ERROR

PERKS ERROR

Farnsworth

TITLE: First Knight
HOUSE: Lockheart
LEVEL: 144

RACE: Human
TRAIT: Versatile – All stats develop equally.
CLASS: Shield

STATS
Hit Points: 5888
Skill Points: 280
CONSTITUTION: 184
STRENGTH: 128
DEXTERITY: 62
DEFENSE: 196
WISDOM: 0
FOCUS: 0
ARCANE: 0
AGILITY: 11
LUCK: 14

ACTIVE SKILLS
SLOT 1: Death Grip (CONTRACT) – Can't be unslotted.

SLOT 2: Taunt – Gives weight to your words to draw the attention of an enemy. PVE only.

SLOT 3: Feral Edge (CONTRACT) – Unleash your inner beast.

HOUSE SLOT: Sure-Foot – Hold your ground while fighting on any surface, may ignore gravity.

PERKS
SLOT 1: Damage Absorption, level 5 – Your shield blocks 90% of damage taken.

SLOT 2: Annoyance – Increases the likelihood of getting an enemy's attention by attacking it.

SLOT 3: Protector – Increase defense by +15 when standing between an enemy and a party member.

Kegan

TITLE: Deadly Wind
HOUSE: Lockheart
LEVEL: 129
RACE: Elf
TRAIT: Control – At creation, choose one stat to receive a bonus for each upgrade point used and choose two stats to receive a soft-cap.
CLASS: Leaf

STATS

Hit Points: 3168
Skill Points: 270
CONSTITUTION: 99
STRENGTH: 140 (+25% racial bonus = 170)
DEXTERITY: 100
DEFENSE: 97
WISDOM: 0
FOCUS: 0 (-25% racial bonus = 0)
ARCANE: 0 (-25% racial bonus = 0)
AGILITY: 50
LUCK: 24

ACTIVE SKILLS

SLOT 1: Camouflage, level 3 – Temporarily change your skin and equipment's coloring to blend into a variety of terrains. Must be holding still.

SLOT 2: Piercing Strike – The next arrow fired will continue moving through your target to hit another behind it. The arrow will continue until it runs out of momentum or hits an obstacle. Each consecutive hit decreases damage by -10%.

SLOT 3: Light Foot – Remove all sound produced by your movement for five minutes for better stealth.

PERKS

SLOT 1: Speed Chain – Increase damage by 5% for each arrow fired within three seconds of the last.

SLOT 2: Charge Shot – Increase damage by 10% for every second you hold the bowstring back.

SLOT 3: Sticky Quiver – Arrows will not fall out of your quiver.

Corvin

TITLE: Nightmarebane
HOUSE: Lockheart
LEVEL: 115
RACE: Reynard
TRAIT: Nine Tails – All nine attributes gain a bonus equal to half your lowest.
CLASS: Blade

STATS

Hit Points: 3200
Skill Points: 220
CONSTITUTION: 80 (+20 racial bonus = 100)
STRENGTH: 85 (+20 racial bonus = 105)
DEXTERITY: 40 (+20 racial bonus = 60)
DEFENSE: 60 (+20 racial bonus = 80)
WISDOM: 40 (+20 racial bonus = 60)
FOCUS: 40 (+20 racial bonus = 30)
ARCANE: 40 (+20 racial bonus = 60)
AGILITY: 40 (+20 racial bonus = 60)
LUCK: 40 (+20 racial bonus = 60)

ACTIVE SKILLS

SLOT 1: Phantom Blade – Launch a blade of malicious intent at a target. Damage and range dependent on skill level.

SLOT 2: Hone – Temporarily hone the edge of a blade to increase sharpness and damage. Last for a number of cuts equal to skill level.

SLOT 3: Shockwave – Unleash a wave of destruction.

PERKS

SLOT 1: Awareness – Hear better than most.

SLOT 2: Quick Draw – The first cut executed within three seconds of drawing a blade has a chance to deliver double damage.

SLOT 3: Follow Up – Gain an additional 25% damaged when attacking within 3 seconds of a previous attack.

Ginger Snaps

TITLE: Lady of House Lockheart
HOUSE: Lockheart
LEVEL: 144
RACE: Human
TRAIT: Versatile – All stats develop equally.
CLASS: Coin

STATS

Hit Points: 3488
Skill Points: 310
CONSTITUTION: 109
STRENGTH: 65
DEXTERITY: 149
DEFENSE: 101
WISDOM: 0
FOCUS: 0

ARCANE: 0
AGILITY: 70
LUCK: 71

ACTIVE SKILLS

SLOT 1: Blur – Decrease a target's ability to target you. PVE only.

SLOT 2: Paralyze – Immobilize a target after a successful back stab. Removes critical hit bonus.

SLOT 3: Five Finger Discount – Will cause an NPC to turn around. Common items are fair game.

HOUSE SKILL SLOT: Royalty – You may claim the throne of any city in Noctem. If you can take it, that is.

PERKS

SLOT 1: Grappling Hook – Fire a line from a wrist mounted launcher.

SLOT 2: Sticky Fingers – Any material taken from an enemy can be converted to an item to be used or sold.

SLOT 3: Backstab – Increase damage by 150% when doing it from behind.

Royal Assistant Seven

TITLE: Born in Blood
HOUSE: The Silver Tongues
LEVEL: 11
RACE: Human
TRAIT: Versatile – All stats develop equally.
CLASS: Venom Mage

STATS
Hit Points: 50

Skill Points: 180
CONSTITUTION: 0
STRENGTH: 0
DEXTERITY: 0
DEFENSE: 0
WISDOM: 0
FOCUS: 18
ARCANE: 33
AGILITY: 0
LUCK: 0

PERKS
NONE

Magnificent Seven

TITLE: Born in Blood
HOUSE: Lockheart
LEVEL: 13
RACE: Faunus
TRAIT: Imbalance – Plus 10% to all stats for each that remains 0.
CLASS: Whip

STATS
Hit Points: 1234
Skill Points: 2
CONSTITUTION: 22 (+70% racial bonus = 37 total)
STRENGTH: 0
DEXTERITY: 0
DEFENSE: 42 (+70% racial bonus = 71 total)
WISDOM: 0
FOCUS: 0

ARCANE: 0
AGILITY: 0
LUCK: 0

ACTIVE SKILLS

SLOT 1: Summon Pet – Summon a monster that has been raised from birth or tamed in the wild. A summoned pet will gain upgrade points equal to your own. If killed, a pet may be resummoned after cooldown. Cooldown will decrease as rank improves.

PERKS

SLOT 1: Friend in Need – Increase the damage of a summoned pet by 20% when your health is below half.

BESTIARY

Nonhostile Creatures

LAGOPIN – Being half rabbit and half bird, these mounts are seriously fun to ride. So, saddle up and hang on tight.

JEROBIN – A small kangaroo-like race, these sentient creatures are often seen working in the cities of Noctem.

FLINT – A rare Dire Scalefang belonging to the player Magnificent Seven.

Basic Monsters

SCALEFANG – A large lizard bearing a mane of bright feathers. They attack with their entire bodies from their tail to their teeth. Their rotating elemental weakness makes them particularly hard to deal with, especially in large groups.

BASILISK – An enormous black snake with a paralyzing stare. Avoid direct eye contact at all costs.

GHOUL – These animated corpses of the dead are known for their physical attacks, but they have been observed using magic as well.

POPLO – A spherical manifestation of elemental energy, capable of a number of spells that match their affinity.

MISFIT – A cave dwelling monster that likes to bite and kick.

SILVER ANGEL – A silent observer who watches those who travel down the spiral.

PLAGUE TOAD – Wet, slimy, and vicious, these creatures exist to eat. They will try to lure you in with their tail and attack from below. They especially like easy targets.

MIND FLAYER – A squid-like creature that inflicts madness on a target by spraying it with ink. Resides in the caverns beneath Rend as well as many other parts of Noctem. Not particularly dangerous in and of themselves, but the madness status can easily kill a target or innocent bystanders, as it alters the perception of the target. Players may look like monsters and vice versa. Environmental hazards may also be manipulated.

MIMIC – A monster disguised as a common treasure chest. Recognizable to any experienced player by a bent handle on one side. Highly lethal ambush predators, mimics give up relatively easily if they have not caught their prey quickly.

MARIONETTES – A low level monster found in the city of Rend. A simple ball-jointed doll with a hostile nature. Appears in groups, usually with a leader.

PORCELAIN BEAST – A conglomerate of Marionettes. If too many of these weak monsters are brought together, they may combine into one mass of writhing bodies.

Nightmares

RASPUTIN – This mad monk exists to tear and rend all asunder, earning him the title of Destroyer.

SENGETSU – Sometime sacrifices cannot be avoided. It is up to you to fear them or not.

KAFKA – Change is necessary for growth, but will that growth create a monster?

RACKHAM – Not all battles can be won, but that doesn't mean you should accept defeat.

THE DEEP – The fear that lurks beneath the water's surface. Did something just touch your foot?

THE VOID – The unseen and unknown. Fear it or embrace it, the choice is yours.

Unique Nightmares (The Horsemen)

FAMINE – The bell of Famine rings a steady rumble in one's stomach. Nothing can be eaten in this Nightmare's dungeon.

PESTILENCE – The horde is coming and it's hungry.

DEATH – Like a force of nature, this nightmare claims everyone in the end.

WAR – The embodiment of war, this Nightmare consists of two dragon kings locked in combat for centuries. There is no stopping them. It's best to just run.

CITIES

Valain

The unofficial capital of commerce, Valain runs like a well-oiled machine. Its citizens work hard and party hard. This city and its territories are the only parts of Noctem that are fully under the control of Checkpoint Systems. (Current Ruler: Alastair Coldblood, Lord of House Checkpoint.)

Lucem

The city of light, Lucem stands as a shining example of what can be done through clever negotiations and diplomacy. Artists and entertainers have flocked to its peaceful and vibrant streets. If you're looking for a night out, you can't do much better. (Current Ruler: Leftwitch, Lady of the House of Silver Tongues.)

Sierra

Previously lost for generations, the city of Sierra hid below ground where its people, the Deru, thrived and innovated. Now known for its unique architecture, which makes use of the cavern ceiling as much as it does the floor. A complex system of railways connects the city. Its towers are filled with crafting workshops for the diligent, while its streets are lined with games and food reminiscent of a carnival. (Current Ruler: Promethium, Lord of House of Forge.)

Thrift

A city-wide bazaar where cultures of all worlds mingle. All are welcome, none are turned away.

Whatever you might seek, you can find in Thrift. (Current Ruler: Murph, Lord of House Saint.)

Reliqua

The city of rest and relaxation. Its inhabitants walk the streets of this tropical paradise at a leisurely pace. Home of the Jewel of the Sea, a crystal pyramid that towers over the tranquil streets. (Current Ruler: Amelia, Lady of House Winter Moon.)

Torn

A winter kingdom not for the faint of heart. Its throne has been in near constant dispute since Carpe Noctem was released. (Current Ruler: Tusker, Lord of House Boar.)

Tartarus

While not an official city, Tartarus defies logic by existing in the wilds on the dark continent Gmork. It has been constructed of entirely farmed and crafted materials. Enter at your own risk.

Rend

Once the sister city to Torn, the majestic kingdom of Rend fell to the greed of its ruler, who attempted to offer the city to the Nightmare Rasputin to form a contract. Its palace, Castle Alderth, has become a frozen tomb, home to nothing but death and darkness. Even now, it remains waiting for the day that someone breaks its curse.

CLASS LIST

Melee

FURY – Fast, loud, and full of style. In the right hands, this class can dish out an impressive amount of damage. That is, if they can actually hit their targets.

Weapon: pistols

LEAF – At home sniping from the trees, this class will attack from where you least expect it.

Weapon: bows

COIN – Don't take your eyes off this class for a second, lest you find yourself a few items lighter. Coins excel at stealth and mobility.

Special equipment: grappling line
Weapon: daggers

BLADE – You can't argue with a classic. This swordsman class is best suited for attacking.

Weapons: sabers, rapiers, and katanas

SHIELD – Built to last, this class specializes in protecting others.

Special equipment: shield gauntlet
Weapon: straight swords

WHIP – A trainer class capable of keeping a familiar.

Weapon: whips

RAGE – Known for its capability to equip anything as a weapon, this class is built for all-out attacks.

Primary weapons: anything and everything

FIST – This unique class has two different paths. On one hand, the MONK is capable of infusing their hits with mana. On the other, the THUG is a brawler through and through.

Weapons: gloves, brass knuckles, and their bare hands

RAIN – Death from above. This class can use their mana to augment their movement, often launching themselves into the air to attack when least expected.

Weapon: polearms

Magic Users

BREATH MAGE – This frail but kind class can keep their party alive through whatever the world may throw at them.

Special equipment: casters

Weapons: clubs, canes, and additional casters

CAULDRON MAGE – Specializing in destruction, this mage class is slow but dangerous.

Special equipment: casters

Weapons: clubs, canes, and additional casters

VENOM MAGE – This mage class excels at slowing the enemy down, weakening a target, and causing damage over time.

Special equipment: casters

Weapons: clubs, canes, and additional casters

Made in the USA
Columbia, SC
25 July 2024

66ddc528-7779-4af8-8726-fadf7f7aa697R01